# The Seed of Joy

WILLIAM AMOS

ISBN-13: 978-1517624569


Printed by CreateSpace, an Amazon.com Company

This book may be ordered in paperback and eBook formats through
Amazon.com

# DEDICATION

For the people of Korea
and for their brothers and sisters –
the men and women of Peace Corps/Korea.

# ACKNOWLEDGMENTS

I would like to thank many people who helped in the writing of this book:

Fellow Peace Corps Volunteers, too many to name, whose reminiscences fleshed out the details of the story; Elaine Neville, Susan Skaggs, and James Amos, for reading the book from an American perspective, and Chung Tae Don and Kim Nam Hee for reading it from a Korean one; David Gettman, editor and publisher at Online Originals, who published the first ebook edition; Paul Courtright, Donald Baker, and innumerable other people along the way who gave help and encouragement over the length of the project.

I must also acknowledge my debt to the following sources: Former Volunteer Tim Warnberg's fine article "The Kwangju Uprising: An Inside View" in the journal *Korean Studies*; a compilation of scholarly articles entitled *The Kwangju Uprising: Shadows Over the Regime in South Korea*, edited by Donald N. Clark; Tim Shorrock's detailed articles, "The U.S. Role in Korea in 1979 and 1980" and "Tim Shorrock and the Kwangju Stories: A Personal Response and Update;" *Korean Patterns*, by Paul S. Crane, which was our cultural textbook during Peace Corps training; and Simon Winchester's excellent book, *Korea: A Walk Through the Land of Miracles*.

Whatever historical accuracy is evident in these pages is due to their contributions. The mistakes are, of course, my own.

# PROLOGUE

"She died well."

The well-dressed, well-fed Korean man cupped his chin in his hand and gazed affectionately across the dinner table at his American guest. His fingertips brushed a scar that traveled the length of his face from temple to chin, a scar that he sometimes showed off with pride and sometimes tried to cover with his wife's make-up, depending on the mood of the times; it was an old one, received eight years before on a day he would remember forever.

A shadow crossed his face. He feared he had made himself misunderstood.

"... It was a good death."

The American said nothing. He stared out the window. From their vantage point high atop Namsan Tower, at one of the better restaurants of Seoul, the city spread out far below them on the cusp of twilight, the time before the lights start twinkling on, when one can barely see the city in the gloom.

"Who would have thought that an old radical like me, a veteran of the Kwangju Uprising, would be where I am today?" the Korean continued. "A politician — a member of the very class I once despised. It was a long road to this point. By some miracle I managed to escape from the police dragnet after the Uprising. Eventually I became an aide to a member of the City Council in Mokpo — your old home town, *neh?* His fortunes rose, and so did mine ..." As he went on, he became dimly aware that talking of himself, of his own success, was not what the American needed to hear. *Her* sacrifice had to be for something bigger.

"Her favorite saying — remember it? 'Trouble is the seed of joy.' I'd say we were entitled to a garden, a forest of joy after what our country went through. Well, we had free presidential elections two years ago. Just what

1

we were fighting for all along. For the first time in living memory, all the political parties had candidates in the election, candidates who ran their campaigns as they saw fit. The government's old nemesis, Kim Dae Jung, ran. So did Kim Yong Sam. They were in prison when you were here last, *neh?* And so what if the bad guy, No Tae Wu, won in the end? That was the Kims' fault. They and another opposition candidate split the vote." The Korean chuckled. "We are so innocent, so unaccustomed to free elections, we completely forgot to do the math. But who knows? Perhaps one of our guys will be president next time. That will be something to see, won't it?"

The American knew what his dinner companion was trying to do, and he smiled.

"Is this your first trip back since ... well, since the Uprising?" the Korean asked.

"Yes, it is. How could I miss the '88 Summer Olympics? I had to come, to watch the Games. And to see how the landscape and the people have changed."

"Changed? The people? You're joking, of course. We Koreans will always be the same: short on patience, long on memory ..."

A busboy at the next table prepared to change the linen. He snapped out a fresh tablecloth, a blue one the shade of the sky in autumn: that jewel-like, infinite blue that so many years ago the American had found so captivating.

He closed his eyes as the mixed blessing of memory washed over him.

# CHAPTER ONE

Mokpo is the black sheep of the family of South Korean seaports: an outpost dangling upon the southwest corner of the Korean Peninsula, the subject of many venerable folk songs in which a woman weeps because her lover has been exiled there. The city has a reputation (well founded, in most people's minds) for being seedy, provincial, and rebellious — a crowded, noisy, sorry excuse for a city, teeming with more than any city's share of unruly sailors, paupers, and prostitutes.

Most of Mokpo's quarter-million residents are native-born or have moved up there from the numerous islands that lie off the southern coast. Mokpo-born residents of Seoul, such as President Pak Chong Hui's great political enemy Kim Dae Jung, are many. Seoul-born residents of Mokpo, on the other hand, seem almost as scarce as Americans in that forsaken city.

One American, a United States Peace Corps Volunteer, had gone against common practice for the first time in his life by coming down to Mokpo from Seoul in July of 1979. Paul Harkin soon found that under almost any normal criteria, Mokpo was at worst an unfortunate excrescence and, at best, a curiosity; yet since he was not in a "normal" situation, he could think of no other place he would rather live. Mokpo was precisely what he had joined the Peace Corps to find: a place — any place — fundamentally different from his home town of Lafayette, Indiana.

Mokpo had none of the familiar comforts associated with a home town; it was different, and that was enough for him. Mokpo had a mountain, for one thing: a big double peak called Mount Yudal against which the city seemed backed into a corner. With its noises, smells, and the ease with which he could get lost in it, it was in countless ways a troublesome place in which to live. But within its shortcomings lay Mokpo's saving grace: for the past sixteen weeks, ever since his arrival, Paul had never once been bored.

From day to day, even from hour to hour, he never knew quite what to expect from this place.

Autumn came to Mokpo with an unexpected splendor, a benign blend of serenity and vibrancy. After spending days confined to the bland, rather dilapidated cocoon of the Mokpo City Health Center, where he worked, Paul jumped at the chance to go outside. The warm sunlight of the season danced all around him, even on the crowded street that Paul and his coworker, Mrs. Mun Yong Ok, followed into one of the poorer sections of town. Everything around him stood out in sharp relief: the yellow sunlight cast contrasting blue shadows all about, while overhead the sky retreated into space like a vast sapphire bowl overturned above the earth.

"*Chon go ma bi*," Mrs. Mun said. She had caught Paul staring flat-footed at the sky. She pointed up and repeated: "*Chon go ma bi*."

Paul reached for his dictionary, his ever-present companion. "'High sky, fat horse.'" He looked at Mrs. Mun, puzzled. "This is right?" he asked, in halting Korean.

Mrs. Mun nodded. That ancient phrase, she believed, described the fine weather perfectly.

Paul and Mrs. Mun had set out from the health center to check on tuberculosis patients who had not come to the health center to pick up their medicines and to take samples of sputum from potential patients they would meet along the way. Mrs. Mun looked on such trips as unpleasant chores that took her to bad parts of town; Paul sought them out as rare adventures. He had never once turned down an invitation to go out. Indeed, he had initiated most of the trips himself by learning by rote the translation for "Shouldn't we go out home visiting today?" and repeating it until Mrs. Mun finally agreed, just to shut him up.

Buk Kyo Dong, one of Mokpo's most wretched districts, clung like a gray scab to one of Mount Yudal's spurs. It was a dirty jumble of red tile roofs and concrete walls, its narrow alleys turning into paths and stairways as they ascended from the bigger streets below. From the fresh sea breeze of the open street, Paul and Mrs. Mun climbed into the musty smell of humidity trapped in concrete. Open ditches carried waste water downhill to the sewage channels that eventually emptied into the sea. That was the intent, if not the result: Paul, crossing one of the countless footbridges that spanned these ditches, saw that the water lay motionless and foul. It bred insects that shimmered in clouds, illuminated by shafts of golden light.

"I'm sorry to give you such a bad impression of Korea," Mrs. Mun said. She rushed Paul along in an effort to make that impression as fleeting as possible.

Paul flipped through his dictionary as they walked. "That is all right," he said, still gamely struggling in Korean. "Tuberculosis patients if there are, I go anywhere. Things in Mokpo make me not worry no more." Mrs. Mun laughed. Paul was nothing short of comical whenever he opened his mouth to speak.

Mrs. Mun carried a half-dozen large yellow cards. Each one bore the name, age, address, and medication history of an actively infectious patient. She selected one, showed it to Paul, and headed toward the front gate of a nearby house. The outside wall fronted onto the little street; it enclosed a small cement-floored courtyard in which a single water tap and a wash basin presided over a scattered bunch of red peppers, *gochu*, drying on the ground. A white-haired grandmother squatted before the tap, washing clothes. Judging from the information on the card, this was the patient's wife. Mrs. Mun stopped at the gate and called inside:

"Good afternoon, Grandmother. I am Nurse Mun and this is Mr. Pak Jong Shik," Mrs. Mun said, using the Korean name that the Peace Corps had given Paul. "We're from the Mokpo City Health Center. Is this Kim Myong Sun*shi*'s house?"

"*Yeh.*"

"Is he at home?"

Deep lines of sadness creased the old woman's face. She shook her head and turned back to her work. "*Anni. Jinan ju tola kattnundeh.*"

Mrs. Mun's face fell. She shook her head sadly and drew her breath in through her teeth.

'*Tola kattnundeh,*' Paul thought quickly. The phrase sounded familiar — like something he had learned in his language classes some months ago, something that meant 'he went away'.

"Grandmother," he piped in helpfully, in Korean, "his new address, may we have?"

The look of profound disbelief in the woman's eyes — mirrored in Mrs. Mun's — swiftly turned into one of blind fury as she fixed a withering gaze on Paul.

"*Nuguya?* Who the hell is this? You bring this foreigner here to mock me? What the hell is this?" She launched a torrent of invective which got worse with each passing second. The woman spoke so rapidly and with such fervor that Paul caught a few references to *paboya* — you fool — and *keh-sekki* — son of a bitch, but the more cutting obscenities were lost on him. Her voice rang through the neighborhood like a bugle call, summoning curious stares from nearby rooftops and windows.

"Huh ... ?" Paul froze where he stood. He was aware of nothing but the woman's surprisingly strong voice, a sudden pounding in his head, and an electric charge of panic. Mrs. Mun grabbed his arm and jumped with him to the front gate. She managed to push him out and join him just before a chunk of lye soap skittered past them on the street.

"Mr. Pak," Mrs. Mun said in a hard voice, her lips pursed. "*Sajon chuseyo.*" Give me your dictionary.

She flipped through the pages and placed her finger next to the verb root *tola kada*: "Read this."

"*Tola kada*. One: 'to go back, away.' Two: 'to die, expire' ..." Paul's jaw dropped.

"Holy crap. I'm sorry."

## Two

"I have made a list of sentences," said Kwajang-nim that afternoon, pulling a sheaf of papers from his desk drawer. "We will practice English pronunciation today."

'Kwajang-nim' was not the man's name. It was his title — administrative chief — with an honorific *nim* added to it for good measure. His name was Kim So Nam. By tradition, and no less because of his forceful personality, no one at the health center called him by his given name.

Paul sighed. Every afternoon at two o'clock for the past sixteen weeks he had trudged to the health center's front office to sit at a low table beside Kwajang-nim's desk. A delicate bonsai tree, the only piece of natural greenery in the entire room, adorned the table. Paul had never seen him actually sitting at his desk; he almost always sat in his cushioned chair behind this table, passing the hours reading newspapers and paperback novels.

Kwajang-nim was a well-fed, self-satisfied man in his mid-fifties. He was, in Paul's opinion, peculiar and a little spoiled, but not a bad sort. He could be much worse. Paul had heard stories from his Peace Corps colleagues in other towns, most of them probably exaggerated, about the antics of the *kwajang*s at their health centers: some of them went on violent rampages at the slightest departure from routine; others never came to work at all, and still others demanded sexual favors from their female employees. Kwajang-nim's eccentricities were not that outlandish. He did come to work every morning, though late and chauffeured by the ambulance driver. He raged occasionally about small matters, but Paul suspected he did so only to keep his workers from ignoring him. He seemed to take little notice of the women who worked for him. His most annoying traits, in Paul's eyes, were his utter lack of interest in the work of public health and his assumption that Paul's role was to be his personal language tutor.

Paul dreaded Kwajang-nim's daily English lessons. At the head of the room, literally at center stage before an audience of twenty or thirty low-level bureaucrats, he sat patiently and listened to his boss rattle off a string of sentences copied from a textbook.

"You visited patients today," Kwajang-nim said in English — he always used English with Paul. "How did it go?"

"Very well, Kwajang-nim."

"I heard you wanted an address for a dead man. Ha, ha." He looked at his papers. "'Some toil for fame, while some toil for money.'" He turned to Paul. "How was that?"

"Perfect."

"Ah. Thank you. 'Through wine they had a quarrel with each other.'"

"Okay."

"'He was killed with a sword by a burglar.'"

"The 'w' in 'sword' is silent," Paul said.

"Are you sure?" Kwajang-nim cocked his head and looked at the word doubtfully.

"English is my native language, Kwajang-nim. The 'w' is silent."

Kwajang-nim chuckled, obviously enjoying the hint of acid in Paul's voice, and made a note on the paper.

Mr. Jong, one of Kwajang-nim's assistants, came to the table and waved to get their attention. He made a pantomime of speaking on the telephone.

"*Na?*" asked Kwajang-nim. Me?

Mr. Jong shook his head and pointed at Paul. He told them that a woman was on the telephone and she wanted to speak to Paul.

"He'll take it here," Kwajang-nim said.

"That's okay, Kwajang-nim. We really should finish this lesson. Mr. Jong, will you ask that person to call me back? Thank you."

"Do you enjoy visiting patients?" Kwajang-nim asked.

"Good."

"No. I am asking a question."

"Mm? Yes, Kwajang-nim. Very much. It is what I came to Mokpo to do."

Kwajang-nim pursed his lips and shook his head, as if surprised that anyone could actually enjoy tramping about the city meeting the lowest classes of people. He also looked disturbed at the prospect of giving Paul some bad news.

"I have decided that you should stay here during the day. You are very useful here. Yes — " he added, seeing Paul's jaw drop, "you are. Your co-workers say you are very valuable to them."

*Like hell they do*, Paul swore inwardly. Kwajang-nim was nothing if not totally transparent: he wanted Paul around for English conversation on demand. Paul took a deep breath.

"Kwajang-nim, I was sent to Korea to do health control work. How can I do that if I do not visit patients?" He knew that he was risking Kwajang-nim's anger by speaking so; the Korean way — which had been drilled into him during training — was to accept orders without argument.

The room suddenly fell silent. Even though few of the office workers could understand English, they saw the conflict in the men's body language.

Kwajang-nim pretended not to hear him. He shuffled his papers and put them back in his desk.

"We will study more tomorrow."

## Three

"Hello, Mr. Halkin?"

A woman's voice, rendered tinny and unpleasant by the ancient telephone on Mrs. Mun's desk, was unfamiliar. She mispronounced his name, as Koreans typically did, by substituting an 'l' for the more difficult 'r'.

"Yes?"

"Ah. Good afternoon. My name is Han Mi Jin. I am an English teacher at the Chung Ang Girls' Middle School."

"Yes. What can I do for you?" Paul immediately deduced the purpose of the call, and was tempted to hang up. The woman almost certainly wanted English lessons. Almost every young person with a modicum of skill wanted to engage Paul in English conversation, not out of friendliness, but to practice a language that would someday be useful: he became a glorified bit of homework. The whole business grated on him, and he felt new chunks of his humanity break off with every new imposition.

"I want to meet you."

"Gosh, I'm sorry, Miss — er — Han? I'm already giving English lessons to my boss here. I really don't have time to give more."

"Oh!" came the voice, after a pause. "But I ... don't want lessons. I already know English. I can give you Korean lessons."

"Beg pardon?" Paul frowned.

"Yes. Do you need it ... them?"

"Oh, sure," he stammered, thrown off by the woman's agility. "Are you serious about this?"

"Yes. Very serious."

Something made Paul stop and consider the offer. Korean was an astoundingly difficult language. Peace Corps gave its volunteers a small allowance for language tutoring, but he had not yet found a teacher. He needed help: even after ten weeks of training and four months' immersion in Mokpo, he relied more on gesturing and 'Konglish' — the mishmash of Korean and English words that most people could figure out — than on the language itself.

What the hell, why not? he finally decided. There could be no harm in meeting her; and if she were not sincere about giving lessons, he would enjoy telling her to get lost.

## Four

Clouds gathered steadily over Mokpo during the day. By nightfall, a cool drizzle started to fall, ringing the street lamps in halos of cold light. Paul paced impatiently in the alleyway beside the health center. He had dashed back downtown after finishing dinner at his boarding house. Though he had been suspicious of Miss Han's proposal at first, his natural curiosity took hold as the day wore on. By the time he rounded the corner at the agreed rendezvous spot, he was wondering if she were pretty.

At the stroke of eight, a slight figure hurried around the corner at the far end of the alley. She wore a tightly belted raincoat and Paul could tell, even without having a clear view of her feet, that she was wearing the stiletto-heeled shoes then in vogue among Korean women: she picked her way over the loose gravel and around the puddles in the street with the practiced agility of a little mountain goat. Paul could not make out her features at that distance because her umbrella shielded her face from the street lights.

"Mr. Harkin?" She stopped a short distance away.

"Yes. *Annyong hashumnikka? Chonun P'yonghwapong satanwon Pak Jong Shikimnida.*" How do you do? I am Peace Corps Volunteer Pak Jong Shik.

"I am Han Mi Jin." She shook Paul's hand and laughed. "Your pronunciation is perfect!"

"It's one of the few sentences I've learned by heart. I practice it all the time."

"'Pak Jong Shik'. Where did you get a Korean name?"

"My Peace Corps teachers gave it to me during training. All volunteers have Korean names."

"Pak Jong Shik. I like it. It is pretty."

"Thanks. Well ..." said Paul. "Shall we go to a *tabang* for some coffee?"

"You know *tabang*," Mi Jin smiled. "That's tearoom."

"Right. Do you know a good one?"

"The door next to the health center —"

"— Next door to the health center. Eh — do you know a better one, perhaps downtown?" The *tabang* she had mentioned was the favorite of the health center staff. The last thing he wanted was for one of the waitresses to amuse his co-workers tomorrow morning with stories of his "date" tonight. The health center thrived on gossip; all these past weeks in the fish bowl had taught him that.

Mi Jin led him to the main street. From there they walked briskly with the evening crowds toward the foot of Mount Yudal, through an older district of the city which was crisscrossed with shop-lined streets. The lack of street lights and the eerie illumination of fluorescent lights from an occasional open air market thwarted Paul's hopes of getting a better look at Mi Jin's face. Mi Jin, meanwhile, kept up a shy patter of small talk.

"Where is your home in America?"

"Indiana-*chu*, Lafayette-*shi. Missu Hanui chip odi issoyo?*" Where is Miss Han's home?

"Ha, ha. My house is in Muan Dong district. It is not far from the train station. But my family's house is on Chindo, a big island in the sea. When did you come to Korea?"

"*Jinan sawol-eh.*" Last April. For someone who wants to teach me Korean, he thought, she's using a lot of English.

"You are in Korea for seven months. That is a long time. Do you miss your home?"

"Uh-huh."

"Do you have brothers and sisters?"

"*Yeh. Oppa hanna hago yo dongsaeng hanna issoyo.*" One elder brother and one younger sister.

Mi Jin closed her eyes and laughed behind her hand. "You mean '*Hyong hanmyong kwa yo dongsaeng hanmyong.*' Use '*hyong*'. '*Oppa*' means elder brother for a girl. You are not a girl."

"Right." Now, he thought, she'll ask me either where I went to college or whether I have a girlfriend.

"Do you have a girlfriend?"

"Bingo!"

"Excuse me?" Mi Jin said, puzzled. "Is that her name?"

"No. *Yoja chingu obsoyo.*" I have no girlfriend.

Soon they arrived at a small *tabang* near the foot of Mount Yudal. The waitresses wore modest uniforms of dark blue skirts and white blouses, but the proprietress glided about resplendently in a traditional dress, a *hanbok*, of pink satin: a voluminous floor-length skirt topped with a short collarless jacket with full sleeves and a long bow in front. She escorted them to a table. A disk jockey in a glass booth played American popular music for a college-aged crowd. Paul saw envy etched in the eyes of many students who watched Mi Jin walk in.

"Why do I feel like Daniel in the lion's den?" he muttered.

Paul helped Mi Jin with her raincoat, then sat down and stole his first good look at her. She had a clear pink complexion, quite unlike the light brown of the people native to Mokpo and the islands. From wide, high cheekbones her face tapered to a pointed chin. Her eyebrows shot straight across her face over eyes that riveted Paul with intelligence and emotion. He perceived in a moment that she would not rest until she got what she wanted from him.

Mi Jin stole a glance at Paul as they settled in and ordered coffee. She saw a man not much older than herself — she was twenty-three — who still bore a few pimples on his face. He looked tall, about a head taller than she, and thin. He had light brown hair, as she had expected the *miguk salam*, the American, to have, since to her most Westerners looked very much alike. In only one respect did Paul deviate from her expectations: his eyes were brown, not blue. She had so wanted her *miguk salam* to have blue eyes.

"*Munjeh issoyo?*" Is something wrong?

"No." Then Mi Jin added: "You have brown eyes like a Korean."

"*Chongmal-iyeyo.*" That's true. "But only the color is the same. My eyes are round and my eyebrows hang down over them when I get angry." He made a mock frown for her and saw how easily he could make her hand fly to her mouth to cover a laugh.

"Well ..." Paul said, after a lull. "What are your hobbies, Miss Han?"

"My hobbies include reading, music listening, and foreign languages."

Ah-ha, Paul thought.

Mi Jin looked closely at Paul's face and noticed a faint change of expression in his eyes: something inside him turned suddenly cool and distant, as if his *kibun*, his inner spirit, had retreated into a separate, isolated spot in his soul.

This is it: she's going to hit me up for language lessons after all, Paul groaned inwardly. *Damn!*

"Foreign languages," he sighed. "Like English?"

"Yes. Also Chinese and some Japanese. I am able to speak these languages, also."

"But you would like some help with your English, wouldn't you?"

Surprised at the sudden edge in his voice, Mi Jin smiled nervously and began to speak, but Paul interrupted her.

"I'm sorry, Miss Han, but as I told you earlier today, I have no time to give lessons."

"Excuse me, but as I told you today also, I am willing to give you lessons. In Korean."

"Really, Miss Han —"

"I meant it," she said, and leaned forward. "I am not a lying person!"

"Okay, okay. I didn't mean to imply ..." Paul sputtered.

"Here is the plan I am thinking of. We can meet for one hour every other day, and I would help you with grammar and vocabulary."

"For how much?"

"Excuse me?"

"How much would you want to be paid?"

Mi Jin recoiled at the unexpected mention of money. "Ah ... I don't know. I did not think of that."

Paul paused, suddenly aware that he might have misjudged her. "Well, I'd like to give it some thought. You see, what you're offering is a bit unusual." He glanced at his watch and was startled to find that the time had passed quickly: before long the front gate of his boarding house would be locked for the night, whether he were home or not, and he would have to raise a clamor to be let in.

"It's getting late and I ought to get going," he said. "Tell you what: I'll call you. Can I have your telephone number? Good. Thank you." He rose, helped Mi Jin with her coat, and escorted her to the street. He shook her hand. "I promise to call you soon. Goodnight."

Mi Jin watched Paul's back merge with those of the crowds on the street. In the gloom, she reconstructed his face in her mind's eye.

"You have the gift of reading *nunchi*," her grandmother had told her in a quiet moment many years ago. "You got it from me. You and I, Jin-a — we can look into a man's face, into his eyes, and read his soul. Not as he tries to show it to others, but as it truly is. What a gift we have! We can never be deceived. We can live in peace with those whom we draw close to us because we can sense needs before they are spoken. And we can avoid those who would harm us. Aren't we lucky?"

Mi Jin had read Paul's *nunchi* thoroughly. It was easy, for he seemed utterly lacking in guile. Mr. Harkin has big moist eyes, she said to herself, filled with wonder at the world but also with a shadow of pain and longing. A good fellow, at heart; his guardedness a while ago was not typical of him. A nice boy far away from home — that sums him up well, I think.

He needs me, she smiled. That is fair. I need him.

## Five

"How was your date yesterday evening?"

Paul started rudely from the state of boredom in which he normally gave Kwajang-nim his English lesson.

"Excuse me?"

"Your date with the Korean girl. How was it?"

"It's — em — true that I had a *yaksok*, Kwajang-nim," Paul replied cautiously, "but it wasn't a date."

"Ha, ha. You're using the Korean word. But '*yaksok*' is a date."

"Excuse me, Kwajang-nim. '*Yaksok*' can mean 'date,' but it can also be a meeting or appointment or any commitment to meet somebody. Am I right?"

"But you went with a girl. That is a date."

"A date has romance in it. *Yonae*," Paul added after searching desperately through his dictionary. "There was no '*yonae*'. None. Just talk."

"Ha! What did you talk about?"

"This and that," Paul said nonchalantly. He fidgeted and fought an urge to tell Kwajang-nim to mind his own business. "About my home and about our hobbies. About — um — language lessons."

"Language lessons?" Kwajang-nim frowned.

"She wants to tutor me in Korean."

"But I already am giving you lessons. Every morning like now. Why do you need more?"

And lessons in what, Kwajang-nim? Paul fumed silently. In mauling English, perhaps, or in driving an American to drink, but never lessons in Korean, as you originally promised. Mi Jin, in her desire to exchange language lessons with Paul, never knew how great an ally she had in this portly dilettante in English.

"I never said I did, Kwajang-nim. We just talked —"

"If you need more help, I can give you lessons for one hour and one-half, instead of one hour." He looked at his watch and put his papers away. "But I have no more sentences today. Tomorrow I will bring more. You may return to your duty."

Paul rose, gave a shallow bow, and trudged back to his desk in another room of the health center. "Your damned sentences," he muttered when he got safely out of earshot, "you and your damned sentences ..."

The office workers watched his face as he walked out of the room. They exchanged knowing looks. "Mr. Pak's *kibun*, his spirit, is bad again."

*Six*

"Where might you be going on this fine afternoon, Miss Han?"

Mi Jin, at Mokpo Station, buying a round-trip train ticket to Kwangju, felt the hairs on the back of her neck rise at the sound of a familiar voice behind her.

"Vice-Headmaster Kim." She wheeled away from the ticket window to face a short pudgy man whose smile and habitually friendly expression agreed completely with the insincerity in his voice.

"*Annyong hashumnikka?*" Art thou at peace? "It is a surprise to see thee here," she said. "A pleasant one."

Kim nodded, not believing a word of it.

Mi Jin did not like Kim Son Kwan, and did not trust him. He was not a native Mokpoan, but a transplant from Taegu, in Kyongsang Province. If that were not enough, his politics were, in her view, of the most repellent variety. He considered himself a patriot, the most fervently patriotic member of the Chung Ang Girls' Middle School staff. Just last week he had stood up in the middle of a teachers' meeting, a routine affair to discuss textbooks for the next term, and had proclaimed:

"All the texts we order must state throughout that communism is an evil philosophy and an enemy to freedom." A few heads nodded in agreement, but for the most part the teachers let his remark pass without comment. "This is the belief we must drive into our students at the earliest possible age. To do anything less would be shirking our duty. Perhaps if we did a better job at this stage of their lives, there would someday be fewer communist sympathizers at the university."

Mi Jin knew he was referring to Chonnam University, her alma mater in Kwangju — and by association to her — but dared not react to the insult.

An instant animosity had sprung up between them at their first meeting the previous spring. He, among several other men, interviewed her for her present teaching position. The elderly Headmaster Shin, who was genuinely pleasant, liked her; Vice-Headmaster Kim, who was even more pleasant and outgoing, obviously loathed her for her university affiliation and the political sympathies that he could very well guess.

Kim walked with her to the train platform. "You're leaving Mokpo for the weekend?"

Mi Jin knew that the question would be asked a hundred times in a hundred ways until he got an answer. Lying to him about her destination would be useless: he would wait to see which train she boarded.

"Yes, sir. I am going to ... Kwangju."

The Vice-Headmaster's eyes narrowed for a split second, then relaxed.

"I am going there to visit my aunt, whose son needs help in English," she said, looking away so that Kim could not read her eyes. "He hopes to attend Seoul National University someday."

"Excellent, excellent," Kim said blandly. He had detected the lie instantly.

"Art thou too traveling today?"

"No, no. I have come to meet the brother of my son's mother, who is visiting us this weekend from Haenam. Ah, here is your train, Miss Han. Travel well."

"I thank thee, Vice-Headmaster Kim. Stay in peace."

Mi Jin felt Kim's eyes follow her into the coach. She shivered when she took her seat. Perhaps, she thought, it had been a mistake after all to tell Mr. Kim that she was going to Kwangju. Anti-government riots had been creating chaos in the city of Pusan recently, and sympathetic demonstrations were being staged in Seoul and Kwangju. He would naturally assume she was getting involved: and that would be the truth, after all.

Headmaster Shin had promised to keep her at the school through the spring semester, but she held out little hope for staying there afterward. She wanted — needed — to take part in the student movement. But she still had to make a living in an honorable occupation, and to be dismissed from her first job would be too disgraceful to bear.

"Of all the people to meet at a time like this ..." she muttered. "*Damn!*"

## Seven

Mi Jin's train groaned to a stop at Kwangju Station, an elderly stone structure built just after the Korean War. Its large waiting room smelled darkly of dilapidation even on a cool October morning. The odor was an unsettling end to an uneventful two-hour journey that had taken her through fields of rice that carpeted the ground with gold under an infinitely blue sky.

If Mokpo were an ant-hill swarming with people — as Mi Jin often thought while looking down on it from the heights of Mount Yudal — Kwangju was a beehive swirled about with busy, purposeful bees. The city had a bad attitude, like Mokpo: it could not truly be the capital of South Cholla Province without one. But it could ill afford the cockiness of its smaller neighbor.

Kwangju's people had mixed loyalties. Seoul's vast bureaucracy employed a large part of its population of eight hundred thousand souls, and jobs were always scarce in this depressed region. For this reason, at least, the people tolerated the governmental tentacles that might one day strangle them.

Still, it was a Chollado city, and its people cherished the ancient rivalry that set it at odds with the more privileged regions of the country like Seoul to the north and Kyongsang Province to the east. It landed Kwangju on the wrong side of the political divide and made it a focal point of defiance against President Pak Chong Hui. The abundance of colleges and universities in Kwangju only added to its problems. Chosun University and its rebellious sibling, Chonnam University, provided twin cauldrons where students and a bad provincial attitude could mingle in a volatile brew. It prompted the few foreign journalists who bothered to visit Kwangju to refer to the region as a 'simmering cauldron of rebellion'.

Upon her arrival, Mi Jin went first to a *tabang* not far from the Chonnam University campus. The unprepossessing sign outside said "*Pyong Hwa Tabang*", Peace Tea-Room.

The dirty plate glass windows of the Peace Tea-Room let in the slanting afternoon sunlight every day as classes ended. A wall-sized plaster *bas-relief* modeled after Botticelli's painting "The Birth of Venus" brightened up a side wall. Venus' breasts, made comically heavy by the anonymous artist's imagination, caught the sun's rays and over time sent shadows across her belly like a sundial. Most patrons went out to dinner or to political meetings by the time her shoulder fell into darkness.

The students and middling intellectuals who frequented Peace Tea-House called it their *Jang Nan Chip*, or "Trouble House". They gathered there to talk politics, to share world views, and to laugh. For a gathering place of student activists, it was surprisingly light-hearted. They took pleasure in stirring up trouble.

Mi Jin quickly caught the eye of Yun Tae Don, a good-natured senior at Chonnam University who had friends in the democracy movement.

"Is everything set?" Mi Jin asked. "Everyone knows what to do and at what time?"

"Everything, as far as anyone can plan a demonstration," Yun replied. "It's going to be fantastic! We've composed some new songs — wait till you hear them. One's about President Pak being a Nazi. He kills Chollado people instead of Jews. Another one compares the military to Nazi stormtroopers." Yun laughed. "We've posted the lyrics on the wall of the library. Almost everyone saw them and copied them before they got torn down. And a very well-known guy from Pusan is going to speak. He goes by the name 'Cho'. Then we'll march through the front gate of the campus and head downtown to the park next to the Provincial Office."

"Just a moment," Mi Jin said. "You're taking the demonstration off-campus? That's asking for trouble, you know."

"It's not my idea. At first, I wouldn't have done it that way, either. The police would move in too quickly and start arresting people, saying we've violated the latest security law, or some nonsense like that. But when I consider it, I believe it's a stroke of genius. Think about it." Yun glanced around casually with a practiced eye, looking for eavesdroppers. He beckoned Mi Jin to leave the *tabang* with him and take a convoluted walk up and down the alleyways of the neighborhood; if anyone followed them more than a block or two, he would know about it.

"There's a very good reason for taking the *demo* off-campus," he explained. "The first is purely practical. If we start and end it on campus, the police will eventually line up at the gate and keep us inside. Then they'll break it up. No one outside the university will be the wiser for the trouble we've gone to."

"But the police will break up the *demo* as soon as it moves off-campus," Mi Jin said. "Probably even more violently."

"That's just the point I was getting to. Nobody fools himself that demonstrations alone will ever do any good. The government won't be persuaded. But letting ordinary people see the whole bust-up in all its ugliness — that will be a revelation to everyone and may help us."

"Most people don't care about the democracy movement."

"They will when they see it all with their own eyes," Yun said. "Think about it! No more newspapers' lies about how delicate and polite the police are when they break up the *demo*s. Let the public see a few busted heads. Let them get a whiff of tear gas. Then see how quickly they side with us. They're ready for this."

They walked in silence for a minute.

"Elder Sister. How would you like to meet some of the leaders?" Yun asked.

"Leaders?"

"Sure. Not the 'middle managers' you see running around here. I mean people like the president of the Chonnam Student Union, his counterpart at Kwangju University, and Cho. I could arrange it."

Mi Jin's breath came quickly at the thought. "When?"

"Now. I know where they're gathering for a pre-*demo* strategy meeting. I'm in tight with one of the top guy's lieutenants."

"Take me there!" Mi Jin whispered.

Yun smiled. "Are you wearing comfortable shoes? We're going to walk a good distance to make sure we're not followed."

"Let's go!"

## *Eight*

Mi Jin and Yun took a convoluted path through the streets and alleyways of Kwangju to Chonnam University.

"From almost any other part of the city, we could walk straight to the campus," Yun explained, after ducking into a street market and lingering at a noodle stand. "But from Trouble House we have to be careful. Some people think the police have Trouble House staked out as a hangout for student radicals. It'd be smart of the cops to do that, *neh?* But I don't think they're onto us. They'd have shut us down long ago. Still," — he looked in all directions before starting out again — "it pays to be careful."

Finally, inside the campus grounds, in an upper-floor room of an administration building, Yun knocked four times quickly, then twice slowly, on a door that opened to a cramped, untidy conference room filled with people. A nervous-looking student, after asking their names and looking them over carefully, let them in.

"Yun Tae Don!" called one young man seated at the head of the table, "*Oso-wa!*" Come on in!

"That is Om Song Nam," Yun whispered to Mi Jin. "One of the best organizers in the movement."

Om motioned Yun and Mi Jin to sit. They found a place at the fringe of the group and listened.

"We'll march over to the plaza after a few short speeches," Om said to the students. "Cho will come with me and join the people in the plaza just as the crowd reaches the size we expect."

Cho, a tall, shaggy-haired graduate student from Pusan National University, nodded.

"How many people is that?" someone asked.

"In light of the furor over Kim Yong Sam's expulsion from the National Assembly, we expect over five hundred. Cho will address the people without an introduction from me," Om continued. "We know the police are going to crack down pretty quickly, and we want to put Cho on for as long as possible before things get rough."

"What happens when the police try to round us up?"

"The usual. We put up a fight for as long as we can, and then melt away. One good thing about that plaza is that a dozen side streets and alleys are within a block of it. We'll run off. The police will in effect be trying to catch water and tie it in a bundle. They won't get us.

"Another thing: face masks. Cover your nose and mouth with a wet cloth. There will be tear gas. You can count on it."

"Weapons," a glowering, earnest student named Lee Byong Guk prompted.

"The usual," Om replied. Anything we can get our hands on. There's a couple of construction sites along the way to the plaza. I suggest we load up with rocks and large sticks as we go, and tell others to do the same. I think a few people are bringing Molotov cocktails."

"Guns," Byong Guk persisted. "I wish we had guns. Can you picture the damage we could do if we had only a dozen army-issue rifles among us?"

Everyone in the room thought silently of the havoc they could cause, and of the repercussions.

"No guns are available," Cho said matter-of-factly, with only a tinge of regret. "Never were, never will be. Maybe it's just as well. A stray bullet hitting a child or some old woman would turn everyone in the world against us. We couldn't afford that."

"Bullshit," Byong Guk snarled. "Pardon me, *hyong*, Elder Brother, but one day it's going to come down to a battle of firepower between the student movement and the government. They win every skirmish. The government overpowers us because our weapons come from the Stone Age. If we get guns and if, unfortunately, a few other people get hurt, that's an acceptable risk, *neh?* They will have given their lives for a good cause."

A few students nodded.

"In giving one's life for a cause, the operative word is 'give'," Cho said sharply. "It must be given willingly. Killing an innocent person to prove a point would completely negate that point. Let the government make that mistake. It's far better to let them make victims of us. Guns may win battles, but victims can win wars. We have the moral advantage. It's the only advantage we do have. We can't afford to lose it."

"Why are we arguing about guns? We'll never get them, anyhow."

## Nine

Mrs. So, the proprietress of the Pyonghwa Inn and, to the Kwangju-based Peace Corps Volunteers who lived there, a well-known and beloved madwoman, fluttered about her small courtyard in a state of high agitation. Trying to talk herself into calmness only made it worse. She was washing dishes, and when she carried the wash water from the tap to the kitchen, she splashed most of it on the ground. Her young daughter got in her way and was blamed for the puddles that seeped quickly into the cracks in the concrete. The girl ran indoors crying, her ears boxed for her clumsiness.

"What's the matter?" an American asked Mrs. So but the woman squinted through swollen eyes and waved him off with an evasive laugh:

"I'm just getting old. Nothing to worry about. I feel like a *halmoni*, a grandmother, before my time, that's all."

Mrs. So was getting ready to go to the university campus. She had heard that speeches were going to be given there that afternoon, and that her son, a university student, was planning to take part in a demonstration.

Her friends in the neighborhood had tried to persuade her not to go. You have to be quick on your feet, they told her, because the riot police always put a stop to *demo*s by rushing in and chasing the students. You're sure to be trampled. Leave the boy alone, they said. Let him and his friends protest about the lopsided Yushin Constitution, or democracy, or whatever the favorite cause is these days. Protesting about one thing or another is just part of being a student.

She did not understand what the students were protesting about. She had never lived under real democracy, never knew a Korean who had, and had no idea what a constitution, much less the "Yushin" one, had to do with the cost of rice. From chatting with the Americans in her house, she figured that democracy was good and the Yushin Constitution not so good. If the students wanted to get democracy for Korea, more power to them. But she wanted her son to have no part in it. Myong Gun was a good boy, a smart boy. He had a future. Mrs. So could not stand by and watch him throw it away on some vain political quest. The boy needed to come home.

Under a warm afternoon sun and a cool October breeze at the far end of the quad at Chonnam University, a few hundred people milled around a speakers' platform hastily constructed of wooden packing crates. They chanted slogans that made Mrs. So's pulse quicken with fear for her son: "Down with the Yushin Constitution!" and "Down with martial law!"

A young man, lanky to the point of scrawniness, mounted the platform and called for silence. He identified himself as a philosophy student at Pu-san National University, and thus earned Mrs. So's scorn, for she cared little for intellectuals who kept their heads in the clouds and caused trouble for hard-working people.

"I am Cho," he proclaimed through a bullhorn. He balanced nimbly on the rickety rostrum and struck a self-consciously heroic pose. "Our nation, my friends, is at a crossroads. Korea must choose now between freedom and slavery, between national pride and the craven dependence that forces us to *saebae*, to bow, before a foreign power."

Mrs. So knew the tack this young man was going to take, and could not restrain herself from shouting loudly toward the platform: "Come on, now. Don't be coy. Do you mean the United States?" Everyone heard her; her voice, conditioned by the raising of four mischievous children, carried well over the distance that separated her from Cho.

The crowd tittered at her raucous tone. No one took her seriously enough to quiet her.

"Yes, Ajumoni. *Miguk*," Cho replied, smiling. He continued, addressing the crowd: "Who, I ask you, is responsible for the suppression of freedom in Pusan — ultimately? You know as well as I do.

"Our government never acts alone. The United States pulls the strings that make President Pak Chong Hui jump like a puppet! America supplies tanks and guns to Korean troops to put down a just struggle for Korean democracy."

"But America is a democracy," Mrs. So called out. "Why would they be against democracy in our country?"

Cho smiled darkly and took a one thousand won bill — worth about two American dollars — from his pocket. He waved it in the air.

"We are slaves to a foreign economic dictator. American businessmen come to our country. They stay in fancy hotels in Seoul and can't wait to sleep with Korean women. They meet with rich Koreans who own vast *chaebol*, the family-owned conglomerates. Around coffee tables they make deals. They buy our labor at bargain rates and take home all the profits ... except for spare change they give to the wealthy sons of bitches who own the *chaebol* and are friends of the ministers in our government. The Americans give us more work, and we do it — cheaply. If we do something they don't like, they say 'Maybe we'll go to Taiwan, eh?' and President Pak grovels on cue. But the bastard also ensures that he has no political opposition by creating the Yushin Constitution, which makes him president for as long as he likes.

"The government, the wealthy elite, they're all rotten with corruption. The Yushin Constitution ensures it will stay that way forever."

Mrs. So grudgingly agreed with Cho, for she lived in a district where young girls, making barely enough money to live on, sewed sweat suits and underwear from dawn to night every day. But she shook her head.

"America doesn't look upon us as a nation of humans," Cho continued. "How many of you have ever met an American soldier? Ever been addressed by them in *panmal*, low language? That's all they learn. They use it

20

on college professors and prostitutes alike. No, friends, South Korea is a big military base. Nothing more. Jimmy Carter says, 'You take these troops or we stop investing in your country's economy.' Our government hears and rolls over like a dog."

Cho had his facts wrong, and the crowd knew it. President Carter had actually proposed, against fervent opposition from the Korean government, pulling all thirty-five thousand American troops out of Korea by the spring of 1980. They saw the truth as a flexible thing, however, and would not spoil the point of Cho's speech by disputing with him.

"Therefore, my friends, Korea can never exist as one nation — with no separation between north and south — as long as American soldiers and guns remain on our soil. Who was it who tore us apart from our northern brothers after World War II? The United States —"

"And *Sokyon*, the Soviet Union," Mrs. So interrupted shrilly. "Have you read your history books? Of course not, you're too busy making speeches." The crowd gave her a good-natured laugh while Cho began to lose patience. "Papa Josef Stalin — or was it Kim Il Song, I'm always getting those guys confused — split our country in two after the Japs got kicked out. By the Americans, I might add. Oh, and then there's all the Christians who had to move down south because Kim Il Song didn't like them. Were you there when all that happened, Sonny? *Eh?* I was."

Mrs. So shook her head and started to walk away, secure in the belief that she had won the impromptu debate.

"First of all, Ajumoni, I have no friends in the Soviet Union," Cho called after her. "Secondly, I prefer one Korea over two Koreas. How many families have been split apart by the meddling of the big powers? Ten million? Fifteen million? Are you, Ajumoni, separated from a close family member because the United States says you should be?"

Mrs. So's anger began to boil over. Her parents lived and died in North Korea, and she had not seen them in the last years of their lives; her uncles and cousins were probably still alive, but she had no way of knowing.

"Why, you little pup! What do you know about such things? Listen, I'm not the only one with family in the north. Lots of people, including your despised rich people and government leaders have family up there. Don't you tell me that they would sell their loved ones for money or power!"

A voice in the throng nearby muttered "Get her out of here," and was echoed by louder ones further off. But when someone approached Mrs. So, it was a young man, a student, who spoke gently to her:

"Let's go, Ajumoni. Don't get so excited. You made some excellent points. But let us have our time. We know what we're doing."

He escorted her quietly away from the campus.

*Ten*

Mi Jin watched with mixed emotions as the *ajumoni* was led away. She supported the student movement; yet unlike many of the students she knew, she neither hated the United States nor admired North Korea. Weeks later, when thinking of this incident, she would feel a stab of uneasiness that she agreed more with the *ajumoni* than she did with Cho.

A wave of chanting started, on cue. The chants were the standard ones that Mi Jin knew well: "Down with Pak Chong Hui!" and "Tear up the Yushin Constitution!" After a few minutes, however, she heard a new one. Cho handed the bullhorn over to another student and stepped down.

"*Shine-ro kaja!*" the student shouted. "Let's go downtown!"

The crowd turned slowly and moved *en masse* toward the main gate of the campus a short distance away. A group of students unfurled a twenty-foot wide banner that read "DEATH TO THE YUSHIN CONSTITU-TION!" in large red letters. Chanting loudly, they marched in neat rows a dozen abreast. The first to reach the gate was a group of freshmen girls who walked together linked arm in arm. The crowd constricted and then flowed through the narrow opening behind them like honey from an overturned jar.

A long green line of police in riot gear waited for them a block away from the gate. They wore heavy green fatigues and held rectangular shields. Wire grille face plates and helmets that hung down behind, covering their necks, made them look like modernized Japanese samurai in battle gear. Their faces were obscured by gas masks.

"Sons of bitches!" Mi Jin whispered, then louder, as a warning to the people around her: "Police! Get ready!"

Cho saw the phalanx of riot police move and felt the familiar quickening of the blood that presaged a fight. He got the bullhorn back and shouted through it the more extreme slogans the crowd had been waiting all afternoon to use: "Death To Nazi Pak Chong Hui! Throw Out The Yushin Constitution!" The throng, which Mi Jin estimated at a couple of thousands, replied in kind, over and over, with raised fists as they marched on.

'Death To Nazi Pak Chong Hui! Death To Nazi Pak Chong Hui!'

The riot police commander and his men held their place across the street.

A half dozen students ran through the crowd, each staggering under the weight of boxes containing small glass bottles filled with gasoline and stoppered with rags. One student passed by Mi Jin and offered her one.

"Molotov cocktail?"

She shook her head. She hated those terrible weapons. They caused too much damage, and were utterly horrendous when they set people afire. "That's what they're for," friends had told her many times, friends who had

22

made and thrown many of them throughout their college careers. "Police have guns, we have Molotov cocktails. They even the odds in battle."

Mi Jin still would not touch them. Instead, she ran over to a street corner where some people were pulling up sections of the sidewalk with a pickax. She picked up a few fist-sized chunks of concrete and turned a watchful eye toward the riot police.

"Death to Pak Chong Hui! Throw out the Yushin Constitution!"

The battle lines formed on opposite sides of the wide plaza outside the campus gate. A demilitarized zone of roughly fifty yards separated the two wary groups, the one side a tight formation of green and the other a shifting, amorphous mass. For a minute they stood still and stared, waiting for the other to make the first move. Cho acted first. He held a Molotov cocktail out to a colleague for a light. The firebomb leapt to fiery life in Cho's hand, spitting fragments of gasoline-wet cloth to the ground. He took a few running steps toward the police and let it fly. It fell well short of its target, intentionally, but the sight of the flames spreading out on the street toward the patrol spurred the crowd and the police to action.

The chanting stopped and the banners came down. The demonstrators now concentrated on well-honed tactics of attack and retreat. Several more firebombs popped out from the crowd, drawing lazy yellow arcs over the park. The police started an inexorable advance toward them, quietly and without fuss, like a machine.

One firebomb struck the pavement a few feet from the police line and splashed against a policeman. His riot shield bore the brunt of the fiery spill, but some of it onto his fatigues. With a shout he retreated into the folds of his phalanx where, after someone pried his shield from his hands, he was hurriedly tamped out. Before long he was back on the line, none the worse for the experience.

A dozen policemen in the front line raised tear gas launchers to their hips and fired. *Pop! Pop! Pop!* The sound was like a toy gun shooting rubber balls. Trails of smoke arced over the street. The canisters landed a few feet away from the demonstrators and quickly engulfed them in thick, acrid gas.

The breeze carried the gas into the crowd. People scattered like chaff. Mi Jin saw it coming and closed her eyes and held her breath. She reached into her purse for a wet handkerchief that she had put there for just such an attack. Many of her colleagues too slapped rags over their noses and mouths and dabbed at their eyes when the stinging got too bad.

Mi Jin, still carrying her load of rocks, ran to an alleyway that opened onto the plaza. Several dozen demonstrators were there already, hiding quietly in doorways and around the crooks and corners of the street. Most had rocks or Molotov cocktails at the ready.

The mass of riot police moved quickly across the length of the plaza and jogged at double-time past the alleyway's opening onto the street. Mi Jin looked up and saw Cho breathing heavily and waiting a few feet away, holding another Molotov cocktail. He smiled at her and nodded. He waited a few more seconds, lit the fuse with a cigarette lighter, and with a loud "*Kaja!*" — Let's Go! led the demonstrators out into the street. They caught the police off guard. A group of demonstrators had done exactly the same thing at the next alleyway a few hundred feet ahead, but had not waited for the police to pass them. The police, caught between two groups of demonstrators, were forced to turn back to back and defend themselves on two fronts.

"I can't believe they let themselves get caught like this." Cho took several running steps and hurled his firebomb. It landed in a plume of flame and ignited the trouser legs of two policemen, who retreated into the mass of their comrades. Mi Jin followed Cho and handed him a rock. He accepted it without a word and threw it deep into the police ranks, where a loud thud told that it had made contact with a helmet. Mi Jin threw another rock. It bounced against a shield.

They ran back to the alleyway together and Cho picked up another Molotov cocktail. He lit it and held it out to Mi Jin. She recoiled. Cho shook his head and bounded out into the street.

The police did not stay in their defensive formation for long. Presently a black army jeep mounted with a tear gas cannon rumbled into the plaza. With a fiery *fraaaaaap! fraaaaaaap! fraaaaaap!* it sent clouds of gas into one side of the student ranks that held the police at bay. Mi Jin, coughing and sputtering, ran out onto the street and into another alleyway with most of the other demonstrators. Her wet handkerchief gave little protection against this more penetrating type of gas.

She ran as far into the alleyway as she could to escape the tear gas, then sat down to rest. Steps approached. She got ready to run again, but stopped when she saw that it was Cho. He too had had enough of the gas for now.

"My grandfather fought in the streets against the *jjokbalb*, the Japs," he said, sitting down beside her. He dabbed his swollen eyes with a damp cloth and let out a grunt of pain. "The only difference between him and me is that he dealt with bullets instead of gas."

"Pray heaven it doesn't come to bullets for us."

"It will," Cho said. His face was a mask, expressionless. "Sooner or later it will."

## *E*leven

Paul was largely unaware of the riots that had taken place the previous Saturday afternoon in Kwangju. He picked up on some small arguments among his coworkers, and he gathered that they were talking about the picture on the front page of the newspaper. It showed a policeman in riot gear, his leg set aflame by a Molotov cocktail. It was only mildly interesting to him; he was more interested in doing his work.

Paul liked Mrs. Mun, his co-worker and the sub-chief of the health center's tuberculosis control section. There was something maternal about her that let her serve as a stand-in for his own mother, whom he missed terribly. She was a middle-aged registered nurse, married to a martial arts instructor. Her two sons, a sophomore and a senior in high school, were her pride and joy. Paul discovered that the easiest way to get on her good side was to speak well of her sons. He did so sincerely, for he had seen the boys several times and liked them.

Mrs. Mun spoke no English and had no interest in learning any. Her best attribute, the one that had smoothed Paul's way at the health center from the beginning, was something like a sixth sense, an uncanny ability to penetrate his atrocious Korean grammar and limited vocabulary and understand almost anything he tried to say. She continually gauged his level of skill and chose her words and structured her sentences at a level that he could understand. "Why can't they all be like her?" Paul often wondered.

"*Kajong pangmun hagoshipoyo?*" Would you like to go home visiting? She always knew exactly what Paul's response would be, and she delighted in it.

"Yes! *Kapshida!* Let's go!" Then his face clouded. "I cannot. Kwajang-nim going home-visiting, he won't let me."

Mrs. Mun tossed her head and gave Paul a look that said, "Just what is that spoiled so-and-so dictating now?" He packed a medical kit and Mrs. Mun summoned Miss Choi, one of her younger health workers, to go out with him.

Out on the street, Paul pulled his sweater tightly around his neck. A stiff October wind blew cold from the sea under an oppressive layer of clouds, ruffling Miss Choi's hair in what she considered a most unbecoming way. They rode the bus to Yang Dong district, a middle-class neighborhood on the eastern slope of Mount Yudal. Paul was glad to get out of the health center; Miss Choi was almost inconsolable.

"Mr. Pak, why do you insist on going out in this weather?" she asked, in Korean.

"This kind of weather I like. The air is good-smelling."

"You must have come from the North Pole. Are you an Eskimo?"

"Excuse me? I do not understand."

Miss Choi handed Paul a green patient treatment card. Its corners had become dog-eared through age and use. Kim Son Hum, a sixty-two year old male, first came to the health center for treatment in early 1975. Now, more than four years later, his sputum tests still came back positive for tuberculosis.

"Mr. Kim is on secondary drug treatment. See, Mr. Pak, he started taking regular drugs a long time ago. After a few months he stopped. Half a year later he started again. Then he stopped again. This went on for three years. He has become resistant to the regular drugs. So now he gets the secondary drugs, which are ... ?"

"Continuing INH, ethambutol, rifampin, and kenomycin."

"Correct. Kenomycin is a hypo." She took out a hypodermic syringe from her medical bag and showed it to Paul.

They soon arrived at their patient's front gate, a rusty door that opened noisily to a courtyard lined with potted trees. An elderly man sat on the front step of the house smoking a cigarette.

"Are you Kim Son Hum*shi*? *Neh*. We are from the Mokpo City Health Center. How are you feeling today?" Miss Choi bowed to Mr. Kim and walked into the courtyard. "This is American Peace Corps Volunteer Pak Jong Shik."

Paul bowed to the old man while trying to hold his breath.

"Have you been eating your medicine, sir?" Paul asked.

"Yes, young sir, but *ehhh* — I don't like it. It makes my stomach hurt."

"That's because the medicine we're giving you is strong," Miss Choi said. "It's special medicine."

"*Ehhh* — whatever it is, it makes my piss orange."

"What did he say?" Paul asked. Miss Choi shook her head and continued:

"Even so, Grandfather, you must take it. The orange pee-pee is not harming you. You have a dangerous disease that must be controlled."

Mr. Kim nodded his head glumly.

"We've come to drop off your month's supply of medicine and to give you your injection," Miss Choi said. "Mr. Pak, will you please do it?"

Paul was startled. He had never given a shot to a person before; in a college bacteriology class he had inoculated a few laboratory animals, but they were incapable of cussing, kicking, or any other thing that Paul feared a Korean man in pain could do with a snapped-off needle in his rear. He was not sure, but he thought that Peace Corps rules forbade volunteers to give injections. Two pairs of eyes bore into him, waiting for him to act.

He broke the ampule of sterile water, drew 100 cc into the syringe, and injected it into the bottle of freeze-dried medicine. He shook the bottle and drew the proper dosage back into the syringe. Miss Choi handed him an alcohol swab with which he dabbed the flank that Mr. Kim offered to him. Holding the syringe like a dart, he jabbed it at Mr. Kim's skin. The needle did not go in.

Paul swabbed the skin again. The skin on the man's buttocks was old, but not especially tough. He held the tip of the needle up to the light. Poor fellow, he thought. It looked no sharper than a toothpick.

This time the needle pierced the skin, but Paul had to push hard.

"Did that hurt, sir?" he asked when he finished.

"No! It didn't hurt at all."

"Good. Well, we go now. Eat your medicine every day, okay?"

"Okay."

"*Annyonghi kyeship-shiyo.*" Stay in peace.

Miss Choi laughed as they walked back to the main road. "You should have seen your face when the needle didn't go in. *Waugh!* I could have died!"

"For cleaning the needles you boil," Paul said, "but do you make sharp?"

"Of course. Like this." She made motions that looked like she was filing her fingernails with an emery board. "You just don't push hard enough!"

After a few more calls, Paul and Miss Choi took the bus back downtown to the neighborhood of the health center.

"Let's stop at City Hall, Mr. Pak," she said. "I want to see someone."

City Hall was completely indistinguishable from the rest of the cluster of drab government buildings across the street from Mokpo's train station. Its halls echoed when women *click-clicked* along on their high heels. Occasional laughter or speech boomed through the rooms like the noises of a haunted house. To save electricity, only a few lights were turned on. The glare of sunlight never made it far into the interior of the building; the central hall lay plunged in eternal dusk. The place was cool in the summer, albeit in a musty, mildewy way; today, in October, it was almost as cold as the outdoors.

Miss Choi excused herself and went off to chat with a young woman behind a counter in the main room. Paul looked around patiently, trying to read the signs and the pamphlets that told citizens things that he could scarcely guess at. A small wooden box with a slot cut into its padlocked cover drew his attention. It looked like a mail drop-box. On its front, in bold block letters, it bore a sign: *Bangchop Ham.* Paul looked it up in his dictionary: *Bangchop* — counter-intelligence; *Ham* — box. Counter-espionage Box. He peered into the slot. A few folded slips of paper lay there. The purpose of the box suddenly dawned on him: if you suspected some acquaintance of being a North Korean spy, you wrote his or her name on a piece of paper, and dropped it in the box.

Paul smiled impishly. On a slip of paper, he wrote in large unpracticed letters: "*Choi Song Kumun puk han spy imnida*". Choi Song Kum is a North Korean spy. Not knowing the word for "spy," he left the word in English. He waved the paper above the slot in the box.

"Miss Choi," he called. "This place right for the paper it is?"

Miss Choi looked, started, and dashed toward Paul to grab the paper from his hand. "Mr. Pak," she hissed, but barely able to suppress laughter at his impertinence, "do not do that. That is very serious business. You could get me in trouble."

27

Paul obligingly tore the paper up and put it in his pocket. "Trouble?"

Miss Choi dropped the laughter completely. Her eyes bore into him with the intensity of a mother scolding an infant for running out into the street. "Very big trouble. This is not a matter for *nongdam*, joking."

Paul swallowed. "Sorry." He returned to the health center feeling very small.

## Twelve

Paul lay on his foam mattress on the floor of his room, and pulled his heavy quilted *ibul*, his comforter, around his shoulders. He was warmed against the autumn chill by the heat that radiated from the floor - heated in traditional fashion by a *yontan*, a glowing brick of charcoal set in a receptacle outside that drew in air, warmed it, and circulated it through an air space beneath the floor. The high school students who rented the next room in the boarding house sang together and chattered. Paul heard every sound through the thin walls. He was trying to concentrate on the international edition of Newsweek that had arrived from the Peace Corps office in the morning's mail.

He scanned the magazine's cover and turned to the table of contents. The wide black slash of a marker pen obliterated a paragraph next to a photograph of President Pak Chong Hui. He flipped a few pages forward and held the magazine up to his lamp's feeble light. A straight tear ran along the length of one page. The page numbers jumped from sixteen to nineteen.

His magazine had been mangled like this before, and he knew what it meant: students were rioting in Pusan again. News of it had fallen victim to the Korean government censors. He would know nothing about it unless he could find an uncensored magazine somewhere.

"Damn the censors," he grumbled. Normally he took censorship in stride, but today had been an especially rough day and his threshold of annoyance was low. He tossed the mutilated magazine aside and turned out the light.

In the darkness his thoughts turned to his first language lesson with Han Mi Jin the night before, a few days after her return from a trip to Kwangju. Her first task had been to probe the state of his knowledge of Korean vocabulary and grammar. The poor woman's face looked pinched and worn by the time she had finished the test, conducted entirely in Korean.

"Will you describe your work at the health center to me?" she asked.

"*Neh?* Excuse me?"

"Tell me about your work at the health center, please."

Again, Paul drew a blank.

"At the health center, what work do you do?" Mi Jin asked, obviously on the verge of giving up and trying a simpler question.

"Ah! What work. A tuberculosis control worker I am."

"Very good," Mi Jin said, relieved. "What did you do today?"

The conversation went on like that, by fits and starts, seemingly for hours. After covering the minutiae of the day, Paul had finally managed to turn the topic of conversation in a direction that interested him. "*Missu Han. Bangchop hami muoyo?*" What is a counter-intelligence box?

Mi Jin raised an eyebrow, wondering how he had come across one of them. After a couple of abortive tries at explaining in Korean, she switched to English, and the linguistic tension between them eased noticeably. "South Korea is always having trouble with North Korea. You know this, *neh?* Sometimes spies come down from the north and cause trouble in our country. They get information, they destroy things, they cause ... not resting ...?"

"Unrest."

"Thank you. Unrest among people against the government. So sometimes if people act strangely, other people can put their name in the bangchop ham, the counter-intelligence box, so the police can watch them."

"Is that a good thing?" Paul had asked. "People snooping on each other? What if they finger the wrong guy?"

"Snoop ...? Finger?"

Paul rephrased the question.

"Yes. It is bad. Many people are innocent, but the police and KCIA — the Korean Central Intelligence Agency — watch them and arrest them. I know people who do not like North Korea, but were arrested anyway. They worked with students and labor unions, and spoke out against President Pak. They got arrested because they did things that our government did not like."

She drew her head close to Paul's and said in a low, hard voice: "I myself, I hate President Pak. I hate his spies." She straightened and caught Paul with her hooded eyes, swearing him to secrecy with her look.

Paul paused as the importance of her statement sank in. Koreans rarely talked freely about their politics, especially to foreigners: a dismissive wave of the hand and a murmured "I don't know about such things ..." usually closed a political discussion quickly. For Mi Jin to volunteer such opinions to Paul sent a thrill of sudden intimacy through him, as if she had just presented him with a dangerous peek behind a veil.

"Spies?" Paul asked. "The people who use the *bangchop ham?*"

"No. The KCIA. They are everywhere. Everywhere. Every company, school, government office ... They all have one person or more who watches people and gives information. These people are supposed to catch North Korean spies, but they usually watch people who disagree with the government. There is one such spy in my school. I am sure of it."

"Isn't it possible you're being a little paranoid?" Paul looked the word up in the dictionary. "*Pyonjipbyong.*"

"It is not para- paranoia," Mi Jin replied simply, "if you know it is true."

# CHAPTER TWO

To Ajumoni's way of thinking, the American was without question the strangest human being — if that word could be rightly used to describe a foreigner — that she had ever seen.

Paul had come last July to live with her family and a few high school students at her boarding house on the outskirts of Mokpo. It was a small L-shaped building, with each room opening onto a porch running along the L's inside length. A walled-in courtyard filled in the rest of the area to fit into a rectangular lot. The outhouse, or *pyonso*, was a tiny room built into the wall next to the front gate. The house was made of timber, cement, and plaster, and the roof, covered with red clay tiles, curved up gracefully at the corners. It looked like nearly every other old middle-class house in Mokpo.

She had never dreamed of a more impossible mixture of knowledge and ignorance than she found in Paul: at their first meeting he had bowed and said with exemplary politeness, *"Choum paepgae-sumnida"* — I'm delighted to make your acquaintance — but stumbled in the most hilarious pidgin Korean when he asked where the toilet was. He knew the Korean alphabet and had learned that it was invented by King Sejong the Great in the year 1446, but he could hardly read anything in it.

She watched curiously on his first day as he set up his portable closet and unpacked his belongings. He owned a fabulously expensive-looking camera, a small cassette tape machine, a stack of books all in English, and a large number of snapshots. The pictures piqued her interest more than anything else. How did he live in America? she wanted to know. What did he leave behind when he came here? How does my home compare to his?

He showed the pictures to her after his first supper at her house. One was of a woman with hair the color of a thundercloud: *Omoni*, mother. And a man with a huge belly: *Aboji*, father. A beautiful blond teenager, *Su-san*, his sister, and a man in an American Army uniform, *Jon*, his elder brother.

31

She felt drawn to one snapshot more than any of the others: it showed his mother standing at the door of a large house. Her gray eyes were swollen and shiny. "The day I went to Korea," he told her, "this picture I took." Ajumoni gazed at that photograph every time she had occasion to come into his room, and compared herself to that gray lady. "Poor woman," she had often thought, "the boy ought to have stayed home."

"Song Min's mother!"

Ajumoni looked up from the water tap in her courtyard, where she was hunkered down low on her heels washing laundry in a large plastic tub. Her neighbor called her from the open gate.

"*Yeh*, come in. I've just been scrubbing the American's clothes."

"Ah," the woman said. She squatted at the tap with a noisy grunt. "How is he these days?"

"Who can tell? He keeps to himself most of the time, and his habits are so strange that I can't tell from one day to the next if he's well or not."

"Oh?"

"He misses his family, I can tell," Ajumoni said. "It would help if he had friends here in Korea, but his language is poor and he has very odd ways." She half-rose on her haunches, turned her head, and, blocking one nostril, cleared the open one with a ragged bugle-like blast.

The neighbor moved next to her and picked through Paul's clothes. "Tell me something, Song Min's mother. I'm dying with curiosity. The American — is he clean?"

"What do you mean?"

"Is he dirty?"

"Well, yes and no. He goes to the bathhouse every other day."

"That often?"

"*Yeh*. And he never fails to wash his hands every time he visits the outhouse." She shook her head, bewildered. "But in some ways he's so dirty. Do you know, when he sat down to his first meal here, he turned his head and blew his nose!"

"You're joking!"

"No. I almost puked up my supper."

"Did he clean up the floor?"

"He didn't do it on the floor." Ajumoni gingerly pulled one of Paul's dirty handkerchiefs from a trouser pocket and brandished it at arm's length. "He blew into this. Americans carry their snot around with them!"

"*Chuk kae neh!*" the neighbor exclaimed. I could die!

"Can you believe it? And the Americans are trying to teach us Koreans about hygiene!"

"They'd be better off learning from us."

"Ha, ha. You got that one right."

"Has your son spent much time with the American yet?"

Ajumoni's eldest son, Pak Song Min, was a high school student in Kwangju. He had earned top grades at his middle school in Mokpo the year before and that had got him into one of the better technical schools in the province. He lived cheaply in Kwangju with relatives; the rents paid by Paul and his fellow boarders went to pay the school's exorbitant tuition.

"He's been with him a little, between July and the beginning of the school term." The mention of the boy instantly brought a mother's proud smile to her face. "He'll be home soon on winter vacation. That's three solid months that he can be learning English from the American. With that kind of boost, he'll go far!"

The neighbor rose to her feet, her knees popping as she stood. Ajumoni's talk of her son grated on her sometimes, for she had only daughters and had little hope for their future: only that they marry into respectable and possibly wealthy families. She saved no money for their education beyond that needed for a mediocre local high school; she and her husband did not believe they were worth more than that. When Ajumoni started yapping about her favorite subject, her son, she took it as her cue to go home.

"Tell the American hello for me."

## Two

Kwajang-nim, seated comfortably in stockinged feet in a small private room at the Neja Tabang, sipped his tea placidly. A young woman sat beside him. She worked there; her tight blouse and short skirt were part of the decoration of the place; her attention was the entertainment. She kept his cup filled and, while chattering on with empty compliments about his stylish suit and strong hands, she managed to rub herself against him. Kwajang-nim's hands wandered and his tips were always more than generous.

"I'm tired," the *tabang agashi* sighed. She snuggled against him and made sure a firm breast made an impression on his arm. "Are you going home tonight?"

"Yes, I am," Kwajang-nim laughed. He chucked her under the chin. "My wife would murder me if I slept out. Then you'd get no more of my company."

"Who's coming tonight?" the girl asked.

"The usual bunch. Mr. Lee from the bank, Mr. Kim from the school, and a few friends from church. Are enough of your girls here to take care of them?"

The girl poured him another cup of tea and lit his cigarette. "Of course."

"Speaking of Mr. Lee!" Kwajang-nim rose to his feet and gave a short bow to his old friend, who had just slipped off his shoes and entered the room through the sliding wood-and-paper latticework door. "Good health to you."

"And to you, too. Hello, Agashi." He lightly slapped the girl's rear. "Get me some coffee, will you?" He paused to watch her hips swing when she left the room, then took a seat beside his friend.

Lee Won Il by all appearances belonged to Mokpo's upper crust: a member of the local chamber of commerce, a friend of the mayor and several city councilors, and a major in the National Reserves. But like many men in Mokpo, even those with wealth and powerful friends, there was still an underlying coarseness about him, like a man in a smart suit who wears frayed underwear.

The noise of the television drifted in from the next room. A snatch of a commentator's speech touched on the expulsion of a legislator, Kim Yong Sam, and his followers from the National Assembly in Seoul a few days before. The commentary was decidedly anti-Kim.

"The bastard is getting it where he deserves it, *neh?*" Mr. Lee observed. "Right up the ass. The President showed him a thing or two."

Kwajang-nim grunted, amused. "In the hindquarters. That's what he deserved, that's where he got it, all right." They laughed. "Here's Mr. Kim. No doubt he's got something to say about it."

Kim Son Kwan, the vice-headmaster at the Chung Ang Girls' Middle School, smiled politely at the *agashi* who took his jacket and eased himself onto a cushion next to Mr. Lee. He allowed the girl to light his cigarette.

"Something to say about what, my friend?"

"Kim Yong Sam," Kwajang-nim replied, shoving an ashtray across the table. "I knew you'd frown like that, Teacher. You are completely predictable." He turned to the *agashi* who had now reclaimed her seat next to him. "Mention any political figure from the Left - or even just the Opposition - and Vice-Headmaster Kim goes crazy. Mr. Lee and Mr. Kim are hilarious when they talk politics, but the latter is the better of the two. He throws the most entertaining fits." Kwajang-nim, the *agashi*s, and Mr. Lee laughed heartily.

"There is no difference between the Left and the Opposition, as far as I can tell," Kim corrected him with a peevish growl. "Both are a pain in the rear and a real danger."

"Lighten up," Mr. Lee said, and motioned to a newly arrived *agashi* to take a place next to his old friend. This one wore a daringly open blouse that displayed a lacy white brassiere when she bent over, which she did frequently. "I don't find your fits as amusing as our friend does. I really fear you'll have a heart attack." The two men laughed again.

"Let's get off this subject," Kwajang-nim said. "We shan't give Vice-Headmaster Kim bad *kibun*, bad spirits. That wouldn't be right. Come, have something to drink."

The new *agashi* poured another cup of tea and made sure she did not extend it too far from her bosom when she handed it to him.

## Three

"Repeat after me. Pak Jong Shik. *'Chonun yogan kippuji anayo.'* That means 'I am very glad.'"

Mi Jin sat across the table from Paul and smiled thinly at him. The smile hid her dismay at his struggle with the Korean language. As far as she could tell, he knew little more than stock phrases, a few basic words of vocabulary, and only the simplest constructions of grammar. What he did know he said mostly in ultra-respectful High Korean — not improper, but ludicrous in most situations. His understanding of spoken Korean was poor, even when she enunciated each syllable slowly. Much to her embarrassment, the other customers of the *tabang* heard every word they said.

"*Chonun yogan kippuji ana* ... wait a minute," Paul said. "'*Kippuji anayo*' means 'not glad,' doesn't it? Even I know that much."

"You are correct. However, *'yogan'* makes it different. When you place it before the verb and make it negative, it makes the verb stronger in the positive meaning."

"Huh?"

Mi Jin shook her head. She needed to take a new approach with Paul. He was not stupid — she knew that — but the approach she took with her students, of painstaking instruction in grammar and parts of speech, simply were not working for him. He knew plenty of simple words, but he was trying too hard to fit them together in some linguistic puzzle.

She reached across the table and tapped his forehead.

"Jong Shik*shi*. You are thinking too much. While you're thinking, you're falling behind. That is partly my fault. Let's start again. Do not use your head so much." She tugged at his ears. "Use these instead. I will say a couple of sentences. Clear your mind and listen. Then tell me what I said."

"Okay."

In Korean, Mi Jin spoke clearly but at a normal rate of speed: "'I went to the department store today and bought a pink dress. It was too small, so I exchanged it.' Now, Jong Shik*shi*, what did I say?"

"You went to the store today," Paul said uncertainly. "You bought a dress...a pink one? A small pink one. And you sent it back."

Mi Jin smiled. "You see? Very close. You understand more than you know. Stop translating each word as you hear it. Listen without stopping. Do this, and you will master Korean quickly."

They continued like this for more than an hour. It became a game for them. At last Mi Jin took a piece of paper from her purse and unfolded it.

In two columns she had written twenty Korean words in over-sized, neat letters.

"Here is a list of words for *sukjae*, homework. Do you know any of them already?"

He read the words slowly, mouthing them one by one: his mastery of *hangul*, the Korean alphabet, was still shaky. He shook his head. "No. I suppose I should."

Mi Jin sighed. The words were indeed simple ones, words like *segyeh*, the world, and *jibang*, neighborhood.

"Learn these words for next time. I will give you a test."

"What if I flunk your test?" Paul asked. In response to a moment of incomprehension in Mi Jin's eyes, he added, "I mean 'fail'. Don't pass."

"I will hit you on the head and send you back to Podu University," she smiled.

"That's Purdue."

"Yes Podu, Pak Jong Shik*shi. Podu taehakkyo-eso muol kongpu hessoyo?*" What did you study at Purdue University?

"Biochemistry." He looked the word up in his dictionary. "*Saenghwa-hak.*"

Mi Jin raised her eyebrows, impressed. "That is a very difficult subject."

"No. Korean is a very difficult subject."

"You will become a bio ... biochemist when you go home?"

Paul shook his head. "It's not that easy. A professional 'biochemist' is someone who has a PhD — a *paksa* — and does research. All I've got is a bachelor's degree, and it's impossible to get a job in the field with that alone. Unless I want to be a laboratory technician — a *shihom-ja* — for the rest of my life. No, I won't be a biochemist."

Mi Jin's look invited further comment.

"That's not my goal anymore. To be honest with you, I got bored with the subject halfway through college. By that time it was too late to switch majors without having to spend another year in school. I did not want to do that. So I finished." An edge crept into his voice. "I got my degree, with distinction, and my parents were happy for a while."

Mi Jin burned to know what had upset his parents' happiness, but she kept her peace. We're still strangers, she told herself, and I can't yet ask him to draw aside this veil.

Paul stirred from his reverie and noticed that Mi Jin had been listening with rapt attention. He paused, unsure whether to go on.

From the time he had learned to read — early, at the age of three and a half — it had been decided in the Harkin household that Paul should go to medical school. The idea started with Paul's father. Because he had never attended college and had suffered from chronically poor health, he held the medical profession in high esteem. He saved his money for almost two decades, read every book and magazine article he could find about the best medical schools, and boasted to all his friends that his 'smartest kid' would be seeing patients one day. The proud man believed in his mental picture of a stethoscope-wielding Paul as devoutly as he believed in Holy Scripture. He could not be shaken from either.

When Paul broke the news to him that he did not want to be a doctor after all, the man could not believe what he was hearing. When the disbelief cleared and anger started to boil, he glared at his son as a medieval pope would have glared at the author of some loathsome heresy. When Paul declared that all he wanted to do now was seek some unnamed adventure outside the confinement of Indiana — perhaps with the Peace Corps — his anger exploded and the fallout polluted his household until the day Paul left for Korea.

Funny, he often thought sadly, how I dream of going home until I think about those last months.

"You said biochemistry is not your goal. What is your goal now?" Mi Jin asked.

"I don't know," he said, and closed his notebook.

She studied Paul's face for a moment, then tugged at his sleeve and said, "*Kaja.*" Let's go.

Mi Jin loved walking. It helped clear her mind, and she hoped it would do the same for Paul. She led him out.

"Where are we going?"

"Come with me and see the harbor," she said.

A rush of cold air met them when they stepped out into the dark street which, even at nine o'clock, was still full of people. The smell of the sea, with its rich, fetid mixture of fish, seaweed, and water grew stronger as they approached the harbor. They walked along the street that ran parallel to the water, lined with three-story warehouses. Only older docks with ramshackle boats in their slips populated this area behind the buildings; bigger ones, and the great Mokpo-Cheju ferry, were several hundred yards away along a newer, far less picturesque area of frontage.

Paul and Mi Jin walked slowly past the commodities shops that opened out onto the street. Their proprietors, mostly gnarled older women trying unsuccessfully to baby-sit their grandchildren while squeezing in the last transactions out of the day, huddled under heavy blankets against the sea wind. Bright tongues of propane flame lit the interiors of the shops and cast shadows that danced across the curb. Large plastic tubs filled to overflowing with rice, chickpeas, malt, and other grains and powders sat on sawhorses. On the ground, tubs filled with seawater held small live *nakji*, octopi, destined to be eaten — live or freshly killed — by customers in the nearby bars. Paul knelt beside one tub that contained a particularly skittish octopus and watched it flit from one end of its prison to the other.

How interesting he finds everything, Mi Jin thought as she watched him stop at every stall and look around. A simple *nakji*, a mere trifle, fills him with wonder. She began to see the creature with new eyes herself, and she knelt down beside him.

Fresh fish peered at them with pale eyes from every corner of the marketplace. "This *shijang*, market, is mostly for fish," Mi Jin said. "The other markets and the restaurants buy fish here."

"People in Mokpo eat lots of fish," Paul remarked, noticing too late that he had merely stated the obvious.

"At every meal."

Mi Jin saw the crinkle in Paul's nose. Even after four months in this city, he had not become accustomed to the odor of the sea and its inhabitants; the smells that permeated the harbor had permeated her life, both here and at her parents' home on Chindo, a large island well south of Mokpo in the vast archipelago off the mainland. She hardly noticed them anymore. She smiled at his discomfort.

"Let's go and look at the sea."

They turned at the end of the block and followed a broad passageway that led to the old dock area. The warehouses that lined the way were of an indeterminate age and woefully dilapidated. Paint peeled off in layers that must have gone back for decades — and none of it applied with much apparent care. Glass windows relieved the surfaces with gray, unlit smoothness, but even that smoothness was relative: encrusted with dirt and dingy with brine, they added to the buildings' decrepitude.

Mi Jin noticed how Paul looked at the buildings, attentively, as if drinking in a level of decay far beyond his experience. "I'm sorry to have to show you such ugliness," she said.

"No, no. Don't apologize. They do look old."

"Have you ever been to Pusan, or Pohang? No? If you went there, you would see much better places than this."

"Oh?"

"The government in Seoul hates the people in Chollado — Cholla Province, that is — especially the people in Mokpo. When the government gives money away to improve places like docks and warehouses, we don't get any. These buildings were built a long time before the War. Maybe they are as old as the Japanese occupation. I don't know. They are dirty and dangerous."

"The government won't give Mokpo any money because it hates Chollado?"

"That is always the way it has been. Even hundreds of years ago, when the kings in Seoul wanted to get rid of people, they sent them here, to Mokpo. This is a place of exile. It is the farthest spot from Seoul."

"That isn't right, is it?," Paul said. "Pusan is even farther away."

"Yes, but many of the important people in the government come from there, from Kyongsang Province. Those people help their own *kohyang*, their home region."

"But aren't there riots going on now in Pusan?"

"Yes." Mi Jin heard the implied question: If people in Pusan are more closely connected with the government, and conditions are better there, why are they rioting? For the first time she herself began to appreciate the complexity and inconsistencies in the situation. "It's the students who are demonstrating. They want democratic changes to the government."

"What about Mokpo? Why is this city worse off than Pusan?"

"Because Kim Dae Jung is from Mokpo."

Paul had heard the name, but could not place it.

"He ran for president against Pak Chong Hui several years ago," Mi Jin explained. "He won. But President Pak would not let him take office. He was upset that Kim, a man from Chollado, might take the government from him." She made an encompassing gesture with her hands, taking in the worn-down city around them. "This is his revenge," she said bitterly. "He punishes us for his own corruption."

The pair rounded the corner of the warehouse and walked out onto the dock area. A cold salt wind hit them in the face, and they drew their coats tighter. Rusty fishing boats bobbed in the water before them.

"It's too cold," Mi Jin said. "Let us go back."

## Four

Paul was convinced he would never understand how a typical Korean public health center works. At the very top of the organizational heap sat the *sojang*, the director. Paul had never met the *sojang* of his health center; he was a shadowy figure who never seemed to be around. Kwajang-nim, his administrative chief, actually ran the place. There were several *kyejang*s, or department heads, under him: pharmacy, laboratory, X-ray, communicable diseases, TB, and leprosy control. Most of these people never went out and did anything. Their main job seemed to be sitting at their desks in front of Kwajang-nim and writing numbers in large loose-leafed books.

Paul took refuge in the laboratory. His skills shone there, thanks to the hours of lab work he had done to earn his college degree. Laboratory Mr. Kim (not to be confused with the health center's Dr. Kim and Pharmacy Mr. Kim) immediately recognized Paul's value. They became fast friends. "*Shihom-shil eso ilul yogan choha haji anayo*," Paul said to him, using the grammatical construction Mi Jin had recently taught him. Laboratory Mr. Kim grinned and replied, "I'm glad you enjoy working in the lab. Well said, Mr. Pak!"

Laboratory Mr. Kim was a square-jawed man in his early thirties who clearly kept up his military physical training several years after leaving active duty. His hands were large and muscular, yet he handled the lab's medical equipment and biological samples with the delicacy of a surgeon.

Once, when he was alone with Mr. Kim, Paul had asked quietly, "In the health center, KCIA people are there?"

At first, Mr. Kim did not seem to understand the question. He shook his head. "*Neh?*"

Paul repeated it. Mr. Kim held his hand close to his chest and waved it as if brushing away a fly. He chuckled mirthlessly and shook his head. "No, Mr. Pak. Please don't concern yourself."

Paul did not know if the "No" meant no KCIA operatives or "no, don't ask." He let the matter drop. Mr. Kim had already slipped out of his lab coat and was pulling on his sweater. "It's almost quitting time, Mr. Pak!"

The crackle of a loudspeaker being turned on and adjusted through screeches of noisy feedback came from a tower atop City Hall and echoed through the health center's courtyard. Paul heard some unintelligible Korean words, and then a pause. The radio, sounding through the loudspeaker, marked off the hour: *beep-beep-beep-beeeeeeeeep.*

The National Anthem, solemn and stately, came on. Mr. Kim rose and stood beside his desk at attention, and reminded Paul to do the same. Paul rather liked the song: it was easy to sing and it surprised him in sounding less like a military march than a hymn. In a minute it was over. Mr. Kim bolted for the door.

"See you tomorrow, Mr. Pak!"

## Five

Ajumoni rapped gently on the frosted glass door of Paul's room. The music of an evening radio program played softly in the background. "Have a snack," she called.

"Thank you." Paul cleared his table of the books and papers he had been poring over — more homework from Mi Jin — and invited Ajumoni in. They sat across from each other on the floor. She placed a plate of sliced apples on the table between them; a little fork stuck out of one wedge.

"Please ... eat with me," Paul said. Ajumoni demurred, but Paul jumped up and took one of his own forks from a drawer of his bureau. He speared a wedge and pushed the plate toward her and smiled.

"You are working hard!" she said, looking over his papers. Are you writing a letter home?"

"No, Ajumoni. Studying Korean I am. It is very difficult."

"Ah." She smiled.

"Ajumoni. Your son, how is he these days?"

"Song Min is very well, thank you. He loves his school and he studies hard, like you are doing. The boy is very smart, very happy; Heaven is blessing us. We found a good *hasuk chip*, a boarding house, for him in Kwangju. Very close to downtown, close to three churches. Every day he sees the churches and remembers God's goodness and works hard to please Him."

Paul smiled and nodded. He understood only a few phrases here and there, but he gathered that all was well with his young friend and that he was probably working too hard. "Glad I am, Ajumoni. My little brother coming home soon, he is?"

"Two more months. Too long, too long."

"*Song Min-hante anbu chonhae chuseyo.*" Give Song Min my greetings.

Ajumoni thanked him and left. Over the months he had been living with her and her family, he had learned much about how they lived. Ajumoni's husband, whom he called "Ajoshi," was rarely at home. He was an automobile mechanic at one of the taxicab companies in town and worked an extra shift most nights of the week. The family rented out two of the rooms of their house — Paul's and the students' next door — and themselves lived in a small suite of rooms on the other side of the kitchen. In the courtyard, Ajumoni fermented large jars of soybean paste to make *toenjang*, the bean paste that served as a stock for soup; she sold it at a friend's stall at the marketplace. The family scrimped, saved, and scrounged for money, all to send Song Min to a fine high school in Kwangju — better than any available in Mokpo — and on to a fine university in Seoul. They had their hearts set on Seoul National University, the "Harvard of Korea." It was almost too much to dream for, as this was also the aim of every intelligent, hardworking student in Korea. But the family could not be shaken from the belief that prayer, hard work, money, and luck would do the trick.

Paul went back to his studies but soon became distracted by a newspaper lying on the floor. A picture on the front page showed a squad of riot police chasing students across a wide street. The police wore riot gear, including gas masks; clouds of tear gas hung over the scene. Several students lay on the street, many of them bleeding.

It was a Korean newspaper, so Paul could make little sense of the writing. He scanned for familiar words and soon found "Masan," the location of the demonstration. He looked up other words in his dictionary and jotted the words for "martial law," "injured," and "civil order" in his notebook.

"So these are the demos Mi Jin has been talking about," he told himself. He made a mental note to ask her about them the next day.

An explanation would come sooner than he thought.

*Six*

Paul ripped open the envelope that arrived for him at the health center in the afternoon mail. It bore the return address of Evan Barker, a member of his volunteer training group, who was now teaching English at a college in Pusan.

*Hey Paul:*

*How's it going? You asked for some info about the riots around here. I would have written sooner, but things have been just a bit hectic lately.*

*As you've probably heard, all hell broke loose a couple of weeks ago. 5,000 students from Dong-A University and Pusan U. started the whole thing when a demo got out of hand.*

*Students are supposed to keep their demos on-campus — that way most people don't find out what's going on. It's the law. These kids broke that law in a big way. They smashed through a line of police barricades and marched downtown, picking up more students as they went. What a sight! Wall-to-wall humanity flowing like a big river up and down the streets near City Hall.*

*The riot cops didn't approve. They told the students to disperse. Have you ever seen riot police in action? They didn't say, 'Please go home now, OK?' Their attitude was more like, 'Here's my billy-club, here's a student. The two just go together.' They waded into the crowds with sticks flying and tear gas canisters going off all over the place. I was there in the middle of it. Have you ever been gassed? Jesus. Try to imagine chunks of raw onion crammed up your nose and rubbed into your eyes. It's worse than that, actually.*

*The cops arrested at least a couple hundred people in the first few days of the riots. Some big shot government guy made a special trip here to check things out, and then the government declared martial law. Martial law — that means more soldiers than usual hanging around.*

*They've extended the curfew. Used to be 11 pm to 4 am. Now it's 10 to 4. Shoots my social life to hell, that's for sure.*

*Last Wednesday, on the second day of the riots, a student from Pusan University was clubbed to death by a cop. His girlfriend saw it happen. Don't expect to read about it in the local papers. I read it in The New York Times. I've got a friend in the US Consulate in Pusan who takes uncensored newspapers and copies all the articles about Korea for me. Then I make copies and sell them to students at the Korean equivalent of ten bucks a pop.*

Damn, this guy is cold, Paul thought.

*I'm enclosing copies of all the Times articles and a few other goodies in this letter. As a token of my esteem for you, I won't charge you for them.*

*This letter is getting too damn long. What do you want to know all this for, anyway? If you sell copies to your friends in Mokpo, I get a cut, OK? I'll see you in Seoul for Thanksgiving. Take care, man.*

    *Evan*

## Seven

"Pak Jong Shik. Would you like to teach my English class someday?"

Paul shook his head. He hated teaching English.

"Please?"

"I'm not a teacher."

"But this will be easy for you," Mi Jin said. "You know your own language perfectly. You would be a good teacher. A very good teacher." She saw by his *nunchi*, the look in his eyes, that he was wavering. Work on a man's ego, she said to herself, and you can make him do almost anything.

"You speak English very well already, Mi Jin. What would you need me for?"

"One must learn English from an English-speaking person and Korean from a Korean. Were your Peace Corps language teachers American?" she asked.

"No, they were Korean. I see your point."

"All the girls in my class would love you."

"How many are there?"

"About eighty."

Paul's eyes widened. Whatever thought he had of teaching the class was evaporating fast. Mi Jin laid her hand on his arm and squeezed.

"You would be doing me a big *putak*, a favor."

"Well ..."

She almost had him. "Please?"

"All right."

## Eight

"I'm very sorry, Teacher Han, but no."

Vice-Headmaster Kim leaned back in his chair and folded his hands over his stomach. "Are the books we provide for your use not good enough?"

"They are adequate, Vice-Headmaster, but it's always good to listen to a language spoken by its native speakers, is it not?"

"Your students can go to approved American movies anytime they wish," Kim responded. "They have Korean subtitles, so the students can hear the English and follow in Korean. It's a very good teaching tool."

43

"But it is not the same. I myself have learned a great deal from just talking with Mr. Harkin informally."

"Is he your boyfriend?"

Mi Jin pursed her lips against the temptation to tell him that it was none of his business. "No, Vice-Headmaster. He is an acquaintance."

"Really. Teacher Han, I still believe that a class taught by him would be unnecessary and too costly. We don't ..."

"Excuse me, sir," Mi Jin broke in. "The American will teach for free. It is against his rules to receive payment for this sort of thing."

"But it is our rule to give an honorarium. We don't have the funds in our budget for that."

Mi Jin looked out the window at the two automobiles, one for the headmaster and one for Vice-Headmaster Kim, parked just outside the window. Two of the school janitors, who doubled as drivers, busily polished them in the cool sunlight.

"I think it's a good idea."

Mi Jin and Vice-Headmaster Kim wheeled and saw Headmaster Shin Chang Sop standing in the doorway. His lined face wore its customary slack grin, but his eyes hardened when his gaze met Kim's.

Headmaster Shin was short but thin. His perpetually tousled hair and wide eyes made him look like a fool or a madman, depending on his mood. He and Vice-Headmaster Kim regarded each other with mild contempt, for completely opposite reasons. Shin considered Kim overqualified and too ambitious for comfort. He himself had obtained his position not from ability or experience, but from good connections. He had been a teacher of geography for most of his life at a high school in Haenam, a small city on the southern coast. The school administrators there thought him too easygoing on his students. He was lazy.

His break came when a classmate from high school became a *kyejang*, a department head, in the South Cholla Provincial Office of Education. He sent his friend an enormous bouquet of flowers with a banner saying 'Great Fortune In Your New Exalted Position — Congratulations from Shin Chang Sop'. At least once every winter vacation he left his wife and sons in Haenam and took his friend out for a week of revelry in Chonju, where he was on good terms with several beer hall women who dressed in shockingly revealing girls' high school uniforms. When an opening appeared at the Chung Ang Girls' School in Mokpo, his friend offered it to him. "Do me a favor, though," the man urged him. "Put your Chonju lady-friends out of your mind when you're at work." Shin gratefully accepted the position and the advice and became a mildly ineffectual headmaster.

Headmaster Shin liked Mi Jin. His liking was not sexual, and that surprised him. She reminded him of his wife when she was young and betrothed to him by their parents. He had hardly any sexual interest in his wife then, and had even less now, but he had found her smart, capable, and a bit of a dreamer, all qualities that he admired. Mi Jin had these qualities as well.

"Excuse me, Headmaster Shin?" Kim said, rising from his chair.

"I said I think it's a good idea."

"Headmaster, I was just telling Teacher Han about the extremely tight financial situation of the school ..."

Shin waved the matter aside impatiently. "Miss Han, ask the American when you next see him. You may offer him a small honorarium of, say, five thousand *won*. Enough for a nice dinner."

Mi Jin smiled gratefully but came back to cold reality when she turned back to Vice-Headmaster Kim to take her leave. He did not relish defeat.

"Did you have a good time in Kwangju?" He whispered.

Mi Jin hurried to hide the scratches that still marked her hands.

## Nine

"Your mastery of the vocabulary words is very good," Mi Jin said slowly in Korean.

"Thank you," Paul replied, also in Korean. "On them hard I worked, pleasing you ... to be?"

"I am pleased. Let us practice conversation now by speaking entirely in Korean. Do you understand me?"

"Yes." Paul started with a question that had nagged him all day. "About Masan my friend wrote a letter. What do you think about the demos and the ..." Paul said the words in English: "martial law?"

With one last check of Paul's *nunchi*, Mi Jin said cautiously: "The *demos* are good, like the *demos* at American universities during the Vietnam War. Yes, very much like them. The students — we — are fighting for political freedom, for a voice in our government. Do you understand?"

"Yes. Mi Jin, you are involved in the *demos*?"

"I am." She did not like the look of surprised interest in Paul's eyes, but she pressed on in English, and soon the words came tumbling out. "Ever since I was in college, in Kwangju, I have seen the bad things the government of Pak Chong Hui has done. You saw some of it at Mokpo Harbor the other night. Do you know how many people are in prison because they disagree with him? Thousands! Put there only because they wanted to say something about the government that Pak and his people didn't like.

"I hate President Pak. That's only fair — he hates Chollado people. I hate the Korean Central Intelligence Agency and the crimes they do inside our own country. Do you remember I told you about Kim Dae Jung?"

"The political dissident from Mokpo," Paul said. "He ran for president against Pak a few years ago, and lost."

"Yes. And no. He won. He would have been our president, if Pak had not cheated on the election. Yes, he cheated! The results were so close. Everyone wanted to count the election again, but he refused. He wanted to make sure that nobody found out about his KCIA agents. They forced people to vote for him and they destroyed bal ... bal ..."

"Ballots?"

"Yes, ballots from parts of the country that voted for Kim Dae Jung."

"Is that true?" Paul asked.

"Yes. That is what I meant when I said that President Pak hates Cholla-do people. He didn't want to see our Kim Dae Jung become president. And because Kim Dae Jung was so popular — and he himself was not — he neglected the Cholla provinces ever since. And that's not the worst thing he's done. President Pak decided to stay in power forever. So he wrote the Yushin Constitution to ensure it. *Yushin* means 'revit ... revitalization. It revitalized his political power, not our country. He gave himself the power to appoint most of the National Assembly, to put dissidents into prison without trial, and to censor the press whenever he thought it to be in the 'national security' interest."

"So that's what the Masan riots were all about."

"Yes."

"Time magazine agrees with you." He withdrew several sheets of paper from his jacket and grinned at Mi Jin's mounting curiosity. "So do *Newsweek* and *The New York Times.*"

Mi Jin gazed hungrily at them.

"I knew these would interest you. I have a friend who can get American magazines that are uncut, uncensored, and unexpurgated." He waved them in the air in front of Mi Jin's face and lay them on the table with a flourish. "For you, my friend."

Mi Jin unfolded the papers carefully, almost reverently, and recoiled at the picture of troop carriers and riot police on the first page of the *Newsweek* article. With hushed exclamations of "Good God!" she read the first article and moved on to the second. "Five thousand demonstrators," she said. "It was larger than I thought."

"I'm giving these to you to keep," Paul said, tapping the table with his finger. "You don't have to read them right this minute."

Mi Jin did not look up. "Five people died! Oh, no!"

"Hello. *Yoboseyo, Mi Jinshi. Hanguk mal yonsup do hapshida,*" Paul said. Let's practice some more Korean.

Mi Jin looked up, puzzled. "Have you read these articles?"

"Yes."

She paused. "And they do not make you upset?"

"Well ... yes, they do."

"And — ?"

Paul groped for words. "I feel bad about all this. Really, I do. But how can I feel the same way you do? I'm an outsider in this country. Maybe I always will be. I hope not. Someday I'll tell you about politics in the States. The whole country is quiet right now, and that's how most people like it. Sure, we had our own protest marches and *demos*, but they're all over now. These days, frankly, we're a bit complacent."

Mi Jin looked up the word in Paul's dictionary. She sighed.

"But Jong Shik, *manjok*, complacency, is wrong. It is President Pak's best friend. This is why my country is falling into ruin. Someday it may ruin your country, too."

## Ten

Paul supposed it was inevitable that Mi Jin would eventually persuade him to teach one of her English classes at Chung Ang Middle School.

"Talk about anything you want, but make it simple."

Mi Jin's instructions were direct, but they left Paul in the dark about the appropriate subject matter, the students' level of skill, and even the political undercurrents within the school. That last point became clear when he arrived at the school and greeted Mi Jin's superiors. The headmaster shook his hand and thanked him warmly for giving a boost to his young teacher's classroom. Vice-headmaster Kim, though effusive in his thanks, cowed Paul with a gaze of pure ice from beneath hooded eyelids.

"Stay out of school politics," said Althea Wittberg, a fellow Peace Corps Volunteer who taught deaf children at a school in Seoul. Paul had called her the night before for some last-minute advice. "There's no more political place in the world than your typical Korean school."

Paul and Mi Jin arrived at her classroom early. She placed him in a chair next to the podium, a "seat of honor so the girls could see him as they came in for their 10 o'clock class. "I will introduce you, and then you can teach. The class lasts for fifty minutes." Paul sat down in the chair and tapped his foot nervously against the podium while he looked around.

The classroom was long and wide, far bigger than any of the classrooms from his own school days. Five rows of double desks stretched eight rows back. Paul asked if the students would be sitting in the chairs closest to the front of the room, as he did not want to shout.

"No, they are all filled," she replied.

The girls filed in, a swirl of navy blue skirts, blue jackets, and starched white collars. Each girl's hair was bobbed; each carried an identical book bag. The egalitarian sameness of the girls, inherited from the Japanese school system, impressed Paul. They took their seats, watching Paul and giggling amongst themselves. Vice-Headmaster Kim followed them in and closed the door.

"Class, this is Mister Harkin," Mi Jin addressed the students. in loud, carefully enunciated English. She made a small wave with her hand.

The girls stood and bowed in perfect unison. "Good morning, Mister Harkin."

Paul rose slightly and bobbed a small bow of greeting.

"Mister Harkin works at the Mokpo City Health Center. He came to Korea with the United States Peace Corps." She pronounced "corps," as expected, as "corpse." "He will talk today about life in his home." Mi Jin nodded at Paul and sat down.

"What should I talk about?" Paul had asked Althea. "Well, your work is out," she replied. "The kids wouldn't understand; they wouldn't have the English medical vocabulary. American politics is out: they wouldn't know and wouldn't care. Religion is out: Peace Corps would be on your ass for preaching. American government is out: the school staff would think you're making unflattering comparisons with Korea. What you do in your spare time is out, unless you're a goddamned Boy Scout. Shit, Paul. You're stuck. Why on earth did you volunteer for this?"

Paul cleared his throat and grasped the podium. "Hello, everybody."

The girls watched silently.

"I am very happy to be here today. I would like to thank Vice-Headmaster Kim for making my visit possible." He made a polite bow, this time in the direction of Kim, who stood in the rear of the classroom with his arms crossed. The severity of his expression relaxed slightly as he waved and returned the bow.

"When Teacher Han asked me to lead a class, I did not know what to talk about. Then I remembered the things I liked when I learned English. When I was a child. I liked stories. My favorite story was Snow White and the Seven ... er ... Very Small Men. Do you know that story?"

Some of the quicker girls in the class shook their heads, while the others, knowing a question had been asked but at a loss to understand it, glanced around sheepishly.

"It started a very long time ago in a king's house in a different country ... a place very far away. The bad queen was beautiful. She had a magic mirror on the wall. Every day she asked it 'Am I the most beautiful lady?' The mirror always said 'Yes', but one day it said 'No'. It said 'Snow White is the most beautiful lady in the world.' This made the queen very angry. She said to her servant: 'Take her far away and kill her!'"

As Paul warmed up to the story, he gestured with bravado, mimicking the wounded shriek of the jealous woman. The girls smiled, and a few ventured to laugh. Mi Jin was horrified at such clownishness in front of the students, but she could not help laughing with the girls. Vice-Headmaster Kim, planted at the back of the room, remained unsmiling in a most determined manner.

## *Eleven*

A gunmetal gray layer of clouds covered most of Mokpo like a dirty blanket in the hours before sunset. Ridges of white clouds scudded low over the sea. A salty wind blowing out of the south-west hinted at another typhoon moving across the southern islands. So typical of Mokpo, Paul mused: close enough to the brink of disaster to be exciting, yet happily placed to capture just the refreshing part of a storm.

Standing outside the Gukjae Theater downtown, he whistled as he waited for Mi Jin. He was in a good mood. The sense of pleasant disquiet at the sight of a far-off thunderstorm reminded him of Indiana during the tornado season: again, he felt the expectation of danger, though distantly. Disaster would strike somewhere, but not near him.

"Good evening, Pak Jong Shik." Paul wheeled around to see Mi Jin, dressed in a trim blue woolen suit, walking briskly toward him.

"*Annyong haseyo?* How are you? Are you ready for dinner?"

She had never seen Paul smile so pleasantly. She hummed happily to herself as she led the way to a restaurant where she ordered *pibim pap* for both of them.

"Do you know what *pibim pap* is?"

"Sure," Paul replied. "It's everything in the kitchen dumped into a big bowl with rice, all stirred up together with hot red pepper paste. I've had it many times."

"You had no spicy food at your home?"

"Mexican. But that's baby food compared to Korean."

While eating quietly, Paul studied her face. Over the past few weeks, Paul had seen her features in a variety of situations, reflecting a wide range of emotions, and he admired them. Her beauty was not overly refined; no one would ever take her for a fashion model or movie actress. Her eyes, nose, and mouth lined up perfectly, as if her maker had used a plumb line and carpenter's rule. Black wiry eyebrows, carefully controlled, shot straight across her brow like an arrow. Her face was square at the temples and tapered off at the jaw line; her chin was strong. When quiet or thoughtful, she looked somber, almost sad. Smiles came rarely: whenever she gave one to Paul, it was like a gift.

"Tell me about your home," Paul asked, in Korean.

"In Muan Dong, here in Mokpo, I live in a *chachi*. It is a room that shares a kitchen and a *pyonso* — the rest room, you know — with the other people in the house. The house is traditional Korean design. Probably it is similar to your *hasuk*, boarding house."

Paul nodded. The L-shaped design prevailed, almost without variation, among all dwellings more than ten or twenty years old.

"My parents live in a farmhouse on the big island of Chindo, in the sea south of here. It is very primitive. The roof is made of straw, like the old, old style, and the walls are clay."

"I have a friend who lives on Chindo," Paul said, "a Peace Corps Volunteer like myself."

"My father moved there with his brother from Jasong Gun in North Korea before the war. Almost all of his family members — uncles, aunts, cousins, sons — are still in the north." She paused.

A flash of insight told Paul that a relative in North Korea would be completely inaccessible to anyone in the south, and therefore a delicate subject for conversation.

"Oh...does it bother you to talk about this?"

"No, Jong Shik. Thank you for being concerned. My father is a very sad man. He gets depressed sometimes because he misses his old family. He does not even know if they are still alive."

Paul tried to think what his life would be like if his parents and siblings were separated from him by such a political division, but it was beyond his comprehension. "That must be a terrible burden."

"It is," Mi Jin shrugged. "It is with us all the time, deep in our hearts. Most people have got used to it."

"Impossible."

"True."

"What's Chindo like?" Paul asked.

"The small town, also called Chindo, has only a few paved streets. It's mostly farmers and shopkeepers who live there. My father and mother want me to go back to Chindo to live someday so I will be close to them."

"Do you want to?"

Mi Jin paused before answering. "No."

Paul was too interested in Mi Jin's family in north Korea to stay off the subject for long; the tragedy of it all seemed to him an aspect of Mi Jin that he should try to understand. "I gather you don't communicate with your relatives in the north," he said.

"Never. We have not even met."

"Then which place is your *kohyang*? Chindo or Jasong?"

Mi Jin managed a flicker of a smile at Paul's correct use of the word for "ancestral home."

"I consider my ancestral home to be Jasong County, even though I will never go there. Most people nowadays would not think the same way, but this is the way I choose. There is much anger and hatred between north and south." She toyed with her food in silence until she looked up into his saddened eyes.

"I wish there was something I could do," he said, with utter sincerity.

Mi Jin fought to control the tears that suddenly rose in her eyes.

"Finished with your *pibim pap*? I see that you are." Paul's voice suddenly took on a welcome brightness. "What shall we do now? The evening's still young."

"Have you ever gone to Mount Yudal?"

"Of course."

"When?"

"Last August, I think."

"That is too long ago," she smiled. "Let's go there now."

"It'll be dark soon," Paul protested weakly, but he allowed himself to be pulled by the arm out into the street.

The sun hovered over the horizon of the Yellow Sea as the pair climbed the stone steps that meandered up the southernmost of Mount Yudal's twin peaks. At two hundred and thirty meters, the mountain was not a grand one, yet it had a picturesque cragginess to it. Jutting out from Mokpo's small peninsula, it offered a fine view of the city and the outlying islands. The view was so popular that simple covered pavilions made of stone and concrete had been built along the trail up the mountainside every hundred meters or so.

In silent imitation of Mokpo's capriciousness, the sky had changed in the past hour: formerly overcast, now ridges of pink, yellow, and magenta clouds criss-crossed it and converged at some unseen spot far past the horizon. As Mi Jin mounted the steps ahead of Paul she turned and smiled as if to say, "Look around you: Mokpo has something of beauty to offer, after all." Paul smiled back. He could not disagree.

They stopped at a deserted pavilion halfway to the summit. The distant typhoon had washed the air of impurities, so that every feature of the terrain below stood out with such clarity that even the mountains on the eastern horizon seemed close enough to touch with a fingertip. To the south and west, innumerable dark islands dotted the water that had now become incandescent orange under the setting sun. Below them, a sea of red and gray roofs glowed as if on fire. Pinpricks of light flickered on in the shadows as Mokpo prepared for night. Close scrutiny revealed the streets to be teeming with life: with taxicabs, buses, and people. From this height the city looked like a gargantuan colony of insects, its inhabitants swarming, flowing in disjointed streams, converging here and there to join the traffic that surged in every direction.

But the mountain stood resolute against Mokpo's onslaught of noise. The darkening silence of the pavilion was palpable, accentuated rather than broken by an occasional blast from a distant taxicab's horn.

Mi Jin gazed dreamily out to sea. She seemed to forget Paul's presence in the twilight, even after he joined her at the balustrade. She began to hum to herself. It was a simple melody, suffused with the melancholy of half-forgotten loss. She glanced at Paul and sang softly in Korean:

"Seh no yah — seh no yah
*We live in the mountains and the sea;*
*To the mountains and the sea we go.*
*If it is happiness, give it to the mountain;*
*If sadness, to your love.*
*If it is happiness, give it to the sea;*
*If sadness, to me.*"

"That was beautiful," Paul murmured.

"Do you understand the words?"

He shook his head.

Mi Jin translated the song. "How do you like it now?"

"Maybe it's too subtle for me," he whispered, puzzled.

She turned around. With her back to the sunset, her face lay in shadow. Paul struck a match and held it up to illuminate her features. The flickering light revealed an unguarded expression of mixed pity and tenderness. She smiled and playfully blew out the flame.

She stepped closer to Paul and laid her hand on his arm.

An unfamiliar voice called out from the gloom far below them on the steps: "Hello! Excuse me ... the park closes at sunset. Please make your way down to the exit." The call was repeated and grew more distant as the park official made his rounds.

Mi Jin sighed. Paul took her elbow and began to walk with her down the dark stairs.

"Don't they have any lights on this mountain?"

The pavement was made of irregularly shaped rocks that protruded at every angle a full two inches above the surrounding mortar; the effect was pleasing in daylight but treacherous at night. The pair inched toward street level one slow step at a time in near total darkness.

"DAMN!"

Paul's foot scraped against the edge of a step. He scrambled to regain his footing, but then he found himself sprawled momentarily in mid-air. With a *thummmp* he skidded heavily onto a landing several steps below.

"Jong Shik!" Mi Jin bounded down the stairs and knelt beside him. "Jong Shik, are you hurt? Oh, no! Oh, no!"

Paul sat up. "I'm okay, I think." He had scraped the palm of his right hand, and parts of his arm, hip, and thigh smarted from being knocked against the pointed rocks in the pavement. Mi Jin cradled his bleeding hand and dabbed at it with a tissue.

"I should not have brought you up here, Jong Shik. I'm sorry, so sorry!"

"No, no," he protested as he tried to stand. "I'm just clumsy, for heaven's sake. *Oof ....!*"

A flash of pain stabbed at the instep of his right foot and shot into his calf. He hobbled to the balustrade and clung to it.

"Your foot! Does it hurt?"

"Yeah," he gasped.

"Let me help you." Mi Jin wrestled his arm around her shoulder and, putting her arm around his waist, hoisted him off his injured foot. She possessed surprising strength for her size. "The street is not far from here. We can walk together. Like this, see?"

They took the remaining flight of steps in unison. She hailed a taxicab and gently trundled him inside.

"Thank you, Mi Jin. Good lord, this is embarrassing." He slipped his shoe off and gingerly probed his foot. "If it doesn't feel better tomorrow I may have to go to the Peace Corps doctor in Seoul. I'll let you know what happens."

"Yes, Jong Shik. Go to a doctor."

The taxicab's interior light gave Paul a fleeting glimpse of the anxiety in Mi Jin's eyes. He wanted to lean out of the window and kiss her — just a quick peck on the cheek, perhaps — but he checked himself. Instead, he reached out and squeezed her hand hard, and received a squeeze in return. Their eyes locked for a moment before the car pulled away.

# CHAPTER THREE

"So this Korean guy — a college student — comes up to me in a beer hall. He's got this earnest, straight-on focused look on his face, like he's got to talk to me, okay? He asks me — with a straight face, now — 'May I have Englishie intercourse with you?'"

Althea Wittberg, unsteady after three strong drinks, almost fell over laughing. Most of those clustered around her joined her. "I just about shit!"

Joel Reynoso stood at the edge of the crowd and smirked, his black eyes, as always, cold. He knew he would find her holding court at this evening's 'Thank God It's Friday' party in an apartment at the US Marine Compound in Seoul.

"What did you say to him?" he asked.

"I'd been there for a couple hours already, so I was wasted. Wasted, just like a Korean. I said '*Neh. Condomul isso?*'" She laughed raucously.

"'Sure. Got a rubber?'" Joel translated for the others. "Did he accept your invitation?"

Althea shook her head. "I've never seen anybody run away so fast. It was beautiful!"

Joel felt his faith in Korean common sense vindicated.

The tall, profoundly reserved man worked in the Peace Corps' leprosy control program. Both his home and workplace were the Korean Leprosy Institute, a hospital and research center fifteen miles south of Seoul outside the city of Anyang. With a tight smile and a nod of dismissal he turned from Althea and squeezed through the crowd of chattering embassy employees to the shaven-headed Marine in a disco shirt who tended the bar. He ordered a beer.

Althea was a volunteer at the Kwangwha School for the Deaf in Seoul, a position, Joel thought, perfectly suited to one as loud as she. The two of them were the only volunteers at the party at this early hour; others were certain to join them later after traveling most of the evening from down-country. In a country only the size of Indiana, Seoul was within reach of almost every volunteer.

Presently a thin young man hobbled through the door and searched the room for a familiar face. He leaned heavily on a cane as he pushed through the crowd. Joel's eyes warmed at the sight of him.

"Paul!" he shouted. "Over here! ... What happened to your foot? Has Dr. Paek seen it?"

"First thing when I arrived this afternoon. It's just a really bad sprain," Paul said, dropping heavily into a chair. "My *kwajang* wanted to send me to St. Columban's Hospital in Mokpo — it's run by Irish nuns, so he thought I'd enjoy the English-speaking company — but I told him 'No, thanks. This foot requires special care.' It's been too long since I've been to Seoul. So I used my foot as an excuse to spend some time here. I told him that the PC doctor has to treat all cases like this. Peace Corps rules." He winked.

"Good. I've used that line myself. Let me buy you a beer."

"No, thanks. the doctor has me on codeine. I'll have a Coke."

"How did it happen?"

Paul blushed. "I fell down some steps into the arms of a young lady."

"Oh, sure you did."

"No, really. She's a middle school English teacher. She's giving me Korean lessons."

"Heh. Have you had 'Korean intercourse' with her?"

Paul looked up, puzzled. "Excuse me?"

"Sorry," Joel said hastily. "It's a stupid joke. Althea's fault. Forget it. How much has she taught you so far?"

"Quite a bit, actually," Paul said. "People are already seeing an improvement."

"She's pretty, isn't she?"

Paul bristled.

"I swear, Paul, I think I know you better than you know yourself," Joel laughed, and pressed Paul's shoulder. "Don't be upset. I'm sure she's doing a fine job."

Paul's drink arrived. He drank it greedily. "It's seven-thirty and I'm getting sleepy already."

A group of embassy people lingered in the open door. A wave of cold air sent a shiver up Joel's back.

"The air feels good," Paul said. "Can we leave pretty soon? All this heat and noise are getting to me." Joel, himself eager to leave, gave Paul an arm up. "I knew you wouldn't mind." The pair waved to Althea and stepped out into the night.

"That's better." Paul breathed in sharply. They walked slowly along the street toward the Capitol building. "Winter's coming."

"President Pak's glad, no doubt, that school vacation is coming," Joel said. "Less trouble for him with all the college students at home in the countryside rather than rioting in the cities. Hang on a second —"

The scream of a siren cut through the noisy rush of traffic in front of the Capitol. A government limousine, its windows darkened, bracketed front and back by army jeeps, careened out of the street that led to the presidential mansion and rushed headlong toward the center of the city.

"How about that," Joel remarked. A flash of insight told him they were going to a hospital. His practiced paramedic's eye saw in the spectacle the nimble driving of an ambulance driver. "I wonder if somebody got shot.

"Have you heard the latest rumors about Pak?" he continued. "Some of the goons in his inner circle are unhappy with the way he's handling the Masan crisis. You know he sent in tanks and paratroopers and imposed martial law, don't you?"

"Paratroopers? Not riot police?"

"Kyongsang paratroopers. The meanest, roughest, toughest kind. From North Kyongsang Province, Pak's home turf. They're his guys; he's got their loyalty, especially when fighting his enemies way down south, where that little extra touch of brutality makes all the difference. The moderates and liberals ridicule him for over-reacting and refusing to negotiate with the students. His generals think he should have sent troops sooner and kicked more ass. The poor bastard can't please anybody."

"What do you think?" Paul asked.

"Me? Hell, it doesn't matter what I think. The wheels of Korean society will grind along whether I have an opinion or not. President Pak or General Whoever's Next — it doesn't really matter. They're all the same. Grab power, use it any way you like, and hold onto it until somebody comes along to pry it from your bloody, lifeless hands. The way of a true dictatorship." They paused at a street corner.

"Are you staying at the Cheil Inn?" Joel asked. "How about letting me stay with you tonight? We can split the cost, and I won't have to go all the way back to Anyang tonight. Jesus, it's cold. Winter's coming."

## Two

Paul and Joel awoke simultaneously with a start.

The commotion of Seoul's downtown traffic had dwindled to near silence by eleven o'clock, the curfew hour, and the pair had settled gladly to sleep. The room they shared was one of a dozen at the Cheil Inn, a small tidy place across the street from the Peace Corps office and a few hundred yards from Taepyong Street, the great main street that shot like an arrow through the middle of the city and ended at the front gate of the Capitol.

Suddenly in the darkness the inn had begun to vibrate, faintly at first, but with mounting force as the minutes wore on. The window rattled furiously in its frame. Joel woke instantly. He soon recognized the sound: one huge diesel engine after another, all of them thundering hard and fast up the street, just out of view from their window.

"Whazzat?" Paul mumbled from a medicated sleep. "What time is it?"

Joel sat up. "Three-thirty."

"What's that noise?" Paul whispered, now fully awake.

"Tanks. Lots of them."

"Where are they going?"

Joel paused to listen, his heart thumping. He sensed something wrong.

"Toward the Capitol." The two fell silent. The clamor went on unabated for several more minutes. They were not the only ones awakened by the commotion; the floor and walls of the inn creaked with the sound of other guests moving about, and a few of them held a hushed conversation in the hall. Paul spoke quietly, more perplexed than fearful:

"What's happening?"

At last the noise ended and the vibrations ceased to shake the fragile inn. Joel and Paul sat still for a long time in the darkness, their ears cocked to hear any more activity outside. The street was silent. The other tenants went back to bed.

"Night-time defense maneuvers," Joel said as he lay back under his covers. "Like they have during the day once a month. Go back to sleep." He pulled the quilt over his head and, as he often did when he was nervous, he began to hiccup.

## Three

Joel and Paul lounged comfortably the next morning in the common hot pool of the public bathhouse. The pool was much favored by old- and middle-aged men for soaking the chill out of their bones. The place was usually crowded, for nearly all Korean homes, including the Cheil Inn, lacked running hot water.

Bathers came and went. Joel saw them only as indistinct shapes: without his contact lenses he was almost blind. One shape that came through the sliding glass door from the dressing room appeared taller and lighter-skinned than the rest. It hastened to Joel's side.

"You look pretty calm." The thick Brooklyn accent identified him as Mark Follett, a volunteer stationed in the city of Chunchon.

"Shouldn't I be?"

"You haven't heard the news, have you?" Mark's voice, always loud, carried such excitement in it that Paul splashed across the pool to join them.

"News?"

"President Pak's been shot!"

"What!" Joel and Paul cried in unison.

"Last night. Around eight o'clock. He's dead! Didn't you guys see all the flags at half-mast on your way over here?"

"Shit," Joel whistled. A momentary sensation of being separated from his body washed over him. He pressed his arms tightly against his sides. The very thought of the trouble outside the walls of the bathhouse made him acutely aware of his nakedness.

"Who did it?" Paul asked.

"Hang on to your soap. Here's where it really gets weird." Mark lowered his voice and emphasized each word: "They say it was the fucking Director of the Korean Central Intelligence Agency!"

"What! The KCIA?"

"Yeah!" Mark whispered, exhilarated, pleased to be the bearer of amazing news. "His name's Kim Jae Kyu."

"Wow," Paul said. "Wow!"

"Did they catch him?" Joel asked.

"He's in jail now, probably being tortured. Can you believe this is happening?"

Joel and Paul dressed quickly and left the bathhouse. "If the North Koreans are going to bomb us," Paul had mumbled, "I don't want to die naked."

Armed with the knowledge of last night's events, they took more careful notice of their surroundings. Every sight and sound made an impression on them.

Small *taegukkis*, national flags, flew from every doorway at half-mast, and Joel wondered how he had missed them earlier. The Saturday traffic at noon, nearly deafening under normal circumstances, was now queerly silent: the numbers of cars, buses, and people had not slackened appreciably — the Acting President, Choi Kyu Ha, had ordered "business as usual" as a show of public strength — but cars and people moved at a measured pace, as quietly as if participating in a vast funeral procession.

Paul glanced at the faces of the people he passed on the street. They betrayed no clue to the emotions behind those impenetrable eyes, for every face was set in a mask made purposely bereft of expression. Even laughter, the most frequent Korean disguise for tension and fear, was absent; an overriding numbness had taken over. Paul remarked on this.

"Look at it this way," Joel replied. "Their president of almost twenty years is murdered; there's certainly a power struggle going on as we speak; the North Koreans are a short missile's flight away, waiting for the right moment to launch an attack. Hell, I'm scared, too."

## Four

The Peace Corps office occupied the seventh floor of an office building in downtown Seoul, not far from the United States Embassy. The volunteers' lounge was an untidy, book-lined room furnished with a few old sofas and a library table. A long time ago someone had decided that the lounge should be a complete refuge from Korea; therefore, it had been meticulously arranged to look like a lounge in some dormitory at a small Midwestern college.

The place buzzed with agitated talk. Althea sat at one end of a sofa spinning out nervous wisecracks and looking wilted. A dozen other volunteers sat around, many of them smoking. A portable radio blared music from AFKN, the American Armed Forces Korea Network. At intervals Althea hushed her companions and turned up the volume as the news bulletins came on.

" ... Repeating our main story: Republic of Korea President Pak Chong Hui and five of his bodyguards were shot dead last night near Korean Central Intelligence Agency headquarters in Seoul. The details surrounding the shooting are sketchy at this hour. According to a Ministry of Information spokesman, the president's assailants are KCIA Director Kim Jae Kyu and two of his assistants. All are in custody. Acting President Choi Kyu Ha declared a state of martial law effective at 0400 hours Saturday. All ROK and United Nations Command forces are at a high level of alert. Leave for all military personnel has been canceled.

"President Jimmy Carter responded to the crisis by ordering two early warning aircraft and the aircraft carrier *Kitty Hawk* to the Republic of Korea. The US State Department issued a statement this morning saying, quote, 'The United States government wishes to make clear that it will react strongly, in accordance with its treaty obligations to the Republic of Korea, to any external attempt to exploit the situation in the Republic of Korea.' End of quote."

John Atwood, the Peace Corps/Korea Country Director, strode into the lounge and looked around. He was a short, wiry man who was part scoutmaster, part Marine Corps drill instructor, and part father confessor to his volunteers. His shirt collar was open beneath a wildly loosened necktie.

"Hello, everybody," he boomed. "I want to check who's here. We're making phone calls to all the volunteers down-country. I don't want to leave anyone out. Let's see: Mark, Chunchon; Paul, Mokpo; Althea, Seoul; Jack, Chechon; Joel, Korean Leprosy Institute; Theodore, Suwon, and Sarah, Anyang — anybody else in town today?"

"Leslie Black is around here somewhere," Althea said. "Leslie, Chindo. It's too bad Korean beds lie flat on the floor. She'd be hiding under hers."

"Scared, is she? Well, troops, I want you to know that we're all perfectly safe, okay? The army's on alert — you heard that on the radio — and there's no sign of any messin' around up north. Everything's under control." He caught sight of Mark opening his mouth to speak and added hastily, "Now, I know you all have a million things you want to ask me about, but don't. Not now. Honest, I don't know much more than you do. As soon as we find out more, I'll pass it on to you. C'mon, Mark, wipe that smirk off your face. I promise I'll keep you posted.

"I want to make sure you all understand this: you are all to stay in Seoul until further notice. Got that? No travel until things settle down a little. The *kwajang*s or *sojang*s — or whatever — at your sites will be notified so they won't think you're playin' hooky. Joel, you and Theodore and Sarah can go back if you want to, since your sites are so close. Althea, you too. Sorry to ruin a free vacation. But keep in touch, okay?

"You all know that curfew's been moved up to nine o'clock, right? Observe it. All right. Thanks, everyone." Atwood flew out of the lounge as abruptly as he had entered it.

"He knows more than he's letting on," Mark muttered to no one in particular. "He's got to. If he's worried, I'm worried."

## Five

Mrs. Kang Yon Shim kept lists. She started each day at the Peace Corps office with one entitled "Things To Do," and even though it frequently ran two pages or more in length, she managed to cross off every item by the day's end.

It was by the strength of her organizational skills that she landed her position of Health Programs Director for PC/Korea when the agency first came to her country in the mid-1960s. Being the wife of an Assistant Minister for Health and Social Services helped — she knew it did — but she preferred to think that she had made a success of herself solely through her own accomplishments. Other "host country nationals" working in the office had come and gone over the years as the political winds shifted. Mrs. Kang alone, with her neatly ordered lists, kept her place.

"Mrs. Kang," John Atwood's voice cracked over the intercom on her desk. "Would you please come to my office in five minutes? Staff meeting."

Mrs. Kang looked about her and wished that the meeting would be held in her office. Fifteen years' worth of plaques and certificates lined the wall behind her desk and spilled over onto the adjacent walls. The Ministry of Health and Social Services had awarded her most of them. It bothered her little that her husband had had them conferred on her every time her contract with the Peace Corps came up for renewal: she saw it as nothing more than recognition, on demand, of her outstanding service under the most difficult of circumstances.

She gathered some files and strode into Atwood's sparsely decorated office, purposely late.

Atwood, puffing on a pipe, sat in a leather chair at the head of a coffee table. The Educational Programs Director, the Executive Director, Dr. Paek of the Medical Office, and the Assistant Country Director, Howard Perry, sat in overstuffed chairs. Mrs. Kang favored Atwood and Perry with a friendly nod and ignored the others as she took her place in the chair opposite Atwood's.

John Atwood suited her perfectly. "Call me John," he had said when they first met. "Thank you, John," she replied with a smile that revealed sharp silver-capped teeth. "Call me Mrs. Kang."

"Well. How is everybody?" Atwood said. "I don't think I need to comment much on the crisis we've got going here. We all know how bad it is. Everything's up in the air right now. My chief concern is our volunteers' safety."

"You are articulating our concerns, too, John," Mrs. Kang chimed in. "We share your caring about how the abrupt termination of President Pak's presidency will impact on the volunteers."

"I've been in contact with the main Peace Corps office and with the State Department in Washington," Atwood said. "The Peace Corps brass wants my opinion on whether to order an evacuation."

"Evacuation of the volunteers?" Mrs. Kang repeated, aghast. She had a momentary mental picture of the volunteers, and her career, flitting away on the wind. "What time-frame are we talking about?"

"Immediate."

"Why, John," Mrs. Kang laughed, her laughter hiding her anxiety, "effectuating an evacuation at this jun ... juncture would be premature."

"It has been nearly a full day since the assassination took place —" Mr. An, the Executive Director, said.

"And the perpetrator has been arrested," Mrs. Kang broke in. "Also, the unrest potential in Korea, even in Pusan, has gone down to almost zero."

"Can we be sure it'll stay that low?" Atwood squinted at Mrs. Kang while he polished his glasses. "What if the assassination spurs the Pusan crisis on? That hasn't gone away."

"Oh, pooh," Mrs. Kang smiled. "Pooh, pooh. You have much to learn about Korean politics, John. Politicians often show extreme drastic ... drasticness in their behavior. They are always conflicting. And it's the students' natural pastime to protest against the government. As long as the volunteers stay away from the demonstrations —"

"— As they're required to do, anyway."

"Thank you, John, I knew that. As long as they avoid the demonstrations, they will be perfectly safe."

Atwood squirmed in his chair, aware that Mrs. Kang was avoiding the issue that worried him most.

"What about North Korea?" he asked. "That's the biggest problem here, in my view. How do we know that Kim Il Song won't get it into his head that the time is ripe for another stab at conquering the South? I don't want a bunch of dead and dying volunteers on my hands."

"John, I applaud your devotion to the volunteers, but my husband, the Assistant Minister of Health and Social Affairs —" Mrs. Kang tapped the arm of her chair with each syllable for emphasis, "— has close ties to experts in the Korean government, and he assures me that the North Koreans know the strength of the United Nations forces, especially in the light of the current tragedy. Any effort to attack our country will initiate a terrible conflict. North Korea will not take that chance, because it is still an impoverished, backward country that cannot stand the strain of a war."

"I think I should put the evacuation process into motion, though: call the U.S. Eighth Army Command and the Embassy ..."

"Totally unnecessary, John," Mrs. Kang said, almost shrilly. "There is no danger to the volunteers either from North Korea or from the political situation."

"I can always terminate the procedure, Mrs. Kang. I just want to be prepared for the worst. I'd be neglecting my duty to the volunteers if I didn't."

"But John —"

"But Mr. Atwood —" the others protested.

"I agree with our Country Director," Dr. Paek said. The room fell silent with surprise, for Dr. Paek rarely spoke during staff meetings. "True, North Korea probably will not attack us. True, the political situation in our country does not directly affect us yet. But who can be certain? The volunteers' safety is our first concern. Their safety is more important than our careers."

Mrs. Kang glared at him.

"Howard?" Atwood said.

"I'll get on to it right away," Perry said. "I'm already in touch with some people at the Embassy."

"Good. Well, then." Atwood slapped his knees and rose from his chair. "I think we've accomplished something. It's business as usual, but with an escape route handy if we need it. Just the way I like it. Don't worry, Mrs. Kang. I'm sure it won't be necessary in the end to send the volunteers home."

"I know, John," she smiled. "You would not end a fine program like Peace Corps/Korea through a lack of courage. I will be in my office if you need me."

## Six

"There's more to this business than meets the eye, I tell you," Mark Follett declared as he stubbed out his cigarette with nervous staccato jabs. He sat cross-legged on the floor of Leslie Black's small room at the inn across the street from the Peace Corps office.

Most of the volunteers who were still stuck in Seoul surrounded him. It was past eleven o'clock at night, and curfew had long since begun. The only sounds from the street were the occasional rattle of an army jeep speeding by on its way to a checkpoint at the end of the block.

"The papers say that Kim Jae Kyu had an 'argument' with President Pak's chief of security — what's his name?"

"Cha," Sarah Conlon said.

"Right — 'Cha-Cha' — and that Pak just kind of got in the way. Right. Is that horseshit or what?" He added in a whisper: "Even Paul wouldn't believe a story like that." Paul had curled up in a corner and fallen fast asleep. The remark brought a murmur of agreement from the others.

"Kim is the damned Director of the KCIA!" Mark continued. "Anybody ambitious enough to get a post like that isn't gonna draw a gun right in front of the guy that put him there. He's not gonna start blasting away just because he's pissed at somebody."

"I wonder if he was drunk," Sarah said. "Korean men are amazing drinkers. Sometimes they do terrible things when they're drunk. Not long ago a cab driver in Suwon was drinking and weaved through the traffic of the main street for miles. Then he drove his car into a crowd of schoolchildren. Do you remember that, Theodore? It was horrible."

Mark shook his head irritably. His theory required a sober assassin. "No, no, no. There's a big difference between a bunch of little kids and a head of state. You don't kill a president on impulse, even if you're stoned. A political act requires a decision first. You don't do something that big under the influence. It just doesn't make sense."

Althea brandished a half-empty bottle of *soju*, the clear potent liquor she drank when she wanted to get drunk quickly and cheaply. "If you've had enough of this," she mumbled, "you can do just about anything."

"What do you think is really going on?" Leslie asked in a hushed voice. She had been silent all evening, huddled in the corner opposite Paul. Her prominent eyes made her look all the more frightened, an impression that was accentuated by her tangle of unbrushed hair and the glare from the naked fluorescent light overhead. "Do you think there's a conspiracy going on? Like, you know, a big one?"

"Who can tell?" Mark shrugged. "A lot of shit has to be sifted through to get to the truth.

"There are plenty of other questions I'd like to have answers to, though," he continued, ignoring Leslie but glad for a springboard from which to launch another monologue. "Did Kim act alone? If he did, was it out of envy of Pak's power — or was it idealism, to knock off a despot for everyone's benefit? Did the North Koreans get him to do it? Or maybe somebody in Pak's government?" He blew a cloud of cigarette smoke in Sarah's direction.

"But you want to know what I really think?" He did not wait for an answer. "I think the military's behind it, and Kim is the fall guy. They wanted Pak out of the way because he bungled the Pusan riots and because the economy's taking a nose dive. So they got Kim to blow him and his security chief away. That's what I think." He picked up Althea's bottle of *soju*, drained it, and leaned back against the wall.

"I think you're wrong," Joel said.

"Huh? What do you mean?"

Joel put down the book he had been pretending to read and stretched slowly. "Let me re-phrase that. I think Paul has spoken more intelligently than anyone here tonight."

"He's asleep."

"Yeah."

The others smiled at the insult, but Mark spat out a cloud of cigarette smoke in preparation for a riposte. Joel continued before he could speak.

"The fact is, none of us know a damned thing about the assassination — and the politics of this country — beyond a few censored news reports and what we can see with our own eyes, and that's very little. Will the country be better off, and will we be safer, if Mark figures it all out? I don't think so." He rose to leave.

"Hey, you listen to me, Joel," Mark began. "Get back here, asshole!"

"Stop it!" Leslie's low voice cut through the room and startled Mark out of his belligerence. "Stop it. I think it's time to go to bed. Will somebody wake Paul up? And Sarah, stay for a moment, will you?"

When the room emptied, Leslie leaned toward Sarah and whispered nervously, "Do you believe what Mark was saying about the big conspiracy?"

Sarah hesitated, for the question caught her off guard; she was the 'baby' of the group — even younger than Paul — and she was not accustomed to hearing her opinions count for much. "I agree that there's more here than anyone's been told," she replied cautiously, "but I don't know about any conspiracy. Mark just likes to listen to himself talk. I agree with Joel. It's pointless to over-analyze it."

"Oh, how I want to go home," Leslie whispered. "I hate this country! I hate it! The people won't leave you alone. The politics are dangerous. It smells, there's filth everywhere ... If it turns out to have been a big conspiracy, Peace Corps would send us all home, wouldn't they? It'd be dangerous to stay here, right?"

Sarah sat down beside Leslie and put her arm around her shoulder.

"I seem to be the only one who's frightened about the — you know, the situation here," Leslie said.

"What nonsense! We're all scared. Why, Paul told me earlier today that he'd gladly listen to his dad's entire collection of Guy Lombardo records if he could just go home now. Isn't that funny?"

Leslie nodded, unconvinced.

"And you heard Joel, Mr. Inscrutable, just now," Sarah went on. "This is the most he's talked that I can remember. He's nervous, just like everybody else. So you see — you're in good company."

"You don't look scared."

"Well, looks are deceiving. Believe me, there are times when I'd like to go home, too, danger or no danger. It's a rough life here." She gazed at Leslie sympathetically. "Look, I think you ought to see Dr. Paek tomorrow morning. He can put your mind at ease, and if he can't, he'll find someone who can. Theodore and I are right next door. If you want anything, just knock on the wall, okay?"

Leslie nodded, and Sarah pressed her cheek with her hand. Left alone in her room, Leslie kept the light on all night long.

## Seven

Paul awoke at mid-morning from a drugged sleep. He had dreamed of home all night long. He saw his bedroom with his old oak desk in the corner and the flowering dogwood tree outside his window. His mother and father were at home, and his brother and sister. They were all sitting in the living room watching *The Carol Burnett Show* on television when suddenly they heard a series of explosions come from the bedroom and, running to investigate, stared with horror at the world map on his wall: a smoking crater gaped where South Korea had once been.

"I've got to get up," he mumbled when he finally came fully awake.

Dr. Paek Ju Il peered kindly at Paul through wire-rimmed glasses that perched unsteadily halfway down his nose. Mrs. Kang had given him the cold shoulder all day yesterday, and in spite of the day's shocking news, he felt almost light-hearted.

"How's your foot today?" he asked in a British-accented chirp while gently probing Paul's instep.

"It's still sore. I had to take codeine to get to sleep last night. Say, what are you doing in the office on Sunday?"

"I thought you volunteers might like to have me around today." Dr. Paek declared that the sprain was healing well in spite of its soreness. "See, the swelling is going down. Give it a couple more days, and the tenderness will go away. Don't walk too much." After a pause, he asked a question Paul had never heard from a doctor before: "How's your *kibun*, your spirit? Do you wish you were home?"

Paul stirred. "Yeah, I guess so. I'd feel safer there, that's for sure. But —" He felt the cold tightening in his stomach and the quickening of his pulse and breathing that had been with him constantly since Saturday morning.

"But you know what? I feel alive ... for once. It's like going down a steep turn on a roller coaster. My senses are wide awake. It's exciting. Nothing like this has ever happened in Lafayette!"

## *Eight*

Paul wanted to walk. He invited Sarah Conlon to go with him.

"If I don't get out, I'll go crazy," he said. "Everybody's in the lounge, yammering about things they know nothing about. There's so much more going on outside."

"Why, Paul, how defiant of you."

"It's not that, really," he grinned. "The fact is, I'm as jumpy as hell, and I have to get up and move around, to go and see how the Koreans are dealing with all this. Does Theodore want to come?"

"I doubt it. He's working on applications to medical school. They've been piling up — fifteen at last count. He's using our forced 'vacation' to catch up on them. Each one is different, you know, with questions and essays and what not."

"I know." Paul tried to block out the stack of them on his own desk at home in Indiana — and the look of disappointment in his father's eyes in the weeks before his departure for Korea.

They went up Taepyong Street past the heavily guarded intersection near the government buildings, up toward Kwanghwa Mun and the Capitol. A shrine half the length of a football field had been hastily constructed of plywood the night before and festooned with black crepe. A dozen copies of President Pak's official portrait glowered down from black-wreathed frames over a crowd of people who, even at this early hour, offered flowers and prayed silently. Several legions of students stood at attention in neat rows with bowed heads, their black uniforms adding to the bleakness of the spectacle. The air smelled heavily of incense blown about on a brisk wind. Now, at mid-morning, the crowds poured into the shrine in a great confluence of humanity; it went on for several blocks on either side of the great gate whose massive wooden doors, which were normally closed, had been flung open to accommodate them.

"Was President Pak really this popular?" Sarah wondered aloud.

"The state deity doesn't have to be popular," Paul said, not seeing the arrogance in his statement, an arrogance he had picked up from Joel. "Just powerful."

## Nine

"Good afternoon, Paul. Thank you for coming again."

Dr. Paek looked up from a stack of papers he was filing, uncharacteristically trying to impose order on the Peace Corps medical office. The rest of the Peace Corps office, and the whole country, for that matter, had started giving the impression of dishevelment, of distraction from comforting routine. The new martial law authorities were trying to return to a sense of orderliness. Dr. Paek was, too, in his way.

Paul smelled creosol and clinical cleanliness, and took comfort in it; it was the smell of safety in the cocoon of the lab, of work getting done, of everything being in its proper place.

"You've been outside, haven't you?" Dr. Paek asked. "You look a little sweaty."

Paul nodded. "I couldn't stay in. I've never seen so many tanks in my life, parked all over the place. And the shrine — that monumental shrine and all the people there. It's ... exciting."

Dr. Paek smiled. "Would you step into my office?"

A pinkish filtered light came through the paper-covered lattice window next to the doctor's desk. A small peephole had been cut out of a corner of the paper, allowing Dr. Paek to look outside without opening the window. Dr. Paek followed Paul's glance.

"I can't keep from watching, either," he said, "though I'm more worried about what I can't see.

"I have a favor to ask of you, Paul." Dr. Paek sat down and rummaged through a stack of medical records on his desk. "You know Leslie Black, in Chindo, don't you?"

"Sure."

"Do you know her well?"

"Fairly well," Paul replied. "We went through training together. She's not in trouble, is she?"

"Oh, no," the doctor replied. "But I am worried about her. She seems nervous, on edge."

"Who isn't?"

"True, a certain level of anxiety is normal for everyone right now. But she is not reacting like an American Peace Corps Volunteer, one who has a natural detachment from the situation."

"I see."

"You are not the only one I've seen who is full of excitement and fright. Almost all your colleagues are treating this like a dangerous, exciting roller coaster ride. Leslie is not. She is fearful and withdrawn almost to the point where I might have to recommend that she be given a medical discharge and sent home."

"It's that bad?" Paul asked.

"Yes. I would hate to do that. Her *kwajang* tells me that she is very good at her job and is well liked by her co-workers. She deserves to stay and be successful."

"What can I do?"

"You are stationed very close to her, in Mokpo," Dr. Paek said. "That's only an hour from Chindo by boat. Chindo is a little isolated, and you're the closest volunteer. I'd just like you to keep an eye on her. Call her up on the telephone every couple of days to chat. Go visit her on a weekend from time to time. Will you do this *putak*, favor, for me?"

"Of course."

"Thank you."

"Dr. Paek," Paul said, after a moment. He lowered his voice without thinking: in the country's present state, candor was invited in hushed tones. "What's going to happen to us?"

As Dr. Paek leaned back in his chair his face fell into shadow and exhaustion became more apparent in the dark pouches under his eyes. "I don't know. If North Korea decides to attack after all, you volunteers will have to go to the nearest US military base, where you'll be evacuated."

"What about you?"

Dr. Paek shrugged. "My family and I will probably do what my own parents did when I was a teenager. We will leave Seoul by car or on foot and go south. And we will pray constantly."

"But if North Korea doesn't attack, we're all okay?"

"Well," Dr. Paek held up a finger. "We still have to deal with our own government. It has been my observation in this country that martial law is easy to declare but very hard to give up. We will pray constantly no matter what. You do, too. Okay?"


## Ten

Mi Jin awoke slowly, painfully on Saturday morning. In the darkness and in the shadowy state between sleep and wakefulness, she wept.

She had had another dream about her grandmother.

Mother's mother was the best woman who had ever lived. No one had ever told more exciting love stories about the princes of old Korea, nor been so generous with candies and affection, nor listened so attentively to a little girl's secrets. And suddenly, almost two years ago, Grandmama had collapsed while washing clothes in the courtyard of her house. The pain she had been hiding for months came from a massive tumor in her belly that had metastasized into her lungs and intestines. She died slowly in a hospital room in Chindo in the company of her family and a dozen patients suffering from tuberculosis, gangrene, and who knew what else. For weeks after that, Mi Jin stayed home from school and wished she could join her Grandmama in the Great Void. The pangs still came, especially after a bad, sleepless night like this one.

"Jin-a!"

The beloved voice had come from out of a mist in the dim blue light of dawn.

"Grandmama!" Mi Jin responded not with her voice but with a thought that attained the same measure of tangibility as the mist at her bedside. "Grandmama, I miss you so."

"I'm here."

"But I want you with me all the time."

The presence in Mi Jin's dream paused, then said tenderly, "Come with me, Jin-a."

Mi Jin felt her dream-self stand and walk toward the voice. She saw first her grandmother's face, the kind eyes leaping out at her, then the rest of the body clad in a white homespun *hanbok*. She felt not the touch of Grandmama's hand on her arm, but rather the warmth of association with past touchings. "Come with me, Jin-a," the lovely voice said. "I feel your absence, too."

Tears welled in Mi Jin's eyes and she drew back. She remembered well what Grandmama herself had told her many years ago about the strange power of dreams: that accepting the invitation of one who has passed into the Great Void is a sure sign of one's own imminent death. How many times in the past months had she wanted to go with her dear Grandmama!

"No. I'm not ready," she sobbed. "I have to stay here."

"Come with me."

"I can't."

The image faded. The sad eyes were the last features to dissolve away.

"*Annyong*," it said. Peace.

Mi Jin, now awake, lifted her head from her wet pillow. The silhouette of a moth fluttered on her frosted window and disappeared. She did not know what had invited her away from the world: an apparition of her grandmother or a manifestation of her own mind.

## Eleven

The Chung Ang Girls' Middle School was dead quiet on Saturday morning in the hour before classes started. Vice-Headmaster Kim Son Kwan sat nervously at his desk listening intently to the radio. He did not bother to empty his ashtray of the small mountain of cigarette butts that had accumulated since his arrival at dawn.

Pak Chong Hui was dead. He could not believe it.

He prodded a bundle under his desk with his foot. It was his Homeland Reserves uniform, which he fully expected to put on by this day's end.

A hurried clomping of footsteps in the hallway announced the arrival of Assistant Vice-Headmaster of Student Affairs Choi Hui Gon, a man who, to Kim's surprise, had been allowed to return to the school after the KCIA had questioned him at his, Kim's, instigation. He watched warily as the little man of uncertain loyalty approached his desk at a trot; it was obvious what news Choi wanted to tell him. He wished he knew what was going on in that man's head.

"Vice-Headmaster Kim," Choi said, winded, addressing his superior in High Korean. "Hast thou heard what happened last night?"

Kim grunted in the affirmative. He watched Choi pace back and forth in front of his desk while trying to catch his breath. Something in Choi's demeanor suggested to Kim an inappropriate excitement, a lack of shocked grief or fear. He had never seen Choi so stimulated.

"May I have one of thy cigarettes?"

Kim wordlessly extended his cigarette box and lit one for Choi. He noted with dry satisfaction the contrast between the tremble in Choi's hand and the steadiness in his own. He, Kim, could contain his inner turmoil — the true mark of a *yangban*, a noble.

"I cannot believe that such a thing has happened!" Choi said. "And for the President to be killed by the head of the KCIA ... it's shocking, simply shocking!" He rambled on and on.

Kim strained Choi's words through a sieve of skepticism born of habitual suspicion. How interesting, he thought, that you don't mention the loss to our nation, Mr. Choi, or the likelihood that the North Koreans will practice some treachery on us — only that you can't believe it. Interesting.

"Has Headmaster Shim been notified?" Choi asked.

"He has surely heard about the tragedy already. As soon as he arrives he will probably want to assemble the students and tell them the news. It will be good for the school to put the matter in the proper perspective for them: to assure them that everything is under control, and that vigilance is now more important than ever."

"Vigilance," Choi repeated. "I could not agree more."

Slurred words in the outer office announced the arrival of Headmaster Shim Oh Nam. He was giving orders that the students be assembled in the schoolyard at the stroke of eight o'clock, in just over a half hour's time.

"Headmaster Shim," Kim called out. A disheveled and red-eyed man appeared in the doorway as Kim rose from his seat. Shim's hair was thoroughly gray, even though Kim knew for a fact that he was only fifty years of age. Kim regarded him with a mixture of contempt and fear. He despised the man's reputation for lechery and marveled at his incompetence in running the school. Yet the Headmaster had friends in high places who kept him from being removed in disgrace from his position. Any man with friends who could perform such a miracle must be powerful, and therefore worthy of his respect.

"Headmaster Shim, this is truly a terrible morning, *neh?*"

Headmaster Shim nodded. "Is all the staff here yet? I want them standing with the students when I make the announcement."

"All are here except for Teacher Han," Choi piped in. "Han Mi Jin."

## Twelve

Mi Jin plunged headlong from the bus into the press of people swarming at the corner of Mokpo's train station downtown. She made a dash for the vast concrete plaza that fronted the station and hoped that by dodging suitcases, bundles, and passengers she might make up for the time she had lost this morning composing herself for class.

"Vice-Headmaster Kim will kill me this time," she muttered. "He never liked me in the first place."

The look in Kim's eyes when she told him at their first meeting that she had graduated from Chonnam University stabbed through her thoughts as she reached down and pulled off her high heeled shoes. His words about her credentials had been complimentary, but his *nunchi*, the look in his eyes, told her: "Too young ... unsettled ... a product of a politically suspect university." Though she had Headmaster Shim's esteem, the image of Kim's frigid reaction to her lateness this morning spurred her into a run across the plaza.

"*Yah!*"

The sharp, commanding bark of a policeman stopped Mi Jin in midstride.

"Why are you running?" he demanded.

The eyes, almost completely hidden by the black visor of his cap, darted from Mi Jin's face to her handbag to her stocking feet and back to her face. She noticed with a thrill of anxiety that he had a rifle slung over his shoulder.

"Well?"

"I am late for work, Officer," she responded, affecting meekness. She felt overpowering curiosity and dread over the rifle — unusual equipment for a street policeman — but she dared not ask him about it.

"I don't care if you're late for a funeral," he said harshly. "No running."

"Yes, Officer. Thank you very much, Officer."

Mi Jin put on her shoes and, cursing silently, walked the rest of the way across the plaza. She looked at her wrist, cursed herself again that she had forgotten her watch, and glanced instinctively at the large clock on the train station's facade.

A cold shiver of fear gripped her spine as her hand flew to her mouth. Two .50 caliber machine guns, each manned by a pair of soldiers, perched like gargoyles on the corners of the station roof.

"...What's happening?"

She was unaware that she had asked the question aloud, but a young woman paused at her side. "Pak Chong Hui is dead," she said. "Haven't you heard? One of his own men shot him last night. The whole country is under martial law."

At the word "dead," Mi Jin had stopped listening, for a loud rush of blood had flowed into her ears. Her heart pounded in her chest like a panicked animal in a cage. It took her mind several minutes to clear enough to remember that she had prayed for this event countless times; but slowly, as she walked across the plaza, she found that she was not happy, not ecstatic or joyful, as she dreamed she would be, but anxious.

"The President is dead." She suddenly was not the liberal who wished the government could be transformed in the blink of an eye, but a Korean who suddenly felt rudderless and frightened. One of the machine gunners on the train station roof spit carelessly onto the plaza below.

"What's to become of us?"

## Thirteen

"Students!

These are tragic times for our country. Our beloved President Pak Chong Hui 'went away' last night."

Headmaster Shim paused. A murmur of shock rippled through the column of black-uniformed girls arrayed in formation before him. Inwardly he glowed at the effect of his words on his students. For once he was certain they were listening to him.

"In the face of this tragedy, students, our duty is to ... er ... to do our duty.

"First, we must honor our fallen leader. It is only right and proper that we do so; as we honor our ancestors for making a bequest of our world to us, so we must honor the one who brought order to it. The Father of our Republic, whose life touched each and every one of us in ways that you can scarcely understand, deserves all the glory we can give him.

"At this very minute our city government is constructing a large shrine to President Pak Chong Hui. When it is finished, our whole school will go there to bow heads together and pay our respects. In addition, volunteers will be chosen from among you to construct our school's own shrine. All students will be expected to contribute flowers for its beautification. We shall show all of Mokpo that the Chung Ang Girls' Middle School grieves for its departed hero with more sincerity than does any other school in the whole city.

"Secondly, students, we must pledge our wholehearted loyalty to our Republic's new president, Mr. Choi Kyu Ha. I have heard a great deal about him," Headmaster Shim lied, "and I know for a fact that our nation is in good hands. Choi Kyu Ha has accomplished ... many great accomplishments. And besides being a great leader, he is a *yangban*, a gentleman, and is exceptionally kind-hearted. You all would like him if you knew him."

Headmaster Shim saw Mi Jin out of the corner of his eye as she hurriedly took her place with the faculty. He fought an urge to wave to her, and continued:

"Lastly — and this is most important, students — it is our personal duty to combat communist infiltration of our country in these troubled times. Each and every one of you must be on guard every hour, every minute of every day. I cannot stress this strongly enough, students. The North Koreans and their sympathizers — who are more numerous than you know — are glad at our President's passing. When they heard the news they jumped up, clapping their hands and shouting for joy. They remember how vigorously Pak Chong Hui fought communism, and now they are breathing more easily. Unaware of our people's strength of spirit, they may choose this time to destroy the democratic institutions that our late President single-handedly built.

"Do not let them. Be wary of those who say bad things about President Pak Chong Hui. Such people are trying to cast doubts on the rightness of our way of life. They want us to live someday as the people of North Korea are forced to live, and to worship their dictator, Kim Il Song, as a god. Don't be fooled by them. We in the free South, thanks to the example set by Pak Chong Hui, will not tolerate propaganda or mind control. Individuals who say nasty, untrue things about our late President must be reported to the authorities at once.

"Students, now it is time to pray in silence."

## Fourteen

"What does it all mean?"

Mi Jin sensed excitement in the voice of her friend, Choi Un Mi. In the space of a few short words Un Mi expressed a paradox of anxiety, joy, and helplessness.

The two women huddled over coffee at the same *tabang* in which Mi Jin gave Paul his lessons. The sun had just set; before long, curfew would begin. In the shadows slouched Lee Byong Guk, puffing on a cigarette in the self-absorbed manner of a youth convinced of the complete originality of his every thought. He replied:

"It means that for the first time in over fifteen years, the Korean people have a chance to write a new destiny for themselves. One tyrant is gone. All we have to do now is to prevent the rise of another."

Mi Jin winced. "'All we have to do now,'" she repeated. "You make it sound so easy. It won't be." She admired him for his closeness to Cho, the student activist from Pusan. Byong Guk's exploits during the Pusan demonstrations enthralled her: the word on the street had it that, among other deeds, he single-handedly saved a dozen demonstrators from a squad of riot police by driving an abandoned city bus between the combatants and using it as a moving barricade to protect the students from the worst of the attack. He was wounded badly in the arm, they said. He neither confirmed nor denied the story, though a freshly healed scar ran from wrist to bicep, and this added to the mystique that he hoped would serve him well some-day as Cho's successor. But he was an ideologue of the type Mi Jin detested, one who saw only the white and black of human affairs, and none of its grays: his favorite assertion, one that he tried to bring into every conversation because it was one of the few ideas he had, was that all workers were unhappy with their lot, and those who were not were aberrations, or lackeys of undemocratic forces. You were either against the Yushin Constitution in its entirety — or, if you found some parts tolerable, you clearly had sided with the oppressive government. All his philosophy seemed to embrace what at base was a diffuse sense of injury.

Mi Jin was never completely sure whether he worked for the North Koreans or, as she hoped, merely agreed with them.

"Who is Pak's successor?" Choi Un Mi asked. "Choi Kyu Ha? I've never heard of him."

"A political nonentity. Part of Pak's government, but not one of his cronies," Byong Guk said. "When Pak chose his Prime Minister he made sure to find someone with no political power to threaten his own. It worked against him in the end, didn't it? Since he didn't anticipate his own death, he left a gaping hole in the President's office."

"One that's likely to be filled by someone from the KCIA or the military, if they're not careful," Mi Jin said. "You should know enough of human nature, Byong Guk, to realize that anyone ambitious enough to make it to the top of those organizations is going to find the 'gaping hole' in the President's office too enticing not to fill himself. Especially if he's been given a 'national emergency' like the assassination of the president."

"Stop interrupting me. What do you know about these things? Have you spent any time with Cho, as I have? Have you learned anything directly from him? Eh? We're in the middle of a national emergency, all right.

That's why the time to move is now. We can have tens of thousands of students demonstrating on the campuses of South Cholla Province tomorrow, if we want them. Students in other provinces can follow suit the day after. Cho has friends in every major student organization in the country. By the end of the week the whole government can be on the edge of collapse."

"What then?" Un Mi asked.

"Well, a more progressive government will take its place."

"Or a more repressive one will move in to restore order," Mi Jin said. "*Yah!* Byong Guk, why do you and your kind walk around with your eyes closed? Don't you think the Korean people should look past the *demo*s and work on creating a democratic republic? 'A more progressive government will take its place.' *Yah!* It won't happen by itself, and it won't be built by a bunch of students who committed suicide by tangling with the martial law authorities."

Suddenly remembering where she was, she lowered her voice, fearful of attracting attention in the *tabang*. "Listen. I've marched in demonstrations at Chonnam University — big ones, and many of them. I'm proud of it. I've even seen Cho in action. Picking a fight is not the only answer. The *demo*s have to fit the times they're in. And now, with the KCIA and the Army looking everywhere for subversives, is not the time. We're all sitting on the sharp edge of a knife. Risk your own neck if you want to, but I'm not going to risk mine. Not on the feeble hopes you're peddling. And don't risk the democratic movement for your urge to play in the streets." She gathered her purse and overcoat and stormed out.

"A comfortable liberal," Lee Byong Guk sneered after a moment of stunned silence. "She'll never do our country any good."

"Are any demonstrations planned for tomorrow?" Un Mi asked.

"No. People in the movement who think as your friend does have put an end to those plans. We're losing one hell of an opportunity. You just watch."

## Fifteen

The white buildings of the Hanguk Nabyong Yonguwon — the Korean Leprosy Institute — gleamed like a scattering of a child's toy blocks before the shaggy mountainside against which it nestled, serenely poised within a small closed valley near the city of Anyang, about twenty-five kilometers south of Seoul.

A cluster of houses, pig farms, and small factory workshops flanking the KLI and its hospital comprised the 'leprosy re-settlement village' called St. Lazarus Village. Patients from all parts of Korea came to the hospital to be diagnosed and treated and, if Catholic, to live in the village. At the hospital they received antibiotics to render them non-infectious and physical therapy to ease the discomfort of their deformities. In the village they relied on Father Lee and his chapel for spiritual comfort and on eight Daughters of Charity for daily care. The ones whom leprosy had mangled the most — the elderly, the blind, those lacking fingers or toes or feet who could not care for themselves — lived higher up the side of the mountain in clean, modern dormitories.

All who came to live in the village knew that they would die there, but no one seemed to mind. They were lucky, they believed, to live out their lives in the village — debilitated, perhaps, but happy in a little paradise of a valley far removed from bitter years of being shunned on the outside. It was better to live and die peacefully among one's fellows than to endure a living death in the outer world.

"Good morning, Grandfather," Joel called to the white-haired old man who peered sheepishly into the hospital's physical therapy room. "*Annyong hashumnikka?*" Art thou at peace?

"Yes." The man started. He had never seen an American so closely before, much less one who had learned to speak in the respectful convolutions of High Korean. He jerked a bow and hobbled into the room. "Thou speakest Korean very well!"

"Truly thy words are too kind," Joel replied. "I speak Korean terribly." He smiled at the confusion written on the man's face. "Please be seated here, Grandfather. Knowest thou what we will do together?"

"No. All this medical stuff is a mystery to me. But you'll explain it to me, *neh?*"

"With pleasure, Grandfather. This," Joel said, indicating a creamy yellow substance in a heated tub at his side, "is wax. It is warm, but not hot. We shall dip thy hands into the wax to make the skin soft. Then I will move thy fingers to make thy joints less stiff. Please sit down. May I see thy hands?"

The skin on the old man's hands was dry and callused. Old ulcers that had become infected and then healed left patches of horny scar tissue. His fingers were reduced to curved sausage-shaped stumps without nails; what was left of the little finger had already begun to meld into the palms of his hands. One effect of leprosy was the deadening of nerve endings in the extremities. Physical pain, a fearful enemy to most people, was a lost boon to this man. For years he had burned his fingers with cigarettes, rammed them against solid objects, scalded them, and in countless other ways abused them without sensing it in time to prevent permanent injury.

Joel looked carefully at his face. The man's eyebrows were completely gone, and his nose sagged at the bridge due to a breakdown of cartilage. The conjunctiva of his eyes were inflamed and his pupils slightly clouded: the continuing depredations of leprosy would make him completely blind in a few years.

"Do thou tell me if this hurts," Joel said as he lowered the man's right hand into the wax. He withdrew it and poised it briefly over the tub in the open air. "When the wax hardens on thy hand, we shall dip it again a few times."

The old man stared at his glistening hand, now white and smooth from wrist to fingertips.

"Why?"

"The warmth of the wax loosens thy joints, Grandfather," Joel replied, putting the hand into the tub again, "and it softens thy skin so that we will not damage it when we move thy fingers back and forth. Now ..." he satisfied himself that he had accumulated enough layers of wax. "Let us peel this off."

The wax sloughed off easily. Several pieces of dead skin came with it. The skin left behind looked good: it was soft and the horny edges of old ulcers were more pliable. A faint pinkish glow was just visible under the brown outer layers.

Joel rubbed what was left of the thumb. It was pressed hard against the side of the palm and curled in a state of permanent flexion. He grasped the thumb and gingerly pulled it away from the palm, then bent it backwards in as full a range as he thought possible.

"Does this hurt, Grandfather?"

"No. Art thou a physician?"

"No," Joel replied. "*Pyongwhapong satanwon-imnida.*" I am a Peace Corps Volunteer.

"Ah! How is thy impression of Korea?"

"It is a beautiful country, Grandfather, and its people among the friendliest I have ever met." Joel paused, watching his patient's face, and then decided to jump into normally forbidden territory:

"The government concerns me, however."

"Yes," the old man sighed. "Thou knowest that our president 'went away.'"

"Yes."

"How tragic for our country!" He fell silent.

Joel knew that he could not enter the man's private thoughts by asking open-ended questions: Koreans were by nature circumspect, even secretive, when discussing politics with outsiders.

"What will happen to the man who shot the president?"

"He will die," came the hard-edged response. "The son of a bitch ended the life of a great man."

"President Pak was a great man, thou sayest?"

"Yes! May he live forever in heaven with Jesu Christu and all the blessed saints, even though he wasn't a Christian.

"You see, sir, I am a farmer. I grew rice and potatoes in Kangwon Province, in Hongchon Gun, before I caught this disease. Farmers like me honored President Pak. He was the first leader we ever had who saw that the poor farmer was as important as the mighty rich man in the city.

"Our lives were filled with terrible hardship before President Pak came. There used to come a time every year when the farmers' food ran out. We called it *polikogae*, and our families starved until we harvested the new crops. I remember those days well."

"What were they like, Grandfather?" Joel asked as he worked the fingers back and forth one by one.

"There came a day every spring when the grain in my father's storage bin got down to the depth of one finger. If that day came too early my mother wept the whole day, for she knew what the future held for us. It happened like that many times in my childhood. From that day until the new crops came in, the rice had to be divided very carefully — when we had rice at all. The biggest portion went to my father, to keep him strong enough to tend the fields. The next biggest went to my elder brother, who was old enough to help; and besides, he was the eldest son. Since I was the second son, I got the next portion. My mother and two tiny sisters shared what was left. One year my youngest sister 'went away'."

The old man paused thoughtfully. "During those days we foraged for food. We gathered berries, roots, and edible weeds from the fields. One year we were forced to eat straw from the old crop. Many, many people died. Canst thou understand? Nothing like this has ever happened in thy rich country."

Joel shook his head, astonished at the old man's candor. It's the temper of the times, he mused; much in Korea has gone awry lately.

"The farmers with the smallest fields suffered the most. It was most sad when babies were born to them during those days. One day, when I was a young man, I found a new-born girl-child lying on the side of the road. It was dead. Many Koreans believe that any evil deed is permitted in times of famine or war. I am a Christian, so I do not. Taking the life of a child, even if it is a girl, is a sin against God. That is what I believe."

"Does this time of starvation still happen, Grandfather?"

"No! When President Pak came, everything changed. This is the point of my long, long story — so sorry, sir. Knowest thou of Saemaul Undang? The New Village Movement? It helped us — the farmers — grow more food. We got better irrigation and more fertilizer. The time of starvation came later and later every year, and now it never comes at all. We got more money for our crops; we could buy food on the market when our own ran out. No more hunger, thanks to President Pak Chong Hui!" The old man's wrinkles deepened suddenly and his voice turned grave. "How could anyone take the life of such a man?"

A nurse arrived to tell Joel that it was time for another patient.

"We did well, Grandfather," he said as he rose and returned his patient's smile and bow. "We conversed most interestingly. *Do mannapshida.*" Let us meet again.

## Sixteen

By the sixth day following the assassination, the capital had been judged sufficiently calm for normal work. John Atwood put his evacuation plans on hold and decided to let the volunteers travel again. It was time for Paul to go back to Mokpo.

He left Seoul at half past ten that morning and returned to a Mokpo seemingly untouched by the turmoil in Seoul. Once out of the bus terminal, he delved again into dusty, noisy streets.

"Mr. Pak!" The health center receptionist, who was watering some potted flowers out front, caught sight of Paul as he rounded the corner. She ran indoors to tell the others of his arrival.

"Mr. Pak, *annyong haseyo?*" Mrs. Mun said. She had run out to the foyer of the health center followed by her fellow TB workers and everyone else who happened to be in earshot of the receptionist's call. "How are you, Mr. Pak? Goodness! We were worried about you."

Paul bowed politely. "Thank you. I too worried I was. The problems in Seoul ..." he consulted his dictionary, " ... 'frightening' they were."

"Tell us," TB Mrs. Lee prompted.

"In the late night, I heard tanks. *Brrrrrr. Brrrrrr.* Very noisy." He shook himself to convey the sense of vibration from the tanks' powerful engines. "Next day, I could see — President Pak ... er ... went away."

Paul noticed a half-hidden smile on Mrs. Mun's face. His incorrect use of the euphemism for 'he died' had caused a great deal of embarrassment for the health center a month ago. He led his entourage into the TB Control Office and sat down at his desk, glad to be the center of attention.

"Next day, too, we thought about North Koreans much." He cupped a hand to his ear and mimicked an air raid siren: "*Wooooooo, wooooooo.* But no fighting airplanes. Whew!"

His audience laughed nervously, and he pressed on:

"My Peace Corps *sojang* said, 'Do not travel to work!'"

"I said, 'Please, Sojang-nim, I must go to Mokpo for working.' He said, 'No! In Seoul you must stay.' So I stayed. I am sorry."

Mrs. Mun crossed her arms and tried not to burst out laughing.

"In Seoul, the streets they were very quiet. Downtown, a HUGE ... er ..." he opened his dictionary again, "shrine was built. Many people came — oh! *Annyong haseyo*, Mr. Hong."

Mr. Hong, the health center's Disease Prevention Chief, had walked into the room.

"I'm well, Mr. Pak. How are you? Kwajang-nim wants to see you now."

The familiar figure sat behind the usual low table, but Paul now approached him not with the dread connected with a language lesson, but with anticipation. He at last was coming to this table with a unique experience that might spark some interest or admiration in this strange, impassive man.

"Good afternoon, Mr. Harkin." Kwajang-nim motioned Paul to a chair.

"Good afternoon, Kwajang-nim."

Kwajang-nim tilted his head back to one side and looked at Paul as if he were a half-forgotten acquaintance. "You were gone a long time. I have many sentences to study with you today, because you were gone." He drew a stack of papers from his desk drawer. "Today's lesson will be two hours in length."

Paul blinked.

"'Some are fond of playing baseball, whereas others are fond of playing soccer.'"

"Okay."

"'Whichever you choose, you should use it carefully.'"

"Okay."

"'If you look after the house while we are out, you may play indoors at will.'"

"Itwouldbebetter ifyousaidyoucanplay indoorsasmuchas youwant."

Kwajang-nim shook his head. "Please repeat what you said."

"I said: "Itwouldbebetter ifyousaidyoucan playindoorsasmuch asyouwant."

"Your English pronunciation is not clear enough. Say the words slower."

This only spurred Paul on. "I said, 'Itwouldbebetter ifyousaidyoucan playindoorsasmuchas youwant."

Kwajang-nim frowned. "Ah ... I understand.

"'It is true that he is young, but he is old enough to understand the feelings of his parents.'"

"Good."

"You know, Mr. Halkin, you received some calls on the telephone while you were gone."

It took Paul a second to realize that Kwajang-nim was not reading another sentence to him.

"Good ... Oh?"

"From a young woman," Kwajang-nim said slyly. "I think she is the one you went on a date with before."

Mi Jin called here! Paul thought. Damn!

"Er ... what did she have to say?"

"I do not know. Miss Oh, the telephone answering girl —?"

"Receptionist."

"Thank you. Miss Oh, the receptionist, talked with her. She told me that your girlfriend called."

Paul groaned. No doubt she had also told everyone else in the building.

"She said your girlfriend sounded worried." Kwajang- nim picked up his papers. "Let us study some more sentences."

## Seventeen

When Paul met Mi Jin outside the gate of the Chung Ang Girls' Middle School the evening of his return, she almost hugged him.

"I am so happy you're safe," she said. "I was worried first about your foot, then I worried about your safety in Seoul. But you've come home safely."

They walked together through Mokpo's semi-dark streets toward a small restaurant that specialized in *mandu*, dumplings stuffed with seasoned meat and cabbage. She walked briskly, as always, and in an effort not to lose her in the after-work crowds, Paul slipped his hand into the crook of her arm. She held it fast, glad that it was already dark, and that no one could see it.

A few blocks later they passed within view of City Hall, where a group of fifty or more people was waiting to go inside. "Did you see the shrine?" Paul asked.

"Yes."

"What do you think?"

"I will tell you later."

"You should see the one in Seoul," Paul said. "It's huge. Right in front of the Capitol. It's hung with black and white banners, and takes up the whole plaza. Thousands upon thousands of people came to see it." He went on in this vein for some time, letting his observations spill out as they walked. When they got to the restaurant and seated themselves in a corner away from the other customers, Mi Jin spoke to him quietly.

"Do not be fooled by the big crowds you saw," she said. Most people go there because it is expected of them. They go there in groups from their work; or army veterans go there with their old comrades in arms. They want to be seen giving respect, because it helps them."

"Helps them?"

"It shows they have respect for the top power. To get a better position, sometimes that is needed."

"But I saw people crying," Paul said.

"Who were they?"

"I don't know; mostly old women and people who might have been farmers."

"Koreans will cry at anything," Mi Jin said. "And the farmers had reason to respect President Pak. He improved their standard of living."

"Did you go to the shrine here?"

Mi Jin nodded.

"But you went with the school? And you bowed because you had to?"

"That is right."

"I'm lucky," Paul said. "If I don't do it, people don't care. He wasn't my president. All I had to do is stand still and keep my mouth shut."

Mi Jin smiled.

"The number of people at this shrine in Mokpo is really small, though," he said. "Why is that?"

Mi Jin smiled humorlessly. "I already told you that Chollado people don't like President Pak very much." She pointed across the street at the train station. "Do you see the machine guns on top of the roof?"

Paul nodded. "That's the first thing Mrs. Mun showed me when we went out today. It's scary."

"What better proof of what the government in Seoul thinks of Chollado people?" Mi Jin lowered her whisper further. "Those guns are not to guard against a North Korean invasion."

It took a moment for the importance of her statement to strike Paul. They ate their meal quietly.

"Will I see you again on Saturday?" Paul asked when they rose to leave.

"No," Mi Jin replied. "It is President Pak's funeral. No place will be open for us to sit and talk. Besides, I am going home to Chindo for the weekend. I will miss you."

## Eighteen

The third day of the eleventh month of the Western calendar, a Saturday, dawned on a Seoul smothered in black crepe. The city was darkened by a featureless gray sky and made wet by an early rain shower. Exactly one week had passed since the tanks had entered the city to enforce martial law. Taepyong Street, the thoroughfare that terminated in front of the Capitol and Kwanghwa Mun — the Gate of Transformation by Light — was cleared of traffic. A million people crowded the sidewalks along its entire length, all the way across the Han River to the National Cemetery. A great many wept. *Han*, the spirit of pathos, of bitter regret, swept through the capital; it lay always just under the skin of every Korean and surfaced at times like this when events conspire to prove what everyone already knew: that life is a string of tragedies, that the mighty are destined to fall, and that the Great Void is but a step away from even the most powerful man in the land.

Althea squeezed through a tight knot of people and joined Leslie, Sarah, and Joel at the corner near the Peace Corps office. "I see Peace Corps is well represented,"

"How did you find us in this crowd?" Leslie asked.

"Easy." She reached out to pat Joel on the shoulder. "Mister Six-Foot-Three stands out."

"Where's Theodore?" Leslie asked.

Sarah cocked a thumb at the office, half a block behind them. "Up there. He's watching the procession from the men's room. He says he can see everything from there."

"True," Joel agreed. "There is a good view from the window over the urinals."

"All these people ..." Leslie said. Her wide eyes seemed wider than before, for crowds frightened her. She came to the street only because Sarah and Joel had coaxed her, saying that being by herself in the Peace Corps office would be worse.

"They're just finishing the ceremony in front of the Capitol." Joel inclined an ear toward a man nearby who held a transistor radio. "They're forming the procession now."

"Be careful what you say here, Althea," Sarah said. "'Deaf men' are all over the place. One of them has been keeping a pretty close eye on us." She nodded in the direction of a middle-aged man nearby who wore a dark blue wind-breaker. A coiled white cord ran from his ear to his breast pocket.

"What a nice surprise!" Althea said shrilly. "A KCIA *kae-saekki!*"

"*Shh!*" Leslie tugged at Althea's arm, not just in fear, but in anger. "Don't go calling a KCIA agent a son of a bitch practically to his face. And remember you're at a funeral, for heaven's sake!"

Althea laughed.

In Chindo, Mi Jin sat on the floor in her parents' living room. The funeral was playing on television. She turned the channel knob to KBS and then to MBC, the two major networks. Both carried exactly the same shots and nearly the same commentary.

"Put it on one channel and leave it!" her mother commanded.

"Make it MBC," the father said. "The reception's better."

One by one dignitaries from foreign countries walked past the coffin and across the television screen. Mi Jin recognized representatives from Europe and the Middle East, but her interest was piqued when the commentator identified the representatives from the United States, who were Secretary of State Cyrus Vance and President Carter's son, Chip. "They sent only a Cabinet secretary?" Mi Jin frowned.

She took offense for her country's sake; Korea rated at least Vice-President Mondale.

"What a strange name for a man," her mother commented. "*Cheep*. Like 'house.' Jin-a, is 'House' a common name in America?"

"I don't know, Omma. I don't think so."

"Strange name. Strange president. A bad one," she grumbled. "He was making all that noise about taking the American troops out of our country. Think of it! Leaving us to fend for ourselves! An open invitation for North Korea to attack us, that's what it would be." Mi Jin rolled her eyes and fought the urge to argue. She turned her attention back to the television.

The new president, Choi Kyu Ha, was delivering a speech from the steps of the Capitol. The words glorified President Pak, lifted his memory in shining phrases that made little sense to Mi Jin: "National hero," and " ... tragedy for our country and the world ..." he said.

"The tragedy is that he didn't leave office — one way or the other — sooner."

"Jin-a!" Sharp words from her father. She was unaware that she had been mumbling aloud.

"What were you saying? Eh?"

"Nothing, Appa. Really nothing."

"Mmph. Be quiet while we watch this," he retreated. "This is an historic occasion, one you'll want to tell my grandchildren about."

"Yes, Appa." She sat in front of her parents so they could not see her face. "He's gone, the bastard's gone, and his corrupt administration with him," she exulted silently. Yet as the funeral wore on, she, like her countrymen, could not crawl out from beneath the *han* that covered the nation like a shroud that day. She watched the rest of the ceremony with her face drawn in a heavy and unexpected mask of grief.

In Mokpo, Paul sat with his boarding house family in their living room watching the television. They watched with interest and sadness. They were Mokpoans, city dwellers who had not done well under Pak's rule, and Pak had never sat well with them; but they too felt the *han* and gave in to it.

Ajumoni nudged her husband and pointed at a glum Paul who watched the screen absorbed in thought.

"What's wrong with the American?" she whispered. "You'd think he'd just lost his best friend."

Paul was indeed present and his face was turned toward the television screen, but his thoughts were not on the funeral. He knew that he was watching an event of singular importance, the end of an era, whose significance was largely beyond his comprehension. He watched, and thought, and wished Mi Jin were there to help him think.

# CHAPTER FOUR

"I'm glad that President Pak is no longer here," Mi Jin said. She and Paul huddled together over tea at their usual tabang. A shaggy-haired and willfully unkempt DJ spun records in the sound booth in the corner; someone had requested the Bee Gees' "Too Much Heaven" for the third time in an hour, which did not seem to bother him in the least. A small black and white television sat on a shelf in another corner. It was turned on, playing at full volume, competing with the music.

Despite the racket, Mi Jin whispered low out of habitual caution. "But part of me is worried that worse will come. Do you know Chong Seung Hwa? General Chong?"

"I've heard the name."

"He is bad," Mi Jin said. "He is in charge of the martial law. We are all in trouble."

Mi Jin talked at length about her opinion of General Chong, punctuating her discourse with careful glances at the tables that surrounded them. She knew little about him. Some of her information came from the sketchy local news reports that painted him as a capable, fair-minded leader. The rest came from stories she had heard from her friends in the student movement who believed him to be a monster. Lacking a reliable source, she believed the sources she agreed with. Paul blushed under her relentless, passionate gaze.

He looked away from Mi Jin for a moment when he noticed that the *tabang* had suddenly gone quiet. The music stopped playing. All faces were turned toward the television in the corner. They watched a middle-aged bespectacled man, his face badly bruised and swollen, sitting at a low table amid several military officers. He was handcuffed. Paul motioned toward the picture.

Mi Jin looked, gasped, and listened intently. Paul gently shook her arm to get her attention. "That is Kim Jae Kyu," she said, without turning her head. "He shot President Pak. Now he is telling the martial law police how he did it."

The drama on the television made no sense to Paul, so he watched Mi Jin's face. Her handsome features, lit rakishly by the candle on their table, changed with almost every moment, at times showing disgust at Kim's treachery, at other times moved by the signs of the violent beating he had received, apparently while in custody. "*Ommo, Ommo,*" she gasped from time to time as the story unfolded. Kim had argued with Cha Chi Chol, Pak's chief bodyguard and, at the climax of the argument, shot Pak in the chest and head. Pak, dying, fell into the lap of the *kisaeng* girl who had been entertaining him. Kim next turned his gun on Cha and shot him dead. His co-conspirators, hearing their cue in the gunshots, butchered five of Pak's bodyguards in an outer room. Kim's story continued with his flight from the house where the shooting had taken place and ended with his arrest. Through it all, he spoke haltingly, indistinctly, his mouth swollen from his beatings. He never raised his voice above a monotonous mumble.

"It is terrible," Mi Jin finally said.

They left the *tabang* when the broadcast ended a short time later. The place never did regain its old good-natured commotion.

## Two

"*Yah!* How's that Peace Corps kid of yours doing?"

It was late; the Neja Tabang had nearly emptied of customers, and the girls who worked there wanted to get attached to a well-paying man or go home. Kwajang-nim was sleepy, and Vice-Headmaster Kim of the Chung Ang Girls' Middle School had long ago become sullen, as he always did when he was tired. The annoyingly cheerful voice of Lee Won Il, the banker, cut through the dull quiet and the cigarette smoke like a klaxon. Kwajang-nim and Kim jumped.

"How is he? Oh, fine," Kwajang-nim mumbled.

"I think he's seeing Miss Han," Kim said. Lee and Kwajang-nim exchanged questioning glances. "Han Mi Jin, that radical teacher in my school, if you two idiots can't remember our last conversation."

"Oh, really," Kwajang-nim yawned.

"That girl is mixed up in this 'student movement' business," Kim went on. "A month ago, I caught her getting on a train to Kwangju by herself."

"Lots of people go to Kwangju," Lee said, looking disparagingly at the remnants of the snacks that had been served with the tea. "It's one way to get halfway decent food." He and Kwajang-nim laughed.

"But that very afternoon there was a major *demo* there," Kim said.

"There are lots of *demo*s in Kwangju" Lee pointed out.

"She came to work the following Monday with cuts and bruises on her arms and hands."

"So she had a fight with her boyfriend," Lee said. He and Kwajang-nim laughed again. "Big deal."

"But the American is her boyfriend. That's what I was trying to tell you."

"Hm?" Kwajang-nim became fully awake. "Mr. Harkin is her boyfriend?"

Kim nodded. "He gave a guest lecture to Miss Han's class. This was a couple of days before President Pak was assassinated. I opposed the whole thing, but Shin, that old fart of a headmaster, overrode my refusal. The depraved bastard would let her get away with murder, I swear.

"Anyway, the American gave this talk. I couldn't understand a word he was saying. He told a story and carried on like a fool. But you should have seen the look on Miss Han's face through the whole thing — she was mooning over him like a lovesick cow. I picked up on it because I can read faces. I only hope the students didn't get corrupted by her behavior."

"So the boy has a girlfriend to keep him company," Kwajang-nim shrugged. "That's fine. It keeps him grounded here. I've heard that Peace Corps people are notorious for their restless feet."

"He's a bad influence, I tell you," Kim went on. "America is full of radical students. Anybody who goes to college over there has connections to the underground groups that start those huge *demo*s. Don't you remember seeing them on television?" Kwajang-nim and Lee tried to remember the last time they had seen something like that, but the war in Vietnam had been over for many years. Still, they were reluctant to spoil Kim's point. He seemed to know what he was talking about.

"You think Mr. Pak is a bad influence on your teacher?" Kwajang-nim asked doubtfully. "He doesn't seem such a bad fellow. He works hard and shows respect for authority — at least, as much as Americans are capable of. And his command of Korean is getting better all the time. I must claim responsibility for that. I tutor him every morning for at least an hour."

Kim smirked and shook his head. "You must be blind. Miss Han is teaching him. They meet at a *tabang* several times a week and she tutors him. He laps up her attention like a little shit-dog."

"Huh? She gives him lessons?" Kwajang-nim sat upright and searched Kim's face for a sign of a malicious lie, but found none. "I thought ... but our lessons were going so well. Why would he want to learn with anyone else?"

"About this Miss Han," Lee broke in. "If she's such a damned rebel, why not fire her? Why not just kick her out of the school?"

"She's under the protection of the bastard Shin," Kim grimaced. "He likes her for some reason that I can't see. As long as he's headmaster, she's got a secure position. But the day he leaves is the day Miss Han finds her ass on the street."

## Three

Kwajang-nim was called away from Mokpo on business the next day; in his absence, Paul jumped at the chance to go home-visiting. He and Mrs. Mun quickly worked through their scheduled patients on the outskirts of town near the bus station, and when they found themselves near Paul's neighborhood with only an hour left in the workday, she sent him home.

A wave of raucous laughter hit Paul when he opened the sliding front door of his house. In the main room, surrounded by other middle-aged men, sat the man he addressed as "Ajoshi", the *ajumoni*'s husband and head of the family. Paul rarely saw this man; he spent most of his time at work, where he was a mechanic for a local taxicab company, and the rest of his time he kept to the family's section of the house, venturing out only at the beginning of each month to collect Paul's rent. Paul did not even know his full name; he knew it was Mr. Yi, but he referred to him only as Ajoshi.

"Mr. Pak!" Ajoshi called, interrupting whatever lewd story had gotten his friends laughing. "Come join us!"

Ajoshi and his friends, four of them, all sat cross-legged on the floor. They broke the circle to make room. In the center was a low table with a half-dozen large bottles of beer. A pile of well picked-over peanut shells littered the table and floor.

"Thank you, Ajoshi," Paul said. "What is the occasion? You have such a party here!"

The others in the group murmured in surprise at Paul's speech. The man seated next to him slapped Paul's knee and said with beer-soured breath, "You speak Korean very well, Lord Teacher!" The others laughed so hard that at first Paul thought he was being mocked.

"You should have heard him when he first came here," Ajoshi said. "Could hardly say a word straight. Couldn't even ask where the shithouse was. Haw! Let me tell you, he has improved a lot. Now we can talk like old friends."

Paul had never traded more than a few words with him, but he let it pass.

"Have some," one of the fellows, a lanky, greasy-haired man said. He ran to the kitchen and brought a glass. Paul held it with both hands while the man filled it with beer.

"We got off early today," Ajoshi explained. "The power went off in the shop. *Blam!* No light to work under the cabs, no juice to run the tools.

There was nothing to do but go home. Thank God!" The others hooted and roared.

"Happy days," Paul said in English. Then he added, "*Chukhahamnida.*" Congratulations.

The men soon forgot about him and resumed their conversation.

"So who was this lady who caught the president in her lap?" one man asked.

"She was no lady," Ajoshi said. "She was a whore."

"No! I heard she was a singer."

"She was a singer," Ajoshi rejoined, "who did more than sing. She was a *kisaeng,* a high-class whore. Why would Pak Chong Hui be interested in a woman who only sang?"

The others snickered and nodded in agreement.

"What a shock she must have had!" Ajoshi went on. "*Blam!*" He pretended that the man next to him had slumped his head into his lap. With a comical expression of horror he let out a shrill woman-like scream. Again his companions collapsed in laughter.

At that moment the door flew open with the suddenness of a pistol shot. The men jumped in fright and sprang to their feet.

"What the hell are you guys doing here?" Ajumoni roared from the doorway, loaded down with parcels from the market.

"We're just having a little drink together," Ajoshi mumbled. He jumped up and, red-faced, helped her put the packages down.

"More than just a little drink," she shot back. She glared at the bottles and glasses, and the peanut shells strewn all over the floor. "You look like you've been caught in the act, all right! Look at the mess in here. Get out! Take your friends and go someplace else to get into trouble!" She heaped an extra dose of invective on Ajoshi, pointing out his laziness, his love for alcohol, the many low points in his ancestry, and several other faults that Paul lacked the vocabulary to understand.

Ajoshi puffed out his chest and made a show of answering her allegations with accusations of his own: she did not keep the house clean enough, and why was she not at home to prepare food for his friends? Everyone in the room, including Paul and Ajoshi himself, knew from the start that the skirmish belonged to Ajumoni; Ajoshi's half-hearted defense was only an effort to save face. Satisfied that he had done the best he could, he feigned disgust at the injustice laid upon him and herded the others out to the street. The scare made them more giddy than before.

"Whew! That was a hot one!" one of them exclaimed.

"A world-class scolding," agreed another. "Where shall we go now?"

"It's a beautiful afternoon," the lanky one said. "Let's have a drink on Mount Yudal!"

Ajoshi prodded Paul. "You come with us!" He pushed him to the street and hailed a cab.

Over the protests of the driver, who recognized the men as the mechanics from his own shop and wanted nothing to do with them, the six men squeezed into the car. "Let's go!" shouted Ajoshi, and they sang obscene drinking songs in the late afternoon traffic. The driver stopped at the base of the mountain, even though the entrance to the mountain park was a half-mile up the road. "I can't push this car any higher up the hill," he said. "If you guys did your job right, there'd be no problem." Ajoshi and the others took the insult in good humor, and stiffed the driver only half his fare. Two of the men ducked into a *kage*, a small streetside market. They emerged with four plastic jugs of a milky liquid.

"*Makkoli* is here!" they cried.

"You like *makkoli?*" Ajoshi asked Paul.

"A little," he replied. Paul had tried the cloying, acrid liquor often enough before, and knew that its quality varied: it could be sharp but smooth or, as Althea had once remarked, it could taste "like last night's dinner preserved in cold vomit". He sipped cautiously, and drank more. This batch was not bad. The white solids did not detract from the pure fiery liquor at the heart of it. He took a long gulp. The men approved.

"You'll be a Korean before you know it, *neh?*" one man laughed.

The men walked unsteadily up the steps of the mountain, tripping over each other and laughing at their growing clumsiness. They stopped at an open-air pavilion about fifty yards below the one from which Paul and Mi Jin had looked out over Mokpo and the sea on the night before President Pak's death. That had been barely two weeks ago; to Paul it felt like an eternity.

Ajoshi caught Paul looking up the mountain at the higher pavilion. "You want to go up there?" he mumbled. "*Aigo* — this is good enough. Nice view, *neh?*" He gestured over the sea with its multitude of islands, toward the late sun, and without a second look sat down heavily on a bench with the others.

Paul looked out to sea. The view was indeed fine enough from that spot. A chill wind swept up from the water and carried with it the smells of the living things it held. The brine in that wind braced him and cleared his mind. He looked out contentedly, reluctant to share the higher sacred place with these drunken men.

Sacred place? Paul slowly realized that many things he associated with Mi Jin were becoming dear to him, if not sacred: the *tabang* where they had their lessons nearly every night, the alley behind the health center where he had first caught sight of her, even the spot on Mount Yudal's treacherous staircase where he had lost his footing and leaned on her in pain. He looked out over the jumbled streets of Mokpo. Somewhere in that labyrinth of streets and houses was Muan Dong district, where Mi Jin lived. Beyond, in roughly a straight line along the coast and over the horizon, lay Chindo. This large island was Mi Jin's parents' home; she had told him that she would be staying there this coming weekend. It was also where Leslie Black was stationed, at the Chindo County Health Center.

"How long does it take to get to Chindo?" he asked aloud.

The others stopped their conversation. "Why would you want to go there?" asked Ajoshi.

"I have friends there. I would like to go visit."

"By boat it's what — an hour? Yes?" The others disagreed, volunteering estimates that ranged from forty-five minutes to two hours. "An hour or so. You catch the boat at the passenger dock down there."

"Thank you. Maybe I will go this weekend."

## Four

Mr. Han studied his farmer's hands — large, gnarled, and tough as leather stretched over rock — while he listened to the argument between his wife and daughter. He was certain everyone on the island of Chindo could hear them.

"Omma, I'm not ready to get married."

"Don't you dare contradict me!"

"But I'm only twenty-three; I just finished college last year. There's so much I want to do before I settle down!"

"Such as?" her mother scowled.

"Well ... I want to continue teaching, for one thing. My scholarship to the University was such a blessing, Omma, and I worked so hard to win it each year. Surely you don't want me to throw it all away now that I'm finally putting my education to good use."

Mr. Han had heard the same row a dozen times over the past several months. His wife and daughter used the same arguments and counter-arguments each time, almost without variation, as if reading from a script.

"Why did you let me go to college if you only wanted me to be hidden away as somebody's *anae*?" Mi Jin continued, referring to the ancient tradition of keeping the wife, the "inside person," secluded forever within the four walls of the home.

"That was the biggest mistake we ever made, let me tell you! We sent you to college because that school money wasn't good for anything else, and it's stupid to turn down a free gift. But I never thought you'd use it against your father and me. I should have listened to my own common sense: the more schooling a girl gets, the harder it is to get her married It's enough of a shame to have only one child left, a daughter, without her being too smart for her own good."

"Then why did you let me finish school," Mi Jin cried, "when my friends stopped at junior high? Why did you send me to a fine university? I keep asking you, but you never answer me."

"I told you. We sent you because you did so well on the college entrance examinations that they gave you a scholarship. Free money! I wanted to throw it back in their stuck-up faces, but he —" she jabbed an angry thumb at Mr. Han "— said no. He didn't believe me when I told him that an educated girl is impossible to marry off.

"But even so," she continued, "I'm not finished with what I was saying: Mokpo is no place for you. It's rough and dirty. Too many of the wrong kind of people roam the streets. And the politics! Thank the Lord you're no longer in Kwangju, with its packs of troublemakers. But Mokpo is not much better."

"Omma, I'm fine in Mokpo. I stay out of trouble. As long as I'm a teacher at the Chung Ang School I don't dare to be seen participating in any street demonstrations ... in Mokpo. I'd lose my job. And I couldn't stand the shame of that."

"You need a home and a family," her mother said, "even though your father and I realize that once you join your husband's family, you'll have no obligation to care for us when we grow too old to support ourselves."

"I'll take care of you and Appa. You know that. I'd never let marriage release me from my obligations to you. I'll be both a son and a daughter to you."

"Good. That's why I've called the matchmaker."

"Omma, no!"

"The matchmaker, I say, who has already found a good prospect for you. It wasn't easy. You were born in the hour of the cow, a very unhappy hour, and not many men's families would take a chance on such a marriage. Especially with an educated girl."

"I am not ready for this, Omma!"

"Shut up. His name is Kim Hyong Chol, of the Haenam Kims. His father owns a clothing store, a successful one, here in Chindo. He has an elder brother who would have inherited his father's business."

"Can't you hear me, Omma? I don't want to get married!"

"But he came down with polio as a child — poor fellow — and is crippled. He can't be expected to run the business. It will go to Kim Hyong Chol."

"I don't want to be a shopkeeper's wife. I don't want to live in ..." Mi Jin paused.

"What? Out with it. You don't want to live in Chindo, is that it?"

Mi Jin remained silent, her head bowed.

"Then what's to become of your father and me? What will happen when we become old and frail and have no son to take care of us? Who will we turn to? Our daughter? Ha! Our daughter who would force us to live our last years in ... Heaven help us ... in a big city like Mokpo or Kwangju? *Eh?* What kind of daughter are you? What happened to your promise to be both son and daughter to us? *Eh?*"

Mi Jin hid her face in her hands. Tears rolled off her chin and spotted her blouse.

"Omma, Omma, why are you talking to me like this?" she sobbed. "I love you and Appa. I wouldn't ever do anything to hurt you. It's just that —"

"It's just nothing," Mr. Han broke in sharply. "I'm sick of this bickering. Meet Kim Hyong Chol. Stop bawling. You'll thank us one day for putting you on the right road. That's that. Now — where's dinner?"

## Five

Old Mr. Han went for a walk after the meal, down to the sea whose quiet shore was not far from his house. His footsteps clumped heavily on the sand. In the fading light of sunset, he sat down on a boulder and stared out over the gray sea. Tiny uninhabited islands dotted the horizon and faded in and out of view through the offshore fog like ghosts of the ancient sea gods that the native townspeople had once worshiped. He absently lit a cigarette and drew in the mingled smells of seawater and tobacco that had comforted him through most of his life.

"Trouble," he muttered. "Nothing but trouble. I was cursed the moment I left my *kohyang*, my home."

In the spring of 1950 Han Ki Tae loaded the last of his provisions onto a rickety horse-drawn pullcart outside his farmhouse in Jasong County, in the newly emerging nation of North Korea. His brother and young cousin loaded their belongings, too. Together they had enough supplies to last four months.

A knot of townspeople, mostly family and close friends, milled about, packing extra bags of food onto the overloaded cart, talking, and drying tears. They spoke in hushed tones of better times to come in the south, of safety from the political winds that were blowing against them, as Christians. At last the sun broke through a tear in the low clouds, illuminating the poor horse with an almost absurd brilliance. Mr. Han took this as a sign to get under way.

"We'll be home soon, dear," he said comfortingly to his young wife, Sun Ja. "As soon as we find a good piece of land at a good price down south, we'll come back for you and the boys. Then we'll all be safe. And rich someday, too."

Sun Ja would not be consoled; and even though she said nothing, her swollen eyes spoke volumes for her. She gave her husband a chaste hug and herded the children toward him. Mr. Han picked them up — Dae Il, who was four, and Do Ma, two — and kissed their dusty faces. "Take care of Omma," he said, and choked as he set them down.

He never saw them again after that day. It had been twenty-nine years.

"My Sun Ja, she was a beauty and a fine wife," Mr. Han sniffled, wiping his eyes with a leathery old hand. "And my boys. My boys."

Within weeks after he and his kinsmen passed south of the 38th parallel, the artificial boundary between the communist-led north and the Western-led south, war broke out. On June 25, 1950 the armies of the north swept down upon Seoul and soon conquered all but a tiny region of the Korean peninsula around Pusan. Then the United Nations landed a major force at Inchon, on the sea near Seoul, and drove the North Korean army almost all the way up to its border with China. Suddenly China joined in the fray, and the battle line wavered back and forth around the mid-section of the penin-sula for the next two years. Mr. Han never did get a chance to return home to bring his family to safety. The signing of the armistice that ended the war completely cut off those in the south from their people in the north.

"Is she alive?" he wondered. "Are Dae Il and Do Ma in the army up there? Are they all brainwashed into being happy that I'm gone?"

He yearned for a bottle of *soju*.

The trouble this evening between his second wife and his daughter rein-forced his conviction that the Almighty had singled him out for a life of misery and loss, a life like the one handed to Job when Satan taunted God, saying that a good man would never lose faith, however extreme his misery. God scourged Job to prove a point. "What is the point in my troubles?" Mr. Han muttered bitterly. He spat. "No point."

He had had a son in the south, one born to him and Mi Jin's mother long after he had finally given up hope of regaining his original family. Jin Ho was a fine boy, quick-witted and athletic, not at all like his quiet and stubborn younger sister. The boy was always getting into dangerous spots and then extricating himself as if it were a mere trifle. He was destined to be a great military leader, Mr. Han had assured himself, a first-rate battlefield commander if, heaven forbid, war came again. But one day, playing with some friends on the nearby rocky cliff that jutted out over the sea, he had fallen and smashed his head against the rocks. His friends brought him quickly out of the water before he drowned, but the damage had already been done. By the time they had got him to Chindo Hospital an hour later, he was in a deep coma. He lingered in that state for several days before he died. He was eleven years old when that happened, and his sister, Mi Jin, was eight. She became the family's only child. "Thank heaven the child has her mother's strength," old Mr. Han often thought. "Without it, she would never have survived her mother's grief."

The sky had turned dark. Mr. Han got up from the rock and gingerly made his way up the path to his house. His willful and ungrateful daughter again dominated his thoughts. If her brother Jin Ho were alive, she would be free to do as she pleased, but that was not possible now. She had responsibilities, and responsibilities had to be met at all costs. He tried to think of a way — any way — to keep this remnants of his tattered family close to him. Misfortune had to stop with Mi Jin.

## Six

"No wonder Leslie's going crazy."

A drab landscape greeted Paul as he approached the Chindo County Health Center: a gray building, a lowering gray sky, dun-colored dirt at his feet. The trees behind the health center reflected only a bare gray-green half-light on this unusually dark day. Even Paul, who normally enjoyed the muted colors of cloudy weather, found the scene oppressive. Mokpo, at least, had a fairly constant hum of activity going on to balance out the doldrums. This place was as silent as a tomb.

"Paul!"

Leslie Black appeared at the door of the building, looking like a wretched castaway who had just been thrown a lifeline.

"I'm so glad you've come. You have no idea how lonely this place can get. Come inside. I'll introduce you around."

Everything inside the building, from the walls to the desks to the primitive medical furnishings, was coated with the same shade of gray paint, which was peeling. Leslie took Paul to the Tuberculosis Control Room, which was another study in dilapidation: a few chipped pieces of wood furniture blended in with the walls of the darkened room which was heated by an ancient kerosene heater. A middle aged woman peered at chest X-rays while holding them up to the window.

"Mrs. Kim, *i buni dongryo P'yonghwapong satanwon 'Paul Harkin' imnida.* This is my fellow Peace Corps Volunteer Paul Harkin."

"I am delighted to meet you," Paul said, in Korean.

"Likewise," Mrs. Kim replied. "Miss Mun has told me much about the work you do with leprosy patients at the Korean Leprosy Institute. They are very sad cases, *neh?*"

"Excuse me?" Paul did not understand everything she said, but he caught a reference to leprosy.

"Oh, no, no, no," Leslie blushed. "This is not the volunteer from the KLI. This man works at the Mokpo City Health Center." She spoke Korean rapidly, pausing briefly only once to grope for words.

"Ah, Mokpo. So sorry."

"She got you mixed up with Joel. Mrs. Kim, may I be excused for the day? Peace Corps business."

"Of course. *Caseyo*." Go.

Paul and Leslie walked down Chindo's sole paved street, past the county administrative office, to a *tabang*.

"I'm impressed with the way you spoke Korean back there," he commented. "Do you have a tutor?"

"Yes. One of the local girls who graduated from college in Mokpo and then lived in Kwangju for a while. She got married a few days ago. How's … um … Joel these days?"

"Joel? He's fine. I stayed at his place right after President Pak got shot. Didn't you see him? You were in Seoul, too."

"Yes, I saw him," Leslie said moodily. "But I didn't see much of him."

The two sat quietly sipping coffee.

"What makes him tick?" she finally said.

"Hm? Who?"

"Joel," Leslie said. "I don't understand the guy. He's harder to figure out than most Koreans."

"I agree with you: he's an enigma, all right. He and I talked quite a bit when I stayed with him. At night, after he'd turned the lights out, but before we fell asleep, that's when he talked the most. During the day he's a man of few words, and the words he chooses don't illuminate him much. But in the dark, when he can't see who he's talking to, I guess he can convince himself that he's talking to himself. I don't know. That's the impression I got. He went on and on about all sorts of things: his travels, his most exciting or bizarre cases as a paramedic.

"But you want to know something funny? I don't know much about him. Even after all those long talks, I don't know where he was born, who his parents are, or even whether or not he was ever married. He's old — probably between thirty and thirty-five, but I'm not sure."

"Then what did you talk about?"

"Life," Paul shrugged. "Experience. He's traveled all around the world, you know. I was always asking him about the places he'd gone to and the things he'd done. 'That's all bullshit,' he'd say. Then he'd ask me about one thing or another: whether I thought President Carter's human rights policy was right or wrong, to what lengths we should go to rescue the hostages in Iran, and things like that. It always seemed that we carried on two discussions at once. I wanted stories about exotic people and places, and he wanted — what? An 'innocent' outlook on the world, I guess."

"You two are good friends."

"Yeah. Isn't that strange? We're about as different as two people can be, but we took to each other right off. He's a man of vast experience. Adventures everywhere. Never a tourist, always an explorer. As for me — well, I went to Chicago once. I've made a career of being naive. Yet in spite of our differences, we're close. I'd do just about anything for him — anything — and I know he'd do the same for me.

"So there you have it. I can't figure him out," Paul concluded. "It sounds like you'd like to give it a try."

Leslie blushed.

"I wish you luck," Paul said. A television in the corner of the *tabang* was tuned to a musical program, some kind of talent competition among high school students. Paul had been watching it idly as he talked. Now a girl student, surprisingly attractive in the severe white blouse and dark skirt of her school uniform, took center stage and prepared to sing. The song's introduction sounded familiar to Paul. When the girl sang, Paul's heart lurched with recognition:

*Seh no yah—seh no yah*
*Sangwa pada-eh uliga salgo*
*Sangwa pada-eh uliga kaneh ...*

"'If it is happiness, give it to the mountain; if sadness, to your love,'" Paul murmured.

"What did you say?"

"Nothing. That's a beautiful song." He got up and paid for the coffee. "Let's go for a walk. I want to look around."

## Seven

Kim Hyong Chol was a giant of a man, standing almost two heads taller than Mi Jin. His face bore the placid, kindly expression of one who has spent his entire life in one of Korea's rural towns and has therefore dealt more with the unchanging rhythms of earth and sky than with the caprices of humanity.

"Art thou at peace, Miss Han?" he asked politely. Etiquette demanded that their first conversation be conducted in High Korean.

"Yes. Art thou at peace, Mr. Kim?"

Mi Jin thought reflexively of her first meeting with Paul Harkin, similar to this one in so many respects: the strain of making the acquaintance of a total stranger, the uncomfortable silences, her reliance on reading his *nunchi* to glimpse his character. She hastily put Paul out of her mind.

"My mother tells me that thou art a teacher of English," Kim Hyong Chol said in a soft, clear voice. He walked with Mi Jin to the larger of Chindo's two *tabangs* and ordered coffee with extra sugar. "I'm afraid I know little of English besides 'How are you' and 'I love y—' Ahem."

Silence ensued.

"Speak to me about thyself," Mi Jin said at last.

"I spent many summers on a farm not far from Haenam. We grew rice and raised pigs. I liked caring for the pigs best of all, and truly it is those creatures that make a farm a farm, *neh?* My clan has lived on the same land for many, many years; nobody can say for how long. My family lost much during the War, but now all is well. 'Trouble is the seed of joy,' as the saying goes. My father was the second son, so he moved off the farm and opened a clothing store in Chindo. We worked hard, and the family prospered."

Hyong Chol's eyes told Mi Jin what his words could not: that he had genuine love for his animals and for the earth, and that he liked the world and his lot in life. This was a man quite unlike the stridently dissatisfied men in her circle of friends in the student movement: he was happy. He lit a cigarette, but took care not to blow the smoke in her direction.

"My elder brother was ill as a child. He is crippled now, so my father's shop will be my responsibility when he is ready to retire. I would prefer to return to the land, but one must do as one's parents demand, *neh?*"

Hyong Chol's voice betrayed no hint of resentment, only an unquestioning respect for the traditions of his family. Mi Jin began to envy him his acceptance of the natural limits of his world.

"...Yes. Of course."

"Even now I have several ideas for the shop to make it grow. I have been studying on my own with books I borrowed from a friend of mine. One is a textbook on business administration published by Seoul National University Press. I can show it to thee sometime, if thou wishest."

"I thank thee."

"Listen to me talking about books and education to a teacher," he chuckled sheepishly, "a graduate of the great Chonnam University. I had only one year at a tiny college in Kumsong. Thou are smarter than I, *neh?*"

"Not at all," Mi Jin said politely. "There are plenty of things in life as important as education."

"Like family and land and flooded rice fields in springtime. The simple view of life I learned from my grandfather dealt with earth, sky, and wind, as if nothing else matters."

"I'm afraid I do not know much of such things. I have been off the land for many years now."

Hyong Chol's eyes gently invited her back.

"Now tell me more about thyself," he said. "My mother's speech has been full of thee lately."

"Then thou must know more than I can tell thee in a short time. I live in Mokpo and like it there. Being hired at the Chung Ang Girls' Middle School was a stroke of good fortune, for its reputation is equal to schools even in Kwangju; my career has a good beginning there."

"Chindo has good schools, also."

Mi Jin ignored the statement and pressed on: "Someday I hope to live in Kwangju, or even Seoul. Tell me," Mi Jin said after a pause, putting aside the conventions of polite conversation, "how dost thou feel about the 'October 26th Affair?'"

Hyong Chol stroked his chin in silence before answering.

"President Pak could not live forever," he finally said. "Powerful people come and go. It is a shame that he departed in the way he did. Thou art eager to hear me talk about him, the better to find out more about my ... politics, *neh?*"

"Er ... well —"

"Pak did both good and bad. Which of us has not? He created the Saemaul Undang, the New Village Movement, of which I am a member. My family is richer because of him, and I honor him for it. Yet he destroyed many people who disagreed with him, including Kim Dae Jung, whom I admire. He regards students — scholars — as enemies, when everyone knows that scholars are the conscience of our nation. In that respect he was a bad man. I know nothing of our new president, Choi Kyu Ha. I hope he is as good as President Pak ... but not as bad. Have I answered thy question to thy satisfaction?"

Mi Jin smiled fully for the first time that evening. "Yes. Yes, thou hast."

## *Eight*

"Trouble is the seed of joy."

Mi Jin repeated the old proverb to herself over and over again as she and Hyong Chol strolled down Chindo's main street toward the bus that would take her back to the countryside, to her parents' house.

"Trouble is the seed of joy." The thought comforted her as the gray day slid into a deepening gray twilight. Earlier, she had hoped that this prospective bridegroom would be an ogre, a man so undesirable that she could exercise her veto on the match without having to justify her decision. But Hyong Chol was a good man. His *nunchi*, her window to his soul, showed him to be attractively different from the men she knew in the student movement: open minded, open hearted, kind. His *nunchi* called to mind another man with similar characteristics: the American, Paul Harkin.

To her chagrin, she liked Hyong Chol. She could not picture herself loving him, but love was not a requirement for the match that her parents had in mind. Her mother's voice kept intruding on her thoughts: "You'll learn to love him. And if you don't, eh. No matter. With luck, he and his parents will treat you well. You'll have a good marriage." But Mi Jin did not want to marry this man.

Trouble, endless trouble, she lamented. Heaven grant me joy at the end of it!

Two figures approached them up ahead. In the gloom, Mi Jin could see only that they were slightly taller than most Koreans and that they had the light skin and self-consciously casual look of Americans, a man and a woman.

"Han Mi Jin*shi!*" the man called. "*Annyong hasumnikka?*"

Mi Jin instantly placed the voice and the faulty pronunciation. "Mr. Pak! Why ... What are you doing in Chindo?" she asked in English.

"Visiting my friend. This is my fellow Peace Corps Volunteer, Leslie Black," Paul said, in Korean. His eyes narrowed as he waited for Mi Jin to introduce her companion.

"This is Kim Hyong Chol," she said. "Mr. Kim, this is Peace Corps Volunteer Paul Harkin — Pak Jong Shik, he has a Korean name — and Miss Black."

"*Pangap-sumnida,*" Hyong Chol said. I am delighted to meet thee. He bowed and folded his left hand across his chest in the formal manner as he shook hands.

"Delighted," Paul repeated.

"I thank thee for all the help thou art giving my country."

"Thou art too kind. Not important are the things I do."

"No, no, thou and people like thee do much work of great importance for Korea and other countries around the world."

"I thank thee for thy kind words," Paul said, already bored with the contrived, polite argument. "In Chindo thou livest?"

"Yes. My father owns a shop. That one," he pointed up the street. "I will own it someday."

"Congratulations."

Surprised and puzzled at Paul's presence, Mi Jin could not take her eyes off him. "Pak Jong Shik works at the public health center in Mokpo," she said. "I am tutoring him in the Korean language."

"Thou truly speakest Korean very well!" Hyong Chol exclaimed. "Miss Han is an excellent teacher, *neh?*"

"Thy words too kind they are. Han Mi Jin is a good teacher, but a poor student I am. Really very little I know."

The pleasantries dragged on, and at last Mi Jin cleared her throat.

"My parents are expecting me home early this evening. I must leave."

"So be it," Hyong Chol said. "I must go also. Han Mi Jin, we shall meet each other again." Observing traditional etiquette, he did not touch her, not even to shake her hand. He did shake hands with Paul and Leslie. "An honor to meet thee."

The bus, a ramshackle wheeled crate which in its dim past once plied the streets of Mokpo, pulled over to the curb and opened its door for Mi Jin. She shook hands with the Americans. "Meet me here," she whispered low to Paul.

Leslie returned to her boarding house. Paul stood on the corner and waited. Curiosity and a vague unease gripped him. Who was this Kim Hyong Chol? he wondered. Why was Mi Jin so agitated when they met? Her discomfort during the conversation bordered on unfriendliness. He could not shake the impression that she wished the two of them had not met, and he prepared himself to be hurt.

A bus stopped across the street and went on, leaving a fragile Mi Jin behind.

"Jong Shik!" she whispered.

"Yes! Over here."

The lack of street lights had plunged the town into a darkness that the poor lights from homes and a few shops could not relieve. Mi Jin walked briskly across the street and, holding Paul's arm, guided him into an even darker side street. She wanted it that way because she did not want to see his face when she spoke.

"Jong Shik. You are wondering who Kim Hyong Chol is," she said, in words rehearsed on the bus ride halfway home and then back to town again. "This was not a casual meeting. It was a date arranged by my parents, and his. Do you understand? They intend for us to be married."

Paul at first said nothing, but he stopped walking and Mi Jin felt his arm stiffen under her grip.

"When?"

"I do not know. Whenever my parents say. It is their wish that I marry the man they have chosen for me. They are wise, wiser than I am. Mr. Kim's family is a respectable one, and he is industrious and kind-hearted. Our marriage is in ... inevitable. Because of this, I do not think I should give you Korean lessons anymore."

"Do you love him?"

"It doesn't matter."

"You shouldn't have to marry anyone you don't love, Mi Jin," he protested. "It just isn't fair. It's not right."

Paul reached out and found Mi Jin's hand and held it. Mi Jin stood silently, looking at the pavement, but did not remove her hand.

"Kim Hyong Chol is too lucky. What has he done to deserve such good fortune?"

"Don't. Please don't," she whispered.

Paul looked around in the dark street, then tried to make out Mi Jin's features. He could only tell by her posture that she was too miserable to move.

"You don't want to marry this guy, do you? You don't really want to go along with what your parents are demanding. I'm right, aren't I?"

After a few moments of silence, Mi Jin withdrew her hand from Paul's grip and took a step back.

"Please leave Chindo, Jong Shik. Go back to Mokpo."

"Will I see you there?" Paul asked.

Mi Jin shook her head. "I don't think so."

"Your voice tells me you don't want it that way. You see, you can read eyes," Paul said, managing a weak desperate smile and reaching for her hands, more firmly now and not letting go. "but I can read the voice. Let's continue our language lessons. I'll respect your culture and treat you like a near-married person; your virtue will be safe, I promise. In return, you must respect something from my culture."

"Yes?"

"Friends don't abandon each other on account of marriage, or engagement, or any kind of trouble. Walking around with a big burden day after day is no way to live. Keep me. Let me help."

She stood still and solid as a deeply-rooted tree. "American culture has no place here, Paul. It must be as I've said."

"Will you at least think about it?"

Mi Jin said nothing. She turned slowly and walked into the night.

## Nine

Winter came to Mokpo in the second week of November, 1979.

A thick layer of white and gray clouds, looking like masses of cotton soaked in dirty water, heaved into the skies around Mount Yudal at mid-morning. With it, the air suddenly turned cold, and this sent the people in Paul's health center scurrying for kerosene space heaters. They searched by matchlight for fuel in dark closets, for the world outdoors had become darker than twilight under the cloud cover, and no one wanted to ask Kwa-jang-nim to allow the building's electricity to be turned on; rather, they waited for him to put down his book and declare that he did not have enough light to read by.

The first flakes of snow fell shortly after the clouds arrived. "Mr. Pak!" called Mrs. Mun from the window. "*Nuni wayo.*" It's snowing. Large flakes floated lazily to the ground like feathers, hesitating as they approached the ground as if looking for a place to settle. The buildings across the street became difficult to see. The sounds within the health center grew more distinct as the snow muffled the noises outside.

Paul sauntered through the halls and looked into the rooms. Everyone had stopped working. The snow and the quiet outside the windows illuminated the distinction between "inside" and "outside," and drew their attention outward. "Mr. Pak! Have some tea with us!" someone called.

Paul gladly joined the conviviality of the moment. He sat with four different groups in leisurely succession for tea and snacks of oranges and dried squid. "*Nuni wayo*," they said at every stop. They all gathered at their windows and watched.

"It is very beautiful. Let us go outside and build a man of snow," Paul joked.

They laughed politely, wondering why anyone would want to go outside on such a day, and returned to watching the snowflakes drift down. Paul watched, too, content with the silence and the quiet beauty outside the window. That's what I like about the Koreans, Paul thought. They can be as busy as can be, but when something like this happens, they drop everything and become poets.

The snow was still falling at lunchtime, but wetter than before. Paul was freezing in his light sweater and tennis shoes. "I'd like to go home to change my clothes," he told Mrs. Mun.

The snow was lovely but treacherous. It hid Mokpo's rough edges with a white cloak of purity, but when it fell beneath the wheels of the city's taxi-cab drivers, it turned the streets into stretches of dirty slush. Paul saw two traffic accidents on his ten-minute walk, neither of them serious. Mount Yudal, in contrast to the dirty streets, was a distant confection whose trees and crags were dusted with white powdered sugar. He could hardly keep his eyes off it.

Paul's boarding house, like the health center, lay largely in darkness. It smelled of *gochu* — hot red peppers — and green onion and garlic; Ajumoni had spent the morning making one last batch of *baechu kimchi* before the winter made cabbage unavailable. He stumbled against his desk on his way to the armoire in which he kept the two suitcases he had brought from home. Because space was scarce in his room, he had never bothered to un-pack them completely: his goose-down jacket was in there, rolled into a tight coil, along with a stocking cap, his long underwear, and a pair of hiking boots. Taking the rubber bands off the jacket, he unrolled it and held it to his face. It still had the musty, sweet aroma of home. He took a deep breath. Ajumoni rapped gently on his door.

"The weather is cold," she whispered. The snow made whispering seem natural, almost mandatory. "You're getting your winter clothing out, *neh?* Good."

Paul swept the inside of his suitcase with the flashlight once more, then closed it.

"I am sorry it's so dark, Mr. Pak. Electricity is expensive, especially in winter. I didn't know you were coming. I would have turned it on for you." She motioned toward the voltage regulator box mounted on the wall beside the outside door.

Paul shook his head. "That's all right. This light is plenty. ...Do I smell *kimchi?*"

"Yes. Wait right here." Ajumoni jumped up and returned with a small lunchbox. One half was packed with hot steaming rice, the other with *kimchi*. "Take this back with you. This is new *kimchi*. I know you like it fresh, not soured."

Paul took the lunchbox. "Thank you. How is your son? He'll be coming home soon, won't he?"

"In a few weeks. How well your Korean is coming! You'll soon sound like a native. Song Min is doing well. He is excelling in mathematics and all his science courses: he'll win a school prize this year for sure. He's not doing so well in English — when he comes home, he'll have to work on it."

And I'm just the one to help him, Paul thought ruefully. "We'll see what we can do," he said, rising. "Now I have to change and go back to work. Thank you for the lunchbox."

The sun peeked out briefly from the clouds while Paul was walking back downtown. It melted the snow off the pavement and made the normal roar of the city louder with the *shish*ing of traffic on wet streets. The air, scrubbed by the snow, now had an incandescent clarity, freezing the world into crystal. But the clouds were not far off, and by the time he got back to the health center, the city had again fallen under a suffocating gray pall. It remained that way for days.

## Ten

Paul's scheduled language lesson was set that night at their regular *tabang*. He had not heard from Mi Jin since Chindo the previous Saturday, and he hoped the appointment was still on. He went in anxiously.

Everything was different. Paul's visit to Chindo had changed it. When he did not see Mi Jin right away his heart lurched sadly. "I chased her off," he muttered, and turned to leave.

She was not at their regular table. He saw her in another corner under a circle of light from an overhead lamp. Steam from two cups of tea rose and washed into a thin cloud over the table. She seemed more carefully dressed than usual, in a long dress and a flowered blouse, as if she had not come directly from school. She sat still, her hands warming around her teacup, her eyes downcast.

"Hello?" Paul called meekly from a few steps away. "May I sit here?"

Mi Jin looked up. An inner struggle had taken its toll on her features: the pair of furrows between her eyebrows, never prominent before, had deepened and her face was pale. She gestured to the opposite chair.

"How are you?" Paul asked softly. "Are you okay?"

She nodded without looking up. He looked at her for a long time before he spoke again. "I didn't mean to make you unhappy the other night. I am so sorry. Do you want me to leave?"

Mi Jin looked up and shook her head. "No," she whispered. "No."

She had been thinking about Paul almost constantly since Saturday night. She had never thought it possible to be thrilled and mortified at the same time, but she was. Paul's affection soothed her like balm; the unrelenting loneliness that had dogged her through her life diminished when he was with her. She liked him. He was kind-hearted and gentle, and the jokes he told were lame but never cruel. She treasured the hours she had spent with him.

On the other hand, Mi Jin kept reminding herself, he is *oeguk in*, a foreigner. He is not one of us. Foreigners cannot be trusted. They cannot understand Korean people. A deeper voice within her, one she inherited from ancestors who had shut themselves off from the rest of the world in the Hermit Kingdom of times past, was more harsh: He is a *ssangnom*, a nonperson. He was not born like men; he just "happened." She winced, trying to shut those voices out.

"I'm sorry to bother you," Paul continued. "Are you hungry?"

"No."

Paul paused, then pressed on. "I've been thinking about what happened last Saturday. I won't take back anything I told you, but I'm unhappy that you're upset. Do you understand?"

Mi Jin nodded.

"I think I know how you feel. You get engaged to a guy you don't know or don't like. Or maybe you resent him being chosen for you by your parents. Along comes another guy who chooses that moment to say something stupid like 'I think you're wonderful, and I want to help you.'" Paul smiled sadly. "So you've got two men showing you more attention than you want. And one of them is a white guy — not the kind of person a respectable Korean lady can be seen with. Am I right?"

Mi Jin nodded again, hiding her surprise. She had not credited him with being so perceptive.

"What do you want to do?" Paul asked gently. Before she could reply, he continued: "I'll do whatever you ask. The main thing is for your *kibun* to stay good. That is important to me."

Mi Jin smiled in spite of herself. Nobody had ever cared much about her *kibun*, her spirits, before.

"Look," Paul said, "I'll be in Seoul all next week. Peace Corps has something they call the Volunteer Community Meeting, and we all have to be there. Maybe it'll be a good chance for us to think, apart from each other. I'll miss you, but we'll have time to figure things out. Does that sound okay to you?"

"Yes. I think that is a good idea."

## *Eleven*

The Volunteer Community Meeting, or VCM, was a yearly gathering in Seoul of all Peace Corps Volunteers throughout Korea, timed to coincide with the Thanksgiving holiday. In addition to giving the volunteers a real turkey dinner for Thanksgiving, the Peace Corps staff gave refresher training in health care and teaching, and workshops on Korean culture. What the volunteers enjoyed above everything else, though, was the chance to gather and live for a whole week in a tightly-knit American community. Paul had been looking forward to it for weeks. He took the train up to Seoul on Saturday afternoon and spent the entire day before the meeting reveling in the sophistication of the city. The contrast between powerful Seoul and poor little Mokpo always struck him: even the sounds seemed to him the difference between the roar of a distant jet aircraft engine and the close-up rattle of a ramshackle bus, both equally loud but completely different in their source.

Volunteers arrived in Seoul in increasing numbers as the weekend wore on. As a group, and individually, they changed as they grew in number. While living at their sites, they comprised a loose confederation of two hundred Americans scattered in a country the size of Indiana. At gatherings like this one they became more insular and more stubbornly nationalistic, as Americans gathered in a foreign country will do. They stopped speaking Korean. They dispensed with the customary short bows when meeting acquaintances on the street, as among themselves such a gesture would seem wildly out of place. Ugly, arrogant "stupid Korean" jokes came up in conversations. The sense of wonder at their privileged view of Korean society, which they felt strongly at their sites, faded before the urge to complain, to feel homesick, to ridicule the "Host Country Nationals." In isolation, the volunteers were generally exemplary; together, they got on Koreans' nerves.

Seoul gave the volunteers a chilly reception. The wind blew a thick blanket of clouds from the north that threatened to let loose a load of heavy snow at any moment.

"A gift from North Korea," Evan Barker remarked, shoving his hands and neck deeper into the recesses of his parka. He and Paul were walking from the bus stop near the Korean Defense Ministry building to the main gate of the US Army's South Post in the Yongsan district of Seoul. The auditorium just inside the gate was the only one in the area big enough to hold all the volunteers for the VCM's opening session.

"I hope that room is warm enough," Paul chattered. "My room at the inn was cold last night. It felt like the *ajumoni* forgot to change the *yontan*." He was referring to the cylindrical block of pressed charcoal which, when lighted, provided heat to the floor of a good-sized room for several hours. Changing the spent one with a new one, or stacking one on top of another in the *yontan* receptacle, insured that the room would be warm the night through.

"Charcoal is expensive these days," Evan said. "Besides, it's probably too early to start heating houses for winter. You know how Koreans are: winter starts on December first, even if it's colder than hell in November. Gotta stick to that schedule!"

Evan's eyes danced merrily. No one had ever seen him out of good humor. He displayed his wit constantly, though he was never smug about it; laughter was a part of him, like a mole or a cowlick that he accepted as a natural part of the face he presented to the world.

Joel, Sarah, and Theodore joined them as they walked.

"Evan, I hear you had a bit of a scrape in Pusan," Theodore said.

"Yeah. Man, you should have seen those riots. People just blew up. Both the army and the plain old folks. Koreans are so emotional, you know. You tick 'em off and they come at you like lunatics."

Paul disliked the generalization, but he did not interrupt.

"Martial law started a few days after the protests began. I don't know what all went on — there were no newspapers, the radio and TV news was censored — kind of like now, here, since President Pak was assassinated. Tanks rolled in to most of the intersections downtown. There was one outside my school, too, because a lot of high school students joined the *demo*s. Well, I was content to sit the whole thing out and just watch the *demo*s; they were fascinating. But one day, one of the kids in my class was throwing rocks right up there at the front lines. He was my best student — bright, informed, a really good kid. He threw a chunk of something at the wrong place at the wrong time. The army guys chased him inside my building. He burst into my classroom with those thugs clumping up the stairs after him. I told him to hide in the supply closet. When the goons rushed in they demanded to know where he was. I played dumb, like I couldn't speak Korean. They tore the place up and found him. They beat him up right before my eyes and led him away. Then they started on me. I got a couple of chops in the face and a groin punch."

"Holy crap," Paul said.

"Believe me — they know what they're doing when they beat the shit out of somebody! The headmaster came in just in the nick of time. He ordered the fuckers out and took me to a doctor. He was pretty upset that I hid my student like that, but he was more upset that an American got involved and saw the Koreans' dirty little secret: that the government beats the shit out of its people.

"My headmaster has been treating me strangely since then," Evan continued. "He's glad he's got me — a volunteer is a prize, you know — but now I think he kind of wishes I'd just go away."

The auditorium was a light-filled, airy place built in the American style: a quality one could not put one's finger on until one has spent many months in Korea, after which it becomes completely unmistakable.

"Hello, everybody."

John Atwood got up before the assembly and put his hands up for quiet, which was a long time coming. The two hundred faces that eventually turned toward him comprised the largest gathering of Americans he had seen in one place in months. They slouched in their seats and regarded him with markedly casual attention. "These are not your typical federal employees," his predecessor had told him. "They're a lot like cats. When you say 'jump' they'll sit there and think about it — and then decide not to. If you're a former military man, you might have trouble with that."

Atwood was, and he did, and getting over it was his first priority when he assumed his post. He soon discovered that he could get his way by suggesting rather than ordering, and by threatening an early completion of service in a roundabout way when his suggestions were not taken; for although the volunteers complained constantly about their living conditions and kept talking about how badly they wanted to go home, few cared to leave before their time. At length Atwood came to act less like a battalion commander and more like a popular college professor.

"Thanks for coming to your annual Volunteer Community Meeting. You first-timers are in for a treat; the rest of you know what kind of a great time this is. We've got a lot planned for you — some serious things like workshops and brainstorming sessions —" Good-natured boos and jeers came from the audience, "— and some fun things, like Thanksgiving dinner with all the trimmings." Wild applause. "Thanksgiving dinner will be at the Officers' Club on Yongsan South Post. That will be Wednesday night. I know, I know, it's not really Turkey Day, but it's the best we could do. For some reason, the folks in charge had plans for the place on Thursday.

"Before we go any further, lemme say something very important. I know you're all happy to be together here with your friends and away from the fishbowl environment many of you 'enjoy' at your sites. But let me remind you: You are all still volunteers this week, and all the usual standards of conduct still apply. That means no staying out past the curfew, no offensive conduct, and no welching on the commitment to show up on time at all the sessions we're holding. This is not a vacation."

A loud groan went up from the volunteers.

"I realize that it may be a terrible burden to you," Atwood grinned, "so to reward your anticipated good conduct, I've made special arrangements with the Post Commanding Officer. You'll all have unrestricted access to the movie theater, library, and restaurants on the Post all week. Just show your Peace Corps ID cards to the guard at the gate. Don't make me pull that privilege."

A whoop of approval greeted the news.

"I like Atwood," Paul said to Sarah. "I gotta get me a cheeseburger. Soon."

## Twelve

Atwood had got scarcely halfway through his opening remarks when Mrs. Kang turned around in her seat and scanned the faces in the audience. Her jaws worked as she looked around. The volunteers who let their attention stray from Atwood noticed her and knew that someone was in trouble.

"I'm happy to announce," Atwood went on, "that we've arranged to have Greg Friedman speak to us about the assassination of President Pak and the current political situation here. He's a Foreign Service officer with the Embassy ..."

Mrs. Kang got up and moved silently to the end of the row Evan Barker was sitting in. She whispered his name and motioned with her finger to get up and follow her. They went into a sparsely furnished conference room near the auditorium. She sat down at the head of the table and stared at him. As the moments wore on, a growing wave of panic rendered Evan weak in the stomach. He wanted to go to the bathroom.

"How are you, Evan?" Mrs. Kang asked, and upon receiving a lie for an answer, dispensed with pleasantries.

"Evan, I have heard that you participated in the demonstrations in Pusan last month. I want you to tell me what happened."

"Well ... I didn't really participate, Mrs. Kang," Evan stammered. Her name came out harsh and grating from his dry mouth, like the clash of a broken bell, ending in a sound of strangulation: KAAANG. "One of my students was being chased by the police." He launched into telling the story again, trying to make it sound as innocent as he could.

"When you were accepted for Peace Corps service," Mrs. Kang interrupted, "you were told that getting involved in the host country's political situation is strictly forbidden. That is the rule."

"I know. I didn't get involved. Like I said, the soldiers were chasing my student, and —"

"I have reports that you hid a demonstrator in your classroom, and then you attacked the soldiers who tried to detain him."

"What!" Evan cried. "No, no, Mrs. Kang, they came after me. I had to get stitches on my chin, see?" He started to tilt his head back, but Mrs. Kang cut him short.

"Do you understand how bad it looks for the Peace Corps when its volunteers fight with the authorities? I had to spend hours on the telephone explaining to your school's headmaster that you were not acting in the true Peace Corps way. He was very offended with what you did."

"No ... he helped me," Evan protested weakly.

"Evan, I have no choice but to terminate your duty as a Peace Corps Volunteer. We are sending you back to the United States."

"Huh ... ?"

"Our driver will take you back to your site and help you pack your things. Then he will escort you to the airport." She pointed to a lanky man who had been standing in a shadow, unnoticed by Evan until now. She uttered a quick command. The driver laid a courteous but firm hand on Evan's arm and led him away.

## Thirteen

"I'd like to thank John Atwood for inviting me to address your group."

Greg Friedman nervously shifted his weight from one foot to the other behind the podium. He had spoken to groups of Peace Corps Volunteers before. They were an insolent, skeptical audience. Since they lived among Koreans seven days a week — far more than most Embassy officers ever dreamed of doing — they thought they knew everything about Korean society and culture: they challenged every statement he made, even when he talked of political matters beyond their ken. He had to walk the thin line between concealing the information he could not trust them with and giving them enough to satisfy their need to know. When preparing his talk, he had made a list of items that he could not talk about: who conspired with Kim Jae Kyu to kill the president; which factions of the armed forces had sided with the president and which had opposed him; how close North Korea was to launching an attack on the South; who controlled the new president, Choi Kyu Ha. Looking over the list, he discovered that he had very little to say. The volunteers were not going to like that. Atwood owed him a big favor for this little speech.

"As you know, the Republic of Korea has undergone certain changes recently in the political arena. Most of these changes don't impact you directly, but as Americans, you're rightfully accustomed to having access to all the available facts. This level of access is not universal, however, and is certainly not the case in Korea. The information I give you today must not be repeated to any of your host country nationals."

A murmur of anticipation ran through the assembly. Most volunteers immediately started thinking about which of their Korean friends they would talk to first.

"Let's begin with the political situation that led to the killing of President Pak. Last month, pro-Pak legislators voted to expel Kim Yong Sam from the National Assembly. This move prompted 66 members of Kim's party, the NDP or New Democratic Party, to resign from the Assembly in protest. In response to Kim's expulsion and the mass resignation of his followers, pro-democracy demonstrators in Pusan staged violent protests against Pak's government. They burned cars and set fire to some government buildings and offices of government officials. Pak responded by declaring martial law in Pusan; he later extended it to the nearby cities of Masan and Changwon." Friedman continued dryly in this vein through the events of the days before the assassination.

Paul and Joel exchanged glances. "So far he's told us nothing we didn't already know," Paul said, disappointed. "I thought we were gonna get the real shimmy on all this."

"I never expected anything of the sort," Joel snorted. "He can't tell us anything the Koreans themselves don't already know."

"On the night of October 26, at 7:50 in the evening, President Pak was shot by Kim Jae Kyu, the Director of the Korean Central Intelligence Agency. Contrary to reports circulated at the time," Friedman continued in a voice heavy with significance, "the shooting was not accidental. It was an assassination."

"What a revelation," Joel muttered.

Sarah leaned forward from the row behind Paul and Joel. "Can you believe this guy? Is he an idiot, or what?"

"No," Paul replied. "He thinks we are. You know, I bet he's a spook, a spy. Maybe I should talk with him about joining up. I have lots of information I could sell him about my *ajumoni* and her taxicab repairman husband. Earth-shaking stuff. I could use the cash."

Sarah laughed.

"Don't laugh," Mark Follett whispered from a few seats over. "Some of my co-workers think I'm a fucking informer for the CIA and that everything I hear ends up in some file at KCIA headquarters."

Atwood shushed them and they turned their attention back to Friedman.

Paul recalled his conversation with Mi Jin about the *bangchop ham*, the counter-intelligence box, at Mokpo City Hall, suddenly aware that the suspicion of spying knew no political boundary. He endured the rest of the talk in uncomfortable silence.

## *Fourteen*

"I hope you all remembered to bring your copies of the Peace Corps Manual," Mrs. Kang said, once she had gathered her portion of volunteers, about twenty in all, in a circle of chairs around her. The Peace Corps staff had divided the volunteers amongst themselves to talk about updates to the manual. She would have preferred to have them lined up in rows, classroom-style, but a popular management book she had been reading said that openness, or the appearance of it, could be best maintained in a setting where everyone could see everyone else. Paul, Mark, and Sarah had the misfortune of being among the ones in her circle. Mrs. Kang pursed her lips into a thin white line when she saw only Paul and three others pulling manuals out of their knapsacks.

"Well, you will just have to take detailed notes and write them in your manuals later. We are under a very tight time factor."

*We are under a very tight time factor*, Mark wrote in his notebook. He planned to compile a list of such phrases — he already had a lot of them — under the title *The Collected Sayings of Mrs. Kang*, and distribute copies through an underground network of trusted volunteers.

"First we will focus on changes in Peace Corps processes and procedures. Then we will focus on relations with host country nationals through an idea-sharing session. Are there any questions?" She proceeded quickly, not waiting for an answer. "First, regarding the time demands on Dr. Paek. He is impacted by too many volunteers coming to him with unimportant personal matters. Since I am your supervisor, you should bring matters like this to me."

*Unimportant personal matters.* How neatly those words sum up her attitude toward us volunteers, Mark thought.

"... So if you have a concern of a personal matter to talk about, make an appointment to come to see me. I will make every effort to fit you into my schedule. But please do not abuse this privilege." She smiled slightly, pleased to see Mark copying everything down. She motioned to her secretary to start distributing documents.

"Here is a new form I am instituting to help me understand the problems you are having at your sites. On top, put your name, site, date, *etcetera*. In the next section, answer these questions. 'What special problems did you experience at your site this week?' 'How did you feel about your Peace Corps experience this week?' 'Name three major accomplishments.' This information will help us keep our fingers on the life pulse of the field. Please be sure to fill them out assiduously every week."

Paul greeted the form optimistically. "I can write about Kwajang-nim's English lessons and how little home-visiting I'm doing because of him," he thought. "Maybe Mrs. Kang could help change that."

"What a great way to keep track of the malcontents," Mark muttered. "She finds out who's having the most problems and makes life miserable for them. Asshole."

"Now I want to talk to you about relations with the host country nationals," Mrs. Kang said. Her voice carried an edge of exasperation, as if she were scolding a gathering of errant youths. "This is mainly directed at the men. I have received many reports in the past few months regarding much cultural insensitivity against local women. Peace Corps men have been making advances of ... ummm ... a sexual nature against women they meet.

This has got to stop. Korean women interpret American friendliness very differently from the man who gives it. It makes them scared and upset. Korean society is extremely conservative. You have to be sensitive."

"Maybe we should start treating them the way Korean men do," Mark whispered to Paul. "Use low language, tell crude jokes in front of them, haul off and hit 'em once in a while ..."

"It is imperative that you be discreet," Mrs. Kang continued. "Remember that you have come to this country to do a job, and behavior that compromises that job performance cannot be tolerated. Korea is not a playground."

"She can't stand the thought of an American *ssangnom*, a non-person, banging a Korean lady," Mark told Paul after the session. "Neither can the men we work with. She's probably getting calls from guys who are jealous that their ladies like Americans better than them."

Paul wondered if Kwajang-nim had talked to Mrs. Kang about Mi Jin.

## Fifteen

The Peace Corps Thanksgiving dinner was held not on Thanksgiving but the evening before, as the Officers Club's rightful owners had reserved it for themselves on that holiday. The volunteers did not complain: the prospect of an American feast, served up in a luxurious hall, charmed whatever complaints they had right out of them; indeed, having it a day early pleased them all the more.

The Club was located in an older, more residential area of the Post, where diplomatic employees and their families also lived. A bowling alley and movie theater were visible from the gate, which was guarded as if by Cerberus by two American MPs and one Korean KATUSA soldier. They checked each volunteer's identification carefully at first, shaking their heads in amused depreciation when giving directions to the Club. As more volunteers arrived, they grew familiar with the volunteers' ragtag, decidedly unmilitary appearance and waved them through more casually. They addressed the volunteers as "Sir" and "Ma'am" in a thin disguise for "Hey you."

Within a few yards of the entrance gate, Paul wondered whether he had been whisked away to some weirdly familiar Midwestern American town. The streets were straight and had sidewalks. The houses, all graced with front porches and painted white, had front yards of closely trimmed grass. Mature trees dotted the neighborhood. A small chapel on a nearby street corner looked like it had been shipped from New England and reassembled brick by brick here.

"What a wonderful place!" Paul sighed.

"Not bad," Joel nodded, less enthusiastically. "No smell of *kimchi* from the doorways, no packs of middle-school students roaming free and knocking you down with their book bags."

A wave of homesickness rose in the pit of Paul's stomach. "This neighborhood looks just like home."

"Yeah, right. I've never been to Lafayette, but I guarantee it never looked this clean. Remember, this is a military neighborhood. No real place looks this orderly. Don't let sentimentality cloud your judgment.

Paul bristled at the comment, but said nothing.

"You see, Paul, I'm not sentimental about shit like this," Joel went on. "When I see something, I see it for what it is. I don't compare it to some ideal, so I feel no rush of joy when I come to a place like this, and I have no regrets when I leave."

"That's too bad," Paul whispered.

The dinner was served buffet-style in the Club's large banquet room. Paul was one of the first in line. The sight of the food in gleaming stainless steel trays made him talkative, much to his fellows' surprise. He commented on the variety of dishes — four varieties of vegetables alone, not counting mashed potatoes — and their aroma and texture. Wrapped up in innocent enjoyment, he assumed everyone around him wanted to hear how Thanksgiving was celebrated in Indiana. "This is my first Thanksgiving away from home, you know."

There were even some foods that Paul had never seen in his home celebrations: meatballs in shimmering brown gravy, collard greens, marinated mushrooms and artichokes, and several varieties of California wine. "What wine are you supposed to drink with turkey?" he asked Sarah. "Red, white, or pink?"

She replied, suppressing a laugh: "Try pink."

However, dinner turned out to be a problem for the scrawnier volunteers, Paul among them: they could not eat much. Months of picking at Korean food had so shrunk their stomachs that they became stuffed halfway through their first helpings. Paul felt cheated at the sight of his half-empty plate, and he spent the rest of the evening in a dark funk.

The noise and eating lasted nearly two hours, and ended only when the large buffet pans were changed for the last time and the volunteers settled into a lethargy that made them drowsy and complacent. Several of them were quietly drunk.

Atwood rose to his feet. "Can I have your attention, please," he said, clinking his fork against a water glass. "I just want to welcome each and every one of you to our annual Thanksgiving dinner. Looking over at the buffet, which is about as clean as it can be, I gather the food went over well. Am I right?"

The volunteers burst into thunderous applause.

"We've all got a lot to be thankful for," he continued. "I'm thankful for all of you: living under difficult conditions, working hard to make a difference. Very few Americans can do what you do. You folks are unique. I'm proud of all of you.

"But thankfulness doesn't begin and end with me. You all have things to be thankful for, whether it's a warm house, a satisfying assignment, or working with good people. Let's do this: let's go around the room, and each of you stand up and pay tribute to a fellow volunteer or staff member who's had an especially positive effect on your life here, one who you're thankful for. Now, I'm not forcing you to get up and talk. But when you're grateful for someone's help, you should express it. Claire, let's start with you."

"Dear God," Joel moaned.

Claire Aguilar, assigned to a small mountain town called Yangdok, stood nervously and cleared her throat. "I'm thankful for Dr. Paek, who takes good care of us and always listens."

"Thanks, Claire. Next?"

More volunteers praised their favorites. Dr. Paek proved to be the most popular person in the room, with Atwood a distant second. Mrs. Kang was never mentioned, a fact that seemed to surprise her. Each testimonial for Dr. Paek affected her like a physical blow. Paul stood and put in a good word for the doctor and for Joel; Sarah praised her husband.

Joel stood slowly when his turn came. The room went silent. He was the one volunteer everyone expected to take a pass, sneering, with nothing to say.

"I want to raise a toast to a volunteer whom every one of us knew and liked: Evan Barker."

Mrs. Kang's face went white.

"He worked hard and did a fine job at his school. He was a credit to the Peace Corps. I am going to miss him." Then he sat down.

One or two of the more inebriated volunteers began to clap without knowing what they were clapping for. Others joined in, and soon all the volunteers were applauding madly as much for Joel as for Evan. Atwood waited a long time, gave a few perfunctory claps, and quieted the room. Mrs. Kang cast a piercing laser glance at Joel and beckoned him over with her finger in a most condescending way.

*Sixteen*

"Joel Reynoso is really something, isn't he?"

Sarah rubbed her hands together in glee, relishing the thought of what had become known as "The Toast." She was sitting in the nearly deserted Peace Corps lounge on Thanksgiving Day with Leslie. "It's gonna take Mrs.

Kang forever to get over her humiliation last night. She can't face us volunteers in the same nasty way ever again."

"What happened after The Toast?" Leslie asked.

"I saw a little of it. Mrs. Kang called him out into the hallway. She ripped into him like you wouldn't believe. Cussed him out as only a furious Korean bureaucrat could. She told him how disrespectful he was, that he wasn't being a team player, that he was the most culturally insensitive volunteer she'd ever seen, whatever that means. All delivered in a really intense, icy cold blast, like a spray of dry ice. She was kind of shouting in a whisper, because she didn't want the others to hear her. Joel was wonderful. He just stood there straight as a tree, in his cold stolid way. And you know what? I looked at his eyes as I walked past, and for the first time they looked like they were laughing. Oh, he was relishing every minute of it."

"I suppose he's in really bad trouble."

Sarah shook her head. "If it were that bad, he's be on a plane going home right now. He wouldn't have pulled something like The Toast if he didn't know he was covered."

"Covered?"

"Did you ever notice that he can stand up to Mrs. Kang without suffering any consequences? He's always dropping snide comments right in front of her, and when she's on some volunteer's back, he's usually there to smooth things over. Well, he told me once that his boss at the leprosy hospital is one of the old professors of Mrs. Kang's husband. It's one of those complicated Confucian things: the bond between student and teacher is practically sacred. Mrs. Kang's husband looks up to Joel's boss, and Joel's boss thinks Joel is the greatest volunteer who ever lived. If our Joel is unhappy, the boss is unhappy. If the boss is unhappy, the husband is unhappy. If the husband is unhappy, well .... The long and short of it is that Joel wields a hell of a lot of power."

"He certainly is something. I was worried about him. Still am."

Sarah often wondered what made Leslie behave the way she did. She was a bundle of contradictions: reclusive, but anxious for company; passive, but intent on mastering her surroundings; fearful of Korea's state of chaos, but unwilling to call it quits and go home. She reminded Sarah of Peter Pan's Lost Boys, except that Leslie was a Lost Girl: she had been separated from her family, left behind on a remote island to live a rather pointless and static life. She could not help feeling sorry for her.

They got up to leave. The *clack-clack-clack* of high heels in the hallway came toward them. Before they could duck back into the lounge, Mrs. Kang rounded the corner. She didn't greet them, nor even acknowledge their presence; she pressed the elevator button and waited, her face up close against the doors. When the elevator arrived, she went in and pushed the button without inviting Sarah and Leslie to come in. The doors slid closed.

"Goodnight, Mrs. Kang," Sarah and Leslie chirped together, and they dissolved into helpless laughter.

## Seventeen

Paul got his first taste of a full-blown demonstration shortly before he returned to Mokpo.

He had gone to a district near Ehwa University, on the west side of Seoul, to buy a gift for Mi Jin from the small shops that adjoined the campus. They sold the same kinds of trinkets he would find in similar shops near the Purdue campus: jewelry, printed T-shirts, souvenirs. He stopped, trying to remember whether Mi Jin had pierced ears, when he noticed several large hand-written posters taped to a stone wall. Students milled around them, beating their feet on the cold ground, reading and talking cautiously, their eyes darting back and forth from the posters and the faces in the crowd. Paul moved closer to have a look. He scanned the Korean text for familiar words. There were a few that Mi Jin had taught him: *sawuda*, to fight; *minju*, democracy; *daetongryong*, president. Scattered among the words of *hangul* text were a few in the English alphabet; "NAZI" and "FASCISM," for example, appeared several times. Just as Paul began to decipher the text, a hand reached out from the crowd and tore the paper from the wall. The middle-aged man bunched the paper up and crammed it inside his parka. The crowd dispersed quickly.

A few minutes later, a knot of a few dozen students, led by a stocky young man striking a small gong, marched out through the campus' main gate. A woman, shouting hoarsely into a bullhorn, led them in a chant:

"Military junta OUT! Popular elections NOW!"

They repeated the chant over and over. Most of them were women, as Ehwa was a women's university, but they had linked arms with a good number of men. Their pockets bulged with rocks. Several of the men carried thick wooden sticks. The marchers doubled, then tripled their numbers by the time they had gone the length of the block.

Paul had never seen a *demo* with his own eyes. He had heard about them, from Evan and from Mi Jin: he was tempted to follow the excitement. He fell into step with some of the marchers, taking care to stay on the edge of the crowd. They flowed down the street like a river, growing from the tributaries of students who joined them. Suddenly he stopped and remembered Evan. Evan had done more than just watch. Paul had no intention of getting involved, but one never knew what one could be accused of in the middle of the action. As much as I really want to stay and watch, he thought, I'm not ready to be kicked out of Korea yet.

He scampered away from the marchers, down the street that led toward the subway. Suddenly a pair of students sprinted around the corner and nearly knocked him down. A few more followed close behind, then still more until a torrent of them flowed down the center of the street. Unlike the marchers, they carried knapsacks and books in their arms as if they had been on their way to classes. Paul hugged the side of the building and peeked around the corner. A line of riot police, protected by body armor, helmets, and shields, marched slowly up the street towards him. They moved silently and relentlessly, like a wall of lava: no bullhorn announced their presence, nor any message they wanted the students to hear. Their presence was their message.

Paul stood rooted to the spot, caught in the crosscurrents of students fleeing the police and students armed with rocks and sticks rushing to meet them. He pressed harder against the stone wall and looked about frantically for some space through which he could escape.

The protesters harried the police in waves, running up to throwing distance and slinging a few rocks, then rushing to the rear to allow others to come up and take their place. The students with good arms drilled their projectiles hard into the policemen's shields. Those with less strength were just as effective by lobbing their rocks high and letting them fall like rain.

The scene quickly devolved into a chaos of running and shouting. The marchers scattered in an effort to draw the police out of formation, then regrouped, and then broke off again like nimble drops of mercury.

Paul could not take his eyes from the spectacle. He admired the students' tactics, the way they used their lightness and mobility to harry the police, but the violence of their emotions appalled him. Some of the students had murder in their eyes. He tried to picture Mi Jin: did she too look like this in the battles she had fought?

Paul tried desperately to work his way out of the center of the conflict, but every time he spied an escape path it quickly filled up with students or police. He became so confused that he often found himself running toward the conflict instead of away from it.

The fighting continued on this scale for nearly an hour. The students kept splashing up against the police and backing off, over and over again. The police did little but close ranks and hold firm against each new assault. Paul watched from beside the doorway of a restaurant whose shuttered door had been closed at the first sign of trouble.

Suddenly in the distance Paul heard a new, unnatural sound over the uproar, not quite mechanical but much too loud to be human. A black Army jeep sped around the corner several blocks away and stopped. Its driver and crew wore the same riot gear as the police, only without the shields: they wore gas masks instead. Instantly upon the appearance of the jeep, the police in the street beat a hasty retreat and put on gas masks themselves. Then the jeep moved slowly out of the intersection down the street where the *demo* had begun.

*Fraaaaaap fraaaaaap fraaaaaaaaaap!*

A mechanism mounted on the back of the jeep, manned by one of the masked policemen, looked to Paul like an old-fashioned Gatling gun. It belched out a shower of sparks and white smoke at a prodigious rate. The driver had maneuvered the jeep upwind of the riot; within seconds the area was bathed in a heavy cloud of tear gas.

Paul had never been gassed before. His impression from his first whiff was of some foul thing burning. An instant later, there was no smell, but only sharp, overwhelming pain. The gas burned the linings of his nose and throat and eyes and reduced him to uncontrolled coughing and weeping. He put his hand over his face while searching desperately in his knapsack for anything to put over his face. He started running toward the side streets, more desperate than ever to get away.

He stopped short when he turned a corner. In the alley sat a green police bus, its windows reinforced with wire mesh. A squad of armed and masked police was herding a dozen young men into it. The prisoners were bent over at the waist, as if they had been kicked in the stomach; their hands were tied behind them, where they could not wipe their stinging eyes, for the gas, though not visible this far from the street, was still potent. They coughed and hacked in misery, and the amused policemen kicked them from time to time when they could not move onto the bus fast enough.

Before Paul could run away from the scene, a group of about twenty students, handkerchiefs tied around their faces like train robbers from the American Old West, stormed into the alley. They waved stout truncheons over their heads. With a loud shout they fell upon the police and beat them ineffectually around the heads and faces. The police were not hurt, but they were surprised, and those whose gas masks were knocked off ran blindly away with their hands over their faces. The students pulled roughly at the prisoners to free them from the grasp of the police while others ran aboard the bus and pushed more out the front and back doors. The police, surprised and slow-moving in their ungainly body armor, tried to defend themselves and keep their prisoners, but the students did their work and departed with the speed and agility of water sprites.

Paul watched in awe. As he later recalled it, barely two dozen practically unarmed students swept down on nearly twice the number of police and freed most of the prisoners. He had never seen such daring.

So this is the kind of people Mi Jin is involved with, Paul thought. And she's fought these battles herself.

## Eighteen

"I don't feel like studying tonight."

Paul had returned to Mokpo the day before. He and Mi Jin, coming from different directions, arrived at their *tabang* at nearly the same instant.

"What would you like to do, Jong Shik*shi*?"

"It's a lovely night," Paul said. The air was crisp but not too cold. The sky was the blackest he had ever seen it, and it shimmered with stars. "Probably one of the last perfect nights before winter sets in. I want to walk."

Mi Jin nodded. She was silently, unutterably glad to see him again. She gently nudged him toward Chungang Street, the broad avenue that sliced through the center of Mokpo and, at its farthest reaches, led to the dark fields of the countryside. They would have plenty of room in which to walk as much as they pleased.

They strolled past the train station, its broad plaza lit by floodlights and the sentries at the machine guns still standing motionless in darkness. They knew the guns were still there, still waiting for trouble, but they did not give them a second thought. In a city where the signs of martial law intruded everywhere, the gunners had become routine, a fact of life, like the cold, the noise of traffic, and the smells in the fish market. There was no point paying them undue attention on a night like this.

"How was your Peace Corps meeting?"

"It was all right. Parts were good, parts were bad."

Mi Jin gave him a questioning look.

"It was great seeing my friends again. I enjoyed speaking English all day long for a change. And we got to eat all the American food we wanted at the US Army base. I think I gained a few pounds from all those cheeseburgers. Did you notice?"

Mi Jin smiled. It was a sad smile, not much brighter than the one she had left him with before he had gone up to Seoul.

"There were some bad things," Paul continued. "One of my friends, Evan, got sent home to America. One moment he was there with the rest of us. The next day he was on a flight home. He didn't even get a chance to say goodbye."

"What happened? Why did they send him home?"

Paul explained the circumstances of Evan's termination: his involvement in a demonstration and the charge — exaggerated, in his view — that Even had broken Peace Corps rules by participating in Korea's political affairs.

"And the rules are for you, too?" she asked.

"Yes. I have to follow them, too."

Mi Jin drew in a breath of cold air. She had always seen Paul as a free entity: not a member of Korean society, but rather of an American class that had recently fought the same battles she was fighting, only on different campuses and under the protection of the American Constitution. His constitution guaranteed him the right to express himself, but it could not help him here. She balked at her stupidity in thinking that just because Paul had the right to protest against his own government he had also the right to protest against hers. She shook her head.

She was in a quandary. Her political beliefs were a part of her, inseparable from her body and mind. The unstated rule in her relationship with the American had always been that he would take her as she was: a member of Korea's protesting class, latest in a line that began in the Chollado peasant rebellions two centuries ago and struggled through Japanese colonialism and the excesses of the Syngman Rhee regime. Her maternal uncle had participated in the student uprisings that led to Rhee's downfall; her grandparents, in defiance of the Japanese overlords before the Second World War, established a clandestine Korean school when the teaching of the native language and culture was punishable by prison and death. She herself had dreamed too much, marched in too many demonstrations, and got into too much trouble to relinquish her place in that proud lineage for the sake of one friendship.

Yet still she found herself drawn to this gentle man who seemed not to have a political thought in his head, whose only aim was to gather up as many sensations and experiences as he could cram into his memory. The old dream of a life of peace loomed before her when she was with him. It was a secure life filled with love and only tangentially concerned with matters of politics. She dreamed of peace, and imagined it flooding her with warmth; but immediately she forced herself to take up with reality again, and to quiet the gnawing sense of self-betrayal that inevitably followed the thought of giving up her place in the democracy movement.

"What else did you do in Seoul?"

"I got caught in a *demo*," Paul replied.

"How ... did it go?"

"It was fascinating and scary. I got tear-gassed."

She gave him a knowing smile. "Your first time? You should have put a wet cloth over your nose and mouth."

"The voice of experience, eh? I tried, but there was no water. I spent most of my time trying to get out of the way."

"Where did it happen?" Mi Jin asked.

"Near Ehwa University. I'd heard there were some nice shops there. I wanted to get you something." Mi Jin squeezed his arm, touched. "But the *demo* started before I could find you anything. I'm sorry about that."

They walked quietly past the district of the carvers of grave markers. Granite blocks in varying stages of completion dotted the yards near the sidewalk, like miniature Stonehenges that had been scattered by some overpowering natural force. Paul was trying to collect his thoughts.

He described the beginning of the march, the arrival of the riot police, and the menacing sound the tear gas generator made. Then, in a voice tinged with anger and awe, he told her about the blows the police had showered on the demonstrators they had caught, and the heroism of the students who managed to rescue them.

"I have been in *demo*s like that one," Mi Jin said. "Remember the one in Kwangju I told you about?"

"You marched and threw rocks in that one."

"Yes."

Paul nodded. "I admire you. I really do."

Before long they arrived at the Second Rotary, a round intersection where five or six smaller streets converged on Chungang Street. The area swarmed with people visiting the *tabang*s, billiard parlors, and beer halls that abounded there. Children rushed home from their tutors' classrooms, *ajumoni*s strolled to the markets to buy the provisions they needed for the next day, and the evening's first drunks staggered toward the alleyways to be sick. One place, the Chong Yol Tabang, announced its presence in bright red letters, the only neon sign in view. It was on the second floor of a nondescript building that overlooked the swirl of traffic.

"Do you need a break?" Paul asked. "Let's stop in this *tabang* for some coffee."

Mi Jin looked at the neon sign and shuddered. "Not this place. It's a bad one."

"Bad?" Paul looked again. He saw a few men laughing as they climbed the steps and went in. "What do you mean, 'bad'?"

"A nasty, dirty place," Mi Jin elaborated. "Business ladies. Most of the *tabang agashi*s on this corner are business ladies."

"You mean they own their own businesses on the side? What's wrong with that?"

"Business ladies," Mi Jin repeated, exasperated. "You know. They take men's money and ..."

"Oh. That kind of business. So it's a brothel?"

"Not really. They do serve coffee, like our *tabang*. But the *agashi*s sit with the men and let them touch them. That is how they earn big tips." Mi Jin made a face of disgust which Paul could barely see in the darkness.

"Wow."

Mi Jin punched him playfully. "I do not need to stop. Let's go more."

Eventually they reached the end of Chungang Street, out where the suburbs came to an end. The land beyond was so dark the only way to tell where the horizon lay was to see where the stars began. They stood in the shadow of a wall and gazed out over the quiet countryside.

"Mi Jin," Paul murmured. "I did a lot of thinking in Seoul. I remembered how troubled you were when I last saw you. I want to tell you again that you're the best thing that's happened to me in Korea, the best friend I have. I don't want to lose you. If I make you uncomfortable, tell me so, and

I'll stand back. If you only want me as a friend, that's fine with me. I'd rather be here, a friend, than alone as someone who lost you. God, I'm having a terrible time with this, even in English. Do you ... understand what I'm saying?"

Mi Jin stood still for a moment, then turned and silently put her arms around him. She buried her face on his shoulder. They held each other for a long time and then kissed, he with tenderness and relief, she with apprehension and joy.

"Let's go back," Paul whispered.

She put her hand through the crook of his arm and they walked back toward town. She said little. Her heart raced at his presence, but she could not shake a sense of foreboding. "Here I go," she thought; "this is the rough road to the end of it all."

## Nineteen

A frigid December wind raged through Mokpo and flowed through the health center. No amount of effort by the staff could keep it out. Closing all the doors and windows tight did not help; drafts passed easily through the multitude of tiny fissures in the walls. Kwajang-nim had to move his space heater so close to his chair that Paul felt its heat prickling against his shins; having it any further away would have rendered it useless. He begged to go off early to join the nurses huddled around the kerosene heater in the TB Control Room.

Paul passed the lab along the way. Laboratory Mr. Kim, dressed in military fatigues, was stuffing a few books into a duffel bag.

"Going somewhere?" Paul asked.

"Ah. Hello, Mr. Pak. I'm going to Reserve duty. I stopped here to pick up some first aid books. I'll be gone for a week. Dr. Kim will be in charge of the laboratory while I'm gone. If you need anything, just ask him."

"Excuse me, Mr. Kim, I'm curious — why did you join the Reserves?"

Mr. Kim laughed. "I have no choice. If you serve in the military, like all men do, you're automatically in the Reserves when you get out. This lasts until you're forty years old. Then you join the Civil Defense Corps. Even Kwajang-nim is in that one."

Paul tried to imagine the spoiled, pot-bellied Kwajang-nim as a soldier, but could not. Every image that came to mind was too comical.

"I know what you're thinking," Mr. Kim smiled. "It's hard to imagine, neh? But there are plenty of — ahem — older, more settled men in the CDC. He joined because he had to. It's obvious when we see him in fatigues on assignment that he can't wait to get back to the office. He's always very pleasant when he gets back, as if he's relieved to be home. Me — I'd join even if I didn't have to."

"Why?" Paul asked.

"Because it's necessary. We are so close to North Korea, you know. They send spies down here all the time. Yes, it's true. You know those student *demo*s in Seoul and Kwangju and Pusan?"

Paul nodded.

"The northerners are behind them."

Paul shook his head doubtfully, but Mr. Kim pressed on:

"Just look at what those *demo*s do to our society. The dictator of the north, Kim Il Song, wants all the wealth and progress in the south to fall into ruin. Then he can say that his system was the right one all along."

"Do you really believe that?"

"Sure. Don't you?"

"Aren't some of the demonstrators just people who care about society?" Paul asked cautiously.

"They have a funny way of showing it, *neh?* Oh, some of them might think they're doing the right thing and acting out of their own free will, but they're just weak; they're being fooled."

Paul disliked the tone of the conversation. He changed the subject.

"Where are you being assigned this week?"

"Oh, some Marine camp near Kwangju. It's time for their annual physicals. Reservists with lab training go and help out. We also teach basic first aid and field medicine."

Paul backed slowly toward the door and waved nonchalantly. "Well, have a good time. Take care of yourself." He joined his colleagues back at their kerosene heater and could not be drawn into their conversation.

## Twenty

Korean winters follow a unique cycle. For three days the weather seems to come from the ice-cold heart of the Devil himself as the temperature dips well below freezing and an icy wind blasts southward from Manchuria. By comparison, the next four-days are the work of angels: the sun comes out, hats come off and heavy jackets are loosened, and in the slanting rays of sunlight the winter-weary sojourner might sometimes feel the touch of an early spring. Then the devil-cold comes again with a vengeance.

The recent cold snap had driven Paul into a cocoon of clothing. In addition to his regular underwear and T-shirt, he piled on his long johns, a turtleneck shirt, a flannel shirt, a sleeveless sweater, a heavy sweater-jacket, and his down coat. His feet were buried in three pairs of thick socks and thermal socks on top. Yet he still could barely stay warm.

Then the weather changed again. Sunlight and warmth burst upon Mokpo. Paul breathed deeply and reveled in the light. "I've got to get out today," he thought on his way to work.

Within an hour, Paul and a reluctant Miss Choi were on a bus headed toward Muan Dong, a section of the city not far from the train station. Paul insisted on visiting this part of the city because it had been poorly served with home visits in the past. In truth, he wanted to see where Mi Jin lived. He did not know her address, and he had never walked her all the way home; irresistible curiosity drove him to see the surroundings in which she lived.

"Aren't you giving Kwajang-nim his English lesson today?" Miss Choi asked petulantly. The sun and fresh air had no effect on her spirits. To her, winter was winter, and no one had any business being out when one could just as well be indoors sitting next to a heater.

"He is at a conference in Kwangju. Today and tomorrow. We can go out again."

Miss Choi shivered and politely urged him to inflict tomorrow's home-visiting on someone else.

The bus took them to the heart of the district. The air turned cold in Mount Yudal's shadow. The district teemed with people who seemed to be chilled into slow, deliberate movement. The neighborhood of cheap inns and run-down businesses smelled of brackish seawater and the metal and oil of the railroad siding nearby.

This is Mi Jin's neighborhood? Paul wondered.

Miss Choi's mood continued to darken standing in the cold shade. She shuffled noisily through the deck of yellow treatment cards of active TB patients that had been selected for visits. "Let's go to this one first," she said. "Hurry! Don't lollygag!"

Paul and Miss Choi walked into a shadowed alley, whose crooked, twisting way swallowed what little sunlight filtered down from the sky and left it in perpetual twilight.

The first patient they visited was the *ajumoni* of a small inn several blocks up from the main street. A loud hacking cough alerted them to her presence at a water spigot near the front door of her two-story building. She was a heavyset woman who looked ten years older than the age stated on her card. Her gray face was flushed from carrying a load of wet laundry.

"You two want a room?" she asked casually, motioning them into the office that doubled as a living room. "Sign the register. Eight thousand won."

"Oh, no Ajumoni, we're not here to rent a room!" Miss Choi protested, her face turning crimson at the thought. A teenaged boy dressed in a dirty sweatsuit turned away from the blaring television and watched them idly, smoking a cigarette. "We are from the Mokpo City Health Center. This is an American Peace Corps worker; his name is Pak Jong Shik."

The *ajumoni* nodded suspiciously. "What do you want? I run a clean place!"

"That's not what we're here for, Ajumoni. You're a tuberculosis patient, *neh?* You haven't come to the health center to pick up your medicine for two months."

"I've been busy," she snapped, and started coughing again. "Besides, I'm feeling better."

"It's extremely important that you keep taking your medicine," Paul said in nearly perfect Korean. The *ajumoni* gaped at him. "If you do not, you'll just get sicker and sicker. That's not good."

The *ajumoni*, after the first wave of surprise, stood sullenly in the doorway and looked Paul up and down. The boy indoors went back to watching television.

"So give me the medicine. I'll take it," she said.

"We didn't bring it with us," Miss Choi replied. "It's against the rules for us to be medicine deliverers. You have to come to the health center to pick it up. It's still free."

"Free medicine," the woman sneered. "I know how good free medicine is. Why should I waste my time fetching medicine that doesn't work?"

Paul and Miss Choi left after assuring her that it did indeed work, and getting a grudging promise from her that she would come the next day. Paul shook hands with her; when she took her hand back, it held two bus fare tokens.

"I don't think she'll come," Paul remarked after they left the inn.

"But we visited her. That's all we're required to do. Where's the next one? Hurry."

The pair walked through several more alleys that morning, visiting three more patients by lunchtime.

"I'm sorry to give you such a bad impression of our country," Miss Choi said. "This is the poorest part of the city. A bad neighborhood."

"I see a lot of children running around. Why aren't they in school?"

"After primary school, education costs money," Miss Choi replied. "These people don't have any."

"What do the kids do, then?"

"Odd jobs. The boys work in restaurants or run errands for companies. The girls work in kitchens or in small factories that sew clothing. When they get older, the boys will go into the army and the girls will get married. Are you ready to go back to the health center, Mr. Pak? I'm freezing."

They emerged from the alleyway and caught a whiff of the relatively fresh air of the street. The noise of the traffic, which had been mostly muffled in the labyrinth, hit them with its full vigor. Miss Choi seemed to breathe more easily.

"What do people do here?" asked Paul. "What kinds of work do they do?"

"All these questions!" Miss Choi sighed. "Don't you have more important things to think about? Most of the men work in the harbor. They load and unload boats. They don't make much money. Some students live here, too; they spend so much money on college, they can't afford better. That forces them to live around rough and dirty people. I don't think I could ever do it."

## Twenty-one

The following day dragged on, and when the national anthem played over the loudspeakers at quitting time, and the *ajumoni* from Muan Dong had not come for her medicine, Paul went to Mrs. Mun.

"I think it's terribly important that she get her medicine right away," he explained. "She's very poor and has too much work to do. Let me take it to her on my way home tonight. If I make a special trip to give it to her, maybe she'll see how important it is."

Mrs. Mun liked his enthusiasm, and readily agreed. She packed a small paper bag with packets of INH, PAS, and Rifampin and shoved it into his coat pocket. "Be careful," she said. "Those streets get awfully dark at night."

Paul met Mi Jin for a light dinner and a language lesson and afterward told her that he had to make a delivery in her district. "Come with me. I'll walk you home afterward."

Muan Dong was indeed dark when the two set out to look for the *ajumoni*'s inn, but the alleys were not as bad as Mrs. Mun had warned: it was almost like walking down the hallway of a building, as every bar, snack shop, and inn whose doorway opened out on the narrow path was illuminated by a bright outdoor light, and the narrow walls of the alleys carried the brightness a long way. Loud music echoed out from the small bars that dotted the neighborhood, and arguments and vomiting from them as well.

"Here we are," Paul said, and he put his head in the doorway of the inn. "*Yoboseyo!*" Hello!

The *ajumoni* jumped up from the floor beside the television and prepared to welcome a new customer. Her manner changed from friendliness to mild surprise when the American from the health center moved into the light.

"Ah, hello, welcome. Come in out of the cold."

Paul and Mi Jin removed their shoes at the door and quickly stepped onto the heated floor. Paul drew the paper bag from his coat pocket while Mi Jin studied a sign posted beside the door. The sign showed two rows of the expressionless, full-face photographs of people wanted by the police. Inn proprietors, as a condition of keeping their licenses, were required to post the sign and watch for such people seeking a bed in their flight. Most of the faces on the sign were young, around college-age.

Paul introduced Mi Jin as his "associate," making it clear that her presence was entirely proper.

"May I speak with you for a few minutes?" he asked.

"Sure. It's slow now; the drunks won't start coming in until eleven, when curfew starts."

Paul handed the packet to the *ajumoni*.

"You didn't come to the health center to pick up your medicine. It's important that you eat it, so I brought it to you."

"Thank you, thank you. You are working so hard!" She heaved a troubled sigh. "I would have come myself, but I couldn't get away. I am so busy here by myself."

"You have no one to help you?" Paul asked.

"Nobody." She turned and addressed Mi Jin. "My son is a lazy piece of shit. My husband is in jail, and I can't buy a lawyer for him because we can't afford one."

"What happened, Ajumoni?" Mi Jin asked.

"My husband went out drinking with some of his friends. It was a few weeks ago. They all work at the docks, unloading the fishing boats, and they like to tip a few after work, even though we haven't got the money for it. He's always been a boozer, that damned husband of mine, and now he's ruining us. There were some rich guys at this bar, getting drunk together in their starched white shirts and fancy neckties — they work at the big bank downtown, but who knows why they came to our part of town, except maybe to pick up some whores.

"Anyway, the way my husband tells it, these rich sons of bitches were drunk, but there was some other guy at the bar who was even drunker. He couldn't see straight or walk straight, and he was saying all kinds of insulting things to the other people in the room — he didn't even know most of them, probably." She turned to Paul and added, "I'm sorry about this. It isn't a nice story."

Paul told her it was all right and prompted her to continue.

"So this drunk bastard says something that get the rich guys angry. My husband didn't hear it. But these guys start pounding their fists into this drunkard like they want to kill him.

"Now, my husband is no genius when he's sober, but when he's had too much to drink, he's about as stupid as a fucking rock. Pardon my language. He's finishing his third bottle of *soju*. He hears this fight. He joins in. Quick as can be, he's jumping on this old drunk and getting his own kicks in while the rich guys hang back and enjoy the show. When the police come, all they see is a couple of grinning rich bastards and my poor stupid drunk husband beating another drunken son of a bitch bloody. So who do the police arrest? Not the rich guys. They got out of the fight just in time and besides, they probably slipped a little cash into the policemen's hands to see to it that they get off scot-free. It's my idiot husband who goes to jail."

"That's terrible!" Mi Jin said.

"That's not the worst of it. I couldn't buy a lawyer for him without selling our inn, and if I did that, where would we be?" The *ajumoni* struck her breast with a tight fist, and the tears that had been building up over the length of the story cascaded down her chin and onto the greasy front of her sweater. "*Taptap hae! Taptap hae!*" she repeated bitterly. It's a heartache, a heartache!

Curfew was less than an hour away; men started coming in, most of them drunk, many of them escorting young women from the nearby *tabang*s and bars. The *ajumoni* quickly transformed herself from a despairing wife to a gracious if lecherous hostess. "At any rate, I have to make a living from this place," her glance implied. "You two come back anytime," she said to Paul and Mi Jin, in a tone that made the latter blush. "You can stay together here for free."

The night air outside refreshed them. They did not talk about the *ajumoni*'s story: it spoke for itself. To Mi Jin it was merely another in a long line of stories she had heard of the inequities of rich and poor; to Paul it seemed too much to digest all at once. Instead, he remarked that the clement period of weather felt like it was coming to an end, to be replaced tomorrow by another snowfall. They stopped along the main street of Muan Dong at the entrance to another winding alleyway.

"I live up here," Mi Jin said. She made no move to invite Paul any further.

"Why here? Isn't it a rough neighborhood?"

"It is not bad. Many students from Mokpo College live here. The rent is cheap, you know."

"You don't make much money as a teacher?"

"I earn enough money, but I send most of it home to my mother and father. It is my duty to help them, to try to repay them for what they have done for me all my life."

Paul was quiet for a time. "Do we have our usual lesson tomorrow?"

Mi Jin smiled and nodded.

"A *yaksok*, a date." He held his hand up, his little finger in a crook. Mi Jin laughed and linked hers in his and shook it.

"A *yaksok*."

"Goodnight," Paul said. He did not try to kiss her. Mi Jin squeezed his arm.

"Goodnight."

Her smile was all he needed.

# CHAPTER FIVE

Mark Follett lay on a small bed and watched Norina, a pretty but not young prostitute, unbutton her blouse to reveal a frayed brassiere. A baby cried in a room down the hall. He was not paying much for this all-nighter in Seoul — fourteen thousand *won*, or about thirty dollars — but he was satisfied with what he was getting. Norina possessed the twin virtues of an attractive body and a flair for showmanship that made all the difference to his increasingly jaded expectations.

Mark loved Itaewon, the gaudy, raucous district of Seoul that lay between the main gate of the Americans' main military base and the Korean Defense Ministry building. Its boundaries burst with peddlers of cheap clothing, American food, and women — a playground for the lonely GI with money in his pocket. Neon of every color blazed from the storefronts. American, European, and Japanese companies from Nike to Hitachi had their trademarks shamelessly violated from one end of the four-block district to the other. Bass-heavy music blared from discos and dance clubs, all of them well stocked with black-market American beer and attractive, exhausted prostitutes. What amused Mark most, however, were the girls' stilted come-ons: "Hey, GI, you busy? Let's party!" "Come dance with me, sexy guy!" Even the old women worked the streets, acting as rheumatic pimps for the ladies under their charge: "Hey, you looking for teenage girl?"

Norina worked hard on her striptease. The cool gray light from the window cast dark shadows beneath her breasts, making them appear larger than they were. Mark's body tensed with anticipation.

Then the shooting started.

*Pop! Popopopop! Pop!*

Mark glanced at the window.

*Popopop! BOOM! Popop!*

133

The distant report of a howitzer shell shook the room. The bottles of nail polish on the dresser jangled against each other and then fell into an eerie silence.

"What the hell ..." Mark pushed Norina aside and ran naked to the window and opened it to the sharp night air. He put his head out to listen.

"Christ, they're attacking the Post!" he muttered. More heads appeared at the windows around him, most of them American. "What's going on?" he shouted to one of them.

"How the fuck should I know?" the GI shouted back. His head disappeared as he threw on a parka. He came back and turned his head this way and that to get a bearing on the noise.

*Popop! Popopopop! BOOM!*

"Is somebody attacking the Post?" Mark called.

"Naw — South Post is over there." The soldier pointed away from the commotion. "Sounds like it's comin' from the Slopehead Defense Ministry. Hey, fuck the curfew, man. I'm going back to my unit. You?"

"I'm not Army. Peace Corps."

"Huh." The soldier gave a dismissive chuckle and disappeared. A minute later Mark saw him dashing down the alleyway below to join a few others waiting at the street corner. They ran together toward the South Post Main Gate.

Mark closed the window and pulled his trousers on. "Stay here," he told Norina, but the girl jumped up and, nearly nude, held his arm in a tight grip.

"Pay me first!" she shouted. In her anger all her former seductiveness was gone; now she sounded like a fishwife, coarse and loud. "You don't run away no paying!"

Mark wrenched his arm free. "I'll be right back. You'll get paid in a minute." He ran out the door and down a flight of stairs into the dark alleyway.

*BOOM! BOOM! Popopopop!*

The entire district had come awake. Most of the faces at the windows now were women; their customers had all got dressed and headed back to the Post. Light from their windows flooded the streets with stripes of light and shadow. He picked his way toward the main street that led downhill to the Korean Defense Ministry building. In the daytime, the building was a gray concrete edifice whose roof bristled with antennae. It was now partly visible through a stand of trees, illuminated with the greenish glow of searchlights. A number of black holes gaped in the building's facade. Korean armored personnel carriers and a couple of howitzers crowded the plaza in front.

By the time Mark reached his vantage point, most of the shooting had stopped. He heard the noise of military vehicles and voices over a loudspeaker. In harsh, almost hysterical tones, someone on the outside was demanding that someone inside surrender and come out.

Mark felt his normal self-assurance drain away: his knees went weak when he tried to analyze all he was seeing and hearing. An attack by North Koreans? he wondered. A *coup*? Factions in the military fighting amongst themselves? He cautiously discounted the first theory, as only South Korean vehicles were visible. The other two were more possible, but hardly more comforting.

"*Yah!*"

A sharp voice startled him. Near the ring of trucks that closed off the area, about two blocks from where he was standing, a pair of guards caught sight of him. They chased him down the street to one of Itaewon's alleys and then returned to their posts. He returned to the brothel.

"You got a telephone?" Mark asked. Norina had got up and dressed comfortably in jeans and a bulky sweater. She had switched on the room's overhead fluorescent light, bathing the tousled bed and peeling wallpaper in a flat un-erotic brilliance.

"Pay me," she demanded again.

"You'll get paid. Where's the phone?" He dug through his knapsack and found Joel's telephone number at the Korean Leprosy Institute. "Joel's got a shortwave radio," he said to himself. "He'll know what's going on." He checked his wristwatch. It was nearly two o'clock in the morning.

The line rang and rang until at last a woman came on the line. "*Yoboseyo?*"

"*Yoboseyo. Ku miguk pyonghwapong satanwon pakkuchuseyo.*" Please connect me with the American Peace Corps Volunteer.

"*Neh?* I am the hospital night nurse," she replied, in Korean. "He is asleep."

"Will you please wake him up?"

"*Neh?*"

Mark feared that in his excitement he was badly mispronouncing his words. He repeated his request, this time more slowly.

"No ... no, I cannot go to the dormitory to get him. Dormitory people may not receive calls at night. You will have to call back in the morning. Goodbye."

"Shit!" Mark cried. He paced about, wondering what he could do for the next four hours. Sex with Norina was out of the question; she gleefully collected her money and settled down to the rare pleasure of sleeping the rest of the night. Her last words before succumbing to sleep were a curt request to get out.

## *Two*

Joel awoke late but took his time getting dressed. His dormitory, a plain concrete structure used by bachelor researchers and visitors, was only a few steps away from his treatment room at the leprosy hospital. Waking up a half-hour before his workday started, he could dress, listen to the U.S. Armed Forces Korea Network on the radio, walk over to the cafeteria, and have a quick breakfast of rice and eggs before seeing patients.

" ... All United States government employees are ordered to stay in their homes today."

Joel stopped buttoning his shirt and turned up the volume.

"Repeating this announcement: due to a disturbance in the Itaewon and Yongsan districts of Seoul, all United States government employees are ordered to remain in their homes today. Details are sketchy at this hour, and no danger to United States personnel is expected, but the State Department and the Department of Defense are telling all American employees living off-site not to report to work today. Details on returning to work will be provided by supervisors in charge ..."

The telephone in the dormitory's common area rang. It was Mark.

"Joel? Joel! Mark. I'm in Itaewon. Damn, you're hard to get hold of. The phone bitch at your hospital wouldn't put me through till now. All hell broke out here last night. What's going on?"

"I don't know. Hold on a second." Joel brought the telephone into his room and switched the radio to its shortwave band while Mark described the scene he saw during the night. "Just a minute, Mark. I'm trying to get the BBC."

It took a few minutes for the news to cycle around to Asian affairs. Joel held the telephone receiver up to the radio speaker.

"In Seoul, South Korea, an apparent rift between two groups of generals in the Korean armed forced erupted into violence today. The rebel faction, led by Major General Chon Du Hwan, stormed the headquarters of the South Korean Ministry of Defense with arms which included tanks and other artillery. The martial law commander, General Chong Seung Hwa, was apparently placed under arrest."

"Shit," Joel murmured.

"Details as to casualties are unavailable at this time ..."

"Did you see anybody hurt?" Joel asked.

"No, but they shot the place up pretty bad. I'm sure people got killed."

"Mark, the State Department says Americans are supposed to stay off the streets. I think you'd better get your ass out of there."

## Three

Mark ventured out of the brothel after spending the rest of a sleepless night squatting inside the doorway. He had never left Itaewon this early. The place seemed deserted except for a number of Koreans who, seemingly out of dull habit, opened the steel shutters of their shops onto the quiet street. Without the happy bustle of tourists and GIs, it looked forlorn and empty, and the emptiness revealed to him for the first time how desperately dirty and run down the place was.

He cautiously drew near to the main street that passed the Defense Ministry Building, not expecting to get far. Most of the tanks and troop transport trucks he had seen several hours ago were gone, replaced by an eerie, heavily guarded silence. A pair of tanks sat on either side of the plaza, their cannon now pointing away from the building. Sentries in full combat gear stood guard at the entrance and around the tanks. They did not move, but Mark could feel their eyes on him as he passed. He slowed almost to a stop; the sentries nearby visibly tensed into a ready posture, and he picked up his pace.

He walked for more than a half-mile before coming upon street traffic that was running at a near normal level. "Take me downtown, to Kwanghwa Mun," he told a taxi driver.

The driver was a grizzled man well into middle age. He wore a smartly pressed gray uniform shirt and white gloves.

"Driver," Mark said. "Do you know what happened back there?"

"Where?"

"The Defense Building. Something big happened last night."

"Ehh," the driver scowled. "Who knows? They don't check with me when they do something. Let them work it out among themselves."

"There was shooting. Aren't people worried?"

The driver turned toward Mark and tried to address him directly without veering from the street. "Listen. I don't know about you, sir, but I have to work no matter what. One guy in charge, some other guy in charge — it doesn't matter. President Choi won't feed my family for me."

Who knows how much longer President Choi will be around? Mark wondered in a sudden flash of insight.

## Four

John Atwood ignored the urging of his government to stay home. If he knew one thing about his volunteers, it was that they would take such a warning as an invitation to go out and look around. He arrived at his office early and immediately placed a call to Greg Friedman, his friend at the embassy.

"Greg? John Atwood. What's going on? I've got two hundred volunteers who are gonna start calling me in about three minutes."

"Hi, John. Oh, you mean the Defense Ministry thing last night." He paused. "What do you know?"

"What do you mean, what do I know?"

"Have you heard anything from your volunteers?"

"One fellow just came in; he was in Itaewon last night," Atwood said. "He heard shooting and saw the ordnance. Then he high-tailed it back to his inn and hid out till morning. Why do you want to know?"

"Hell, John, we're still trying to piece it together here. The Korean government isn't talking. Neither is the military."

"C'mon, I can't believe you don't know what's going on. You're the expert, for heaven's sake."

"Well, like most *coup*s, this one was kind of a surprise. I'm trying to get as much information as I can. Can I talk with your guy?"

So it was a *coup d'etat*, Atwood thought, and Greg knows more than he's saying. "No, I'll talk with him myself and pass the information on to you. I want to insulate my people from you guys as much as possible. Nothing personal. You understand."

"Whatever. I have to run. I'll get back to you. You might want to encourage your volunteers to stay home today, like we announced on the radio."

"I'll do what I can. Thanks, Greg."

Atwood unlocked his file cabinet and once again took out the procedure book for evacuating his volunteers.

## Five

Friedman leaned back in his chair and rubbed his eyes hard. He had not slept in nearly two days. The last thing he needed now was a call from an anxious Scout leader.

He had known for several days that a *coup d'etat* was coming. Suspected, rather. Rumors had been flying that something was about to happen, that an alliance of factions within the military had had enough of General Chong Seung Hwa. He had been in the man in charge of everything when martial law had been imposed over the entire country the night President Pak was assassinated, and as martial law commander he was the most powerful man in South Korea. He certainly held more true power than the figurehead president, Choi Kyu Ha, did. General Chong was one of the old guard, but to everyone's surprise, he had lately made it his business to relax some of Pak's old repressive policies. To that end, he had started promoting his own men and pushing aside the more fervent Pak loyalists. That proved to be his undoing.

Word leaked out from several sources in the military that some of the younger generals hated Chong's new policies and, more significantly, resented the turns their careers were taking under his command. "Keep an eye on the eleventh class of the Korean Military Academy," one source had quietly told Friedman. "They're about to do something big." Cadets who graduated together shared an extraordinary bond of loyalty, and they tended to rise through the ranks together. Major General Chon Du Hwan, the man who took charge of the investigation of Pak's assassination, was a member of that class; Chong had been about to transfer him to some remote command on the east coast, to virtual banishment. Friedman had passed the information to General John Wickham, the Commander in Chief of the US-ROK Combined Forces Command and of the US Forces in Korea, who then passed it on to members of General Chong's staff, but they practically laughed in his face. "How," they asked, "can the Americans know more than we do about what's going on inside our own armed forces?"

Their complacency ended abruptly. Just after dark, a convoy of army trucks and armored personnel carriers converged on General Chong's heavily fortified official residence. The guards in the compound shut the heavy gate while Chong made an excited call to General Wickham. Wickham could do nothing but tell him that he had no authority to defend him against his own armed forces; he advised Chong to avoid an armed confrontation.

At the front gate, a colonel stepped out from the convoy's lead vehicle and called out to the guards: "I am here to see General Chong Seung Hwa. Summon him at once!"

One of Chong's aides, a Colonel Ho, came to the gate. "What do you want?" he demanded.

The leader of the convoy sneered and answered insultingly in Low Korean, a form of address better suited to children and dogs than to a fellow officer. "Get General Chong out here now. He is under arrest for complicity in the assassination of President Pak Chong Hui."

Colonel Ho stepped back in shock. "You're crazy. Under whose authority do you arrest him?"

"The Chief of Investigations for the crime. General Chon Du Hwan."

The arrest was a sham, of course. It had nothing to do with the assassination and everything to do with Chon's ambition. Colonel Ho knew that and refused to summon his commander.

The troops in the convoy opened fire on the residence. A truck fitted with a ram plowed through the front gate. Soldiers streamed into the compound. After an hour of fighting and the death of one soldier, Chong surrendered.

Friedman had got the news of Chong's arrest shortly after the fighting started. With that news came word that some troops normally deployed at the Demilitarized Zone were moving south toward Seoul. General Wickham demanded to know what was going on, but could not get an answer. Those supporting the coup denied that anything was going on; those resisting it had their hands too full to make a report. Wickham knew that chaos in the South Korean military would be an invitation to the North to attack. With this in mind, Wickham, Ambassador Glysteen, and Friedman sped through the cold night to the US command bunker at Yongsan South Post. In the cramped underground room they feverishly gathered whatever information they could find about the status of forces along the Demilitarized Zone. What they feared above all was that, if the front lines were weakened, North Korean troops would also be on the march towards Seoul. American units along the Demilitarized Zone soon quelled this fear, confirming that the North Korean forces were quiet.

Before long the senior Korean generals came to see the hopelessness of their situation and turned to the United States for help. At about 9:00 at night Lee Chong Hwan, the Minister of Defense, and Shim Che Hyon, the Chairman of the ROK Joint Chiefs of Staff, joined the Americans in the bunker. Their fingers trembled as they puffed on cigarettes, one after another. They asked Wickham and Glysteen for protection from the *coup* leaders. The Americans promised whatever help they could.

"What! Son of a bitch, I knew it!" Wickham shouted into the telephone. He told the others: "Chon's behind this."

Wickham and his staff spent the next several hours on the telephones, contacting American military units throughout the country, trying to plot the movements within the Korean military. Eventually they had a network of observers noting which Korean units were being pulled from which areas, which roads they were traveling on, and the speed and directions they were moving. It appeared that most of the Korean units were from the Special Forces and the Ninth Division, led by Major General No Tae Wu. They were headed for Seoul at speeds that would get them there within an hour or two. No forces challenged them along the way.

That news made Minister Lee and General Shim even more nervous. They conferred privately for a few minutes and then called up units in Uijongbu, just north of Seoul, and within Seoul itself, putting them on alert.

"Gentlemen, what do you intend to do?" General Wickham demanded.

General Shim replied that he was preparing troops in the area for a confrontation with the renegades. Wickham exchanged alarmed glances with Ambassador Glysteen and Friedman. If the troops on the move were not being opposed by now, hours after the arrest of General Chong, the *coup* would appear to have broad support. At any rate, since Chon was head of the Defense Security Agency, he could easily thwart General Shim's orders through the Defense Security field officers attached to each unit, all of whom were Chon's men. And word was just coming in that troops of the

Seoul Garrison who were loyal to Chon had taken up positions on the bridges across the Han River. Others were on their way downtown.

"Ahem ..." Wickham interrupted. "General Shim, any fighting in a metropolitan area such as Seoul could result in civilian losses. May I suggest that you ... em ... reconsider calling out the troops?"

"That is not acceptable!" General Shim exploded. "Chon is a renegade. He dared to arrest his superior officer, and then incited other malcontents to try to take over the government. It is not his place to oppose the legally created government of this country. It is treason. He is a treasonous dog for being disloyal to his commanders ..." He continued on for a space of time. Finally, confronted with Wickham's stolid refusal to equivocate, he heaved a bitter sigh.

"Why, General Wickham, will you not support us?"

Wickham and Glysteen looked at each other again, and the latter cleared his throat.

"Our commitment, gentlemen, is to support you in the event of an attack from North Korea. No such attack is taking place. Apart from that, we have no authority to take sides in this matter. My first concern is to prevent fighting within your armed forces if at all possible. Second, we want to prevent intervention from North Korea." He did not mention the third objective that he had discussed with Friedman many times in the past: to minimize political destruction. A *coup* was bad enough; a civil war within South Korea could only lead to disaster. Glysteen planned to reach out to the *coup* leaders once they were established and encourage them with all the leverage the United States could muster to keep to the middle path as they formed their new political order. There was really nothing more he could do.

One of the telephones rang. A leader of the *coup* demanded to speak with Minister Lee. As Lee listened, his lips turned white. When he spoke, it was in a tone of subservience tinged with outrage. He hung up, conferred briefly with General Shim, and turned to Wickham and the Ambassador.

"I have been 'requested' to report to the Ministry of Defense, to meet certain people who are on their way there. General Shim and I will leave now. We thank you for your protection."

"Minister Lee, I counsel you to stay here with us," Glysteen replied. "If you have the slightest suspicion that your life is in danger, you are welcome to take refuge here."

Lee shook his head. "The situation is not yet resolved. We must be with our men when the renegades come." With that, the two left the bunker.

"The crazy son of a bitch is gonna try something," Friedman said, and the others in silence agreed with him.

What happened after the two men left the bunker was unclear to Friedman. Minister Lee and General Shim took a staff car to the Ministry of Defense Building. The rebel troops had not arrived yet. Lee went inside the building and battened it down for a fight.

A fresh convoy of Chon's troops arrived at the Defense Ministry around midnight. They blocked off the streets and surrounded the building with tanks and armament. There were enough soldiers to fight floor to floor if necessary.

The opening move was a replay of the scene outside General Chong's compound, though on a larger stage. A general stepped forward and by telephone demanded the surrender of Minister Lee, General Shim, and whatever troops were inside. In reply, Minister Lee told them to go to hell.

Friedman could not deny a twinge of admiration for the man when he heard about that.

The stand-off lasted only a brief time. The gunners on the roof trained their anti-aircraft guns downward; the line of tanks trained their guns back at the building. Rifle fire rang out and, after several quick bursts from a howitzer on the plaza, the stand-off ended. General Chon's troops entered the building and went floor to floor, disarming soldiers and herding them into trucks. Friedman was not sure where they were taken. He did know that Minister Lee and General Shim were in prison with General Chong. The *coup* was over. General Chon had won.

Six hours later, in his office on the fifth floor of the United States Embassy, Friedman waited for Ambassador Glysteen to hear officially from the new man in control of the country. He hoped for enough time to take a nap.

## *Six*

The weather had taken a turn for the worse on Friday night when Paul and Ajumoni rode a taxi to Mokpo Station to meet her son, who was returning home from school for winter vacation. A raw wind swirled in from the south, flinging wet globules of snow into their faces as they crossed the broad plaza. Paul could not see the roiling sea in the distance, but he could smell its agitated life and picture its angry black surface. He pitied the sailors who had the misfortune to be out on such a night.

"Hurry, Mr. Pak!" Ajumoni called from behind the scarf that covered her mouth and nose. "The train is almost here!"

Paul carried a vacuum bottle of hot barley tea. Ajumoni took it from him and offered him some. "No thank you, Ajumoni," he said. "I'll wait until Song Min gets here." Ajumoni nodded approvingly, reconsidering for the moment her conviction that all Americans, and this one in particular, were no match for Korean winters.

"You didn't have to come with me, Mr. Pak," she said as they passed through the train station's waiting room and walked out onto the platform.

She strained to see the train coming around the curve a mile away. "You know, I would have been just fine coming here myself."

"That's all right, Ajumoni. Ajoshi was busy. You could not come out into this bad weather by yourself. Besides, it will be good to see Song Min."

Ajumoni nodded and gritted her teeth against the cold.

"Ajumoni, how do you think about the incident last Wednesday night?"

"Mmph? What incident? Oh ... that thing with the soldiers in Seoul." She took a gloved hand out from her armpit and waved it dismissively as if she were batting away a fly. "*Pah*. Doesn't concern me. Good heavens, you are worried about such stupid things! Must be that lady friend of yours, teaching you to stick your nose where it doesn't belong. Don't worry," she said emphatically. "That's a thing only Koreans should worry about."

"Does Ajumoni worry about it?"

She shot him a stern look for his impertinence, then strained again to see the train, praying for it to come quickly to put an end to the questions. "No!" Then she contradicted herself in a low mumble: "I'm a Chollado lady, aren't I? General Chon and his friends are from Kyongsangdo. There'll be no good thing for us ... here he comes!"

The train soon rumbled to a halt. Song Min stepped lightly out, carrying a small suitcase. He wore no coat, only the black Japanese-style school uniform that he had worn since the warmer days of autumn.

Ajumoni did not hug her son, nor cover him with kisses. Following decorum, she scolded him for having left his collar button undone, thanked heaven that at least he had worn a sweater under his uniform, and shoved a cup of hot barley tea into his hand. His red cheeks glowed under his mother's love.

Song Min was a large-boned youth, and tall for his age, reaching well past Paul's chin in height. His quick smile carried with it a hint of mischief, even when he bowed politely to Paul, and Paul — forgetting his station above the boy in the order of things — bowed back.

"Welcome home, Song Min," Paul said slowly, in English. "How was your school term? Did you study hard?"

"Thank you, Mr. Pak," the boy replied meekly, also in English. "Yes! I hardly studied."

"Excellent!"

Laughing, and paying no mind to the worsening storm, they returned to their warm home.

*Seven*

Mi Jin joined Paul for Christmas dinner a week before Christmas Day. They met outside the Hamhung Restaurant, whose windows, covered with a tight wooden latticework and pasted over with paper in the traditional style, glowed invitingly.

"Welcome! Welcome! Come in!" called a gap-toothed *ajumoni* from the midst of the tables.

Mi Jin had dressed up in a fine silken dress of deep blue color. Paul gaped at her as she shed her overcoat. For his part, he had bathed and shaved immediately after work and put on a necktie. She praised him extravagantly for his sense of style. Still, despite their joy in meeting and the restaurant's convivial warmth, she appeared out of sorts.

"What's wrong?"

She shook her head. Several things were wrong. She dreaded going home to Chindo, especially now. Nearly a week had passed since Chon Du Hwan had taken power in Seoul. She waited eagerly for news. In Mokpo she was not far from the network of information, half-truths, lies, and rumors gathered continually by members of the democracy movement. At such a crucial time, remote Chindo was where she least wanted to be. If that were not enough, she suspected that her parents had a surprise waiting for her — good news for them, but bad for her. They had introduced her to Kim Hyong Chol and wanted her to pursue the relationship. No doubt they were preparing to take some further action. She could not bear to think what it might be. She longed to take Paul's hand, but she dared not in the crowded restaurant.

"I know it's a shame we can't see each other on Christmas," Paul was saying. "But we each have to go our own ways this time. Next year will be better. I'm staying with my friend Joel at St. Lazarus Village. I'll be close to Seoul all next week, so I can run some errands for you, if you like. We have uncensored magazines at the Peace Corps office. I'll photocopy the articles about Korea and bring them back for you."

"Thank you," Mi Jin said.

"Have you heard any news from your friends?"

Mi Jin shook her head. "Nobody knows what to make of the *coup*. All they know is that it's bad, and that we should demonstrate. But people are nervous about doing anything yet. General Chon and the new leaders look like harsh men. We have to be careful for now."

She was picking at her food and listening listlessly to the conversations going on around her. A pair of businessmen at the next table were arguing over the cost at which one was to supply rice to the other's hospital. A group of three men at another table joked about some administrative gaff at City Hall. Life continued to move in its old, familiar cycles, despite the *coup* and her own troubles, and nobody but Paul seemed very concerned about it.

"I have something for you," Paul said. He took a small package from his pocket. It was wrapped in crinkled gold foil and tied with a bright red ribbon. "Sorry about the wrapping. I couldn't find any good gift wrap, so I re-used the paper my mother and father used on my present. I hope you don't mind. Merry Christmas."

Mi Jin did not mind at all; she was touched.

In the box lay a gleaming gold necklace on a bed of white satin. A pendant was affixed to it, a delicately-wrought Chinese character that looked like a ballet of brush strokes frozen in gold. It was a rare find.

"Jong Shik. I am ... it is beautiful. Thank you. Thank you so much." She fumbled with the clasp and eagerly fastened it around her neck.

"Do you know what that character is?" Paul asked.

"Of course I do. 'Double happiness.'"

"I wish it for you."

She favored him with one of her rare smiles and reached into her purse. "I have something for you. I wish it were as beautiful as your gift to me. Merry Christmas."

The silk necktie was a brilliant red, shot through with filaments of gold and silver. He took off the one he had been wearing and put the new one on.

"How does it look? Simple, classic, elegant. I like it."

Mi Jin took comfort in Paul's *nunchi*. "He likes my gift," she thought, "but he cares more that I adore the gift he gave me. I must never let him go."

## Eight

Mi Jin arrived at her parents' home late on a gray, blustery afternoon. She had gone the long way, mostly over land, because the sea was too rough. Her bus traveled up Mokpo's small peninsula and then east about twenty miles to the inland city of Yongam. In Yongam she caught a local bus that traveled south past the distant cone of Wolchul Mountain that loomed darkly against an approaching blizzard. The trip was thirty miles in a straight line, but the winding road nearly doubled the distance. A ferry took Mi Jin across the narrow, choppy strait to the island of Chindo; another bus brought her to the town of Chindo, at the island's center, where she caught a taxi to her parents' home within sight of the sea at the north-west corner of the island. She had started her trip from Mokpo early in the morning; it was well nigh twilight by the time she walked through her parents' front gate.

The wind around the house penetrated her overcoat and bit her skin under several layers of clothing. She fared better indoors, but not by much; the old thatch-roofed house was a sieve that let the draft blow in. She disliked the discomforts of winter, but she despised even more the fickle warmth of that old house.

"Good. You're here," her father said when she stepped through the gate. He was sitting on the narrow porch in the crook of his L-shaped house, out of the wind, smoking a cigarette and repairing a scoop that he used for dredging shellfish from the shallows nearby. He looked at his wristwatch and noted the lateness of the hour, annoyed. "Well, we'll put you to work at the dock tomorrow. Your mother's waiting for you inside."

The clinking of utensils in the dark kitchen told Mi Jin where her mother was.

"Hello, Omma," she whispered meekly at the door.

Her mother looked up from the pot of mung bean sprouts that she was turning to encourage growth uniformly throughout the batch. "Ah. You came. Put your bag away and help me with this." Her lined face broke into a smile, an almost undetectable raising of the corners of her mouth, as her eyes followed Mi Jin out of the kitchen. She had news for her, but she wanted to wait for the right moment to tell her.

"So. How was the semester?" she asked.

"Very good, Omma."

"You know, I hear there's going to be an opening for a first-grade teacher at Chindo Primary School in the spring. Mrs. Nam is having a baby, and she's beginning to show."

Mi Jin glanced at her mother's face, then looked down again.

"I think you should apply for it," her mother continued. "You could live at home and save some money. And you'd be closer to Hyong Chol."

Mi Jin's eyes widened and her heart began to beat shakily in her chest. I was right: she means to marry me off, she thought.

"I am not a first-grade teacher," she said lowly. "I am an English teacher."

"Middle school, primary school, what's the difference?" said her mother, who had herself got only as far as the fourth grade. "You're a teacher. Teach."

Mr. Han thumped into the house just then and, grunting loudly, stooped to take his shoes off. He saw with approval that the women had been talking together in near darkness, in the failing light, saving electricity. He reached up to a circuit breaker mounted by the door and threw the master switch. The fluorescent light in the middle of the ceiling flickered to harsh, gray-green life.

"I told her about the opening in the school."

"Good. You are going to apply for it, aren't you?" It was not a question.

"I — I don't know. I need to think about it."

"What is there to think about?" Mr. Han said. "It's something we want you to do."

"Still, I would like to think about it."

"Good heavens, is this going to turn into another foolish argument?" Mr. Han trudged wearily into the main room of the house and turned on the television.

"Just you reconsider, Daughter," her mother hissed. "Get ready for dinner."

No one talked much during the meal. Mi Jin was glad that her parents kept most of their attention centered on a musical variety program on television. The meal was a spicy fish stew and a bowl of rice, with mung bean sprouts and two kinds of *kimchi* on the side. The long trip had made Mi Jin ravenous. She took an extra bowl of rice. She expected her mother to glance at her as if to say, "You'll get fat," or more precisely, "You'll be less attractive to a suitor," as she commonly did. That look was suspiciously absent this time.

"Daughter, we have some good news to tell you," Mr. Han said after the dishes were cleared and the small eating tables put away and the television turned off. He leaned back and let his wife continue.

"It's time you got married. We have made all the arrangements with the matchmaker. It's all confirmed. Kim Hyong Chol is our choice for your husband."

The pronouncement was not unexpected, but its finality struck Mi Jin like a physical blow. She sat silently for a long minute.

"What?" Mr. Han demanded. "What's wrong?"

"Nothing, Appa."

"You don't look happy." He glanced at his wife, prompting her to finish the interrogation.

"Kim Hyong Chol is a good man," she told Mi Jin. "A very good man. He has a business of his own, and it's doing very well. You'll never lack anything with him. He'll take good care of us — you. I can't understand why you're not happy about what we've done for you."

"But Omma, what if I want to choose someone myself?"

"Did you find someone else in Chindo? Who?"

Mr. Han hushed his wife. "Did you find someone in Mokpo? Is that it? No. You will not marry anyone from Mokpo. You must marry a local boy. We can't have you moving away and never coming back. No."

"There is no one else, Appa," Mi Jin whispered. "No one from Mokpo." She hated the half lie she told.

"Then what's the problem?"

Mi Jin shook her head. "No problem, Appa. I just need time to get used to the idea of getting married. I'm very, very tired. Do you mind if I go to bed now?"

She eased shut the door to her cold bedroom and immediately turned out the light. She gathered her rice-husk pillow in her arms and pressed it tightly against her face. Sobs came easily, for they had arisen deep in her stomach when her mother first started talking of Kim Hyong Chol. They surfaced now, and she tried desperately to stifle them. She kept her face buried in her pillow for a long time, raising it only when she had to snatch a gasp of air.

She loved Paul. She had not yet admitted that fact so plainly to herself because she had hoped to test her growing fondness for him over time. Circumstances had sabotaged her cautious plan. Paul's face appeared in the darkness before her, and the fear of loss, that dark underside of love, tore at her. She caressed the necklace he had given her for Christmas as a sort of totem. Sleep came slowly in creeping increments of insensibility, illuminated only by desperate thoughts of Paul.

She woke before dawn after a night visited by bizarre, troubling dreams. Her father, Hyong Chol, and, horrifyingly, her dead brother, rotten from the grave, appeared one by one and lectured her in words she could not understand. Riots broke out in an undefined city. A painful weight pressed down on her chest and another sharp pain came inexplicably to her right leg. She found Paul's necklace in her hand and clutched it. Over her shoulder a small white butterfly flitted by; she knew it was her beloved grandmother, come to comfort her.

She got up at dawn slowly, unsure at first whether she was still dreaming. The palm of her hand bore a backward indentation shaped like the 'double happiness' of the pendant, and it hurt. She dressed quietly and went outside just as the first light of day brushed the hills in a pink glow. On one such hill, overlooking the sea from a high spot, was her grandmother's grave.

The grave of her mother's mother was built in the traditional manner. A mound of grass-covered earth about four feet high and eight feet across covered the woman's remains. A low embankment encircled it, and at the front, facing the sea, a modest stone tablet stood upright bearing her name and the date of her death. The stone was capped this morning with a layer of wet snow.

Mi Jin stood before the stone and tenderly brushed the snow away. Though she practiced Catholicism, she had been raised in the traditional Confucian way, in which ancestors are honored and whose presence is sought during times of trouble. Sinking to her knees in the snow, she threw her arms around the stone and wept softly. Her tears turned to frost on the tablet's cold surface.

"Grandmama, Grandmama," she whispered. "What can I do? Take me with you."

She stayed there until the rising sun bathed the hill behind her in light. Eventually, after her mind had finally settled, a wordless command imprinted itself on her heart:

"Get away. Go back."

It was a call to leave her parents' house and return to Mokpo. She was certain of it. In her own surroundings she could clear her mind and think about a course of action. For now, she would have to let the future take care of itself.

When she joined her parents for breakfast, she was calm. She told them that she had thought of a plan: she would return to Mokpo and spend the rest of her vacation there, earning extra money by tutoring wealthy school-children in English. She would also finish out the school year at Chung Ang Girls' Middle School to take the higher salary there, as compared to what she would make in Chindo. Every extra *won* would go toward her engagement party and the wedding; she wished to postpone the latter until summer. Her parents could not argue with her logic, nor turn their backs on the money. They agreed.

She returned to Mokpo the day after Christmas.

## Nine

Snowflakes started to fall on St. Lazarus Village, just outside the city of Suwon, early on the morning of Christmas Eve. They fell like swirling benedictions that circled in the air at the whim of every breeze that blew in from the head of the valley, dusting the shoulders of the residents of the village who hobbled home after morning Mass. The unfortunate souls, all afflicted to some degree with leprosy, knelt at the manger scene outside the chapel on their way down the mountain. They were happy, for the season had given them the gift of a rural Korean winter's day: a day of snow, peace, and simplicity.

When Sister Miriam invited Paul to help the sisters chop wood, he accepted gladly, happy to be outdoors on such a day.

A number of large logs had been donated to the village by a parish in the nearby city of Anyang. Three men drove a pickup truck up the steep road to the nuns' quarters, unloaded the logs, and departed quickly. The logs lay strewn where they chanced to land, too far from the chopping block and woodpile to finish the task easily; there they had stayed for two weeks until the sisters could find someone to help them. Paul loaded the logs into an old pull-cart and dragged them to the chopping block.

The pull-cart was of the type found on every road in Korea, even in downtown Seoul, sometimes pulled by a pony but more often by a man pushing against a handle drawn out from the front like a tubular metal yoke. It had one axle, large spoked wheels, and a flat bed enclosed in walls of withered old planks. It could carry nearly any sized load, including, as a volunteer with a macabre sense of humor had once pointed out, three layers of three corpses.

Paul made quick work of splitting the logs. After stacking and covering the firewood, he clowned with the younger, more playful nuns, who insisted on pulling him around in the cart. They came dangerously close several times to sending Paul careening down the snowy hill to the valley's floor, until Sister Miriam appeared and put an end to the foolishness.

"This cart is not for people!" she said sharply to the nuns, in Korean. To Paul, she said, "You must be frozen. Come in for some coffee and a chat."

They sat in the parlor of the nuns' quarters. The building was a long gray two-story structure that harmonized with the rock and gray-green foliage of the mountainside; it had been donated to the village by a Japanese charity. The parlor, furnished in Western style with beige wing-backed chairs and a coffee table, was warmed by a wood-burning stove.

"I sure do miss dark, brewed coffee," she said, as she poured hot water from a large kettle on the wood stove and mixed two cups of coffee. "This instant stuff just doesn't cut it." She stirred a bit of cream into Paul's cup and handed it to him apologetically.

"Instant coffee is fine for me. Anything beats barley tea."

"Isn't that stuff foul? But you grow to like it over time, like most things. Now, will you be going to Midnight Mass tonight? It being Christmas Eve and all."

"I wouldn't miss it."

"Wonderful. Will Joel come, too?"

"I'll ask him, but I doubt it. He's not a religious man."

"I didn't ask if he's religious," Sister Miriam said. "Being too religious can work against you. The door is open to him. He's such a fine fellow, very smart, and with a good heart. It'd be a shame not to have him there. Don't forget to ask him?"

## Ten

Joel declined the invitation, as expected, so as midnight approached, Paul trudged alone up the frozen road to the village chapel.

Paul had felt a growing burden of loneliness all day long. He refused to call it homesickness, but Joel saw that it was exactly that, for Paul had prattled on at every hour of the day about the stages of the traditional Harkin Christmas: "By now my Mom should be putting the turkey in the oven," and "The candlelight service at the church would be ending right about now." Paul made those statements with full knowledge that, owing to the difference in time zones between Korea and Indiana, his family was now asleep or just starting the day. Paul was, Joel sensed, seeking immediacy more than exactitude. Even now, alone in the cold, Paul sang Christmas carols softly to himself, in English, fearing he would otherwise not hear them at all this year.

The double row of large globe lights that lined the road — normally unlit to conserve electricity — bathed the snow in warm, joyous light. Paul stepped out of the glare of the lamps and gazed at the mountain at the head of the valley, small but majestic in its way, dusted with snow, looking like it had been draped in lace. In the chill silence he heard the crunching footsteps of villagers from both ends of the valley coming to Mass. It was the only sign of movement in this starry, frozen night.

The chapel filled slowly to capacity. It took a long time for everyone to come in and find seats, for the older, more debilitated villagers were mostly blind and could barely walk. Despite the chapel's absence of steps — only ramps led into the building — their movements were slow and deliberate and were punctuated at intervals by obeisances at the manger scene near the altar.

"In the name of the Father, and of the Son, and of the Holy Spirit, Amen."

Father Kim, a vigorous man in his fifties who reminded Paul of Mr. Atwood, began the celebration of the Mass in a loud, clear voice. Paul had a hard time following it, being unschooled in "church Korean" and in the Mass itself. He kept up as best he could, but his attention soon lapsed. During the sermon, his mind wandered and he began to look at the people around him. On one side sat a nurse from the Institute. On the other, an elderly woman whose body had been ravaged by leprosy sat hunched over, supporting her weight with a fingerless hand balanced on a cane. The bridge of her nose had collapsed long ago; her nostrils were a pair of orifices in the flat expanse of her face. Her eyes were rimmed in deep red from chronic and advanced conjunctivitis, and Paul had no doubt that she could barely see. She listened intently, nodding in agreement with the priest, occasionally whispering "Amen."

Paul's restless eyes swept the sanctuary, but he was drawn back to the old woman at his side. He studied her face in the candles' yellow light. Her expression, what was visible of it through the depredations of her disease, bespoke a depth of acceptance and happiness that shook him to his core. She had every reason, Paul thought, to feel herself cheated by life, for having a disease that had robbed her of her extremities, of her face and most of her eyesight, and had left her bereft of family. Yet her face glowed. She gazed at the manger and the statue of the infant Jesus with the love and expectation of a child. Jesus had healed lepers, and the woman had no doubt wished that he had just one more miracle for her; yet tonight, in church, she seemed the most contented woman Paul had ever seen. At the end of the Mass, when the congregation sang *Silent Night* in Korean, he followed along in English. His eyes were wet.

## *Eleven*

Paul returned to Mokpo early on the day of New Year's Eve. Mi Jin met him at the train station, wearing her new necklace outside her overcoat.

"Welcome home, Jong Shik," she said. They did not embrace, or even touch; an outward display of affection would have been vulgar in that place and time. Instead, she blessed him with one of her radiant, hard-won smiles.

"Did you miss me?" Paul asked merrily.

"Oh, yes."

"Surely your parents kept you busy."

"I will tell you about that another time."

"It's past two o'clock," Paul said. "I don't have work today. Neither do you. Curfew is lifted tonight in honor of the holiday. What do you say we stay out late?"

"I would like that very much. We could go ... how would you say it in English? ... going from one *tabang* to another many times?"

"'*Tabang*-hopping.' How does that sound?"

"College students make a sport of it. You go from one *tabang* to another and have a cup of coffee at each one. It's most fun when you see a variety of them: music *tabang*s, quiet ones, young ones, old ones ..."

"Sexy ones?"

"Not those! New Year's Eve was made for this game. We'll have such adventures tonight!"

Paul soon lost count of the *tabang*s they visited. Some were new and polished, equipped with disk jockeys in glassed-in booths playing American pop songs. Some were tawdry and run down, as if they were kept in business by a dedicated coterie of older businessmen who could not bring themselves to find another place. Still others featured *agashi*s in tight dresses and low-slung blouses, and Mi Jin insisted on leaving those places without even sampling their coffee. After his third cup, Paul started asking for coffee with no sugar, and then taking no more than a sip from each cup, as the coffee was beginning to affect him: he could not stop tapping his foot with nervous energy.

The topic of conversation changed at each *tabang*. Paul wondered if that were one of the rules of the game, and Mi Jin did not say, but he was glad for the variety. At one place, she held forth on the prospects of democratic government under Chon Du Hwan, which she considered dismal; at another, she grilled him on the subject of his relationship with his father and mother. When Paul asked the same questions of her, she suddenly became less talkative, and seemed to regret that she had brought the subject up.

"Tell me what you did for Christmas," she said. They were at their fifth *tabang* of the evening.

"I stayed with my friend, Joel Reynoso at the leprosy village." He described the beauty he found in the quiet valley, and the contentment of the villagers, which had surprised and pleased him.

"Wouldn't it be wonderful to be so content for all of your life?" Mi Jin asked wistfully.

Paul agreed that it would, but he pointed out that the people of the village were stricken with a horrible disease. They had earned their contentment at a price he was not willing to pay.

"I think you have it backward, Jong Shik. They are happy in spite of their disease."

A distant clock chimed eleven times.

"Hey, listen. I just noticed something," Paul said, brightening. "We've been together since mid-afternoon. Now it's eleven o'clock. I've spoken hardly any English in all that time."

"Wonderful! Does that mean you don't need me anymore?" Mi Jin asked.

"No, no," Paul laughed. "I may be getting better at it, but my language is not perfect. I'll always need you."

Mi Jin let his last statement hang on the air for a moment and smiled gently.

"Let's find another *tabang*," she said.

Paul and Mi Jin walked briskly through the streets that were finally starting to empty of traffic as partygoers reached their limits and went home. Their senses were heightened by the infusion of caffeine and sugar. Raucous singing and laughing from a curbside *makkoli* tent sounded tinny and acute to them; the glow of the city reflected in the low clouds seemed to take on a myriad of subtle colors, like the Northern Lights. Paul looked at his watch. It was 12:15 in the first morning of 1980.

"You know, in my country we have a custom," Paul said as they passed a dark alley. "The first person you kiss on New Year's Day will be the most important person in your life the whole year through."

"Is that true?"

"Umm ... I don't know. I made it up." He stopped, gathered her in his arms, and kissed her. It was a long, slow kiss that quivered with nervous energy. Mi Jin kissed back with the same ardor. They held each other for a long time.

"Jong Shik," Mi Jin whispered. "I love thee."

## Twelve

Paul walked about in a fog of joy for the rest of that week. It was only after several days that Mrs. Mun, his coworker at the health center, shook him out of it.

"We have to go to Kwangju tomorrow. Have you forgotten? It's that regional Peace Corps meeting that you've been talking about for the longest time. Where has your mind been this week?"

Paul had been looking forward to going to Kwangju. Mi Jin had told him so much about it that he wanted to see it for himself. He wanted to see her university, the place where her riot had broken out.

"Are you sure you want to stay the whole weekend there?" Mrs. Mun asked. "I don't like Kwangju that much. As soon as your Peace Corps finish the meeting Friday afternoon, I'm going home. You'll be on your own."

He smiled and told her that he had plans.

## Thirteen

"I want to thank you all for coming to this Peace Corps Regional Meeting. I am so very happy to be here with you." Mrs. Kang's voice was flat and abrupt. She stood at the head of a long table addressing the half-dozen volunteers and their co-workers. To avoid spending a night in Kwangju, she had ordered the Peace Corps driver to bring her down from Seoul on a three-hour journey that had begun well before dawn. The driver snored in the corner of the conference room.

The United States Cultural Center, where the meeting was being held, was located in Kwangju a few blocks from the Provincial Office. High walls surrounded it; a small guardhouse stood by the heavy wrought-iron front gate. An elderly gentleman dressed in a wrinkled uniform lolled in the guardhouse and checked identification cards as visitors went in.

"The purpose of this meeting," Mrs. Kang continued, "is to discuss issues that arise from time to time in the relations between volunteers and their sites so as to optimize the usefulness of the Peace Corps programs." She translated the speech into Korean. Mrs. Mun suppressed a yawn.

"What issues?" she whispered to Paul. "We get along just fine."

Paul shrugged.

"Let's go around the room and introduce ourselves," Mrs. Kang said.

"Kevin Palmer, from Kimhae. This is my co-worker, Mr. Pyo."

One by one the others called out their names and the names of their co-workers. No one cared much about who was who; the volunteers already knew each other well, and did not care about each other's co-workers. The pleasantries ended, Mrs. Kang dominated the session for the rest of the morning and appeared to be the only one paying attention during all that time: the volunteers wanted to see the library and their co-workers wanted their free lunch.

While technically the US Cultural Center was open to anyone who wanted to use it, its library and collection of newspapers and magazines were accessible only to Americans and those Koreans who had somehow got clearance to enter the compound. The reason became clear to Paul during a break when he opened the most recent issue of Time magazine: it was uncensored. Older issues told the stories of President Pak's assassination and the military *coup* with all their unsavory details intact.

"You can read those anytime you like," said the librarian, a pleasant, balding man in his forties. "But I have to ask you not to copy them. The Korean government doesn't like that information being passed around."

"Then why have them here at all?" asked Kevin.

"To provide information about the American point of view to the Korean nationals," the librarian replied blandly.

The afternoon session lasted until three o'clock, when Kevin and his coworker had to leave to catch a bus home. Everyone walked out to the gate together. Just outside the gate stood Mi Jin, hugging herself to stay warm. She waved.

"A friend of yours?" Kevin asked.

"My teacher."

"Ah. Have fun, man."

Mrs. Kang laid a hand on his arm to stop him before he left the compound.

"I have heard about your teacher. I thought your *kwajang* was supposed to be giving you lessons."

"Well, he ... umm—"

"Paul, I know what is going on. Do not let your relationship with this girl blind you to your responsibilities at the health center. You were very culturally insensitive when you took lessons from her when you were already learning from your *kwajang*. He was very upset."

"He wasn't teaching me anything," Paul sputtered. "I was teaching him English, not the other way around. She's the reason I can speak Korean so well now, and that's the whole point, isn't it?"

"You cannot let your personal desires upset the balance in your health center," she said sharply. "You must not offend the people you work with. That is most important. You had better be careful." This last sentence was not advice, but a warning.

*Fourteen*

"What's wrong?" Mi Jin asked, once they were out of sight of the Cultural Center and the other volunteers.

"That was Mrs. Kang, the woman I've told you about — my Peace Corps boss."

"What did she say to upset you so?"

"It's nothing. I just hate her, that's all."

Paul's harshness surprised her, but she left that matter for another time. "Jong Shik. I'd like you to meet some of my friends."

They plunged into the stream of humanity that flowed past the center of the city to the vicinity of Chonnam University, where they casually ducked into an alleyway, one of the hundreds that honeycombed the neighborhoods of Kwangju.

"I don't see how you navigate in this city," Paul said. "Which way are we pointed now?" His voice echoed eerily in the high brick and concrete walls on either side. He could have held his arms out straight from his sides and almost touched them. The alley twisted up from the street for nearly a quarter mile. They emerged onto another street, smaller than the first, and again turned into an alleyway. After uncounted turns they emerged into another narrow street. A few doors down was the entrance to Trouble House.

"This is ... what do you call it in English? My 'home away from home,'" Mi Jin said. "Whenever I come to Kwangju, I come here. Let's go in."

The room quieted noticeably when one person, then another, noticed Mi Jin and her American guest. Elbows jabbed ribs and a few *shush*ings ushered in a state of cautious inactivity. Mi Jin put her arm through Paul's and held it tightly, smiling, as if to say, "He's with me, and if I can trust him, so can you." After a minute, the room relaxed and started to buzz again, as much with speculation on Mi Jin's new friend as with the matters they had been discussing before.

They joined Chong Il Man at a table. "Il Man, I'd like you to meet a friend of mine," Mi Jin said. "Paul Harkin. His Korean name is Pak Jong Shik. He is the American I've been telling you about."

Il Man shook Paul's hand with a crushing grip, which Paul returned in kind. He looked at Paul closely from under a mop of hair that fell across his eyes. They exchanged pleasantries in Korean, but the air was charged with tension. Paul sensed himself not trusted.

"So you are in the American Peace Corps. I have heard that the Peace Corps is a front for the CIA," Il Man said smoothly. "Is that so?"

Paul responded in low, guttural Korean that the very idea was the most absurd he had ever heard. Even Mi Jin blushed. "What are you doing?" she whispered.

"The CIA has an excellent foreign language school," Il Man parried, hard pressed to hide his amusement.

"*Shi pal*," Paul said. Shit. "If I were in the fucking CIA, I'd be *listening* to the Korean language, not *speaking* it."

Everyone in earshot held his breath. Il Man at last let out a loud laugh and squeezed Paul's arm. The sound of his laughter put the rest of the *tabang* at ease. "Well said, well said! A friend of Elder Sister's is a friend of mine, especially one who can curse so eloquently in Korean. Let me buy you both some coffee."

They exchanged pleasantness for a while. Paul answered the expected questions from new acquaintances: "Where is your home?" "What college did you attend?" "Do you have brothers and sisters?" He in turn asked his own questions: "What does the democracy movement hope to accomplish?" "How was General Chon able to build up so much power?" In time they were joined by others in Mi Jin's circle: Lee Myong Hi, a quietly energetic woman in her last year at the university, and Shin Sang Uk, her boyfriend.

"Did you ever demonstrate against the war in Vietnam?" Myong Hi asked.

"Well, no. That was a little before my time. By the time I started college, America was pretty much out of the war." Sensing disappointment, he added, "I did participate in a sit-in, though. The teaching assistants were working without a contract, and they needed one badly, but the university refused to agree to one. I sat in a circle with a hundred other students around the administration building."

"And ... ?"

"We sat there for three hours. Then we went to class."

"And did the teaching assistants get their contract?" Il Man asked.

"No, not right away," Paul said slowly, embarrassed now that his story had backfired. "But I guess we got them thinking."

At that moment a young man approached boldly and slid into a seat beside Sang Uk. "Big Sister. Who's the American son of a bitch?" It was Lee Byong Guk, recently come up from Mokpo.

Mi Jin gasped and wanted to warn him that Paul spoke Korean, but she was not quick enough. Paul turned to her and, in a most impolite manner, spoke of him in slightly deprecatory tone:

"So who's this guy? Do you know him?"

Il Man let out a loud roar of laughter. Byong Guk blushed like a girl.

"He got you, kid!" Il Man said.

"I'm so sorry," Paul said in flawless, now respectful Korean. "Let me introduce myself. I am Pak Jong Shik. Whom do I have the honor of meeting?"

"I am Lee Byong Guk," the young man said, his mouth still agape. "Pleased to meet you."

"No, the pleasure is mine."

The levity at the table, gained at his expense, did not sit well with Byong Guk. "Be careful, Big Sister. Americans are bad news."

"Not this one," Mi Jin said tartly.

"As we were discussing, Il Man," Paul said, "I have not had much experience in demonstrating against the government. There were no great political issues during my time in college."

"You are lucky, I suppose. We are surrounded, smothered by the 'issues' our government imposes on us. The Yushin Constitution, the military establishment, the persistent separation of North and South Korea ..."

" ... The continuing presence of American troops in our country," Byong Guk broke in. "You haven't mentioned that. Jong Shik-a. What's your opinion of the American troops in Korea?"

"Well ... not good, I'm afraid," Paul said. "They don't blend well with the Korean culture."

"I'm not talking about the culture," Byong Guk sneered. "I'm talking about the way your troops have been used to oppress the Korean people."

"Excuse me?"

"They back up the Pak regime in Korea. Your government supports the oppression the rulers of our country impose on us. Your troops back them up. The bastards in our government are in power because the opposition is intimidated by their strength."

"Wait a minute," Paul said. "I thought we were here to help defend against an attack from the North. If I remember the history of the war right, the North Koreans ran right over the south precisely because American troops weren't anywhere nearby."

"There are two problems with that," Byong Guk replied. "First, the North overran the South because our military was weak. Your government didn't see fit to supply it and train it. That problem has been solved. The South Korean military establishment is plenty strong now — much too strong, if you ask me, because it has taken over our government and will probably be used directly against us someday soon. Mark my words.

"Secondly, America is responsible for the Cold War that divided North from South, and it is in your interests to keep that division alive. Our government uses fear of the North to justify every kind of abuse against the people. The newspapers are censored — because openness might encourage the North to attack. Student *demo*s are broken up with astonishing brutality — because everybody knows we are controlled by North Korean agitators whose goal is to weaken South Korean society, right?" He blew out a large cloud of cigarette smoke. "Martial law is imposed on us — because the death of President Pak is an invitation for North Koreans to invade and steal our wonderful riches."

Paul wondered how close Byong Guk was to actively sympathizing with North Korea. He glanced at the others. They listened patiently, but the expressions on their faces betrayed their sense that Byong Guk was too belligerent for their comfort. Mi Jin looked back at Paul and gave a short, helpless shrug.

"But an invasion from the North would kill thousands of innocent people," Paul said. "I thought the US was here to make sure that doesn't happen."

"Whoever told you that is telling you bullshit. Your troops were used to back up General Chon's *coup* last month. When the criminal Chon pulled some units off the Demilitarized Zone, your troops stepped right in to fill the gap. The Americans didn't protest, they didn't ask questions, they just did exactly what Chon's cronies wanted them to do. America backed Chon's criminal act!"

"You keep calling them my troops," Paul protested. "I don't have any control over them."

"Settle down," Il Man said, laying a restraining hand on Byong Guk's arm. "Don't get over-excited. Do us a favor, Little Brother. We need some more coffee here. Go get the *agashi*, will you?"

"Pak Jong Shik, I'm sorry," Il Man said when Byong Guk reluctantly left the table. "Lee Byong Guk is one of the brighter flames in the democracy movement. He certainly is on fire most of the time. We hope he doesn't burn himself out with his intensity. But I have to agree with most of what he said, especially that last thing. There is something rotten about the way the American armed forces filled in for Chon's soldiers. If they had not been ready to step in, Chon could not have marched on Seoul. When we get the reforms we want, we will demand that the American military leave our country. We don't really need them, and they complicate our lives too much. Nothing personal."

"Not at all."

Mi Jin and Paul finally left after having a quick, cheap dinner of *mandu* dumplings with Il Man and the others. They had reluctantly invited Byong Guk to join them, but he sensed that his company was becoming vexing and begged off. "To go build a bomb, no doubt," Paul muttered.

"What did you think of my friends?" Mi Jin asked eagerly when they were alone. "I so want you to like them. They are like family to me. We've been through so much together, through *demo*s, and hiding from the authorities, and worrying that we'd be caught. How do you like them?"

"Well ..." Paul paused, searching for words.

"You didn't like them."

"Oh, no. Most of them are fine by me. I like Il Man very much. Now, Lee Byong Guk — there's a character. I get the feeling you don't care much for him, either."

"Byong Guk is a difficult person. But he is well-connected in the radical faction in the movement. Many of the younger students look up to him because his ideas are so extreme. But his heart is good. He would lay down his life for any of us. There's no doubt about that."

"That's the thing I just can't understand," Paul said. His encounter with the students made him a little peevish. "Maybe it's because I'm a fat, lazy capitalist. I can't get past how naive they are, thinking they can overturn a government that has the power to smash them to pieces. We've seen what

President Pak did in Pusan a couple months ago. What did the protesters accomplish there? Not much, in my view."

"What were they supposed to do?" Mi Jin shot back, suddenly infuriated. "Sit down and let the government keep going on as it had been? Haven't you learned anything about Korea? This is not America, where the most you have to worry about is how nasty the election campaigns get. Koreans would love a chance to have a good, dirty campaign. Instead, our elections are meaningless. So if we want to make worthwhile reforms, like improving the status of women, or improving the social welfare system, we run into frightful obstacles because the powers that hold the government oppose such things." She kicked savagely at a pebble at her feet as they walked.

"I'm sorry," Paul mumbled. "Please don't be angry. I'll try to like your friends. Really, I will."

## Fifteen

"Paul! Great news!"

It was Sarah Conlon, calling Paul from the county health center in Suwon, near Seoul.

"Theodore's got an interview with a medical school. The University of Wisconsin."

"Wonderful! Tell him congratulations for me. How are you guys going to get back there?"

"Just him, not me," Sarah said. "He won't be gone long. Now that he has one interview lined up, he'll contact his other prospects. If they're at all inclined to consider him, they can schedule interviews around the time he'll be in the States. Then he'll come back to wait until one of 'em makes a decision. Isn't it wonderful?"

"What does the Peace Corps brass think about all this?"

"Mr. Atwood says 'Go for it!' Mrs. Kang — well, you know Mrs. Kang."

## Sixteen

"John, this is a wonderful opportunity to fine-tune the utilization of volunteers."

Atwood looked balefully at Mrs. Kang, who was uncharacteristically buoyant, even though he was holding in his hand the papers that approved Theodore Conlon's leave of absence. She would normally fight such a request with all her strength. He wondered if she had something up her sleeve.

"What was that again? You want to move one volunteer permanently out of his site and put him temporarily in Suwon to replace Theodore? But Theodore's not quitting. He'll be back in a month."

"He is a very smart person," Mrs. Kang said. "He will be accepted into medical college, and his wife will then leave with him. If we're not pro-active, we will have two sites in Suwon — the county health center and the city one — that have lost their volunteers, instead of just one."

"But that doesn't help the health center that has to provide the replace-ment. Who are we talking about, anyway?"

"Paul Harkin."

Atwood nodded. "He told me that he's been having a little trouble with his *kwajang*. It seems he got stuck teaching his boss English instead of doing his work."

"That is his story," Mrs. Kang said.

Atwood shrugged.

"Paul would be a perfect candidate for trying the special project you mentioned at our last staff meeting," Mrs. Kang said. "A very excellent idea for a project: having a volunteer near Seoul to act as a trouble-shooter among volunteers in the field. You said that many volunteers don't report problems to the Peace Corps staff — although I must remind you my door has always been open to any volunteer with problems. You felt that they would talk to one of their own more freely."

"That's the idea," Atwood said. "Whoever it is would report directly to me."

A shadow of consternation passed over Mrs. Kang's face. Atwood was deliberately cutting her out of the loop.

"Paul would be perfect," she said. "His language skills are very excep-tional. The other volunteers seem to like him. As for how well he gets along with Korean nationals, that is unresolved in my mind. But that can be worked on."

Atwood nodded. "Make him an offer."


*Seventeen*

Paul was late getting home from work. When he stepped through the gate of his boarding house, he smelled cigarette smoke. That was not unu-sual, for the majority of Korean men, including Ajoshi, smoked heavily.

"Oh ... sorry." It was Song Min, Ajumoni's 16 year old son, looking sheepish with a half-smoked cigarette clamped tightly between two fingers.

"What are you doing?"

Song Min made haste to hide the cigarette, then dropped it to the ground and stamped it out. He attempted a smile, but the retch-folds be-tween his mouth and nose made it look like a grimace. This clearly was his first smoke.

"Hello, Elder Brother. It is a beautiful evening, *neh?* Not too cold. Umm ... would you like a cigarette?" He shakily offered the pack to Paul.

Paul took the pack and put it in his pocket. "These things will kill you." He waited for the boy's embarrassed laugh to subside. "I'm hungry. Let's go to the bakery. My treat."

He enjoyed Song Min's company. The boy was bright, friendly, and surprisingly well-read for one his age. Ajumoni had told him that her son was not at all athletic, which sometimes made him the butt of jokes among his schoolmates. "But," she said proudly, "kicking a ball around a field won't get him anywhere. He studies and reads and prays, and the Lord will take him far." What his mother did not know was that between the study and prayer, Song Min had been reading Korean translations of every Western book he could find. He had asked Paul innumerable questions about how Tarzan could survive in the jungle, where he could take fencing lessons to be like D'Artagnon, and whether the Spanish Civil War was as brutal as Hemingway had made it seem. His questions had sent Paul to the Peace Corps library many times.

The bakery around the corner, which styled itself a "German Bakery" for no apparent reason, had a few tables near the plate glass window. Paul brought over two small loaf cakes and cans of orange juice. Song Min kept sneaking glances at his pack of cigarettes in Paul's pocket.

"You don't smoke, Elder Brother?"

"No. My parents told me that if I started, they would throw me out of the house. I listened to them."

They ate silently for a few minutes while Song Min mourned his lost smokes.

"How was school this semester?" Paul asked.

"It went well, thank you, Elder Brother. Just one and a half years to go, and I will graduate."

"What do you intend to do after that?"

"I would like to go to Seoul National University," Song Min said. "Of course, everyone wants to go there. I think I have a chance. Not as good a chance as someone from around Seoul, or from Kyongsangdo, but still a chance, if I keep my grades up."

"Why should yours be worse than anyone else's?"

Song Min sighed. "Not many people from Chollado make it up there. I don't know why. My father says it's because the big guys in Seoul hate Chollado people. I don't think it's that bad. We're all Koreans. Why should they think badly of us? Anyway, I have ambition. I'll make it."

Paul smiled and nodded.

"And then, you know what I want to do? I want to study in America. I'll get a degree in engineering at Seoul National University, and then go to graduate school in the United States. What university did you go to?"

"Purdue."

"Does it have a school for engineering?"

"Yes, it does. Several fine ones."

"Then maybe I'll go to Purdue. Will you help me get in when the time comes?"

"I'll be happy to."

"You won't forget me?"

"Certainly not!"

"I'll make sure you don't." When they got home, Song Min rummaged in his room and presented to Paul a wallet-sized school photograph. In his picture he stared sternly out from a plain gray background, dressed in his black high-collared school uniform. His black cap rested arrow-straight on his head.

On the back he had written in a large cursive hand, in English, with only one mis-spelling:

To My Freind
Pak Jong Shik
From Song Min
January 10, 1980

## Eighteen

Friday dawned gray and dirty. Fresh snow had not fallen on the streets in days, and what was there had melted down into sooty lumps. A featureless blanket of clouds stretched from horizon to horizon. In the flat gray light, people moved up and down the streets in a dark funk. Even Kwajang-nim, normally cheerful because he had so little work to do, chastised Paul for being a few minutes late for his lesson. He read sentences, as usual, and the subjects of those sentences revolved around thieves, sick people, and naughty children.

Paul was freezing. The heating system at his boarding house was not adequate for the bone-chilling weather: it heated only the floor, not the air. His buttocks and legs felt warm when he sat on the floor, and most of his body was all right when he threw his blanket around his shoulders. But the cold air stung his sinuses when he breathed in.

Nevertheless, Paul had spent the day in a happy frame of mind. He and Mi Jin were going to spend the weekend together in Seoul. They began their trip at the highway bus terminal close to Paul's house.

"Is it cold enough for you?"

Mi Jin shook her head. "Excuse me?"

"It's just an expression," Paul laughed. "It means, 'It's cold as hell, isn't it?'"

Mi Jin smiled, but her confusion was not completely dispelled. She thought hell was supposed to be hot.

The sun was about ready to set, but the bus yard had turned dark long ago. The tall floodlamps had already been turned on: they bathed the area with an crisp green glow. The bus left just as the darkness overtook the city boundary marker beside the road. Its gray granite shaft was capped with a stylized statue of a lion in lighter material. It looked like a gravestone. On the body of the marker it said "*Mokpo Shi Annyonghi kashipshio*" in the *hangul* alphabet and "Mokpo City Good Bye" in English.

They arrived at the Kwanghwa Mun area of Seoul, near the Peace Corps office, at around nine o'clock. Paul stopped Mi Jin in the alley outside the door of their inn.

"One room or two?"

"Two," she sighed.

"Oh, well. Two it is."

They spent the next morning at Kyongbok Palace, a sprawling complex of buildings reconstructed after the War from ruins dating from the four-teenth century. Its southernmost precinct was occupied by the national cap-itol, a relatively recent granite-faced domed behemoth that stood at the terminus of the main street of Seoul. President Pak's funeral shrine had been built there last October. Mi Jin regarded the edifice with disgust.

"You don't like it?" Paul asked. "I think it's impressive."

"What is there to like about it? It's ugly. It's the symbol of the govern-ment. And it's Japanese."

"Japanese?"

"Japan occupied our country for many decades before the end of World War Two. This was their colonial capitol. It was from this building that they almost destroyed our culture. My parents and grandparents and all people of their generations suffered terribly under Japanese rule."

While pounding her feet on the ground to keep warm, Mi Jin recounted the indignities suffered by the Korean people in general and by her family in particular. The Japanese forbade the use of the Korean language in any official capacity; they forced teachers to give lessons only in Japanese; they compelled Koreans to abandon their own names and adopt Japanese ones. "My parents both have Japanese names. Do you understand the importance of names, Jong Shik? My parents almost lost theirs. The Japanese tried to swallow up our country into their country and make us second-class inhab-itants of our own land."

"Didn't anybody resist?"

"Oh, yes. We had a strong resistance movement. They moved in packs through the countryside and attacked military convoys on the road, like bandits from long ago.

"But the Japanese were too strong. Most of the resistance eventually broke down. Yet there was one great movement that happened in 1919, here in Seoul. Ten years after they deposed our last king, Japan removed the little remnant of Korean government that was left. They made Korea a colony. Living conditions for Koreans got even worse. In March of that year, there were huge demonstrations right here on this street, and throughout the city. The Japanese called out their troops. They formed long lines and shot their rifles into the crowds. The bloodshed went on for days. We couldn't fight back because we had no weapons. Thousands of people died. The Japanese did still more. They crowded people into churches and then set them on fire. They arrested political leaders and sent them away, never to be heard of again. My grandmother's uncle was one of those men. Nobody knows what happened to him. After that, the resistance movement went even further underground."

"Wow. Well, it sounds like you're keeping up the tradition."

She said nothing, still dwelling on the city's bloody history. She cast one more look at the capitol before moving on. "That thing is rather useless, anyway. The president stays at Chong Wa Dae, the Blue House, and hardly ever comes here. The business of government goes on at the Unified Government Building, that huge skyscraper over there across the street; that's where the bureaucrats work. That son of a bitch General Chon no doubt has an office at an army base nearby, or at KCIA headquarters, wherever that is. And the National Assembly — ha! — for whatever it's worth, it has its own building on Yoido, the big island in the Han River. No, they just use this building for state occasions — funerals and meetings and the like. I wish they'd tear the thing down. If they want a place for ceremonies, let them use this beautiful palace!"

The palace grounds were almost deserted. No one wanted to play the tourist and tramp around in the cold, and the gloomy sky did not show the buildings to their best advantage. Paul and Mi Jin made fresh tracks in the snow, which had a delicacy that struck Paul as something strange and wonderful. At home in the American Midwest, the snow settled on the land in heavy white blankets whose broad folds were broken here and there by spindly remainders of trees. In Korea, and especially in this palace, the snow sat so lightly on the ground and in the evergreen trees, that he imagined being able to blow most of it away with a puff of breath, as if it were made of confectioner's sugar. The ridged tile roofs of audience halls and colonnades were striped in charcoal gray and white. Their curved lines clamped a cap of orderliness on top of the wildly elaborate brackets that supported them, brackets built of layer upon layer of wood painted green and decorated with stripes and rosettes of yellow, blue, green, and orange, splayed out over the corners of the buildings like frozen multi-colored tidal waves. Paul leaned back and gawked until his toes grew cold and he was forced to walk again to get warm.

"Magnificent!" Paul said. "These kings really knew how to live."

Mi Jin accepted the compliment proudly, but asked him to explain what he meant by "knowing how to live."

"They lived luxuriously. Look at all the beautiful buildings, the gardens, the wall around it all. They didn't have to face the dirty realities of life."

"I suppose you're right," she replied. The compliment went sour. She realized that her connection to the place was as a Korean acting as a tour guide for an American; it was a museum, nothing more, though a splendid one. It had no more relevance to her life than the presidential palace did. Her ancestors had toiled on the land; they had no more chance of seeing these wonders than they had of seeing the far side of the moon. Indeed, a great many of the kings, queens, and regents who lived here were every bit as repressive and distant as the generals who now constituted the Hana Hoe, General Chon's First Council.

Mi Jin stopped at the edge of the colonnade that surrounded the great audience hall and looked back. Here, in one panorama, rose symbols of three governments: beyond the hall of kings lay the green dome of the Japanese Capitol and beyond that rose the skyscraper of the Unified Government Building. From king to Japanese overlord to bureaucrat, the government of her country had passed one to the other, and none happily. She heaved a deep sigh and told Paul that she felt very cold.

## Nineteen

The air seemed to get colder as Paul and Mi Jin walked up Sejong Street toward the Peace Corps office. They passed the United States Embassy, a large block of a building a short distance from the Capitol. It looked like a mid-sized company's corporate headquarters, though its roof bristled with antennae. Paul gave it a long, loving glance.

"They have the best cafeteria in there," he said. "I wish I could take you in. Maybe later I'll go in quick and buy us a couple submarine sandwiches for lunch."

"Submarine sandwich ... ?"

"Hero sandwich? Well, it's easier to show you than to tell you. Trust me, you'll like it."

"Hey, Paul!"

A familiar raggedy figure approached them against the current of pedestrians. Paul recognized him as one of the volunteers who had been in the country for just over two years.

"Jim! What's up? Jim Dixon, Han Mi Jin."

Jim bowed deeply and shook Mi Jin's hand.

"I heard your time's up, Jim," Paul said. "So you're going home soon?"

"Yep. And not a moment too soon. I'm gonna miss this place, but it'll be good to be in the States again. Think of it — to go to Burger King anytime I want, and have real beef in the burgers. *Mmmm.* Two years away from that is a hell of a long time. Do you suppose I'll fit back in?"

"Just don't ask for *kimchi* on your hamburger," Paul laughed.

"I'm on my way to the Embassy to buy some traveler's checks. No need to go home the direct route, you know. As long as I'm on this side of the Pacific, I figured I'd hit Japan and then Hawaii. I gotta get going. I'm freezing my ass off out here, and that's one thing I won't miss about this place. Say, Paul, I've got a bunch of stuff I'm trying to get rid of. There's no need to take it home. You want some of it?" He set his backpack on the ground and rummaged through it. Paul knelt and opened his own pack.

"Do you need razor blades? These are good ones. Gillette. I got 'em from some friends on the army base."

Paul took them eagerly. "My supply ran out ages ago."

"Ivory soap? Ninety-nine and forty-four one hundredths percent pure. Here you go. How are you doing on deodorant?"

"You have deodorant?" Paul asked. "I can never find any in the markets."

"Koreans don't use it. They claim they don't have underarm odor. Here. Right Guard. Almost a full can."

People walking by slowed and glanced at the spectacle of two Americans kneeling on the ground dealing in Western products, then moved on. Americans were commonplace in this part of Seoul.

Paul held up the canister, which was copper-colored with a black cap, and looked at it almost worshipfully. "You don't know how long I've been looking for something like this. Thanks!"

They went their separate ways. After walking half a block, Mi Jin leaned close to Paul and whispered, "I think we are being followed."

"What?"

"There is a man behind us who has been watching us ever since you got those things from your friend. Don't look!"

"That's crazy," Paul said. "Why would anyone follow us?" He turned and caught a glimpse of a short, middle-aged man with a gray complexion and an alert, watchful look. A white earphone, the kind that comes with cheap transistor radios, was tucked in one ear, its coiled cord snaking into his open collar. He turned away and pretended to read an advertisement posted on a bus stop when he caught Paul looking at him.

"It is not just you," Mi Jin said, frightened. "If it were only you and your friend passing things to each other, no one would notice. It is me."

"I don't get it."

"They look for young people like me. They assume anyone around my age is a *taehaksaeng*, a college student. Anything that looks suspicious is doubly suspicious when someone like me is involved."

Paul thought of the hunted look in the eyes of Mi Jin's friends at Trouble House in Kwangju and quickened his pace. "The Peace Corps office is close by." he said. "Let's hurry."

## Twenty

"Come on in and meet my friends," Paul said. "It looks like there's a pretty good crowd here today."

A half-dozen volunteers chatted idly in the Peace Corps lounge. Sarah Conlon was there, and Althea Wittberg. As on any typical Saturday, especially one in inclement weather, they complained bitterly of boredom. The complaints segued into grumbling about their co-workers, who did not understand them; their living conditions, which provided too little privacy; and their need for stimulation, which had them quarreling over which bar to visit after lunch. The talk died down when Paul entered the room with Mi Jin.

Mi Jin had never before been the only Korean in a group of Americans. An unexpected wave of shyness suddenly overcame her as she shook hands meekly with those who offered theirs. She glanced only fleetingly into their eyes, and with a glance tried to read their *nunchi*. She liked Sarah, whose eyes showed her to be kind and a bit of an imp.

She took an instant dislike to Althea. Althea's eyebrows arched, and her *nunchi* reminded Mi Jin of the looks in the eyes of the *ajumoni*s who operated the men's *tabang*s. Her small eyes glinted with the habitual seeking of the basest interpretation of anything that came within view.

"Very pleased to make your acquaintance," Althea said in an oily voice. "Paul, I wondered when you'd join the ranks of volunteers with a native cutie." A few volunteers across the room laughed nervously.

"Althea, shut up," Sarah said.

"Ahem ... Althea, I should tell you," Paul said, "that she speaks excellent —"

"Thank you for saying I'm cute," Mi Jin broke in, with a passable imitation of an American accent. "May I say that you're not bad yourself."

Althea drew her breath in and with a flustered "Thanks" sat down. Sarah and Paul let out a loud laugh. The other Americans sat in stunned silence for a moment, then laughed louder than before. Althea peered at Mi Jin from under heavy brows, with murder in her eyes.

"Well said," Sarah told Mi Jin, leading her away. "Most everyone around here was hoping something like this would happen."

"Let's take her downstairs," Paul said. "I want to introduce her to Dr. Paek. Dr. Paek," he explained, "is the volunteers' patron saint. Never mind. I'll explain later what that means. Sarah, are you busy tonight? I was thinking we could take Mi Jin to the Civilian Club for dinner. A nice hot American meal is just what I need on a cold day. I'll call Joel to come join us."

Paul kept talking; Mi Jin followed and watched. Paul was showing mannerisms that she had never seen before. The shy, polite face he exhibited in Mokpo gave way to something more animated and not entirely pleasant. He chatted constantly in an open, easy manner that he never showed with her, and used American colloquial speech with such rapidity that she had trouble keeping up with him. She fought a sudden desire to take him back to Mokpo, where he would once again be himself — or at least the version of him that she knew. Yet she quickly realized that perhaps she did not know as much about him as she thought she did, and that the missing facets of his personality could best be fitted into the whole by observing him with his own countrymen.

Just as they reached the stairwell, Mrs. Kang approached them and touched Paul's arm. He froze as if bitten by a snake.

"Paul, how are you? Did you get time off from your health center to come to Seoul?" It was one of her stock questions. Translated, it meant, "What are you doing away from your site?"

"Umm ... Hello, Mrs. Kang. Yes. Kwajang-nim told me to have a good time and check out the palaces and such."

Mrs. Kang turned to Mi Jin and put on a tight, flat smile. "Have we met? You look familiar to me."

"This is Han Mi Jin. You might have seen her in Kwangju after the Regional Meeting," Paul said.

"Miss Han, how do you do? Are you showing Paul the sights?" She spoke in Korean, at a level precisely calibrated to be faintly deprecatory, but not insulting.

Mi Jin, like Paul, froze in her presence. She could not look into Mrs. Kang's eyes for long: she was sickened by what she found there. Mrs. Kang's *nunchi* revealed a joyless, arid malevolence, born of some pain whose source she could not uncover. More frightening was the scrutiny Mi Jin received from Mrs. Kang: the latter, she could tell, had the same power to read the language of the eyes. She felt her soul laid bare under the penetrating look from those hooded eyes. And within that gaze were unspoken questions, dark and accusatory: "What are you doing with this American? Why are you not with your own kind? Are you a whore?"

"Let's go, Jong Shik," she pleaded after Mrs. Kang left. "I want to get out of here."

## Twenty-one

"Welcome to the Civilian Club," Paul said to Mi Jin as entered a building in a darkened American military compound downtown. "It's the one truly American place in Seoul where just about any American can get in. At least it's never been a problem for volunteers."

The restaurant's real name was the East Gate Club, but volunteers from times long past had called it the Civilian Club because it welcomed non-military Americans and their guests. Its atmosphere was crowded and noisy; it smelled of fatty beef, potatoes, gravy, and fresh-baked bread. The insistent smell of *kimchi* was not to be found here; though on the menu, no one to Paul's knowledge ever ordered it.

"I would like to buy your dinner," Mi Jin said.

"Thanks, but they don't take Korean money here. Only dollars."

"How do you get American money? Do you buy it on the black market?"

"No, no," Paul smiled. "A long time ago I asked my parents to slip a five dollar bill into each letter they send me. Five bucks a week: it adds up."

"Paul, over here!"

Sarah and Joel motioned them over to their table. "Mi Jin, you met Sarah at the office. And this is Joel Reynoso."

"Miss Han, how do you do?" Joel rose slightly as he shook her hand. A slight smile played around the corners of his mouth. Paul knew the smile came from Joel's pleasure at finally having his curiosity satisfied; Mi Jin interpreted it as slightly mocking. She struggled in the low light to trace the contours of his face and read the look in his eyes. What she found there was not malevolence, as she saw in Mrs. Kang's eyes, but something far more disturbing. She saw nothing. His *nunchi* simply did not register: his eyes were like two orbs of polished onyx, having a shiny black surface but no depth. She wondered if he were truly dead inside, as his *nunchi* suggested.

"How do you do?" she replied. "Paul has told me so much about you. He respects you very much."

"It's nice to know that someone does," he replied with a mirthless laugh.

"Mi Jin, would you like me to order something for you?" Paul asked. "The menu here is one hundred percent classic American. How about a nice cut of prime rib with a baked potato? And for dessert, their warm pecan pie is wonderful." Mi Jin nodded.

Later, on their way back to their inn, Mi Jin asked about Joel.

"How did you become friends with him? He is very different from you."

"A lot of people say that. I can't remember what brought us together. It's like we've always been friends."

"He seems cold."

Paul considered for a moment. "Yeah, I can see how you'd get that impression. He's not an easy person to know, and he doesn't exactly shower you with affection. But he's a good person. He gives as good as he gets. He'll give his all to help me if I ever need him. Don't ask me how I know that; I just do. And he knows I'll do the same for him."

Mi Jin linked her arm in Paul's and wondered if his powers of perception were greater than her own or, if not, whether Joel's friendship would one day be Paul's undoing.

# CHAPTER SIX

No sooner had Paul returned to Mokpo than Mrs. Kang summoned him back to Seoul. The call came on a Wednesday morning while he had been out visiting patients in their homes. The health center receptionist gave him a detailed message: He was to meet with Mrs. Kang the next day at two o'clock in the afternoon. He caught the first train and spent the next several hours combing his memory for anything he had done that would prompt such a call. Nothing came to mind.

"Hello, Paul. Come in. Have a seat."

It was the first time he had been inside Mrs. Kang's office. The abundance of decoration struck him, from a wall full of plaques to a row of expensive antiques on a shelf. A second look, however, revealed how untidy the room was. Books were jammed into a bookcase built for half the number of volumes; papers sat in haphazard piles on her desk and coffee table. The room gave the quick impression that Mrs. Kang was too busy to be bothered by visitors. In truth, many of the stacks of paper were yellowed with age and the books were covered with dust.

Paul sat and waited nervously, for her to begin.

"The reason I called you in," Mrs. Kang said, "is to give you some good news: we are transferring you closer to Seoul."

Silence hung on the air while Paul struggled to understand what she had said.

"Have I ... done something wrong?" he stammered.

"Oh, no, not at all," Mrs. Kang said. She laughed with a forced catching of the breath, ending with a falling "ahhhh," like the uncomfortable laugh among strangers at an unfunny joke. "In fact, we have heard some good things about you. We want to promote you."

"Excuse me?"

"Mr. Atwood noticed how excellent your language skill is becoming. He said to me, 'Mrs. Kang, Paul is becoming one of our best volunteers. I want him on my new team.' Let me explain.

"Mr. Atwood cares very much about how the volunteers are maximizing their efforts at their sites. He would like to visit each and every one himself, but he is extremely busy. So he had an idea: why not empower one volunteer to 'make the rounds,' he said, and gather word of the volunteers' concerns? Do you remember the monthly questionnaires we asked everyone to fill out? The volunteers have been very bad at doing what they were told to do. We need someone with good Korean skills to talk with them and their co-workers pro-actively to see what are the biggest challenges. You would not be traveling all the time; it is a half-time position. Consider it being a Volunteer At Large."

"If it's half-time, can I do it out of Mokpo?"

Mrs. Kang laughed again. "No, Paul. Mokpo is too isolated from the rest of the volunteers. We want to bring you back from exile, so to speak. Most importantly, you must be nearby so you can report back to me."

"Report to you?" Paul gulped.

"Mr. Atwood is most anxious to help the volunteers. I can help him by filtering whatever data you present to me. Besides, it is within my authority as the Health Programs Director to manage you."

Paul tried to remain calm, to keep his wits about him, but he felt his resolve weakening under Mrs. Kang's presence. He never was one to stand up for himself; still, he screwed up his courage and asked:

"Do I have a choice in taking this job?"

Mrs. Kang's gaze bore into Paul with a look that said 'No,' but after a heavy pause she spoke in a low, forceful tone. "No one is forcing you to do this, Paul. However, you are absolutely the best person for the job. The hard work you have done with your ... tutor has made you Mr. Atwood's prime candidate. If you don't accept the position, Mr. Atwood would be very disappointed. And we would have cause to wonder about your dedication to the Peace Corps. Is there something going on in Mokpo that you're not telling me?"

Paul sighed. "No, Mrs. Kang."

"Good. I hope you can stay through tomorrow. I have arranged an interview with the Director at the Suwon City Health Center, a Mr. Hong. He's expecting you at one o'clock. You will take over Theodore Conlon's site while he runs back home to chase some medical school application. When he comes back, we'll find another place for him."

"When do I have to move there?"

"Within the next two weeks. Mr. Hong was most annoyed about losing Theodore. It's very important that we do not keep him waiting."

## Two

Kwajang-nim bundled himself in his heavy coat and pushed headlong into a blast of cold winter air. January was well advanced, and with it came the winter doldrums. The charm of the first snowfall had receded into memory. There was nothing now to make the day seem any better than it was. Indeed, this day had held only misfortune and bad news.

Things had started to go sour early in the afternoon, in the languorous period after his large lunch, when he would have expected to be left alone to doze, to putter around with the paperwork on his desk, or to prepare sentences for the next day's lessons with the American. No one in the front office knew what had happened next, except that after receiving a telephone call from Seoul, his mood had suddenly turned black. He moped, he barked at his subordinates, and for the first time in memory he stayed in the office until well past the end of the normal workday. The office workers impatiently waited for the boss to get up and leave; to go before him would have been a serious breach of etiquette. No one dared disturb him. They sat and wondered what terrible thing had upset his normally placid *kibun*.

The telephone call had come from Mrs. Kang. It started pleasantly enough, with comments traded about the severity of the weather in their respective areas of the country. Then Mrs. Kang — much too abruptly, Kwajang-nim thought — jumped to the purpose of her call.

"I'm afraid we are going to have to transfer the American out of the Mokpo City Health Center into a similar facility closer to Seoul."

Kwajang-nim sputtered out cigarette smoke in mid-puff. "What? Excuse me? What did you say?"

"I am terribly sorry. I know how hard the American is working there, and how diligently you have been trying to put some Korean language into his head. You have performed such a miracle! But my American supervisor, the head of Peace Corps in Korea, is now insisting that we take Paul out of Mokpo and place him near Seoul. He has a special project in mind for him, and your teaching of Korean skills will help him a great deal. Now, I argued strenuously against it, but I was overruled. The Peace Corps director does not understand how Koreans work together."

Mrs. Kang talked at length, pausing barely long enough to let Kwajang-nim get in a few simple questions. When the call ended, he calculated that twenty-five percent of it had been straight information, fifty percent flattery, and the remainder simple lies. He was brooding on the lies when he stepped through the door of his usual *tabang*.

"You've kept us waiting. What's wrong with you?" demanded Vice-Headmaster Kim Son Kwan. The question was not one of friendly concern.

"Ehhh, they're taking my American away, the lousy bastards," Kwajang-nim grumbled.

"The American?" Kim waved the cigarette smoke away from his face and sat forward. "The American?"

"What other one is there? The one who's been dallying with your radical little schoolteacher. They're sending him away, transferring him up around Seoul somewhere. You're bound to like that."

Kim flicked the ash off his cigarette and leaned back. "Whatever. It doesn't concern me."

"Liar. You'd be happy about anything that denies your girl some pleasure."

"Ha! Did they give any reasons for his transfer?" Kim asked.

"None." Kwajang-nim took a long draught of his tea. "That's what bothers me the most. They wouldn't even tell me why. Oh, they gave me a load of bullshit, but I didn't believe a word of it."

"You must have done something wrong," Lee Won Il, the banker, said blandly.

"What the hell do you know?" Kwajang-nim shot back. "I did everything right. The language wasn't the only thing. I personally showed him how the health center runs. He wanted to do laboratory work, so I let him. I even let him go out home-visiting, even though it was against my better judgment. Too much sun, too much exposure to the weather, can weaken an American's constitution. Yes, that must be it. He did seem a little peaked a few weeks ago, or so Mrs. Mun informed me. I shouldn't have let him go out. That must be it. His superiors are worried about his health."

"Come now," said Kim. "Don't show everyone how foolish you are. His transfer has nothing to do with his health. It's his involvement with Miss Han. Somehow they got wind of her political 'affiliations.' If I were in their position, I would have done exactly the same thing. Best not to taint him with the crowd she runs with."

"If Miss Han is such a radical," Lee asked, "why don't you get rid of her? She can't be good for her students."

"You think I haven't tried? It's that dotard headmaster of our school. He likes her. He thinks she can do no wrong. I've tried to warn him about her, but the old fool won't listen."

"When she finds out about her boyfriend's transfer, she'll be upset, no doubt."

"No doubt."

On the very next day, Kim Son Kwan called Mi Jin into his office. He had decided to break the news to her slowly, by degrees, so he opened the conversation with talk of her teaching methods, to which he pretended to give mild approval.

"I have heard from a number of sources that English is best learned by listening to native speakers. That American you know, for example ... ?"

"Paul Harkin. His Korean name is Pak Jong Shik."

"Ah, yes. Mr. Harkin. He told that silly story to your class."

"Yes, sir."

"How was the reaction of the students to his talk?"

"Very good, sir. They still talk about it, even after all these months."

"That's nice." Kim leaned back and folded his hands over his belly, ready to move in for the kill. "Have you given any thought to inviting him to come back?"

"Why, yes, sir," she said, brightening. "I would love to ask him to come back again."

"Hmmm." He pursed his lips in mock disappointment and set his eyes on Mi Jin's face. "That could be a problem. It's a shame he's being trans-ferred out of Mokpo. Oh! He hasn't told you? I've upset you. Oh, dear, I am sorry. I heard the news from his *kwajang* last night."

Mi Jin's heart stopped. She could not hear his apology through the roar-ing in her ears. Her face flushed, but she managed to keep her composure.

"I ... I have not heard this. He is in Seoul and has not come back yet."

"Indeed? Then I might be wrong. It is best to hear the true story from his own mouth. I heard it only second-hand, from his *kwajang*, who had heard it from a Mrs. Kang in your friend's home office. I'm very sorry that this has happened, just devastated. It's such a shame that our students won't be profiting from his talents again." He stood, signaling that the con-versation was over. "That is all for now. You may return to your duties."

Mi Jin remained in a state of consternation for the rest of the day; only by a titanic force of will did she manage to keep her mind on her lessons. Still, she was not herself, and her students could see it. When one girl con-fessed, after several mistakes at the blackboard, that she had not completed her homework, Mi Jin raised her voice for the first time in memory. The girl returned to her seat and wept quietly. Mi Jin had no choice but to leave the room for a minute.

What is happening? she thought. Heaven help us. Don't let it be true!

## Three

Suwon was an agreeable old gentleman of a city, slightly larger than Mokpo, and more sedate. Its long history revealed itself at every street cor-ner. The Suwon city fathers took extraordinary pride in the city's wealth of ancient fortress walls, pavilions, and other structures, though not all the wood and stonework in them was really ancient. Most, indeed, were recent reconstructions of what had been nearly demolished in the Korean War. Being new, they lacked much of the patina of age that would normally adorn the capital of one of Korea's old kingdoms. Rather, in a startling in-congruity, most of the city's shops, houses, and government offices looked older by comparison.

Paul liked the place. Mokpo, it had been said, reminded people of San Francisco with its vibrant streets and surprising hills. Suwon, on the other hand, reminded him of Lafayette, especially the older neighborhood where his grandmother lived, paved with yellowed sidewalks and awash with the smell of old wood.

The health center was a new building, less than five years old, located a few blocks from City Hall. The rows of large windows on the first and second stories gave it a light, airy interior. They also made the building cold, for many of them did not seal well, and drafts circulated everywhere. As Paul followed the receptionist upstairs to the chief's office, he reveled in the light and freshness around him. The poor old Mokpo health center suffered by comparison. Where the latter was an old office building converted to a clinic, this building had the brightness and antiseptic smell of a place built for its purpose, where serious public health care was practiced. He liked it immediately.

"Good morning, Mr. Harkin. I am glad to meet you," the health center chief, or *sojang*, said in clear English.

Paul responded in kind in Korean. As they conversed, Sojang-nim saw that Paul felt at home in Korean, so he lapsed away from English.

"You speak with a Chollado accent. How amusing! Let me show you our health center," he said, and came from behind his desk. He was a tall man, almost three inches taller than Paul. He limped markedly, his left leg supported by a metal brace. "A wound from the war," he explained. "I served in Vietnam with your American soldiers.

"Our health center has been in operation for over fifteen years, but our facilities are new. We're very proud of them. It was built to be a model health center, one that other cities and counties could learn from. I'm happy to say that a great many other centers, from Anyang just north of us to the neighborhoods of Seoul, have followed our lead. How are the facilities in Mokpo?"

"Not nearly as fine as this," said Paul. "Even so, we do good work there. Heaven knows there's plenty to be done."

"Of course. Do you know Mr. Conlon? He left just a few days ago to interview for medical school. I wish him luck. We will miss him. He was a very hard worker. I have heard the same about you."

The tour went on and on, and as Sojang-nim stopped at each room and made introductions, Paul grew in his conviction that his transfer had already been approved.

## Four

Another winter storm had begun to assault Mokpo when Mi Jin left school that day, but she scarcely felt the sleet that tore at her face like tiny jagged darts.

"Of course. How could it be otherwise?"

She trudged home and prepared to return to Chindo the following morning. The part of her mind that heeded superstitions and portents, the part most like her beloved grandmother, bowed to what seemed inevitable, mandated by heaven: Paul was making an exit from her life's stage and Kim Hyong Chol, her suitor, was poised to make an entrance, and a lasting one. Marriages had been arranged by parents for as long as memory went back, and uncounted generations of children had honored their parents' wishes.

Her parents had arranged an engagement party for the couple and had invited relatives and neighbors from all over the island. It appeared now to Mi Jin that duty would again win out over desire. She could push against the tide of tradition no longer.

"You're here. Finally!" her mother said when Mi Jin stepped through the gate. Mr. Han had hired a taxi to stay near the boat dock to look for her and whisk her home the moment she arrived. The house had taken on a festive look, every corner spotless, and the very finest embroidered covers placed on the floor cushions. Her mother and an assortment of female relatives had been cooking for days: *ddok*, the traditional cakes made from rice flour, colored in many hues and stuffed with sweet red bean paste or rolled in flour; sliced raw cuttlefish sprinkled with hot sauce; deep-fried shrimp; three kinds of *mandu* dumplings stuffed with seasoned meat; and four varieties of *kimchi* made of cabbage, of chopped radishes, of leeks, and of cucumbers stuffed with shredded cabbage. They laid it all out on three borrowed tables that stretched the length of the house's main room, covered with fine linen tablecloths. Mi Jin stared at the wonderful sight. She had never before seen a feast such as this in her parents' home, and so impressively arranged, as if to say, "We are wealthier than you think!" The food alone looked like it had cost them a month's income — and the wedding, still being planned, was going to be even bigger.

"Well, hurry! Don't stand there looking. You have to get dressed before the guests come!"

Her mother pushed her into the main bedroom and brought out a towering white undergarment, like a full-length slip, from the closet. "Here's your petticoat. See, it's good and stiff; it'll flare out your *hanbok* nicely." Mi Jin quickly stripped down to her bra and panties and reached for it.

"*Yah!*" her mother exclaimed. "What are you doing? Put some pants on, for heaven's sake!" She handed her a pair of white frilled trousers of the traditional style that reached down to her ankles and were made of satin and stiff lace.

"But Omma, these are so hot and uncomfortable! No one will see my ankles under the dress, anyway."

"Quiet! And what if they do? Do you want to look like some — some *tabang* girl? Do as I say!"

Mi Jin's mother went back to the closet and gingerly removed a plastic dress bag from a hanger. The *hanbok* was of smooth, thick satin, of the lavender-pink shade of wild azaleas in springtime. Embroidered in lustrous thread, from the sleeves of the short jacket to the bottom of the long skirt, were innumerable flowerbuds of cherry-red and mauve. Scalloped banding of gold thread ringed the hem of the skirt and the jacket sleeves. Its shimmer bathed the drab old room in a pink glow.

"Omma ... it's beautiful!"

"It cost a fortune. Don't spill anything on it. Let me help you put it on. Hurry!"

Mi Jin let the petticoat fall over her head and straighten out to the floor in a stiff *shoosh!* Her mother checked the shoulder straps to cover her breasts and keep the hem just brushing the floor. She wrapped the heavy skirt of the *hanbok* over the petticoat and fastened it tightly just under the armpits. Mi Jin did a small acrobatic twist to struggle into the short jacket, with its modest V-neck and wide sleeves that reached nearly to her knuckles, and then tied it together with a long bow at the bosom. No sooner had her mother straightened the bow than she ran behind and started drawing Mi Jin's hair back into a smooth, severe bundle in back, which she held together with an ornate hairpin of plastic that was molded and polished to look like jade.

"Hold still, or you'll lose the bun ... there. Ah, you've come," she said to a newly arrived visitor. "You're late. Hurry and do her face. We're running out of time."

The proprietress of the local beauty salon had arrived with a small suitcase full of cosmetics. She sat Mi Jin down and, while scolding her mother for putting the *hanbok* on before the makeup, tucked a napkin into the collar. Then, with a heavily loaded brush, she began daubing Mi Jin's face with a light tan foundation, looking very much like an impressionist painter attacking a new canvas.

"Are you sure that's the right color?" Mi Jin's mother asked doubtfully. "It seems awfully dark."

"It's the popular shade now. Everybody's using it. Besides, if you can't see the makeup, why put it on? So, Little Sister," she cooed lubriciously, "you're the lucky one, *neh?* Or Kim Hyong Chol's the lucky one, is more like it. Such a cute, lovely face you have!"

She droned on with the empty flattery while filling every pore of Mi Jin's face with powder, blushes, and highlights. By all appearances, she had learned her trade in the theater, for the makeup emphasized every feature, and doubly highlighted certain features that she thought attractive, such as Mi Jin's high cheekbones and large eyes. For the finishing touch, she carefully curled her eyelashes and loaded them with mascara. After a professional appraisal from across the room, she declared the work done.

"They'll hardly recognize you!" she said with approval, and Mi Jin's mother beamed in agreement. It was the first time she remembered her mother looking at her with such satisfaction.

Kim Hyong Chol and the guests were already milling about when Mi Jin and her mother emerged from the bedroom. Hyong Chol wore a man's *hanbok*, a loose-fitting suit of satin brocade with light green trousers and vest and violet embroidered jacket. Mr. Han, similarly dressed, stood off by himself with only a few friends from the village; he had no relatives with whom to share the celebration.

All conversation stopped as Mi Jin stepped forward stiffly, her head and eyes lowered, her expression grave. The older members of the party — her mother's siblings, cousins, and an aunt — murmured approval of her modesty. Under coos of admiration and a light patter of applause, she went immediately to her fiancé's side and took his hand.

The engagement ceremony lasted only a few minutes. The couple stood together while the priest from the local church made a speech about the blessings of marriage and the pride the families will have in the happy couple. Hyong Chol slipped a small diamond ring on her finger. They did not kiss. The guests burst into another round of applause and led them to a large Western-style cake excessively frilled with hearts and multi-colored filigree. They cut it and doled it out, and with that ended the official portion of the ceremony.

Mi Jin never lost her air of gravity. While going through the motions of what should have been a happy occasion, she prayed for a miracle of deliverance; but the unstoppable forces of time and ritual and her family's expectations rolled on. In a quiet corner of the room, in a fleeting private moment, Hyong Chol spoke softly into her ear: "I know you do not love me, Mi Jin. But neither did my mother love my father when they were married, and still they were happy. Everything will turn out well, Mi Jin." He squeezed her hand.

Tears welled in Mi Jin's eyes, and her aged relatives, interpreting her shining eyes as a sign of happiness, smiled at one another.

## Five

Paul returned to Mokpo under a cloud of dread. He knew that Kwajang-nim had been told about his transfer; he also surmised that, since secrets were impossible to keep at the health center, the rest of the staff also knew. This was confirmed when he walked through the front door. Where previously he had attained a certain welcome invisibility at the health center after everyone had got used to him, they now greeted him with furtive, meaningful glances.

He called Mi Jin from home that night while taking a break from packing.

"Mi Jin? It's Jong Shik. I ... um ... have news."

The voice on the line was almost inaudible. "I know."

"You know about my transfer?"

"My vice-headmaster told me. He must have heard it from your *kwajang*."

"Bad news travels fast," Paul sighed.

"Yes."

A silence settled on the conversation; both wanted to talk, but neither knew where to begin in the short span of a telephone call.

"When are you leaving?" she asked.

"This weekend. I have to start at the Suwon Health Center on Monday."

"That is such a short time."

"It is. I have to see you before I go."

"Let's have dinner together on Friday," she said slowly.

"Not tomorrow? Today's only Wednesday."

" ... No."

Paul heaved another deep sigh. "Mi Jin, I am so sorry. I did not ask for this transfer."

"Yes."

Paul's last days at the health center bore an uncomfortable air of finality about them. His lack of usefulness, which had always irked him, became worse. His routine duties in the lab seemed unimportant, and he gave up home-visiting altogether. There was simply no point to any of it.

"You've worked so hard all these months," Mrs. Mun said. "Take some time off. Kwajang-nim isn't here. He left for a meeting in Kwangju, and won't be back for the rest of the week. Enjoy your last few days in Mokpo."

"No, Mrs. Mun, I really want to stay and get some things done. I insist."

"*Caseyo!* Go! Have some fun." She smiled affectionately. "You are so funny, trying so hard to fit in. But believe me, a Korean would never insist on working if his supervisor told him to go and enjoy himself."

Paul paused. "Mrs. Mun. I am not transferring because I want to. You know that, don't you?"

"For the hundredth time, yes."

"I wish I could stay. You have been very, very good to me."

"No, no, Mr. Pak. Don't be silly."

"I'm supposed to make a report about my service here. It helps the Peace Corps decide whether a new volunteer will be sent to Mokpo in the future. I will give you all the credit for my success, and it will be the truth. Whether another volunteer will be sent here ... I don't know. If so, I will warn them about Kwajang-nim, and tell them how good you are."

Mrs. Mun made a move to dismiss Paul's speech as just so much nonsense, but stopped herself. The sight of a grown man speaking his heart to someone he did not know well in the Korean sense — of the same gender and intimately associated over years — surprised and moved her. She took his outstretched hand and shook it warmly. "I will miss you, Mr. Pak. Very much."

## Six

Paul's last dinner with Mi Jin came on a bone-chilling Friday night, the night before his departure. His sense of detachment, of being in transit, was now complete. Even in his own dark city, he felt like a ghost.

Mi Jin waited for him under a street lamp, closed in on herself against the cold.

"Good evening, Mi Jin. I've come."

"Yes. Good evening. Let's get out of this cold."

As they passed through the shadows of a side street, Paul put his arm around her shoulders. She did not lean in toward him.

"Is something wrong?" he asked. Her bitter chuckle told him how stupid his question had been.

"What do you think? You're leaving. Perhaps I should congratulate you."

"I'm sorry, Mi Jin. I wasn't thinking."

Dinner at a small noodle restaurant passed in near silence. Paul talked in fits and starts about his duties at his new position. Mi Jin rarely raised her eyes from her food.

Finally, Paul put down his chopsticks and pushed his plate away, his meal half eaten. "Mi Jin, you must understand something. This was all the doing of Mrs. Kang, that ... evil person. She does not like me. So she pulled me out of a place where I feel comfortable. Mokpo is home to me, and you are what makes it so. If it were up to me, I would no sooner leave you than I'd leave my arms or heart or brain behind."

Mi Jin's face softened, but her manner remained detached, almost aloof.

"I know. I do not blame you, just as you must not blame me. We must do as we are told."

Paul gave her a questioning look, but she refused to say more.

They walked out into the cold air, down the main street, and stopped in an alleyway. Across the street was the train station. Two small groups of men still sat silently on the roof, manning the same machine guns that had been in place since last October.

Paul reached out to Mi Jin and held her. She stiffened at first, but softened under his insistent embrace.

"I'm not leaving you for good. I'll call you as soon as I get settled. Then I'll be down here to see you as often as I can. I'm not giving up, honey."

She held him tightly and rested her head on his shoulder.

"Kiss me goodbye, Mi Jin."

The few people out walking who saw the pair shook their heads at the unseemly public display of affection.

## Seven

Paul soon grew tired of the drawn-out goodbyes, especially at work, that lurched along like cold treacle. He became less tolerant of the noise and mayhem of Mokpo and began to look forward to the peace and quiet of St. Lazarus Village, where Joel had found him a place to live.

On the morning of his departure, Ajumoni and her son hailed a taxicab and went with him to the train station.

"Your bags will be sent separately to Suwon Station," she said. She stuffed the claim ticket into his breast pocket and patted it. "Don't lose this. You can pick the luggage up tomorrow or Monday. I hope you remembered to pack some clothes and a toothbrush in your backpack. You did? Good."

The morning sun slanted across the plaza and illuminated the creases in Ajumoni's creased face. Her eyes were shining.

"You're ready to go. Do call when you get settled. We'll be anxious to hear from you. Ah, Mr. Pak. You're a *yangban*, a gentleman, you are. I never had a moment's trouble with you."

"That can't be true," Paul said huskily, in Korean. "My own mother cannot have taken better care of me. I shall miss you." He reached out and hugged her, knowing that she would quickly wriggle loose. She broke away and struck him on the chest.

"Mr. Pak, are you crazy? What will everyone think?"

"I will miss you, too." Song Min stepped up and shook his hand.

"Let's get together in Kwangju after school starts again," Paul said.

"Mr. Pak! Mr. Pak!"

A familiar voice rang through the plaza. A young man ran, then checked his speed under the gaze of the guards. It was Laboratory Mr. Kim, carrying a bundle under his arm.

"You forgot your lab coat," he said. "I made sure our health center's lapel pin is on it."

"Thank you, thank you, Mr. Kim. I am glad you came. You and Mrs. Mun were my best friends at work. I will miss you both."

The northbound train — clean, freshly loaded, and eager to leave Mokpo — blew a blast of its horn. Paul gave one last round of handshakes and was off.

## Eight

"Welcome to Suwon," Joel said. He met Paul at the train station and, seeing his subdued manner, took charge of his luggage and calmly instructed him on the best way to get to St. Lazarus Village.

"Take the Number 4 bus from the Rotary, see? It's just a few blocks from your new health center over there. And we'll get off right outside the gate to the village."

The village's main gate, a pointed arch fashioned of painted concrete, stood next to a statue of Jesus, seated and gathering a trio of children about him. The hospital and Paul's new quarters were a quarter-mile up the valley floor. A winding road led them past an elementary school, a small market, and a broad field covered with a crust of snow. The road followed the valley: to the right, a long, low ridge bristled with pine trees and the low mounds of old gravesites; to the left, past the field, a settlement of houses and a few small workhouses clung to a more gradual incline.

They met Sister Miriam near the hospital, coming out of the infirmary dressed in her white nurse's habit. The smell of disinfectant clung to her, even in the cold air.

"Paul! How good to see you again." She shook his hand and closed the door behind her. "So you're here to stay, eh? Good for you. Welcome. Joel, have you shown him his place? Oh, of course not, you've just come up the road. Well, you're in for a treat. Come along."

She led them up the steep paved road, past a small rose garden decorated with a white statue of the Virgin Mary, into a wooded area across a ravine from the sisters' dormitory. "You remember this place. We're still using the wood you chopped for us."

She stopped in front of a low building nestled in the woods, on a small bluff overlooking the hospital. "This is your home. It used to be the sisters' dining hall before we started eating in the other building; it's just too hard to heat the whole thing in the winter."

The door opened to a large, well-appointed kitchen, though with its major appliances removed. The room beyond was a vast empty cold space, lined on two sides with bookcases crammed with medical books and religious texts.

"Am I going to live in this room?" Paul gasped.

"Good heavens, no. You'll stay in the cook's quarters. Right this way."

The room was small, like most Korean bedrooms, set in the corner of the building just off the kitchen. Sister Miriam took him outside and showed him a sooty space beneath the floor.

"We don't have the _yontans_, the charcoal heaters, in this building. You have to build a wood fire yourself in this pit here. The flames will heat the floor, Korean style."

"This will do nicely. Thank you."

"My dormitory is over there in that building," Joel said as they walked across a small courtyard to the hospital cafeteria. "You're lucky. Most volunteers would kill for a setup like yours. You've got peace and quiet when you get home from work, plenty of privacy, decent food, and attractive nurses running around."

"I'm afraid I won't be chasing any of them," Paul said.

"Sure. How did Mi Jin take the news?"

"Not well. She took it in an unemotional, detached way. It was a little scary, as if a curtain had fallen across her eyes. I couldn't see inside anymore. I want to call her tonight, just to see how she is."

Joel nodded as Salshigi, a skittish dog tied up outside the cafeteria, barked a nervous welcome.

## Nine

Paul's first day at the Suwon City Health Center almost wore him out. He endured a flurry of introductions, made tiresome by the Koreans' ancient protocol of bowing, shaking hands, exchanging florid pleasantries, and bowing and shaking hands again. He renewed his acquaintance with the health center chief — the _sojang_ — and Im Kyong Shik, his co-worker in the tuberculosis program, at a lunch in his honor.

"Tell me about TB control in the Mokpo health center," Mr. Im urged him. "Is their program as good as ours?"

Sojang-nim laid his hand on Mr. Im's arm and laughed. "Why, he hasn't even seen our program at work. How can he compare the two? You've seen our facilities, though, Mr. Pak. How do they compare?"

Paul told them about the dark, cramped space of the building across from Mokpo Station, the Korean War-era X-ray machine, and the lack of heat in the winter.

"The heat situation is common throughout the country," Sojang-nim said. "Our health center has restrictions on electrical power, just like public buildings everywhere."

"The rest of it doesn't surprise me, though," said Mr. Im. "Chollado is a backward area, after all. The people down there like to sit and complain about how hard their lives are. 'Oh, the government doesn't like us, we're so poor,' they say. For crying out loud, they need to stand up and get things done! They've got the brains to do so, that's true. They just lack the proper work ethic. They're too busy conniving, making deals, to make any real progress. Now, I'm from Kyongsang Province ..."

Why am I not surprised? Paul thought.

"...and our people are solid as rocks. If there's a job to be done, we set our minds to it and do it without complaining. Is it any wonder that Kyong-sangdo is better-developed than most of Chollado?"

"You must forgive Mr. Im for his passion," Sojang-nim smiled. "He's always bragging about the sterling qualities of his own people. I sometimes ask him why he doesn't go on back to his *kohyang*, his home. Then he thinks I'm trying to fire him, and he shuts up."

The comment brought a rash of laughter, especially from Mr. Im, whose good nature had quickly returned.

"I feel I must defend my friends in Mokpo," Paul said cautiously. "We all worked hard, and we made good progress in fighting TB, even though we had few resources."

"Of course. I'm sure Mr. Im meant no disrespect. I will direct him to give you plenty of hard work here, too."

"Thank you. I'm ready."

"Haw! Wonderful! We'll send you out home-visiting as soon as you get settled."

## Ten

Shortly after Paul moved to Suwon, the North Korean government made overtures to the South to discuss peaceful reunification. The terse message was delivered to the South Korean government through a neutral third country.

The North had done this before, but nothing had ever come of it. The South Korean government had always treated such offers with suspicion and contempt. North Korea knew that the South had no intention of participating in talks of any sort, and it was content to look like the injured party when the South rebuffed it. For weeks after making an unanswered proposal, the official North Korean news service ranted about South Korea's love of continued war while portraying itself as the gentle seeker of peace.

The game worked the other way, too. South Korea occasionally made offers to talk about peace, and North Korea rejected them out of hand. On these occasions, it was the South's turn to crow about the North's warlike nature while justifying the cost of protecting its people with a massive military machine and watching local sympathizers with a far-reaching internal security force.

"So North Korea has peered out from its pit to make another show of peaceful intentions, like a snake emerging from its hole to strike," Vice-Headmaster Kim, in Mokpo, thought, rubbing the night's poor sleep from his eyes. He had had the same terrifying dream:

Kim was once again the frightened soldier escaping from a burning Seoul, clinging to the steel girders of the bridge over the Han River. And again, with a mighty *whoosh* one section after another collapsed into the water, taking with them hundreds of refugees, most of whom had been recently roused from sleep by the North's attack. But this time the year was not 1950, and he was not a young man — it was modern Seoul's skyline that traced a black silhouette against a fiery sky. The cries of the survivors and the dying hit him with terrific force just as he was almost knocked into the river. Behind the crush of people missiles fell from the sky like shooting stars. They struck their targets with flaming bursts of concrete and steel and glass. The shock waves hit the side of his head like blows from an angry fist. He rode the bucking steel girder as if it were a wild beast. A moment after his section of the bridge fell beneath the water, he felt an even greater wrenching of the steel beneath him, and he sensed the world slipping away as the black water swallowed him up.

Next he found himself far to the north, near the opening of a cave. A column of soldiers, all battle-ready with field packs and rifles, marched four abreast out of the opening and, once they caught sight of him started to give chase. "*Ili wa*," they called in familiar, almost friendly tones. "Come here!" Their voices were gentle but as quickly as snakes they lunged forward with their bayonets trained on his back. Again he lost consciousness, running.

Next he found himself standing in Mokpo, in the plaza before the train station. Students milled about, chattering excitedly about the shelling that came pounding at them from over the horizon. Clearly they had never experienced an invasion before. Their manner was hopeful, almost happy. "Liberation!" they called. "They mean us no harm!" He knew otherwise, but could say nothing: some force clamped down upon him and kept him from moving his lips and his arms.

"We're all brothers," said a familiar voice. "If we greet them with open hearts, they'll see that we want to live with them in peace." It was Han Mi Jin — guilty, as always, of willful stupidity. He almost pitied her for her naiveté. But soon she, like him and all the others, was snuffed out.

Kim woke up. He sat at the edge of the bed and lit a cigarette. Its tip traced trembling red arcs in the darkness.

## *Eleven*

Mr. Han, Mi Jin's father, greeted the news of North Korea's overtures with a pang of consternation. He went out to his accustomed spot by the sea's edge to think. His wife would be upset that he had retreated once again into his own thoughts, but at that moment he did not care. A flood of memories had struck him with the latest news of North Korea, and he needed to go to some quiet place to wait for them to pass.

He did not care whether the two halves of his country ever got back together again, and he surprised even himself at hoping it would not happen in his lifetime.

"Don't you want to see your first wife and your children after all these years?" a farmer in his village had asked him when the specter of reunification had loomed once before. This man had lived in Chindo all his life. Mr. Han was one of the very few from the North who had wound up this far south since the war; his neighbors did not understand him.

Mr. Han shrugged. "*Yah!* Can you imagine what it'd be like to support two families? I'd be torn every which way by endless demands for money. Besides, she's probably remarried, like me. Don't be stupid."

"But still, to see your sons. That would be worth it —"

"Get away from me! You don't know what you're talking about." Mr. Han, shaking his head in anger, turned on his heel and walked away. Every time he thought of his first family the wounds opened afresh; every mention of sons reminded him of the three he had fathered — two lost and one dead. All he had left was one daughter with whom his family name would end.

## *Twelve*

"This is good news!" Mi Jin said, crowded in a booth at Trouble House with her friend Chong Il Man and a few others. They dressed warmly but casually in jeans and sweaters, and carried no books with them, as they were still on winter holiday. The *tabang* was nearly empty, so the few people who were there spoke freely.

"The prospect of reunification is good news only if our government doesn't screw it up," Il Man remarked. "Otherwise, it's an exercise in futility, just like all the other times we've had our hopes up."

"The United States has to keeps its nose out of it," one of the others said. "They're doing just as much as Pak and Chon and all their cronies to keep the country divided."

" ... But don't forget the Soviet Union and China," said Il Man. "They're just as much to blame and have at least as much to gain. Am I right, Mi Jin?"

Mi Jin blushed, disturbed that Il Man was defending the United States and, by extension, Paul, while she was not.

"Yes."

The talk continued, a mixture of youthful faith in the ultimate victory of peace and of acid resentment toward the immutable political forces that were sure to stand in its way. The conversation eventually lapsed. Mi Jin noticed that the woman seated beside her was looking at her hands, which were folded on the table.

"Is that a ring?"

"Um, yes." Mi Jin shoved her hands into her lap.

"Let me see! Come on, Elder Sister, come on." They wrenched her hands into the open. She had turned the small diamond around on her finger so it rested in her palm, but the woman pried her hand open and turned it roughly outward.

"Ow! You're hurting me!"

"Elder Sister. It's an engagement ring." Her companions fell silent.

"Who's the lucky man?" Il Man asked.

"Oh ... a fellow in Chindo. He owns a small business."

Il Man nodded slowly. His earlier high spirits had fallen flat. Among his friends in the democracy movement, especially the women, marriage usually meant a permanent retreat into the world of tradition. Mi Jin would not be with them much longer. He also wondered about her American friend, whom she had once appeared to love. He sighed and turned the conversation to other matters.

## Thirteen

"Paul, I'd like you to meet Mr. Choi, my co-worker, and the district workers in my department."

Claire Aguilar lived and worked in Yangdok, a sleepy town in North Kyongsang Province, not far from the East Sea. Paul was on his first volunteer site-visit, tasked by Mrs. Kang with observing all aspects of Claire's situation.

Paul bowed and shook hands with each person in turn and fell into the customary pattern of polite chatter. He spent the rest of the day shadowing Claire in her duties, by all appearances a trainee on his first visit to a health center.

That evening, Paul joined the *kwajang* and other managers at one of the local beer halls. It was a cramped, dimly-lit place that stank of cigarette smoke and the sour breath of its customers, accumulated over many years.

"Your friend —" Mr. Jong, Claire's supervisor, motioned off-handedly at her "— told me you used to work in Mokpo, Chollado. I traveled a lot through that area a long time ago. It's a rotten place. The people are smart but crafty. They'll cheat you anytime, just like a Jew will."

Claire shot Paul a look.

"Oh ... really?"

Mr. Jong shrugged. "Well, I don't know much about Jews, just what I've been told. But Chollado people are like that, anyhow." He winked a heavy-lidded eye at the serving *agashi* and motioned for more beer.

"Chollado people not so bad they are, I think," Paul said, pretending to speak Korean poorly.

"No wonder he stands up for those people," Mr. Jong grumbled. "He's got a Chollado accent! Can you hear it?" Then, leaning in to Paul and speaking slowly and distinctly, he addressed him with a sly grin: "You speak Korean very well!"

That comment got a good laugh, but the conversation soon turned to other things. The five men turned to gossip among themselves about people they knew. The health center's receptionist gave the beer hall *agashi* a handful of cash, told her to stop serving when it was used up, and left. Paul and Claire were left to themselves.

"How's life here?" Paul asked quietly. "Are you getting along okay?"

"About as well as can be expected, which is not so hot," she sighed. "They're typical Korean males. Whenever I walk into a room, they stare at me and don't stop until I leave. They mostly look at my ... my front. Not that I'm any bigger than the other women — I'm not."

"Maybe they're a little disappointed," Paul said. "They expect an American woman to be busty."

"And they watch to see if I'll suddenly pop up to a bigger size," she laughed. "Yeah, right."

"Does it interfere with your work?"

"Yeah, it does. Women have a terrible time building credibility in this culture; these guys make it worse by looking at me like some kind of American sex object. I've heard little rumors — from the other women — that they think I sleep around. Well, let me tell you something: I wouldn't touch one of these guys or anybody else around here. No way."

"Do you want me to mention this problem in my report?"

"Is Mrs. Kang going to see it?"

"Yes," Paul said. "She's supervising this part of my job."

"In that case ... no, don't bother. She won't do anything. I'll just be accused of complaining, or of being 'culturally insensitive.'"

"Oh, but that's part of the initiation. If Mrs. Kang hasn't accused you of that crime, you haven't become a true volunteer."

Claire laughed, then heaved a deep sigh. "Well, okay. Something's got to be done."

"Mr. Pak." It was Claire's boss again, grown feisty with beer, addressing Paul again. "Let me tell you something else about Chollado people. They're shifty, and they steal from strangers just as if it were a natural thing to do, like farting or screwing ladies."

Paul said nothing.

"You know what? If my son — he's seventeen now — wanted to marry a Chollado woman, I would cut him off." His sweeping gesture almost tipped him over onto the floor. "No college, no support, nothing. If he wants to live with a pig, he has to get down in the muck with her. I won't go with him." His head fell heavily on the table, and with apologetic glances, the others tried to revive him.

"Let's go," Paul said to Claire. "I've seen enough."

## Fourteen

Paul's next site visit, which happened immediately after his visit to Claire's site, took him to the town of Sachon, a dreary settlement that fit the mold of nearly every county seat in the isolated countryside of Korea: low mountains and terraced rice fields surrounded its compact downtown area, which consisted of little more than a few official buildings, storefronts, and a couple of schools. The requisite bank, *tabang*s, and humble restaurants were clustered together within a tiny network of paved streets. The health center was a dark annex of the county office.

Kevin Palmer, a fussy, perpetually vexed volunteer, worked there in the county's leprosy program. Paul had arranged to meet him at the health center, but Kevin spent most of his time in a small leprosy settlement several miles outside of town.

"So you're Mrs. Kang's spy now, eh?" Kevin said with forced brightness.

"What? No way! You know I can't stand that woman. I was forced into this."

Kevin looked at his watch, then glanced around the room he shared with a half-dozen health workers, who were all chatting idly around a kerosene heater.

"It's eleven-thirty. Too early for *soju*. Let's get a beer."

They strolled along the town's main road to a beer hall.

"Tell me what you've been up to lately," Paul said.

"Working like hell. Working very hard. Busy, busy, busy. Treating every leprosy patient with love and respect, spreading good will among the villagers ..."

"C'mon, Kev. Stop it. I'm reporting on site conditions, not on volunteers. I'm not going to judge my friends."

Kevin calmed down a little. "In here," he said.

The beer hall was cramped and seemed to be crusted with grime and mildew. It relied on an outdated bikini calendar for decoration. The page from September of 1977 showed a fresh-faced *agashi* in an orange bikini cavorting in the sand before a mass of blue surf. It was the only hint of brightness in the entire room. Two women in frayed tight dresses waited on a handful of customers, most of them farmers sitting out the cold season until the spring planting season arrived.

Kevin ordered two beers and took a long pull from his when it arrived. Paul sipped his and put it down.

"This town is nowhere," Kevin said, lighting a cigarette. "It's not close to anything. Getting to Seoul takes hours. I really envy you. You're in Suwon now, right?"

Paul nodded.

"Less than an hour to Seoul. Must be nice."

"Yes and no," Paul said. "Easier for Mrs. Kang to get her hooks into me."

Kevin wagged his foot while he sat, and was finished with his beer before Paul had taken another mouthful. He fidgeted until Paul took another few sips. "Ready to go? We have to catch a bus to a spot near the leprosy village, then we'll have to walk a while. I hope you're wearing warm shoes."

As their bus made its way deep into the countryside, no aspect of Korean life around them passed without comment from Kevin. He talked and fretted constantly. His companionship wore Paul out long before they reached their destination.

"My language isn't that great," he said. "I admit it. I just haven't kept it up very well. I know enough to get around, to take care of the bare necessities. My health center just needs a *miguk salam*, an American, to go out to the village and dress lesions. Hardly any local Koreans would look at a *mundungi*, a leper, much less touch one.

"So the people here think I'm strange. They'd think it no matter what I do, so I figure 'Why bother?' Why should I have to do contortions, jump through hoops, you know, to live up to a Korean ideal that they don't expect from me anyway?"

"I can't think of a reason," Paul shrugged.

"So I've decided to live up to their expectations. Or down to them. Whatever." Kevin brushed a strand of sandy brown hair from his forehead and patted it carefully into place. In the bumping bus, it soon came dislodged and he had to put it back again. This happened over and over during the long ride, and he fixed it every time without thinking. "Now, don't get me wrong. I try to do a good job. Mrs. Kang would have no complaints about the leprosy control work I'm doing here. I just choose to pursue my own interests in my spare time. And those interests don't include hanging out at *tabang*s and beer halls with a bunch of guys who'll get drunk and stagger home puking in the street. Do you know how many puddles of vomit I counted between my boarding house and the health center this morning? Seven! That's a new record.

"Gardening. That's what I do in my spare time. I've got plants everywhere. I think my *ajumoni* doesn't like me."

"Oh?"

"Yeah. We've been having running battles about things lately. I live there with a bunch of *haksaengs*, students, you know. They come from families out in the countryside, and they go to the big high school in town. Country boys coming to the big city, right? Man, I tell you: you think *haksaengs* are bad when they roam in packs on the streets? Just try living with them. Noisy, smart-assed kids. I don't like to eat with them. I've been having some digestive problems, and I have to eat in peace and quiet, or else I get really bad heartburn that lasts all night. It was getting so bad with those *haksaengs* that I had to ask the *ajumoni* to serve me breakfast and dinner in my room. I even offered to pay her a little extra. She's squawking about it. She's doing it, but she's not happy because she has to do extra work. Instead of one large dinner table to put food on, she has to prepare two, a big one for them and a little one for me. That means extra little plates for the side dishes, and more work cleaning up. I guess I can't blame her. But still, she's getting plenty of money from me from the rent I pay, which is exorbitant. Maybe she thinks I'm being an ugly American."

"I don't know."

"I think she does think that. But what can I do? We get off here."

The announcement came so suddenly that Paul barely had time to gather his knapsack before Kevin got up and bounded out the door. They stood at a small roadside bus stop. Across the road was a picturesque dirt path, barely wide enough for a car, lined on both sides by leafless trees. All around the path lay frozen rice fields, dotted with neat rows of stubble from the last crop. The fields of brown, surrounded by low dikes, stretched one after another to rows of terraces on the distant mountains. They started off down the path.

The air was cold, but the sun shone warmly around them. There was almost no snow on the ground. "We're lucky it's such a beautiful day," Paul observed.

"It never gets terribly cold here, comparatively speaking. The mountains protect us from the strong winds. It's a good thing, too, because there's no way I'd walk all this distance in the winter if we were farther up north. I don't do cold."

The clinic just inside the settlement was a one-room cinder-block building, primitive in style but well maintained. People were lined up at the door, waiting to be called in one by one. Three frosted windows and whitewashed walls gave the interior a surprisingly light and airy appearance. It smelled strongly of antiseptic.

"Good. Someone's already lit the heater. You want some barley tea?"

Kevin put the kettle on and, without removing his jacket, started seeing patients.

"I don't know how much they taught you about leprosy in your training," Kevin said. "The worst thing about it in the long run is the loss of feeling in the extremities. We have feeling in our feet and hands, and that keeps us from banging them up, burning them, scraping them, whatever. But these people —" he motioned to the middle-aged woman who took the chair in front of him "— don't have that. Their lives consist of one contusion after another. How do you feel about pain?"

The question took Paul off guard. "I don't handle it well, I'm afraid," he said sheepishly. "I tend to avoid it."

"Well, pain is these people's long lost friend, the last thing they needed to lose. Pain prevents self-destruction. Think about it."

The woman before them might once have been pretty; yet no trace of her former beauty, aside from a head of lustrous hair, was visible through the ravages of her disease. She had all the typical deformities: the bridge of her nose had fallen, the result of the breakdown of cartilage — and her eyes were red with conjunctivitis. Most disturbing to Paul was the sight of her hands: her fingers had been worn down to smooth stumps barely half their normal length, and they were covered with tough, inflexible skin. A gaping sore formed a crusted patch on the back of her hand.

"You don't have to watch this if you don't want to."

"I'm okay," Paul gulped.

"Good. Now, we have to be careful here about gangrene. It happens sometimes if these wounds aren't treated soon enough. Phew! What a smell. Have you ever seen a case of gangrene? More to the point, have you ever smelled one? You can spot it with your nose a mile away. The only thing to do is to amputate the limb. Which in the case of these people is not a big loss."

They finished at the clinic around mid-afternoon and returned to town for a dinner out with the health center administrators. Kevin and Paul were exhausted, and their hosts cared for little more than drinking beer. The Americans left early.

## Fifteen

"I just hate to wait," said Mi Jin's mother during her daughter's next visit to Chindo. "There are so many months to your wedding. It's such a long time. To get it all signed and sealed — and then you can get started on your future. I'm sure your fiancé is eager, too."

Mi Jin looked out the living room's small window at the patches of snow that covered the ground in the courtyard. Beyond the gate, the low mountains of Chindo glowed in the orange light of the late-afternoon sun.

"We talked about this, Omma. I need to finish one more term at school, to save money. You don't want us to start with almost no savings, do you?"

"I suppose not," she grunted.

Mi Jin put on her overcoat.

"*Yah!* Where are you going?"

"Just into town, Omma. I need the walk, and it's such a beautiful afternoon. I'll be back by sunset. I promise."

The cold air cleared her head immediately. She strode through the gate with a light step. Spring came early to the southernmost regions of Korea. She imagined a whiff of spring's freshness in the breeze blowing over the inland fields where wet patches of black earth shimmered like oil in the gloom.

Mi Jin had made her decision. She would not marry Kim Hyong Chol, no matter what her parents desired. For the moment it was just an intention, not a plan. She had no idea how she would pull it off, nor even how she would break the news to her parents. All she knew was that come June she would not be Hyong Chol's bride. She did not know what she would be, but she had time to come up with something.

The telephone exchange in the town of Chindo was a small building added as an apparent afterthought to the town hall; the glow from a single kerosene stove in the middle of the room heated it more than adequately. She filled out a form at the desk and, since telephone connections from the island were not instantaneous, waited for a line to clear.

"Miss? Over there." The attendant pointed to a booth by the wall.

After working through a number of people at the Suwon City Health Center, from the receptionist to the tuberculosis control chief, a familiar voice finally came on the line.

"*Yoboseyo?*" Hello?

"Pak Jong Shik! Do you remember my voice?"

"Mi Jin—what a wonderful surprise! How are you?"

"I am well. How are you?"

Paul told her about his new health center and the trip he took to visit Claire and Kevin. "I just got back yesterday. The bus ride was great; the scenery along the way was so beautiful."

"You seem very busy and happy in your new home."

Paul sighed. "Busy, yes, and happy in some ways. But I miss you."

"I miss you, too, Jong Shik."

"You know, I'm going to Chollado next week," Paul said. "Would you like to meet over the weekend? In Kwangju."

Mi Jin swallowed hard. Despite her decision, she was still engaged, and even making this clandestine telephone call to a male friend, much less meeting him for a weekend, was a shameful act. I've already decided not to get married, she finally said to herself; if I've made up my mind, I may as well act like it.

"Yes. Let us do that. Meet me at the express bus terminal in Kwangju on Saturday morning, around ten o'clock." Then she hung up.

## Sixteen

Paul took the express bus from Suwon to Kwangju a few days later. He passed through broad plains of dormant rice fields that were just beginning to shake off the latest dusting of snow in preparation for the next one, which was predicted for the next day. An afternoon of sunshine the day before had melted the snow in the branches of the evergreens into lumps of slush that fell to the wet ground with heavy splashes.

Mi Jin met him on the bus station platform, bundled up in her overcoat and stamping her feet to keep them warm in stylish shoes that were not made to be worn outdoors in winter. She did not touch him, but her smile reached out and embraced him.

"*Annyong haseo?*" Paul greeted her. Are you at peace?

"Yes. And you?"

They left the bus station and joined the teeming streets. Paul remarked, in Korean, on the balminess of the weather here compared to that near Seoul. "My coat's a little heavy. Do we have a place to stay?"

"I got you a room next to mine at an inn," she said. Paul had learned his lessons well; conversing with him in Korean was now as easy as talking with an average Korean student. "It is near the university, so we must take a taxi to get there from here."

Kwangju was as busy a city as Paul had ever seen, much like Mokpo but on a grander scale. Where Mokpo had no streets wider than four lanes, Kwangju had them with six and eight, and all of them were crowded with careening taxicabs and buses. Their cab driver, a pock-faced man in his forties wearing dirty white gloves, shouted florid abuse at the other drivers who tried to usurp his spot on the street. Paul and Mi Jin exchanged amused, anxious glances: Kwangju drivers were of a special breed, more excitable and daring than most.

They skirted the edges of Chonnam University, separated from the rest of the city by a low stone wall.

"It's pretty quiet here," Paul remarked.

"Everyone's away on winter break."

After taking their rooms, Mi Jin led Paul through a maze of alleyways to Trouble House. He cast an appreciative glance at the plaster breasts on the

197

*bas relief* of Botticelli's *Birth of Venus*, but balked at going further. "I don't really like this place," he said. "People are looking at me like I'm a CIA agent, and last time I got into an argument with your friends. Can we go someplace else?"

"Don't worry. My friends know more about you now. They know I trust you, and that's good enough for them. Look, there's Chong Il Man."

Il Man sat idly smoking a cigarette at a table by himself, watching a news program on a television mounted on the wall. The sound was turned up so loud that Paul could barely hear his greeting.

"Mr. Harkin. No ... Mr. Pak. Yes, we'll keep using your Korean name. How are you?"

"I am well, thank you. And you?"

Il Man waved at the television screen, which showed file footage of menacingly well-conditioned soldiers running across the stubble of a frozen rice field as part of a military exercise. "I'm scared shitless," he laughed, in English. He switched back to Korean. "They've been showing a lot of news stories lately about the might of the military. Half of the time they're telling us we're safe if the North gets aggressive — thank heaven for a strong military, *neh?* The rest of the time they're trying to scare us into submission. Who wants to tangle with these guys?"

"The government wouldn't use combat troops to handle demonstrations, would they?" Paul asked.

"Anything is possible. Riot police are soldiers, in effect. If General Chon gets scared enough, he will not hesitate to make war on his fellow Koreans."

Paul felt he was overstating the case, but said nothing.

"What are you two kids doing in Kwangju?" Il Man asked. He glanced quickly at Mi Jin's hand; she had removed her ring. "Is this a romantic getaway? You'd have more fun along the coast somewhere."

Mi Jin colored deeply and tried to laugh to hide her embarrassment, but only made an odd croaking sound. She wanted to slap him.

"I'm going to show Mr. Pak the university, and where we had the *demo* last fall. I told him all about it. He's very interested."

"Tell me, Mr. Pak, do you write letters home?" The abruptness of the question surprised him.

"Why, yes."

"Are they opened, or censored by your government?"

"Of course not."

"Does our government open your outgoing mail?"

"My parents and friends have never noticed anything like that."

"That's good," Il Man said, and he rose to walk with them to the door. "That's very good. It's a good thing to communicate with the folks back home."

When they got close to the university's main gate, Paul asked, "What was that all about?"

"Things might get very bad starting in the spring. There is talk about even bigger *demo*s than we had last year. General Chon will be very, very hard on us."

Paul understood. "The press is controlled by the government, so news of the *demo*s will be full of lies. You need me to report to people back in the States, to tell the truth about what's happening. Is that right?"

Mi Jin nodded.

A grin spread slowly across his face. "You know, I've always fancied myself a foreign correspondent."

"Thank you," she said, squeezing his arm tight.

Paul fell to his task with an energy that surprised Mi Jin. That evening, in Paul's room at the inn, he listed all his friends who had majored in journalism and who therefore would have contacts in the profession, and of the human rights organizations he knew of on the Purdue University campus.

"I think there's even a Korean students' organization," he told Mi Jin. "I'll send this list to my mother and ask her to get addresses for me. If she works on it right away, I'll have the information within a couple of weeks. In the meantime, I'll draft a few letters introducing myself and giving some background on the politics and culture here. I have to establish my credentials early."

He and Mi Jin worked on their project until nearly midnight.

Mi Jin took him the next day to the area where, last October, she had taken part in a demonstration. Bundled up against the cold and wind, they walked from the quad inside the university's walls to the gate, and then to the large intersection where the police on that violent day had descended on the students like phalanxes of a Roman army. Today the area slept in peace under a low gray sky. The wind blew clouds of new-fallen snow into little tornadoes that bumped into houses and walls and quickly died.

"This place looks so empty," Paul said.

"You should see it when classes are in session. People are everywhere. There is a feeling of life like you'll never see anywhere else. A feeling of liveliness, and hope, and intelligence, and anger."

They walked on.

Paul remarked that she spoke as though anger were as healthy a quality as hope. "I've been taught since childhood that anger is a negative, destructive emotion, one to be avoided or covered up," Paul said.

"How wrong that is! Anger can be a force for good. It's the motivating force behind people who seek justice. Sheep never get angry; they meekly let themselves be herded wherever their master wants them to go, even to the slaughterhouse. Most Korean people are like sheep. They are being herded down the road to disaster. But some of us — the angry ones — will not be led to oblivion. Freedom has never been achieved — from the beginning of the world to the present — by people who did not resent their dictators."

The lateness of the afternoon and an approaching snowstorm turned the sky into ever deeper shades of gray. Paul listened while she talked, thinking her words to be the only glimmer of light in the gathering dusk.

# CHAPTER SEVEN

The city of Chunchon, high in the mountains northeast of Seoul, was every volunteer's home town. Here they had taken their first faltering steps in Korea — for Paul, nearly a year before — as Peace Corps trainees. Now, late in the winter, before the snow started its slow dissolution into spring, they all gathered there again for a week of additional training. Mr. Atwood and Mrs. Kang saw it that way; the volunteers, gathering in Chunchon from every corner of the country, saw it only as a chance to kick back and party with their own kind.

Paul had explored Chunchon thoroughly during his first stay there, and knew it well. His spirits jumped when, after a long ride through a late snowstorm, his bus rounded a bank of hills and looked out upon a panorama of mountains. In the distance, rising from the shores of an artificial lake, Chunchon hugged an oddly steep little hill and fanned out from there in a tree-studded jumble of white buildings. Through a break in the snow, against the gray sky, helicopters hovered like dragonflies over a military base on the city's west side. Paul grinned. Chunchon was, in his view, like a child's face, open and immediately comprehensible.

Peace Corps had reserved an entire floor and two large banquet rooms at the Sejong Hotel, which was set on a wooded bluff halfway up the city's central hill. It was in one of these rooms where the volunteers sat cross-legged, chattering among themselves as the program began.

"All right, everybody, can we all take seats now? Let's get started." Howard Perry, a lanky six-foot-four-inch former volunteer, who was John Atwood's assistant, shouted harshly above the din of a dozen conversations. "Let's get started. We have a lot to cover.

"First of all, welcome to in-service training. All of us on the staff are glad you could drag yourselves away from your sites for the week. We've got a lot planned for you, including some new technical training, some cross-cultural training, and a political update from Mr. Atwood. Plus, we've got Mrs. Kang coming up later in the week for meetings, and Dr. Paek will be here on Thursday to treat whoever and whatever needs treating.

"We're holding in-service training alongside some in-country training for new volunteers. That's right, just a few weeks ago they were sleeping in warm houses with indoor bathrooms, and they could dine at McDonald's whenever they wanted. Now they're here. Take pity on them. These people are new and impressionable. Don't scare them off. We'll have a big dinner with them later in the week, and those of you who volunteered to be hosts for their week-long site visits will take them back with you when you leave. It'll give you a chance to feel superior to somebody for a change. Just bring 'em back in one piece, okay?"

Volunteers and trainees fanned out through Chunchon as the days wore on. The focus of their attention was not the city, nor the training they had come for, but on the rather small American Army helicopter base, Camp Page, located on the edge of town. John Atwood had arranged to allow them access to the base for the week. Within the walls of the base, the volunteers and the soldiers regarded each other with mild disparagement: the soldiers saw the volunteers as unreliable and possibly unpatriotic free spirits, yet they secretly envied the volunteers' freedom to come and go as they pleased. The volunteers deplored the soldiers' unwillingness to venture off base except for sex, while at the same time they envied their easy access to American fast food and toiletries.

Even within the Peace Corps ranks, a gulf, though only a temporary one, developed between the volunteers and the trainees. The trainees stood out because of their deficiencies: they dressed either too neatly or too casually, too warmly or not warmly enough for the weather. They wandered about with an enthusiasm that drew snickering from their jaded colleagues. Their laughable mistakes in the Korean language gave the volunteers a pleasant sense of superiority that lasted only until they themselves went home and continued in their old struggles. Paul once helped Rose, a short, grandmotherly trainee from Arizona, negotiate the price of a backpack in the city's open-air market. Instead of asking the shoplady "*Alma-imnikka?*" — How much? — she was asking "*Omma-imnikka?*" — Are you my mommy? "I'll never pick up this language," she muttered after he rescued her from the old shopkeeper's raucous laughter.

"You'll do okay," Paul reassured her. "I had a terrible time at first. Take my advice and get a tutor as soon as you get settled at your work site."

John Atwood came to in-service training late in the week as scheduled, accompanied by Mrs. Kang. They hosted the volunteers and trainees together in the banquet hall at the Sejong Hotel. He mounted the stage with a hand-held microphone and moved freely about like a cross between a military commander addressing his troops and a stand-up comedian working a crowd.

"Good afternoon, people. I'm gonna give you a little update on the political situation in Korea. I suppose you've been waiting quite a while for this talk. Getting the straight scoop from the Korean press is next to impossible these days. Believe me, I understand how hard it is for you, accustomed as we all are to getting uncensored news — *snap!* — just like that. I have a feeling, though, that President Carter wouldn't mind having a little Korean-style press censorship when it comes to his brother Billy."

There were equal measures of groans and polite laughter.

"Now, I've been in contact with the political analysts at the US Embassy, because it's my job to stay current on how safe this country is for you. I would not hesitate to send you all home, or to alternative countries, if I had the least suspicion that you were in any danger. I don't see anything of the sort, and you can be confident that you are all perfectly, er - reasonably — safe.

"On the other hand, the threat from the North is as strong as ever. So let me give each and every one of you an assignment when you get back to your sites. I want you to come up with your own evacuation plan. If something does happen — and this is a big *if* — you will need to take the fastest route to the nearest American military base. Remember: you might not find reliable transport on buses or trains or taxicabs. Be prepared to walk there, even if it's a long distance. And always keep your passport handy. It'll be checked. ... Hey, why is it so quiet here all of a sudden?" Atwood gave one of his engaging smiles, and the room came back to life, slightly. "C'mon, people. I'm telling you things you already know. Just be smart."

Sarah Conlon leaned over to Paul. "Walk to a base? We've never heard that before. Is something up?"

Mark Follett overheard her and nodded.

"One last thing," Atwood continued. "College students are on vacation now, but they'll be going back to school in a few weeks. You can bet there'll be demonstrations. Remember this: it is Peace Corps policy not to get involved in any kind of political activity in the host nation. That means *demos*, rallies, debates, or even betting on the winner of a riot."

"Can we have political discussions with our Korean friends?" someone asked.

"Thank you. Good question. You can talk politics with your friends, but you have to make sure they know that your opinions are yours alone, and not those of the United States Government. Say, maybe you could hire an announcer to say, 'The opinions expressed by this very vocal volunteer do not necessarily reflect those of the United States Government.' How about that idea? Cripes, you're a tough crowd. Any more questions?"

"What happened to the guy who accidentally shot President Pak?" called someone from the back of the room.

Appreciative laughter erupted at the audacity of the remark, and Mrs. Kang, sitting primly near the stage, glared into the crowd. "Yeah, heh heh. That's a good one. Kim Jae Kyu. He was arrested shortly after the incident. His trial is coming soon. You can bet your bottom dollar that the students are gonna take to the streets while that's going on; they didn't much like Pak, and Kim has suddenly become something of a hero to them. Be prudent. The United States' position on the matter is strictly neutral. Okay? Everything at your sites going well? Yes? Good. If you have problems, Mrs. Kang is here. Thanks, people."

## Two

"I want to talk to you, Paul."

Mrs. Kang tapped him on the shoulder during a class and motioned him to follow her to the staff's temporary office.

"I have read your reports on the visits to the sites of Claire and Kevin. Do you expect me to accept them?"

Paul's face began to flush. "Well, I ..."

"When I ... Mr. Atwood gave this job to you, I told you that you were supposed to be balanced in your appraisal of the conditions at these sites. These were both places where the hosts had expressed dissatisfaction with the volunteers."

"You hadn't told me that."

Mrs. Kang dismissed Paul's statement with a wave of her hand. "Why do you think we would send you to a site if not to investigate a problem? You have to think about it. And then you come back to me with a report that is very critical of the hosts. Not only is it culturally insensitive to the people who worked very hard to accommodate the volunteers, it does absolutely no good from an administrative point of view. We cannot turn to the hosts and say, 'You are not doing well.'" She pursed her lips and stared at Paul.

"Claire and Kevin are good people," he stammered. "They're doing the best they can."

"Really. We have known for a long time that Claire is cold and aloof to her co-workers. She has made no effort to be included in the working group. And as you know, that is very important in Korea."

"Her co-workers are all men. They treat her like a sex object."

Mrs. Kang's face puckered into a look of confusion, as if she were unfamiliar with the term.

"They're always commenting on her body," Paul explained, "and invit-ing her to places where the only women around are bargirls and prostitutes. It's in my report."

"Are you saying they are the ones being insensitive?"

"Um ... it's in the report."

"And Kevin. He rarely ever reports for work at the health center.

"That's because he's working all day at the clinic in the leprosy village. It's a long bus ride from the health center. He can get more done if he goes straight from his house. He works hard. I saw him."

"How do you know he works hard every day? Maybe he worked hard just on the day you met him."

"I trust him."

Mrs. Kang sneered and fell into another of her purposeful silences.

"What am I going to do with you?" she said at last.

" ... I don't know. Maybe we should go talk with Mr. Atwood —"

"No! You will not go over my head. I'll send you on another site visit soon. I expect your report to be more balanced next time."

*Three*

The training sessions ended the following weekend with the slow exo-dus of volunteers back to their sites. Paul and Sarah caught the train to Seoul with Martin Budzinski, a balding, athletic man in his forties who seemed incapable of speaking clearly, as if his mouth were full of pebbles; every utterance that came from him had to be repeated or translated some-how. Martin was to be Paul's guest for the coming week in Suwon, getting a taste of the work of the health center, going home visiting, and seeing life outside the somewhat idyllic setting of Chunchon.

Once in Seoul, the three of them took the subway to Suwon and, in the dark intersection dominated by the ancient South Gate, they perched on stools in one of the many beer tents on the side of the street. The tent was small, really little more than a pushcart with a charcoal grill in the middle and crates of *soju* and cold beer stacked all around. On a frail skeleton of metal tubing, a tent-like structure of blue and white striped plastic enclosed the seats and held in the heat from the grill. The robust *ajumoni*, heavily bundled against the bitterly cold air, served grilled marinated chicken and beef along with a seemingly endless supply of drink. A jet of flame from a propane canister lit the tent with bright yellow light and cast harsh shadows across the faces of the customers. Sarah's red hair, escaping in a ring around the base of her beret, danced in the flames with her every move while her eyes glowed a fierce, jolly green. Neither Paul nor Martin nor any of the Koreans around them could take their eyes off her.

Paul ordered beers all around and picked up some of the grilled beef. It was cheap meat, stringy and tough, but its seasonings and the cold wind at his back made it delicious.

"You know you're in Korea when ... the grade of meat that goes into cat food tastes pretty good," Paul said.

"Excuse me?" Martin said, puzzled.

Sarah's face brightened. "You know you're in Korea when ... a five-dollar Hershey bar is a bargain."

"It's a game we play," Paul explained. "You know you're in Korea when ... you don't drink anything after eight-thirty at night."

"Why?" Martin asked.

"Well, let me ask you something. The place you're staying at in Chunchon: does it have indoor plumbing?"

"Yeah."

"No kidding? Well, wait till you get to your site. If your *pyonso*, your outhouse, is a hole in the ground with two slats of wood over it to squat down on, you don't want to use it at night if you can avoid it."

"Mark Follett fell in once during our training," Sarah laughed. "You should have heard him scream. He probably woke up all of Chunchon and most of North Korea. And the smell! Whew!"

"You know you're in Korea when ... after the dog disappears, you'd better ask the cook what's for dinner," Paul said.

"What!"

Paul nodded. "Dog meat, Martin, is a delicacy, kind of medicinal in hot weather. When you go to the market and see cages of little puppies, they're not for pets."

"They're dog soup in the making," Sarah interjected.

"I've never had it myself," Paul said. "Hope I never do."

"That's weird, man," Martin shook his head. "But you know, it explains something. When I was in Vietnam my company was stationed real close to a Korean one. We kept hearing rumors that the dogs in the villages were disappearing whenever the Koreans had some spare time. I thought they were just being sadistic. Didn't know they were chowing down."

"Sadistic?" Paul asked.

"Yeah. Christ, they were something else. When they go to war, they go all out. There's no messing with Geneva Conventions or Red Cross rules, or any of that shit. They've got a mean streak a mile wide. Once, they caught a Viet Cong spy and brought him to their camp. They tied him up by the ankles, strung him up head down from a tree, and skinned the poor sucker alive. No kidding. I saw the skin myself the next morning: it was *almost complete*. You think Mark screamed when he fell into some shit — the screams from this guy made even my tough old sergeant shaky. He went to the bushes and puked."

Paul and Sarah swallowed hard.

"Why did you come to Korea then?" Sarah asked.

"It's where the Peace Corps wanted to send me. Those guys in the war were horrible sometimes — we all were. Doesn't mean they're horrible all the time.

"But lemme tell you something," he continued, his voice low. "You two are gonna give me a lot of advice this week, and man, I really appreciate it. But let me give *you* some. Maybe you've heard this already: Never make a Korean angry. I mean real angry. When that happens, he loses his mind. He goes for blood, and man, he finds a way to get it. He forgets that you're a human being. It happens even to guys you think are nice."

The flame from the gas jet sputtered and nearly went out before the tent lady tended to it.

A week later, after Martin had returned to Chunchon to finish training, the warning still weighed heavily on Paul's mind.

## Four

Fortune had smiled on Headmaster Shin. He had been relaxing at his desk at the Chungang Girls' Middle School on a quiet afternoon when a call came from an old schoolmate who had advanced far in the Ministry of Education office in Kwangju. A position had opened up in his department, a Chief of something — the details did not matter to Shin. Would he be interested in taking it? Certainly. Could he move immediately? He and his wife would like nothing better. Can he get a replacement to fill the position of headmaster at his school? Vice-Headmaster Kim Son Kwan had been waiting patiently for a long time.

Vice Headmaster — now Headmaster — Kim settled into his new office a week later. Lush scrolls of Chinese calligraphy, showcasing bits of old wisdom such as "Peace is cherished throughout the four seas" and "Righteousness will ultimately conquer," shared wall space with smaller framed sayings in Korean script: "Counteract treason with fervent love for our nation" and "Let patriotism govern our thoughts, words, and deeds." A framed portrait of President Choi Kyu Ha hung high on the wall behind his leather chair. On his desk a lacquered nameplate spelled out his name and position in iridescent mother-of-pearl letters: Kim Son Kwan, Headmaster.

His first official act, after decorating the paneled office to his liking, was to call Han Mi Jin in for a meeting.

"Congratulations, Headmaster, on your promotion. I am delighted at the news."

"Thank you, Miss Han. Please have a seat." He motioned her to one of the easy chairs at the low table in front of his desk. He sat at its head. A splattering of sleet mixed with hail pounded at the window, threatening to break it, like someone desperately wanting to be let in.

"How is your vacation? Are you enjoying your time off?"

"Yes, Headmaster, very much."

"Good. The reason I called you here is to give you some bad news. I regret to tell you that we cannot retain you any further as a teacher at this school."

Mi Jin gasped.

"May I ... ask why I am being let go?"

Kim had no intention of telling the truth. "Times are hard, Miss Han. As you know, our nation's economy is in a bad state. This translates into lower wages among the families whose children we serve. We are cutting back on our staff to keep the school operating and out of debt. Since you are the most junior of the teachers — and getting married soon, I hear — it was decided to cut down on our English classes."

"Lies, all lies!" Mi Jin screamed into her cupped hands when she reached the street a short while later. She clutched a pink and white shopping bag that held her personal belongings. It swung at her side like a limp flower, the only spot of color in a vast field of gray, as she walked slowly toward the center of town. People peering out from heavy umbrellas could see it for blocks, swaying slowly like a pendulum.

"He is such a grinning cat. His *nunchi* showed how happy he is to be rid of me. The *kae sekki*, the son of a bitch! Oh, God, what shall I do now? How can I tell my parents about this shame? What will my in-laws think?"

The sleet grew in intensity and lashed at her with the ferocity of a madman.

She tried to think of the things she must do: tell her parents, tell her fiancé, tell Paul. The shame of it was almost too much to bear. She must find a new job — or go ahead and marry Kim Hyong Chol, get pregnant, and not worry about working; but she did not want his child any more than she wanted him for a husband. Or she could abandon everything in her present life and live on her own, without attachments, sustained only by working for the democracy movement, like a nun for the country's new secular religion. Such thoughts quickly ended, for she knew that people like that were not her type; she could no more live for a single idea than she could read only one book or gaze at one flower for the rest of her life. In the deepest regions of her heart she craved normality, if not ease, and once the prize of reform was won she intended to be the first to retire from the struggle. Yet fate seemed to be closing off her most desired options one by one, leaving her only a future painted in shades of gray.

Drenched in sleet, she reached the main intersection, whose streets splayed out like the spokes of a wheel, and suddenly could not remember how to get home. When she finally fell down upon her bed, she did not know how she had got there.

## Five

Paul and Joel took the express bus to Kwangju on a raw morning in the middle of March. It was the ugliest part of the year around Seoul: the air pollution of the city turned the snow brown and gray, but no new snow fell to cleanse the air and hide the dirt under a fresh layer of white. Leslie had called from Chindo to say that spring was coming early to the southern provinces. New buds were already appearing on the trees and bushes after a week of rain. This seemed to cheer her.

Mi Jin met them at Trouble House. Her face had the pinched, expressionless look of one suffering from a long illness. When she drank some barley tea, she did not look down the cup, but straight ahead through windows across the room. On one occasion she raised her cup to her lips and discovered too late that it was empty.

"What's wrong, Mi Jin?" Leslie asked.

She reluctantly told them about her firing and the look of unconcealed pleasure in Headmaster Kim's eyes when he told her to leave. "But it doesn't matter. It really doesn't matter," she whispered flatly.

"What does it mean for you, Mi Jin?" Joel asked. "What will you do now?"

"I don't know. Maybe I will move back to my parents' house. Work in their business until I get married. Then go and live with my husband and give him sons."

Joel had not heard about her plans to marry. He shot a glance at Paul, who blushed brightly.

"Let's go for a walk," Paul said.

He went with her up the gradual slope of Mount Mudung, a few miles outside the city. Just as Leslie had said, spring was making early efforts to win out over winter: under an overcast sky, the breeze carried the smell of rich humus around the side of the mountain, from the ground beneath their feet and from the surrounding rice fields, which the farmers were impatient to flood and plow again. Green swellings on the twigs of trees and bushes promised new leaves in the coming weeks. They had to pick their way carefully, as much of the paved trail was coated with mud. Paul noticed that Mi Jin handled almost everything that came within reach: tree branches, rocks jutting out from the hillside, signs along the way that enjoined hikers to keep the natural area beautiful. It was more than just touching, he observed: she was holding on to them, trying to reassure herself of the solidity of the physical world. A bird a short distance away, resting on its migration to the north, let out a call, a sonorous, sharp melody that seemed to shake Mi Jin out of her preoccupations.

"What are you going to do now?" Paul asked.

"I have three choices," she whispered. "I can go home to Chindo and work for my parents until my wedding. I can live in Kwangju or Mokpo and earn some money tutoring until my wedding. Or I can run away ..."

"Yes?"

"But not the kind of running away you are thinking of. Not Romeo and Juliet. If I run away it will be because I cannot live with the shame of losing my job and killing the hopes and plans my parents have for me."

Paul recoiled at the force of her words. When he replied, he did so weakly, not expecting to sway her thinking: "Mi Jin, lots of people lose their jobs. And lots of Korean women choose their own husbands, even if they go against their parents' wishes. You shouldn't think it's a shameful thing ..."

"Then you do not know me as well as you think you do."

They came upon a pavilion on the side of the mountain that looked out over Kwangju. It reminded Paul of the one on Mount Yudal that commanded a view of Mokpo and the sea, and he longed to be there again with her. Mi Jin looked out over the city, but the view held no pleasant associations for her; the flat gray light gave the city the look of a patch of lichen on a rock. Suddenly the sun shone through a thin patch of clouds and threw their faces into sharp relief. Paul saw the creases around her eyes and at the corners of her mouth. After a moment the sun hid again behind the thick blanket of clouds, and the world darkened.

"I cannot see you anymore, Paul. We can never meet again. This time I really mean it. My mind will not be changed."

"No ...."

"It is time for me finally to grow up, to take the responsibilities that my family expect of me. That means marrying Kim Hyong Chol and starting a family. I will always hold you in my heart, and I am so sorry that I have hurt you, but now our time together must end." Even in her extremity, Mi Jin stepped outside herself and saw that she was living out a typically sad Korean love story. She took some small comfort in that.

"What about the democracy movement? Are you giving that up, too?"

"The movement is becoming too radical for me. I don't fit in anymore."

Her swift responses convinced Paul that she had already worked out answers to any protests he might make. His heart sank and he stood there flat-footed, at a loss for words.

"You have my telephone number if you need it," he said.

"Goodbye, Paul." She turned and stumbled blindly down the mountain by a different path.

## Six

Mi Jin went home to Chindo to live with her parents. Her mother soon fathomed the reason for her firing.

"It's because of your politics, isn't it? *Aigo*, I could die! How many times have your father and I warned you about this? When you run around with that pack of good-for-nothing students, you're bound to get into trouble."

The two women were sorting grades of shellfish that Mr. Han had just brought in from the boat. They sat huddled in blankets and rain slickers beside a glowing *yontan*, trying to ward off the raw wind from the sea. Mi Jin's mother was in one of her states, throwing the shellfish so hard that some of them cracked and splintered like little bomb bursts. This only agitated her more.

"See what you've made me do! We can't sell those broken ones. That's lost money right there."

Mi Jin went on with her work quietly, hating every minute of it, trying to ignore her mother's ranting.

"What are we going to do with you? We can only pray that Hyong Chol's family doesn't learn the truth. They already know that you got involved with some *demo*s at the university. I did my best to play it down so they wouldn't get upset about it — you owe me a huge debt for that. But they always had suspicions about you. That was the hardest part of the deal when we went to the matchmaker. Good country people don't trust radicals. Your father and I practically had to lie to make Hyong Chol's family take you. It was a hard sell."

"I'm sorry Hyong Chol is getting damaged merchandise," Mi Jin whispered bitterly.

"*Yah!* Who told you to talk? *Aigo!* It's times like these I miss your brother. He was such a good boy, so respectful and strong. And so obedient." She wiped her eyes with the back of her grimy hand, leaving a swatch of mud on her cheek.

Mi Jin closed her mouth and eyes tight. A fresh wave of misery washed over her.

"The day he died is the day my life ended," her mother whimpered. Then, in a strained whisper that she hoped her daughter would not hear, she added, "If one of my children had to be taken, I wish it had been this one."

Mi Jin did hear, but said nothing. She deposited her anger and pain in her internal bank and promised herself that her parents would someday draw upon it with interest.

## Seven

Paul had looked ahead with little gladness to his site visit at Yonchon, a small county seat near the Demilitarized Zone. He steeled himself against the expected strictures of security along the way, and the slow, oppressive reinforcement of the paranoia that seemed to lay at the heart of Korean life.

The road to Yonchon flew straight north from Seoul along one of the valley corridors that had channeled North Korean troops southward at the start of the Korean War. Paul gazed at the beauty of the coming spring: the evergreens looked old and worn out compared to the viridescence of budding trees on the mountainsides. The mountains seemed noticeably rockier than the wooded hillsides of Chollado far to the south: whole mountainsides were laid bare of trees. Was the geology of the terrain so different between the provinces, he wondered. Then the answer dawned on him. This region had seen the heaviest fighting of the war. The mountains had been blown apart to the bare rock and had not, even after more than twenty-five years, recovered their mantle of soil.

The road and the valley continued north to a suburb of Seoul called Uijongbu. Innumerable war monuments gleamed from the hillsides above the town.

The bus stopped at a guard station, one of many on the trip northward. Two soldiers, neatly uniformed in silver helmets, shoulder braids, and white gloves, boarded. They both carried carbines. The first soldier stopped beside the driver, saluted the passengers in the abbreviated way reserved for civilians, and excused himself for interrupting their journey. He walked down the aisle, looking hard at every passenger, but paying close attention to young men and women of Paul's age. At a few places he asked to see papers. He approached Paul's seat, near the middle of the bus, and looked hard at him. Paul nonchalantly glanced out the window, wishing he would move on.

"May I see ID, please?" he asked with a heavy accent.

Paul handed over his Peace Corps identification card, helpfully printed in both English and Korean. The guard looked it over and gave it back.

"Do you have passport, please?"

Paul shrugged apologetically and said, in English, "Gosh, I'm sorry. I left it at the US Embassy. I don't have it with me." In truth, his passport lay safely in the inside pocket of his backpack. He had remembered the advice given all the volunteers by their trainers long ago: "Never give up your passport. Furthermore, never speak Korean to an official unless you know and trust him."

The guard hesitated, then moved on.

A moment later, a small commotion erupted near the back of the bus. The guard asked to see the papers of a young man and, after examining them, nudged him on the shoulder as a signal to leave the bus with him. The man tried weakly to argue, saying that he was only going to visit his grandparents in Dongduchon, just up the road. The guard grabbed him under the arm and unceremoniously pulled him out of his seat. The other passengers, grown relaxed after a few minutes of the guards' presence in their midst, became tense. They were quiet for several minutes after the guard saluted, apologized for the inconvenience, and left the bus with his detainee in tow.

Jack Singer welcomed Paul at the front door of the health center in Yonchon. The building looked brand new: it practically gleamed in the midday sun.

"Yeah, the government takes pretty good care of the people around here," Jack said. "People get a bonus for living this far north, sort of like combat pay."

"Aren't they nervous, living up here?"

"I can tell you, I am. But they're pretty used to it. The Demilitarized Zone is only ten miles away from here, but some of the districts I visit with the health workers are right up against the line. There are times I can't get in there because they've sealed it off, usually because they're chasing some North Korean guy through the hills. Maybe you'll see some of that when we go up there today.

"Why did you come here?" Jack went on. "I hear Mrs. Kang is gathering incriminating information on us volunteers. Is that true? Am I in trouble?"

Paul shook his head and promised himself to quit this job as soon as he returned to Seoul. "No, you're not in trouble. I'm visiting as many volunteers as possible over the next several months, just to see how things are going in the field. Everybody does their best, that's the way I see it."

Jack smiled, only slightly more at ease. "So you're not a spy for Mrs. Kang?"

"Shit, how many times have I been accused of that?" Paul said. "No. I feel the same way about her that you do. I'm just trying to help out, that's all."

Jack did not seem completely satisfied. For the rest of the day his manner was reserved, even faintly suspicious. This threw Paul into a black funk that got worse with time, for he had been looking forward to enjoying Jack's good humor. By the time the pair reached the district office near the Demilitarized Zone, talked with the workers there, and had dinner at the inn at which they would spend the night, they had barely spoken except for Paul's pallid observations about the food and the excitement of living so close to North Korea.

"Yeah, it may seem exciting, but it's not," Jack said between slurps of dumpling soup. "Everybody's in a vise up here. Every move is controlled, everybody is suspect. The old timers, the ones who've lived here the longest, are okay, but everybody else gets checked out for security pretty regularly. The government doesn't want sympathizers so close to the border. They don't want any turncoats or safe-houses for infiltrators."

"Do many North Koreans come through here?"

Jack shrugged. "Who knows? Nobody would tell me if they did. Probably not as many as the government want us to believe."

Alongside the district workers, they made their rounds among the health center's small field offices. Paul's awareness of his surroundings was heightened in the almost idyllic fields and forested hills. Despite Jack's assurances, he could not help wondering if the government was right, that the lush greenery hid dangerous men, like rattlesnakes coiled in the spaces of a rockpile. Jack caught him peering nervously at a stand of trees and laughed in recognition of his own first days in the area.

"What's on the other side of the border?" Paul asked as they trekked on foot along a raised dike through muddy rice fields.

"Are you ever gonna get off it, man?"

"No, really. You have to understand. I've never been this close to a war zone before."

"The south edge of the Demilitarized Zone is about a mile that way." Jack pointed to the north-west. "It's marked by yellow flags, and you get shot if you're caught screwing around in there. "A little more than a mile further on is the actual border between the two Koreas. Another mile or so beyond that is the edge of North Korea's side of the Demilitarized Zone. All along the border they have hundreds of thousands of soldiers, tanks, planes, trains, automobiles, push-carts, and all kinds of other shit, including land mines. Watch your step. As the crow flies, we're standing a couple miles from a bunch of guys who'd just love to kill us."

"Wow."

"And here's something more. If they decide to invade, they'll come through here, in this nice, wide valley just like they did in 1950. We'd be dead. They could do it ... NOW."

Paul flinched and almost lost his footing on the dike.

"Are you satisfied? Take that little morsel of excitement back to Mrs. Kang. While she and her high-powered hubby are hunkering down in a deluxe bunker or flying out of town, I'll be here with my poor dead ass hanging from a tree."

When Paul and Jack retired to their inn that night, the latter told him with a malevolent grin: "Don't worry about North Koreans coming through here. Most infiltrators take the sea route and come up the beaches on the west coast. The ones that come this way, over land, are pretty well disguised as ordinary people. You'd never know they're killers. Sleep well." With a nasty laugh he went to his own room.

Paul slept fitfully. In near total darkness, with hardly a breath of sound to be heard, every rustle of leaves or scurrying of a mouse became a matter of significance. In the times that he managed a drowsy state of half-sleep, his dreams filled with images of Mi Jin. He wanted her there desperately, sharing his bed, holding onto him tightly and protecting him from cold and solitude. When he came back to consciousness, he thought about her: Can she or her kind actually be in league with killers in the north? Does she actually know any infiltrators? How could that be?

Then he heard a gunshot far in the distance. It sounded like one, in any event, and it echoed shortly in the mountains. A minute later, he heard another, and then there was silence.

He closed his eyes, but remained awake until a red dawn lightened his window. He did not move even to run to the bathroom.

## Eight

Sarah Conlon had left Korea for good two weeks ago: her husband had gotten into medical school. Paul found a thick envelope from her waiting for him when he returned to his health center. It contained a stack of articles clipped from newspapers and magazines. Some of them were several months old. There was an accompanying letter:

*Hi, Paul*

*I raided my parents' stockpile of clippings about Korea. Now that I'm home safe, they're not so interested in them anymore. When I read through them, I was shocked at how little we knew about what's really going on over there — you will be, too.*

*Some of these are pretty old, but I know you won't mind brushing up on history. Enjoy them. I do hope you'll be careful who you show them to. Theodore and I are well, T sends his regards. Write when you get a chance.*

*Sarah*

His first thought on seeing the small mountain of forbidden knowledge was how greatly Mi Jin would want to see it. But Mi Jin was no longer in his life. With no one to give it to, it lost its luster and became little more than a curio, a mildly interesting expansion on matters that did not touch him directly.

"Mr. Pak. *Waugh!* You have many newspapers."

It was Sojang-nim, the health center chief. Paul jumped to his feet, relieved that the article he was reading carried no photograph on it, only a minor headline: "Student Demonstrations in 4th Day". The rest of the clippings were safely in the envelope.

Sojang-nim's eyes were quick. "You are reading about our country?" He peered into the envelope but did not remove its contents.

"Just a few articles a friend sent me. Nothing very important."

Sojang-nim picked up the one Paul had been reading and examined it. He read slowly.

"This says the students are marching against the new Constitution. That is not quite right. They have undisciplined minds and do not think carefully. Sometimes bad people talk to them about crazy things. Then they get excited and they have to do something. The rest of us try to set them on the right road.

"I know you are worried about our country," he continued, laying a sincere hand on Paul's shoulder. "Do not worry. Do not concern yourself with the silly politics. You are safe with us." Then he went off to a meeting with one of his assistants.

Paul put the newspaper article away and shoved the envelope into his backpack. He would keep it nearby all day and then give it to Joel for safekeeping.

## Nine

News filtered slowly down to Chindo; by the time Mi Jin heard it, it was already a couple weeks old. Cho, the admired student leader, the one alongside whom she had fought in Kwangju, had been captured. The police caught up with him in Naju, a small town not far from Kwangju, which was his parents' home. He had been turned in by a distant relative who had had been on the bad end of a business deal with his father, a rice merchant. Cho was there during the winter break from school. The police, dressed in military fatigues and gas masks, had stormed the house, a large one in a well-to-do part of town, and dragged him out with his arm twisted grotesquely behind his back. His mother lay in bed for days afterward, a hysterical wreck. People who visited him in the Kwangju jail a week later said the arm was broken and clumsily placed in an improvised splint. His face still bore the marks of savage beatings.

Choi Un Mi, Mi Jin's old friend who had recently married Mi Jin's cousin, told her the news in a hurried telephone call. "I can't believe you're not appalled by this, Elder Sister. What's wrong with you?"

Mi Jin told her that her own wedding was coming soon, just a few months away, and that such things could no longer concern her.

"So you're going through with it, *neh?* Oh. Well, I suppose one has to do the right thing. But surely you're not going to give up the cause. If I know you, Elder Sister, someday you'll teach your babies all our slogans and chants. But in the meantime, you have to stay involved. We've just lost Cho. We can't lose you, too."

Mi Jin smiled and felt a flicker of the old spark inside her.

"Listen," Un Mi said. "There's a conference in Kwangju for some opposition candidates on the twenty-second. I've been invited to the reception. Kim Yong Sam's chief of staff will be there, and who knows — maybe Kim himself will show up. You've got to come. That's late next week. Promise you'll try to come. Tell your mother you're coming to see Tae Su and me. Make something up. Arrange to meet your American friend. He can come, too."

Mi Jin thought for a moment, and agreed. "I'll see what I can do."

## Ten

Kim Hyong Chol came to Mi Jin's house a few days later. The sun had finally come out, and the ground hardened; it was now dry and warm enough to hang laundry outdoors. Dressed in a heavy old sweater and with her hair bound in a kerchief, Mi Jin looked like a young wife, an observation that made Hyong Chol pause at the gate before knocking. He looked uncomfortable, even pained to be there.

"Mi Jin?"

She spun around and, seeing him, hurriedly removed her apron and smoothed a lock of hair that had strayed from beneath her kerchief.

"My goodness! You startled me. How are you, Hyong Chol?"

"*Neh. Annyong haseyo?* Mi Jin, may I talk with you in private?"

"My parents are at the docks. We can speak here."

"Thank you." Hyong Chol came forward and stood stiffly before her. In his eyes she read signs of regret, of frustration, even of a little anger.

"What's wrong, Hyong Chol?"

"I have bad news from my parents. I wanted to tell you first, before they talked with your mother and father. They want to break our engagement. We cannot get married."

" ... *Neh?*"

"It's true," he stammered. "I tried to talk them out of it, but they are old-fashioned, and have old views about what a daughter-in-law should be. When they heard that you had been ... dismissed from your school, they thought that it was because you still run with that radical political movement. I don't believe it, but their minds are set."

Mi Jin gaped silently at him, unaware that she had dropped underwear on the ground.

"Maybe it's just as well," he continued. "My parents would not have treated you kindly. You'd join our household, but they would not really accept you. My mother would make your life hard. I don't wish that on you."

Mi Jin nodded.

"Besides, we are not such a close match, *neh?* I like you, I really do. And I think you will make someone a fine wife. But we are so different. I'm a little old-fashioned, I guess, and you are better educated than I am. You would talk about things, and I'd never know what you mean." He smiled wanly.

So he didn't want this marriage, either, Mi Jin thought.

Hyong Chol held out his hand. "Goodbye, Mi Jin. I'm sorry about all this. I wish you well."

She took his hand and shook it, and watched him walk back up the dirt road toward town.

## *Eleven*

"*Yah ... Yah!*"

Mi Jin's mother's lips went white with fury when she heard the news. When she finally managed to speak, she let loose a stream of invective that sent Mi Jin crouching in a corner.

"You fool! You worthless nobody! *Yah*, you're nothing but a leach, a bloodsucker, a black piece of bad luck sent to torment me! How could you do this to us? *Eh?* Answer me! What got into your puffed up little brain that brought such shame to your father and me? You run around with this pack of cats, like an animal, messing things up, screwing things up, making everyone's life miserable. Answer me!"

The first wave of anger passed into tears that flowed copiously down her cheeks, making shiny dark blotches on her shirt. Her muscles tensed again, and without warning she flew at Mi Jin, her fingernails raking across her daughter's face.

"*Yobo!*" Mr. Han cried. He let the attack go on for a few more seconds, then moved in to pull her off. "She's not worth it. Pull yourself together! Stop it!"

Mi Jin tasted salt and blood in her mouth. "Omma ..." she whimpered.

"Don't you 'Mommy' me," her mother screamed. "You're no daughter of mine! You're a piece of shit that came out the wrong hole!"

Even Mr. Han blanched at the obscenity. "*Yobo, yah!* Leave her alone now. You —" he said, addressing Mi Jin. "Go to your room."

She covered her face, wet with tears and blood, and ran off.

Mr. Han's wife was volatile in her emotions; she burned white-hot briefly and then quickly cooled down. She regained some of her composure shortly after the scene. The house lay in a deathly silence for the next several hours, so that Mi Jin eventually gained the nerve to venture out of her room. Her mother regarded her with stern silence, her father with shuffling, inept confusion.

By the next day, the women again acknowledged each other's presence. Neither could forgive the other. Each appraised the other as deeply in debt in the complicated system of balances logged in a ledger of insults.

"Appa," Mi Jin said to her father the next day on his boat. "Daddy, Mama is right. I have to mend my life, to live it better."

"*Mmmgh*," he grunted.

"I think I should pay attention to the Church more. Perhaps if I became more faithful, Mama would feel better."

The confession gladdened the old man's heart. His gaze on her was warmer than she had felt it to be in weeks. "You may be right. We can all go to church together."

"Appa, I've heard about a Catholic retreat being held near Kwangju next weekend. My girlfriend told me about it."

"A retreat?"

"At a place in the hills near the city, out in the country. It's for young people who want to renew their faith. May I go?"

Mr. Han nodded slowly. "It would be good for you to get away for a while. Your mother won't be happy about you going to Kwangju, but I'll talk to her. You have my permission."

Mi Jin had told a lie, a terrible one, but she felt no remorse. She hurried to the telephone exchange downtown and called the Suwon City Health Center.

"Will you transfer me to Pak Jong Shik, please?"

Her heart pounded while she waited.

"Hello?"

"Jong Shik. Do you know me?"

"Mi Jin!"

The dear voice pulsed with joy and relief. She could hardly restrain herself from crying. Her words came tumbling out.

"Jong Shik, I'm sorry about my words to you in Kwangju. I was wrong, terribly wrong. I'm not getting married. I don't want to stay here. I have to see you ..." Paul could not keep up.

"You're ... what? Yes, I'm glad, delighted. What happened? You sound upset. What ...?"

"It's too much to talk about now. Let's meet in Kwangju this weekend. Is that possible?"

"I'll be there!"

"Meet me at the Catholic Center downtown, on Kumnam Street on Saturday morning, around ten o'clock. And Jong Shik," she paused, and continued in English: "I love you. I will not leave you again."

## Twelve

Spring finally arrived, and with it came new stirrings of life in the opposition parties, large and small, that sprang into being like mushrooms under the shadow of martial law. Little had changed since the *coup d'etat* last December that gave General Chon and his circle control over the government; not much, indeed, had changed since President Pak's assassination last fall. Civic life remained dominated by the military. The press remained hobbled under official censorship to such a degree that the newspapers became little more than a vehicle for official government announcements, which they carried verbatim. The hopeful deference with which the current president, the grandfatherly Choi Kyu Ha, had been held by the public was beginning to wear thin as it became clear that the military command had instructed him to shut up and stay out of its way. Kim Yong Sam, the legislator who had been thrown bodily out of the National Assembly the previous fall, was making noises again. As leader of the New Democratic Party, the NDP, he called on President Choi to move the country toward democracy and free elections. To back up his speech, he started a campaign against the current government in areas where he knew he would get support. Kwangju, the famously rebellious capital of South Cholla Province, was one such spot.

The rally in support of the NDP attracted few people — only those brave or naive enough to downplay the reach of General Chon. One of the ballrooms of a tourist hotel downtown easily accommodated it. Men in dark suits and white sashes across their chests, emblazoned with pro-NDP slogans, passed out pamphlets, greeted the attendees, and directed them inside.

One greeter, a young solidly-built man with a watchful gaze, bowed deeply when Paul came in with Mi Jin. He offered a white-gloved hand.

"Are you an American?" he asked in passable English. "We are happy to see American people caring for the future of Korea."

Paul thanked him and accepted a pamphlet. It carried a picture of Kim Yong Sam with the title "Democracy is Korea's Hope."

"Our nation has suffered too long under empty promises for democratic renewal," the paper went on to say. "The time has come for free elections and an end to martial law. True growth and prosperity can come to Korea only when men and women of good will join together to choose the leaders who will guide them into the future. The ruling party has muzzled the people's voice for too long. It is time to support the NDP and call for free elections!"

Mi Jin caught sight of a friend and waved her down. She introduced her to Paul.

"Isn't it exciting?" the woman gushed. "This is the beginning of a great movement. The pro-democracy force is finally moving into the mainstream."

Paul nodded, but felt a twinge of uneasiness. He was glad to be there with Mi Jin, and to see history being made, but it was all against the rules — Peace Corps rules. If Mrs. Kang found out about his presence here, he could suffer the same fate as Evan Barker, the volunteer who had been sent home. He suddenly wished he had not come.

"*Yah ... ahh ... ahh.*" Someone at the lectern was testing the public address system. The hardware squealed and buzzed and soon a man in a gray
suit, also wearing a sash across his chest, stood up on the dais. He wore no
white gloves, and had an air of earnest self-importance. Paul assumed him
to be one of the organizers of the affair.

"Ladies and gentlemen, welcome. The Kwangju Region Support Committee for the New Democratic Party welcomes you to its first conference
and rally in support of free national elections and NDP candidates. I am
Lee Dong Su. It has been my dream for many years to see a rebirth of democracy in our beloved country under the guidance of our Party and its
leader, Mr. Kim Yong Sam." A smattering of cautious applause filled the
room. "He sends his regrets that he cannot be with us tonight. He is being
watched closely, as you know, and cannot risk the trip to our region. But he
is with us in spirit, I assure you. He deeply desires to nourish the seed of
democracy wherever it can be planted.

"The purpose of our meeting is twofold: to show our countrymen and
neighbors that the NDP is alive and well and ready to lead the march toward democracy, and to set up committees for implementing the Party's
plan of action. Mr. Pak Nam Ho, the regional director of NDP campaign
activities, will come now and explain the procedures. Mr. Pak."

"Is this all?" Paul complained. "I was expecting something a little more
exciting."

"*Shhh.* This is historic. Wait for a while until they finish the slow part.
Then we'll see some fine speeches by very important people ..."

Paul thought he heard something, a quiet commotion, in the lobby of
the hotel. Out of the corner of his eye he spied a group of men dressed in
leather jackets moving casually around the back of the hall, largely blending
in with the shadows. One of them carried a camera with a flash attachment
and a long lens. The young man in the lobby who had been handing out
leaflets, his hair now tousled, followed them in, shouting for them to get
out. People turned to see what was going on.

"Something's happening." Paul grabbed Mi Jin's hand and looked for an
exit.

Several more intruders ran in and, with shouts of invective, started over-
turning tables and grappling with spectators. With the exception of a few
men who hung back and talked into portable radios, they were all lean,
square-jawed, and fierce in their attack. One squad of them took up a
fighting stance at the doors, while another circled quickly around to secure
the fire exit. The remainder, after grabbing the literature and trashing the
tables, waded into the crowd of people, using taekwondo kicks and punches
to flatten anyone — man or woman — who crossed their paths.

"Come on — let's get out of here!" Paul shouted. He turned to grab her
arm again, but she was gone. He found her a few feet away, clinging to the

back of one of the men who had thrown a woman to the floor and was kicking her. Mi Jin managed to put the man's neck in the crook of her arm and with her other fist was pummeling the side of his head. He growled in pain and tried to shake her off.

"Mi Jin!"

The petite woman was no match for the man in the leather jacket. In a second he flipped her over his shoulder, thrusting her heavily to the floor on her back. The blow stunned her. His first kick caught her on the thigh and seemed to revive her somewhat, for she rolled with the second kick to her side and managed to scurry out of the way.

Paul jumped into the fray. By the time the soldier had wound up for the third kick, he was upon him.

"Hey! HEY!" Paul shouted. He latched onto the soldier's arm and pulled him around to face him. "HEY!"

The soldier, seeing an unexpected foreign face, paused in surprise. Paul counted on this. A right cross landed squarely on the man's jaw and Paul, ignoring the pain in his hand, followed immediately with his left. The soldier fell backward, slightly dazed, but he recovered quickly. All Paul could remember next before blacking out was the sight of shoe leather approaching the side of his face. When he came to a moment later, he also felt a jabbing pain in his side and saw Mi Jin crying over him.

A flash of light exploded in his eyes. He thought he had been hit again; but when he opened his eyes and peered past the burn spot, he saw only a man with a camera, who quickly ran off.

"Jong Shik! Jong Shik, can you move? Are you hurt?"

"*Ow. Uhhh.*" He tried to stagger to his feet. The world around him, still full of commotion and screaming, spun in slow motion. "I'll be all right. You? Are you okay?"

"Don't worry. We have to get out of here!"

The group of men who had blocked the fire exit had been drawn into the melee. The pair ducked through the door and ran out into the cold night.

## Thirteen

Mrs. Kang called Paul at his health center several days later. "I want you to come to my office. Today. Be here by noon."

When Paul arrived, the receptionist made a hurried call to the back offices and Miss An, Mrs. Kang's secretary, silently led him back.

Mrs. Kang did not invite him to sit.

"What happened to your face?" his inquisitor asked sharply. The swelling had gone down, but not completely. The blue-green remnants of a bruise covered the entire side of his face.

"Umm ... I got into a fight."

Mrs. Kang's eyes narrowed. "Don't lie to me, Paul. I know what happened."

Paul tried weakly to assert that it was indeed a fight, but she cut him short.

"Is this you?" She threw a photograph across her desk at him. It showed him on the floor, grimacing in pain, with Mi Jin beside him and the jumbled legs of brawlers in the background.

"I'm afraid so."

Mrs. Kang pursed her lips and looked straight at him.

"Paul, you know it is against the rules for a Peace Corps Volunteer to get involved in rallies, demonstrations, and riots. It is a serious, serious offense. We know exactly what you were doing when this picture was taken. You were attending a political rally of the opposition party, a group of radicals. You got involved in violence."

"But those goons came in and beat up on people. I couldn't stand by and watch women get hurt."

"You should not have been there in the first place!" she screamed. "And even if you had come upon the scene on an open street, you would have been obliged to walk away. You cannot get involved. I have given this talk many times before, most recently to Evan Barker. Why did you not listen?"

The mention of the dismissed volunteer stopped him short.

"I'm sorry. The heat of the moment affected me. I'll never do it again."

Mrs. Kang paused and picked up some papers from her desk.

"There is no next time. We are terminating you, effective today. The office driver will take you to your living place, and you can pack. He will drive you directly to the airport. You fly home tonight."

Paul could not speak. He slowly gathered his wits. "I want to talk to Mr. Atwood."

"He is not in the office today. Besides," she brandished the termination orders in his face, "he has already signed these. The driver is here. Get going."

## Fourteen

Paul felt sick. The afternoon had been a tempest of activity, riding with the driver to St. Lazarus Village, hastily packing his suitcases and backpack, leaving things he would not take home at Joel's door. He did not have time to say goodbye to him, so he left him a short, desperate note that he later feared might seem too cryptic to follow. The note cursed Mrs. Kang, gave his parents' address and telephone number, and promised that he would call soon. He asked Joel to call Mi Jin, but had no idea how to reach her. Now he was being escorted to the airport in the Peace Corps sedan, watching the sun go down in a blood-red splash behind a line of mountains.

The driver, a friendly, lazy fellow from Pusan, tried to engage him in conversation, in broken English. It did not seem to matter to him that Paul was leaving in disgrace; he kept up a jaunty monologue about the pleasures of American life that Paul would be regaining.

"Beefsteaks, eh? Good chow. I like beefsteaks, you know? Big and thick. Delicious. I go to big hotel in Seoul with friend and I eat it there. But too expensive. If I buy that one, my wife she get angry. Try to kill me." He laughed heartily.

"Good."

"Ha, ha. Color TV You have color TV your house? My house, no. Only blacken white. You watch *Star Trek* ..."

What stung Paul the most, more than being fired, was being unable to say goodbye to Mi Jin. He had her parents' telephone number, but after hearing of the abuse they had heaped on her, he could not bring himself to use it. She had no job, so she could not be reached at work. He thought about calling Trouble House and leaving a message, but his bad luck persisted: the line failed before he could even identify himself to the girl who picked up the phone.

The two men arrived at Kimpo Airport, checked the baggage through, and got Paul's boarding pass.

"Thank you," he said. "I'll be on my way now."

"No, no. I stay with you."

"It's all right, really. Why don't you go home? Your wife will be angry if you stay too long."

"Mrs. Kang more angry. Ha, ha. You know?"

Paul nodded, and sat with him in the lounge. He gazed through the window at the deepening blue of dusk. An insistent and unstoppable train of thought pulled his attention inward.

It occurred to him that his first twenty-two years of life had been an aimless wandering, a period of thralldom to teachers, parents, and the culture of the American middle-class that neither attracted nor repulsed him. He had cheered at baseball games, grown attached to favorite television programs, and generally done what others had expected him to do. His years at home had revolved around entertainment and duty. Rather than experiencing life, he had got wrapped up in depictions of it. All that had changed when he came to Korea.

The events, large and small, of the past months unfolded before his mind's eye: his arrival at this airport, the onerous training in Chunchon, his complicated dealings with Koreans, the vicissitudes of life under martial law. He realized that he rather liked struggle. It suited him. The past months had tested his mettle, and he fancied that he had come out of it rather well.

The past few weeks, however, were a watershed of the changes that had come over him. He had lost his love and got her back, and then been plunged into politics of the most violent sort. He thought of the chaos of the rally, of the government agent kicking Mi Jin, and of Mrs. Kang sending him home, and his face grew hot with a deep, silent rage. It had been there a long time, just under the surface. He had never known that rage and love could live together as brother and sister, but they did, for their parent is passion. Passion had finally come to Paul.

After a few minutes he stood up.

"I'll be right back. I have to go to the *pyonso*, the bathroom."

The driver shrugged and slumped down to catch a bit of sleep.

Paul moved casually toward the bathroom, then turned to check on the driver. He crossed to the escalator, took it down to the lobby, and calmly walked out the door into the night.

# CHAPTER EIGHT

"Joel? It's Paul."

"Paul! Where the hell are you? The Peace Corps office is in an uproar ..."

"I'm in Seoul. In Itaewon, at a dump called the Paradise Hotel."

"What happened?"

Paul quickly sketched the events of the last several days, from the disrupted rally in Kwangju to his escape from the airport. Joel heard a new edge to his voice, a hard staccato rhythm.

"Joel, I'm going to ask a big favor of you. A couple of big favors. First, I need money. I've got a little, but I'm gonna be in this country a while, and I obviously can't work."

"I've got a lot saved. It's yours."

"And I need clothes. All I've got are the clothes on my back. My luggage has gone back to the States without me."

"I'm taller than you are," Joel said, "but you can roll up the legs and sleeves. What else?"

"That's all for now. Can you come and meet me tomorrow? Don't tell anyone where I am. Not Leslie or Mark or anybody. Not even Mi Jin. She'll find out I'm gone when she tries to call the health center. It kills me to think how she'll feel then, but I can't let anyone but you know I'm still here. Do you understand?"

"Yes."

"Good. I'll lay low and try to blend in until I see you."

"Wait a minute," Joel said. "Why are you staying? What are you going to do?"

There was a pause on the line. When Paul's voice came back, it sounded strained, even doubtful. "I'll have to talk that out with you later."

## *Two*

Joel arrived the next day at Paul's hideout, a smelly little inn around the corner from a disco. He brought a suitcase full of clothes and the equivalent of three hundred dollars in cash.

"Are you sure you can spare this?" Paul asked. "It's a lot of money."

"My room and board are free at the Leprosy Institute. All my stipend from Peace Corps goes into savings. You need it more than I do. You sure chose a winner of a place to stay in," he added, looking around at the peeling wallpaper and stained bedding of Paul's room.

"I'm moving out today. Last night was 'Love Night,'" he said wryly. "I guess that's true every night in this place. The moans and groans from the next room kept me up all night."

Joel mentioned that the noises could not be the only reason for him to lose sleep.

"You're right. I'm in trouble. I know it. And I can't explain why I'm doing this. Especially to you. You wouldn't understand."

Joel frowned.

"I don't mean it unkindly," Paul continued. "You're just not the type to act on impulse. You would look at the pros and cons, tally up a balance sheet, and only then decide what's best to do. I'm not like that. I was sitting there in the airport, as mad as hell at Mrs. Kang, at the Peace Corps, at the Korean government for what they did in Kwangju, and I had to do something. To leave would have been an act of ... well, betrayal. It just would have left too many things unresolved."

"Like Mi Jin."

"Yeah, her most of all. I can't leave her."

Joel flopped down on the bedding. Paul's appraisal of him had been sharp as a laser: no, he would not act on impulse, and no, he would never, ever, do anything so foolish for love or even out of anger. He tipped back his head and let out a roar of laughter.

"My friend, you are more human than I'll ever be. If I had a bottle of *soju* handy, I'd drink a toast to you and then get completely drunk out of envy."

Paul smiled uncertainly and paced the floor.

"What's your next move?" Joel asked.

Paul straightened and spoke clearly, his voice crisp. "Over the long haul, I have to get back to Kwangju. I'll do that gradually, as I'm sure people will be out looking for me. I can't stay in Itaewon for long — it's too popular with volunteers. Someone might spot me. I'm thinking of heading over to the east coast and working my way down, staying in the middle-sized towns, avoiding volunteer sites. An American won't look too out of place there, if I stick to the tourist spots."

"What will you do when you get back to Kwangju?"

"I'll be with Mi Jin."

"And then ... ?"

Paul winced. "I don't know yet. Come on, I haven't had time to plan out every damn thing."

"How are you going to sign the guest books at the inns you stay at? The police check those things, you know." Joel said.

"I hadn't thought of that. I'm not sure what I'll do."

Joel dug into his shirt pocket. "Here. Take my passport. I know it's not your picture, but most Koreans think all Americans look alike. If you grow a beard, it'll completely fool them."

"Thank you. I'll enjoy being Joel Reynoso."

"I hope you'll have more fun in the role than I do. One last question. Do you want me to call Mi Jin?"

Paul thought for a long time and shook his head.

"No. Mrs. Kang will expect me to contact her. Maybe I've become paranoid, but I can't take any chances with that crafty bitch. I should wait until the coast is clear. It'll be rough on Mi Jin, but I have no choice. No, don't call her."

Joel turned at the door. "This is goodbye, then. Be careful."

The two men embraced and Joel set off into the bright sunshine.

## Three

Mi Jin stood in the telephone exchange in Chindo, which was cool and damp within its concrete walls, and made phone calls. Before returning from Kwangju she had made up her mind to turn her back on her parents once and for all and move to Suwon, to be with Paul. She had spent the morning deciding which possessions to take with her and which to leave behind, and started packing the smallest articles in a bright red bag. She knew it was premature to do so; she could not think of moving before lining up some work there. The act of packing foreshadowed the pleasure of emancipation. As she walked into town that morning, the world outside had agreed with her, releasing the scents of spring into a warm breeze.

Her first call to the Korean Leprosy Institute brought a terse statement from a receptionist that Paul was not there. She dialed the health center.

"Will you transfer me to Pak Jong Shik, please?"

"He's not here," the woman's voice said.

"May I leave him a message?"

There was a space of silence on the line. "You may, but he won't get it."

"Excuse me?"

"He left the health center for good. Just yesterday."

"Where ... where did he go?"

229

"I don't know. Wait a moment. Let me transfer you to his supervisor."

After another wait, this one more agonizing, a male voice came on.

"This is Im Kyong Shik. How can I help you?"

"Where is Mr. Pak, the American?"

"He was sent back to the United States. It was very sudden. Who are you, please?"

"Han Mi Jin."

"Ah, yes. I know about you." Mr. Im's voice grew cold. "It seems that he got involved in some kind of riot, and the Peace Corps sent him home for breaking their rules. You are the woman who got him involved in such matters, aren't you?"

Mi Jin did not answer.

"Well, I don't know why you dragged the American into your game, but it has done us a lot of harm. He was doing more good with us than he was with your kind ..."

Mi Jin stopped listening and hung up the telephone. She stumbled out into the open.

The dilapidated town and the terraced hills beyond spread out before her. The wind had begun to pick up. Ash-gray clouds had marched in from the west, dribbling rain over the landscape. The scene looked to her like the aftermath of an explosion: everything in sight seemed pulled up by the roots and torn apart, even though the people walked about as if nothing had happened. She leaned her head against a cool wall and moaned:

"Gone. Gone, and there's no hope."

She walked back to her parents' house, though she did not notice the long route she took. Her mind was a tangle of disconnected thoughts, as white and featureless as a snowstorm. A vague condemnation predominated, first of fate, then of the Peace Corps, then of Paul himself. Never trust Americans, they're users, her friends had told her; they suck wealth and dreams from people and then leave when they've had their fill.

She blamed her own government for causing the disturbance that had led to his dismissal. She blamed her parents, whose cruelty forced her to meet Paul clandestinely in Kwangju. Most savagely of all, she blamed herself for being so careless with her heart and, ultimately, for loving the American when all the forces in her life told her that she must not.

By the time she reached the road that led to her parents' door, the blame had run out. She felt only a pit of emptiness in the center of her soul. The prospect of living with loss after loss, to spend the rest of her days at odds with Fate, seeing every good thing come to ruin, was too much for her to bear. She dropped her red bag outside and sat alone in the shadows for hours. She was glad that her parents were not at home when she took her first steps into the numbingly cold water in the shallows near her parents' home.

The sea deadened her toes, then her ankles. She stared straight ahead at the horizon looking west, vaguely aware that, assuming Paul was flying home, she was turning her back on him. She prayed to her grandmother, hoping to hear some voice of solace, and to heaven, begging for forgiveness. Moving forward, the water lapped at the hem of her skirt, then reached her waist. The cold water forced her breath to come in short, wrenching gasps.

"If I'm going to do it, I'd best do it quickly," she told herself.

When the sea wetted her breasts, her heart jumped wildly. She stopped and willed herself to go on. The cold began to overwhelm her. The current under the water's surface rocked her stiff body back and forth like a wrestler trying to overcome a sturdy opponent. She willed herself to calm down, to refrain from holding her breath.

Then something in a corner of her mind, not quite a voice, but more insistent, like hunger, told her to muster her strength and turn around. She caught sight of the house, and her red bag beside it. For the first time since coming home she began to weep uncontrollably, her salt tears mingling with the sea. She waded slowly to the shore and lay crumpled on the rocks until her reservoir of tears ran temporarily dry.

## Four

Mi Jin's parents awoke the next morning to find her gone, with almost all of her few possessions left behind. Among them they found a snapshot of her standing close beside a tall, brown-haired American. They cursed her for straying so far from the right path; they cursed the American, whom they assumed to be a soldier, for seducing her; they cursed the heavens for leaving them alone in all the years to come.

She arrived in Kwangju in a state of despondency. She wanted to lose herself, to retreat from the pretentious individuality that the democracy movement had encouraged in her. The old saying is right, she reasoned, that the nail that stands up gets hammered down; Fate had certainly wielded its hammer upon her. To melt into the crowd of working people, quietly minding her own business and not bothering with bigger issues of democracy and tyranny, or serenity or achievement or love — that was what she wanted to do now. She had once thought of herself as a worthwhile person. Now she knew in her heart that she was not.

A short, foul-mouthed landlady rented her a room with an adjoining bathroom on the top floor of a building a block from Kumnam Street, the main boulevard that terminated at the Provincial Office complex. The traffic and even the top of the office was just visible through one of the windows. The landlady demanded a large security deposit on the room, which consumed nearly all of Mi Jin's savings.

"You have a job, I suppose?"

Mi Jin shook her head sullenly.

"Well, you have to work. What can you do?"

"Nothing."

The landlady scowled and then cast an appraising eye along Mi Jin's full length. "I know what you can do, and make enough for the rent and then some."

"I am not a whore!" Mi Jin shouted.

"No, no, nothing like that. Shit, listen to you talking to your elder like that. No, it's a *tabang* that serves men, but it's not a brothel. The pay is great. A lot of girls who come through the city want to make a bunch of money for whatever reason. They work there and then move on."

The woman's acuity surprised Mi Jin. She accepted a telephone number scrawled on a slip of toilet tissue. When left alone in her room, with nothing but a small armoire and some bedding, she looked in her purse. She had just enough cash to eat tonight, nothing more.

The next day she called for an interview. The Delicious Tabang was well-appointed but dingy, located on the second floor of a run-down office building far from the main street. The waitresses, all thin and heavily made up, wore tight green miniskirts and loose white blouses that fell open provocatively when they bent over. The *ajumoni*, whose teeth and fingertips were yellow from chain-smoking, wore a flowery *hanbok* that made her look at the same time youthful and very old. She gave Mi Jin the same sizing up the landlady had given her.

"You have to buy the uniform," she said in a loud, jangling voice. "If you don't have the money now, I'll take it out of your pay."

Mi Jin nodded.

"What's your name?"

"Ha —"

She held up her hand. "We go by given names here. I don't want to know your family name."

"Mi Jin."

"Ah," she rasped. "What a pretty name. 'Mi' — beauty and 'Jin' — truth. How appropriate for our establishment." She laughed and, falling into a fit of violent coughing, spit a wad of yellow phlegm into a handkerchief. Mi Jin turned away, repulsed.

"Who's the new girl?" A woman had walked up, bedecked in the slinky uniform and filling it well. She looked to be nearly thirty, a round-faced sprite whose eyes sparkled with the liveliness that led men to forget their staid wives, at least for a time. Mi Jin saw instantly that this was an affectation, and trusted her.

"This is Mi Jin. *Yah*, say hello to your elder sister — Monday."

"'Monday'?"

"I made it up. Do you like it, Little Sister? It sounds so sexy ... 'Mon-Day.' Isn't it so?"

Mi Jin smiled in spite of herself. "Ye — yes. It is."

She made her debut after a few quick lessons from her mentor. Her wide hips turned heads among the jaded men who smoked and gossiped amongst themselves. At first she just served coffee, taking care to bend at the knees rather than at the waist when putting the cups down. Soon she started getting the hang of it; if this is all there is to it, she thought, she would not fare too badly. Then a middle-aged man with a hardened, lined face spoke out through a swirling cloud of cigarette smoke.

"*Ili wa*," he commanded.

Mi Jin had never been addressed that way as an adult, with a peremptory, "Come here!" spoken as if to a child. She hesitated.

"*Ili wa ba!*" Come here quick! He tapped the cushion beside him.

She sat on the edge, ready to take flight.

"You're a new one, aren't you?" His voice was a deep, guttural growl that he tried unsuccessfully to soften into something more inviting. "Just like a little bird. Don't perch there. Come sit beside me."

He held her upper arm firmly and drew her in. He was trying to be gentle, but his hands, which were more accustomed to clasping tools and striking his wayward laborers at work, made deep impressions on her arm. She stiffened and reluctantly let herself be guided to a spot close to him. The smell of fresh cologne on top of sweat and liquor and smoke hung heavily around him.

"You're a shy one. That's what I like. Someone fresh, new." He put his arm around her shoulders and played idly with the collar of her blouse.

That was too much for Mi Jin. She cast his arm off and ran toward the back of the *tabang*, where Monday was getting a tray ready. "Hey, come back! Where the hell are you going?" The man cried in mock anger, laughing all the while.

Monday caught the look of terror in Mi Jin's eyes and quickly ran out to the man. "How dare you be so rough with her? You've frightened her, you nasty man!" She pummeled him with her tiny fists, but in an alluring way, and before long she was cuddling with him, laughing at his straying hands.

Mi Jin caught the *ajumoni*'s angry glare. "You'd better treat my customers the way they want to be treated!" her look seemed to say.

## Five

Greg Friedman was at his desk, working late again. The time was 11:35, well past curfew, and he would not leave the embassy to go to his apartment that night. His office had the musty smell of a room where work and sleep alternated. The presence of the Marine guards made the place feel safe. If everyone in the embassy knew what I know, he thought, they'd think about staying here, too.

As if on cue, a Marine in fatigues poked his head in the door from the darkened hallway.

"Spending the night again, sir?"

Friedman smiled and waved.

John Atwood of the Peace Corps had called this morning, asking how things were going. He was not one to make friendly calls; when he asked how things were, he was really asking "Are my volunteers safe?" Friedman knew the question was legitimate. He was torn between keeping official confidences and giving out information that could keep vulnerable Americans from harm.

"Things are pretty much the same as they've been for the past month or so," he had answered truthfully. "Some cracking down on students and religious groups, but there's nothing new about that. Not as bad as what happened in Pusan last fall. If your people stay away from the action, they should be okay."

"How's the government? Stable?"

Friedman pursed his lips and delicately skirted the truth. "Let me put it this way. President Choi is still president, and General Chon is running things. The rest of the government and the military is respecting that. Nothing to worry about for now, John."

In truth, President Choi stood on shaky ground. The embassy had known for months that Chon Du Hwan had every intention of building up his personal power and using force, if necessary, to become president himself.

General Chon was a nationalist in the worst sense, seeing his world as a kernel of Korean purity, always under the threat of defilement by the communists of the North and the insurgents within his own country. He needed the United States to help him defend that inner sanctum, but he had no faith in its will to do so. "The Americans like to throw their weight around, to dominate smaller countries," he said openly on many occasions. "But they leave when the fighting gets hot. If you don't believe me, go ask the Shah of Iran. Ask the people of South Vietnam."

It did not help matters that Chon disliked and distrusted U.S. Ambassador Glysteen personally. When Chon showed up for bi-weekly consultations with the ambassador, they never shook hands. The contrast between the two was never clearer than when the two faced each other across the low office table: Chon the stout, steely-eyed soldier, Glysteen the tall, bespectacled academic. Their meetings followed roughly the same script every time. Glysteen would state for the umpteenth time that the United States backed South Korea through good times and bad but was concerned about the government's — or rather, the military's — treatment of dissidents.

Chon would respond by asking how committed the US could be if it withdrew most American troops from the country, as President Carter had been planning to do, and by pointing out that the suppression of dissent was essential in his beleaguered country. He further stated that the dissidents were being handled far more leniently than was the case last fall when Pak Chong Hui tried to control the riots in Pusan and Masan. Glysteen had to admit that this appeared to be true. With another admonition to use restraint, that was where the meetings usually ended.

However, below the surface, on a level that the ambassador could not officially acknowledge, a great deal of movement on both sides was afoot, and it fell to Friedman to write it up and cable it to Washington. The democracy movement had taken on new life in the past few weeks, fueled by students who returned to classrooms after winter break and realized that nothing much in the government had changed since their last round of riots. Fresh demonstrations were breaking out on the campuses, especially in South Cholla Province, that ancient hotbed of trouble. Chon's military was gearing up for it. Their preparations, which were the subject of Friedman's late work tonight, were most disturbing.

"Hell," he muttered, "what are those bastards trying to pull?"

He had heard from a source in the Korean military, which he confirmed through other sources, that the Martial Law Command was training several brigades of the Special Warfare Command, also known as the Special Forces, for riot control. Riot control. The Special Forces were the rough equivalent of the US Army's Airborne Rangers, highly-trained paratroopers meant to be deployed in wartime behind enemy lines. These soldiers carried out the toughest missions, the ones that called for killing with whatever weapon might be at hand, from artillery to bayonets to bare hands. Added to the potent mix of students versus soldiers was the fact that most Special Forces troops came from the Kyongsang provinces, and were therefore used to the view that Chollado people were somewhat less than human. It was also a fact that the troops were training in the use of CS gas, a vicious formulation of tear gas considered by some experts to be a form of chemical warfare. The dissidents were going to have a rough time of it.

Yet he knew what Glysteen's reaction would be, and the reaction of the Carter Administration. The United States could do nothing but try to nudge Chon and his generals toward moderation. Korean troops under Korean command were off limits to the Combined Forces Command, whose commander was an American. The Koreans had to give notice before using their troops, but they always had "sovereign control" over them. Once they got deployed in Kwangju, or Mokpo, or any of the other rebel strongholds of Chollado, the United States could do nothing but stand aside and watch the melee. The Administration would privately deplore the carnage while publicly supporting Chon, because at the moment Chon's was the only show in town. Not supporting him would almost certainly egg North Korea into attacking the South. And that, if it ever happened, would make the Special Forces' excesses in riot control look like a light spanking. Nobody could win: Friedman was convinced of that. No matter what anyone did — generals, students, the United States, the North Koreans — people would die, and possibly in great numbers. "Within the coming month," he sighed. "I'm sure of it."

## Six

Paul had not shaved in days. His razor was in his suitcase, which by now was sitting unattended in a storage room at the Indianapolis Airport. Someone at the airport had surely called his parents — their telephone number was on the luggage tag — and they would be worried sick at the macabre twist of finding the luggage but losing the passenger. The thought of their agonized questions stabbed him straight through the heart. No one, he thought, deserved to fear that they had lost a child.

"You want razor? Want haircut?"

Paul was in Chechon for the day, a quiet town that glistened with early morning frost among the mountains south of Chunchon. The *ajoshi* of the inn had waylaid him as he was leaving the house. He made a snipping motion with his fingers as if to translate his wildly mispronounced English.

"No, thank you," Paul replied, in English. He had not uttered a word of Korean since he left Seoul. He drew his hand over his chin, now richly covered with copper stubble. "I'm attempting to metamorphose my appearance, you see, so that various personages of my acquaintance will find it difficult to discern my true identity." He grinned at the poor man's bewilderment, and moved on.

He looked around constantly as he walked, like a meek animal crossing an open field, checking up and down streets and scanning crowds for policemen or anyone who could identify him. Now, a week after his escape, he had already had an encounter with the police.

It happened three days before in Wonju. He had just got off the bus and was heading for one of the many inns across the street from the bus station. A policeman, a lean man in his thirties wearing a blue uniform with his cap visor low over his eyes, called out to him from a half-block away. He carried an old rifle over his shoulder.

"What are you doing here?" he asked in heavily-accented English. He intended to be polite, but the question came out sounding brusque.

"I am traveling on vacation," Paul replied, also in English.

"Can I see passport?"

Paul swallowed hard. He slowly unbuttoned his shirt pocket and took out Joel's passport.

"Here it is."

The policeman studied the photograph carefully and glanced at Paul's face. Paul began to feel faint.

"What is your name?"

"Joel Reynoso."

"Oh. I see." He handed it back to Paul, touched his visor, and loped off down the street.

Paul left Wonju on the next bus.

Now, in Chechon, he was a little more at ease. The past couple days had gone well, free of policemen and Americans. He spent his days riding buses from town to town. Once holed up in an inn, he went out only at night, haunting any small bookstores and food stands he found nearby. The program seemed to be working well.

Then he passed the county office building, quite by accident. The early sunlight washed the old concrete-block structure in white light and made a wild pattern of stripes of the front steps. He looked up and saw an American woman standing there, her back toward him. He could tell from her hair color and style that it was Beth Quinn, a fellow volunteer.

Beth was a jolly, wisecracking woman who had gone through training with him. Under any other circumstances, he would have gladly flagged her down and invited her out for a beer. His heart gave a sharp shudder. He flew to the corner of a building across the street, then caught his breath and peeked out. The woman Beth had been talking to, apparently a nurse, had seen him and was gesturing to Beth to turn around. She did so, and saw no one, for Paul was running as fast as his legs could carry him down the alleyway into the rubble-strewn space between two buildings.

Paul stayed in his room for the rest of the day and did not leave it even after dark. The first bus out of town the next day, just after dawn, left with him on board.

## Seven

"See the fat old guy at the corner table? He's ugly, but he tips well."

Monday, the *tabang agashi*, in her role as Mi Jin's mentor, pointed across the room from the small mold-encrusted kitchen where the water for tea and instant coffee was boiled.

"He works at a bank. A vice-president, that one is. Look at his suit and the wristwatch he's wearing! I wouldn't mind being kept by him. Lots of goodies to be had there."

"At what cost?" asked Mi Jin, almost to herself.

"What do you mean at what cost? It's free for us. We just use what nature supplied us with: breasts to grope, asses to pinch, and, well ... so on."
She giggled.

"Do you really go that far?" Mi Jin asked.

"Are you kidding? Of course. I'm not a whore, though. No, I have sex only with customers I really want. And they show their gratitude. That's not prostitution."

Mi Jin sighed. She had not taken that step, and was not sure how she would react if and when she did. After a couple weeks at the *tabang*, she had become good at the suggestive walk, the graceful bending, and the girlish small talk and empty praise that the men hankered for. Her uniform was becoming more comfortable; she no longer felt half-undressed in it. She learned to speak in an infantile squeak, the tiny voice that seemed to bring out the adolescent in a man. And men were ready to tip handsomely anyone who could make them feel that young again. She learned how to sidle up to a man, to rub against him with her hips and sit close to him and lean her head on his shoulder. She even let them brush her breasts with their hands, and then chided them, with a smile for their naughtiness, all the while feeling sick inside.

"Which ones have you slept with, Little Sister?"

"None of them," Mi Jin replied.

"If you want to take the banker, I'll let you have him. You should take the money and pay off your debt to the *ajumoni* for your uniform. I mean it, Little Sister, if you don't get it out of the way, she just keeps adding interest and you'll be forced to stay here forever."

"Like you?"

Monday laughed.

"No. I like it here. The *ajumoni* is a bitch, but the room is nice and the customers aren't too disgusting. I'm really not cut out for anything better."

Mi Jin pitied her and wondered if she herself would follow in the same path. Her future did not look promising. Her original intention, to settle into complete anonymity, was beginning to reach fruition. She never went out. She slept most of the morning and worked from early afternoon till curfew. She had been invited to the rooms of the inn next door by aroused customers, but so far she had refused every request. The more she thought about it, and the deeper she got into the life of a *tabang agashi*, the more she wondered whether holding out was worth the trouble. It was not as though she were saving herself for anyone. That man was now at home in America, never to be seen or heard from again — the symbol of the folly of investing one's heart too ardently in one cause or one person.

"So, Little Sister, are you going to do it?"

"Hush. I'm thinking."

## Eight

Joel traveled to Chollado giving the plausible but false reason that he had to check on the status of a fellow volunteer at a leprosy resettlement village near the town of Naju.

In truth, he went in search of Mi Jin. Paul had called twice in the past week from places in his journey that he refused to name. "Tell Mi Jin that I'm still here," he said again and again, his voice strained with worry. "I'm going to see her as soon as I can. Tell her." In his last call he told him to relay his plans to her: have her meet him at Kwangju Station on April the twenty-second, when the train from Taegu pulls in at 9:10 in the morning.

A call to Mi Jin's home in Chindo had been rebuffed cruelly by a woman whom Joel assumed to be her mother. Then a man's slow, worn voice came on the line. "Did you tell her to run away, you bastard? Do you know how much you've ruined our lives? You Americans think you can do anything you like to us. You son of a bitch! Go back to America and leave us alone!" The line went dead with a loud click. They had mistaken Joel for Paul.

In Kwangju, following Paul's directions, Joel went straight to Trouble House. There hung the voluptuous *bas relief* of Botticelli's *Birth of Venus*, the shadows of her breasts marking the late-afternoon hour on her midriff. His arrival caused a moment's consternation among the customers, but they quickly returned to their conversations, though more quietly than before.

"Is Han Mi Jin here?" he asked the girl at the front counter. Her face clouded and she shook her head uncertainly. "I'll have a cup of coffee, please," he smiled, and took a seat.

"Excuse me."

Joel looked up at a young man whose mop of black hair cascaded in a wide curve over wire-framed glasses. It was Chong Il Man. Joel half rose in his seat. "Yes?"

Il Man sat down. "I was sitting nearby," he whispered. "I heard you ask where Han Mi Jin is."

Joel nodded.

Il Man drew in a slurping breath between his teeth in the manner of one who is reluctant to say much. "You're a friend of the American — Mr. Pak? Mi Jin is not here. When I saw her last, she was terribly messed up. Your friend had left her. She soon stopped coming around here. Some people think she started getting friendly with the martial law guys."

"I can't believe that."

"Nor can I. But we all get a little suspicious around here sometimes. Can you blame us? Why do you want to find her?"

"I have something to tell her," he replied cautiously. "Something that will help her."

"Really. She needs all the help she can get." After a few moments of thought, Il Man wrote something on a corner of a napkin and with a sigh pushed it across the table. "I saw her a few nights ago, by accident. She did not see me. She is a server in this *tabang*." He paused. "When you find her, do not judge her too harshly. She has had a lot of trouble."

Joel thanked him and left.

The air inside the Delicious Tabang was close and smoky. The smell of old furniture, old wallpaper, cigarettes, and cologne hit Joel hard the moment he walked in. He sat unnoticed at a table by a window and looked around. The place had an immediate deadening effect on his emotions; all life and vitality seemed to have been sucked out of it.

He spotted Mi Jin across the room. She sat on the arm of a chair with her arm draped over the shoulder of a well-dressed businessman who turned to her occasionally to cuff her on the chin and run his hand along her thigh. Joel hardly recognized her: he had to watch her, to study her features and movements for several minutes, before he could be sure it was she. Her hair was lifted up off the nape of her neck, secured in a flurry of loose curls. Her lips were painted a bright red and her eyes glinted dully behind dark, plentiful makeup. Joel sighed, disturbed both for her and for himself, for when she got up off the armchair to walk back to the kitchen, he could not help thinking that she filled her skimpy uniform rather well.

Mi Jin returned from the kitchen with a small tray of teacups. Joel stood and waved when her eyes came into view. She caught sight of his tall figure, stopped suddenly, and hesitated. He could not read her expression. She served the tea stiffly, excused herself, and walked uncertainly toward him. The swinging of her hips, so pronounced for her customers, was now gone. She sat down opposite him and glared at him with sad, tired eyes.

"What are you doing here?" she demanded.

"I've been looking for you. I came to tell you something, to give you some news."

"What can you possibly tell me?" she whispered harshly. "That son of a bitch is at home on the other side of the world and will never come back. He's forgotten all about me. I have to start over again, that's all. *Yah*, you shouldn't have come here. You remind me of too much." She got up to leave.

"Paul is here."

Mi Jin stopped and shuddered. "Do not joke about this."

"I'm not joking. Paul is in Korea right now."

Mi Jin dropped heavily into the chair and tried to read the nuances of Joel's face. Tears welled up in her eyes.

"He is ... here? Where? In Kwangju?"

"Not yet. I don't know exactly where he is at this moment. Let me tell you what happened."

Mi Jin wiped away the mascara that had begun to flow in black rivulets down her cheeks. Her tears washed away much of the makeup around her eyes; she began to look like herself again. Joel told her about Paul's escape from the Peace Corps driver minutes before he was to board the airplane, and about his attempt to stay beyond the reach of the Peace Corps and the police, who were no doubt still looking for him. He gave her the time of his arrival in Kwangju.

"So you see, you must keep this a secret. He's coming to see you, but he has to go carefully. He'll be here at the time I just told you. He calls me sometimes, but he never tells me where he is. Just a few days ago he felt safe enough to let you know that he's still in the country. He said, 'Find Mi Jin, and tell her I'm here. Tell her I love her.'"

Mi Jin's face bloomed with fresh joy.

"Thank you, Joel. Thank you so much."

She looked down at her blouse and miniskirt, which were blotched with dissolved makeup, and suddenly turned grave.

"I had to do this, Joel. I lost my job and my engagement was broken off. My parents had nothing but hate for me; I had nowhere to go. I was so ashamed to see anyone, even my friends. I wanted to die."

"Mi Jin ..."

"When you talk to Paul, please tell him that I stayed faithful, even though it was hard and I had no hope."

"I'll let you tell him."

Mi Jin stood and motioned Joel to wait. "I have to do something." She turned brightly, strode to the front counter, where the *tabang ajumoni* sat, and gleefully told her to go to hell.

## Nine

Taegu had obligingly allowed Paul to lose himself in it. Third in size of all South Korean cities, after Seoul and Pusan, the city streets swallowed him up, and he lived there in secure anonymity until the day came for him to emerge in Kwangju. He took the early train, carrying nothing but a half-empty backpack. The amount of money he had left would have paid for a night in a cheap inn, but nothing more, not even a meal. If Mi Jin did not meet him at Kwangju Station, he would have to turn himself in and accept whatever punishment Mrs. Kang saw fit to impose on him.

The railway platform in Kwangju swarmed with people. In the warm, misty sunlight of spring they seemed to exude the sharp smell that Paul associated with Chollado, the smell of hot *kimchi* just a little past its prime. He immediately felt at home. Passengers jostled him as they raced for the terminal. He stood there for a moment: drinking in the fragrant air, pulling at his beard, searching the faces on the platform.

Mi Jin emerged as a shadow against the sun. She stood three cars down, and when she found him she started walking slowly toward him. Paul watched her. Something about her movements told him that she had aged greatly in the month since he had last seen her. She wore the same blue woolen dress she had worn on that October evening when they first met.

As they drew closer, Paul moved to one side to bring her face into the light. A thousand emotions danced behind her moist eyes: love, relief, and reproach chief among them. He could not tear his gaze from her. They stopped a few feet apart, looking at each other, not touching. To embrace would have been superfluous.

"Did you miss me?" Paul asked.

Mi Jin's face dissolved into a tearful smile. "You have no idea."

She stepped up and tugged at his beard. "And what is this? You thought you could disguise yourself so I wouldn't recognize you?"

"Never," he smiled.

People were beginning to notice them. They had to move.

"I live in a small place downtown," Mi Jin said. "We can go there."

### Ten

While Mi Jin and Paul settled into making a home for themselves, the world around them was falling apart.

Hwasun was a small, grimy coal-mining town a half-hour's drive from Kwangju. From morning till evening and long into the night, its streets rang with the rumbling and clanking of heavy mining machinery and its air was a brownish stew of engine exhaust and coal dust. Just outside the town stood a factory that manufactured the *yontan* coal bricks that heated Korea's homes in the winter. The pressing of coal dust into these bricks only added to the discoloration of the sky. It was rumored that a terrible lung disease ran rampant through the population, especially among the miners, but the government took no notice of it. The disease was lung cancer, the bureaucrats said, caused by excessive smoking. Those who thought about that claim remarked that smoking was widespread in the country, and elsewhere the government had denied that the link between smoking and cancer even existed.

Choi Un Mi and her new husband, whose wedding Mi Jin had attended months ago, lived there, working for a shadowy labor union that represented the miners. Mi Jin had been surprised when they announced their intention to live there after their honeymoon.

"That's a terrible, dirty place to go!" she had said.

"Elder Sister, there are no clean places to do the work we do."

Un Mi and Tae Su joined the Labor Alliance shortly after they graduated from Chonnam University. They traveled around the country trying to drum up support for independent labor unions in the textile, automotive, and mining industries. The existing unions were sponsored by the government and were therefore useless — worse than useless, in the Alliance's eyes, for along with doing a poor job looking after the workers' welfare, they quelled dissent within their ranks and guaranteed that the government would win in any dispute.

Mi Jin received a telephone call at the room she shared with Paul, a few days after his arrival. The bloom of their reunion had still not left her face when she excused herself to take the call in the hallway.

A muffled cry filtered through the half-open door. Paul jumped up and ran to her. She was speaking rapidly, in a panic. She slammed the receiver down and clutched at Paul as she hurried back to the room to find a sweater.

"What is it? What's wrong?"

"My cousin, Tae Su." She pulled him out the door and shakily locked it. They ran to the street and sprinted for a taxi stand.

"There has been trouble in Hwasun. A big demonstration. The workers want to go on strike, but their union wouldn't let them. The riot police came and broke it up. There has been terrible violence, and shooting."

They jumped into a cab. Mi Jin told the driver to hurry to Christian Hospital, on the southern edge of the city.

"Shooting?" Paul said in English.

"Yes, shooting." Mi Jin continued, also in English. "Tae Su is wounded. This is terrible, terrible!"

Un Mi, who was visibly pregnant, met them in a hallway at the hospital. Her eyes were red. They could see her husband through the door to his room. Four other men lay there with him, all wounded and connected to intravenous bottles. One breathed in jerks with the help of a respirator.

"How is he?"

"Bad. He has a gunshot wound in his gut. He just got out of surgery. They had to remove part of his colon. It was a gunshot wound," she said angrily. "They used guns against the miners."

"What happened?"

"You won't believe this, Elder Sister. What a calamity at the demonstration. I still can't believe it myself." She glanced suspiciously at Paul.

"It's all right," Mi Jin said, and drew him close. "He's with me."

A shadow of a smile played at the corners of Un Mi's mouth despite her agitation. She went on:

"The miners wanted to go on strike for higher wages. They're justified, of course — they barely make enough to live on, renting company-owned housing at exorbitant rates and buying food at company stores. Meanwhile, the mine owners live like kings in Seoul. The cost of oil and coal has been higher this winter than ever, and these people got hit worse than anyone.

Most of them ran through all their savings to buy heat for their homes. The fact that they mine coal makes no difference. If they get caught taking some home, they get fired and their families are thrown out on the street. Many of them steal it anyway, out of necessity, sneaking lumps home in their pockets. So you see, they have it bad." She nodded toward Paul. "Does he know any Korean?"

"I understand most of what you're saying," he said.

"You speak Korean very well! I'm glad for you, Elder Sister."

"Go on."

"The miners tried to ask their union to get off their asses and negotiate for more pay. Those idiots expressed all kinds of concern, but they didn't lift a finger to help. So the workers started turning to our organization — the Labor Alliance — in droves. Poor Tae Su was hardly ever at home." Her voice broke as her attention shifted to her husband, who had not stirred since coming back from the operating room.

"Our group held a demonstration. We meant it to be a small one, and manageable, but word traveled quickly and over five thousand miners showed up — at first. Three thousand more joined us as they got off their shift, still covered with coal dust. It was just a sit-down *demo* at the intersection outside the mine's main office. We sang some songs, passed out literature, and got ready to march up to the front door. Nothing remarkable.

"Then the riot police came. Seven or eight bus-loads of them, which is twice what we expected. And along with them — armored personnel carriers! We'd never seen them used on a labor *demo* before. Elder Sister, can you imagine the fright we felt from seeing those things rumbling down the street! The bastards who came out of the buses were the usual riot control bunch, all dressed up in body armor and shields and gas masks, strutting like old-style Japanese samurai. But soldiers came out of the personnel carriers. The miners got very quiet. Somebody among the riot police got on a megaphone and told us to disperse. We just sat there. He told us again, throwing in some *yok*, insults, for good measure. Then some miner on the fringe of the crowd got picked up by the collar and thrown to the ground. The police started kicking him. Our guys got mad. We tried to keep them calm, because we knew that was exactly what those bastards wanted — a reaction, an excuse to get rough.

"Our guys obliged them, sure enough. A few groups of men stood up, then more, and pretty soon everyone was on his feet shouting slogans. The riot police started getting into their defensive positions, fitting tear gas canisters into their launchers. The soldiers were excited. I could tell: they moved in the tight, bouncy way cats do when they smell prey. It was exactly like that. Some of them started taking their rifles off their shoulders and setting up to fire."

"My God," Mi Jin gasped.

Un Mi nodded. "So much for the so-called liberal trend in the government. President Choi has been telling the country all about his reforms and the new open feeling in society. Don't be fooled, Elder Sister. He has no power. The real force behind the government is General Chon, and he's worse than that bastard President Pak!

"They set off the tear gas. Some of the miners saw the rifles being readied and tried to run away — back into the crowd, down the streets, wherever. They panicked. I suppose the soldiers saw the commotion as a threat, or maybe as their cue, and they opened fire. Everyone started running away. Tae Su tried to calm them down, yelling at them through a megaphone. He'd been standing on top of a truck, the stupid dear. He made a good target ..."

Un Mi broke down completely. Mi Jin gathered her in her arms and cried, too. Other people milled around them, some related to the other casualties, others attracted by Un Mi's telling of the story. Those who had seen the demonstration nodded during the tale and murmured "That's right!" and "It's just so!" Others glanced around nervously, unaccustomed to such talk being made openly.

The two women cried and held each other until darkness fell and Tae Su moved out of danger.

## Eleven

Tae Su's injury and the disaster at Hwasun were among many reminders to Mi Jin and Paul that their life together was fragile, a feather blown about by the slightest breeze of circumstance. They tried their best to be happy. Mi Jin's small room was their home; they lived there like a married couple. They shopped together, prepared meals together, and made love often. To the shopkeepers in the large city market that ran parallel to Kumnam Street, they became something of a fixture: walking among the stalls, they talked happily to each other in refined Korean. The American was a nice-looking fellow whose only oddity, apart from being an American, was his tendency to glance around nervously from time to time, as if looking to avoid someone. In time, they got used to that, too, for who in Kwangju these days did not feel threatened by outside forces?

"I can't wait until you meet my parents," Paul said late one night, in bed. A gibbous moon shone on them through clouds that filtered the light like flimsy curtains. Mi Jin laid her head against his chest. "Oh, they'll be a little cautious at first, but before long they'll love you."

Mi Jin smiled and patted his stomach.

"And when we get home, I'll take you to Columbian Park. I spent the happiest times of my childhood there, watching the monkeys at the zoo, and playing on the slides and swings. They even have little carnival rides for kids. And the public swimming pool is amazing — a huge circular thing, with the deep end in the middle and benches all around the edge; lots of room for little children. But the most wonderful place is the boathouse."

"What is that like?"

"It's an old building by the edge of an artificial lagoon, tucked off in the corner of the park. You can rent rowboats there. I used to go there at sunset in the summertime. The air was humid and the water rolled around like oil and the buzzing of the cicadas was almost deafening. It was the most peaceful place I knew. I went there to think."

"What did you think about?" Mi Jin whispered. "About me?"

"Maybe. Only I didn't know it then. I used to wonder what the world was like, what people in other countries were doing right at that moment. I used to look at the moon and think, 'That's the exact same moon that people in China are looking at.' It's sounds silly to say it out loud, it's so obvious. But when I understood it deeply, it was like a revelation."

Mi Jin caught a glimpse of the moon that had just come out from behind a cloud. "Maybe your parents are looking at this moon." She stopped herself before saying " ... and thinking of their son." But the thought came to both of them.

"I'm ready to go home," Paul said. "But only if you come."

They turned and kissed, long and hard, and then settled to sleep, still deep in an embrace.

Mi Jin's slow, steady breath blew past Paul's ear. In the *shushhhh shushhhh* he heard the wind blowing through an Indiana cornfield, through the tall cornstalks and the mysterious place where the stalks meet the earth. Home.

Likewise, Paul's breath blew past Mi Jin's ear. She heard the wind blowing over sea and mountain, muffled in life-giving rain. Home, also.

## *Twelve*

Chong Il Man had an itch to move, to get outside and do something. Springtime affected him that way. As a child on his father's farm, he could hardly wait for the rains of April to end so he could go out and peer over the low dikes at the newly flooded rice fields. The world was stretching and straining to wake up after a winter of huddling in upon itself. So was he.

The students at Chonnam University seemed to come out like the azalea blossoms that dotted the campus grounds and blanketed the surrounding hills in pink. Il Man walked across the quad with his friend, Lee Byong Guk, the radical. Even the latter, usually wrapped up in his own world of political animosities, drank in the sweet smell of the season and was moved to make a favorable comment about the weather.

"I agree," Il Man said. "Springtime in Chollado is without a rival anywhere. I've been to Seoul and Taegu this time of year, but something was always lacking. This place is unique."

To Il Man's disappointment, Byong Guk could not stay on the subject of the weather for long.

"Perfect weather for a *demo*, I think. The rain, the humidity helps keep the tear gas down."

"I suppose. You know, I'm getting a little tired of going through the same routine every year: we come back to classes, we go out in the rain, we demonstrate. It's a never-ending cycle."

Byong Guk stared at him. "Are you saying you don't want to demonstrate this year?"

"I don't know."

"How can you say that? Surely you know what's at stake. We're deep in the middle of the biggest crisis our country has ever faced. It's our duty to go out and protest. How else will we ever get the reforms we're after?"

"Byong Guk, that's exactly what you said last year, before General Chon came to power."

"And there was a crisis," Byong Guk replied. "Pak Chong Hui was in power then, remember? Ready to give himself a lifetime presidency and crush anyone who got in his way. That was the Yushin Constitution. It was worth protesting then, and it still is now. But now it's even worse. You're not going soft, are you? You're beginning to sound like Han Mi Jin, all moon-eyed about her American boyfriend."

"Ah, Mi Jin," Il Man smiled. "She seems happy now, doesn't she? Age and love and an eventful life really round a person out."

"I can't believe you. You sound like you envy her."

"What if I do? Let me tell you something, my friend. The democracy movement is like a slow-moving train. The train just keeps moving and moving toward its goal. You have to step off sometime; if you don't, you'll spend your whole life on it. And even if it did reach its destination — say Democracy Station — would it stop?"

Byong Guk considered the question. "Probably not. We'll move on to other issues. There are plenty of them, you know. Reunification with our people in the north, for example."

"So it reaches Reunification Station. What then?"

"Il Man, will you get off it? Look. We've got four thousand years of history behind us. Four thousand years of oppression — from China, Japan, the United States, and from the ruling class in our own country. We'll always have the crust and filth of all those years to scour off any way we can. It's our duty as students to protest. We've been doing it throughout history. We rose up against the Japs during the occupation. We overthrew Syngman Rhee. We'll do the same to Chon."

Il Man nodded.

"I've heard news," Byong Guk said in a low voice. "The Martial Law Command is going to crack down on protesters.

"That's not news."

"I mean crack down hard. Our friends at Seoul National University are telling me they see troops everywhere. It's getting harder to make a move without the police jumping on them. And get this: even the student newspaper — the bland, innocuous one — is being censored. Every word about student unrest is being taken out. The government is telling them what to print.

"You heard about Cho, the firebrand from last fall. He's in jail. The government has special military camps for the protesters they catch. But they're rougher than any regular boot camp. A friend of mine went and saw Cho at one of them. He was hardly recognizable as Cho: he was bruised, his nose and arm were broken, he had a big scar across his face that looked infected. He was as thin as a skeleton. And his speech was slurred, like he was on drugs. That is what's ahead for demonstrators."

"You make it sound like we should all stay home," Il Man said.

Byong Guk wheeled on him with startling force.

"No! All the more reason to get up and struggle against it. If we don't fight them, they'll just herd us all into those camps like sheep. It'll only get worse if we stay home. If we fight, we may change it. The whole world will be watching."

Il Man admired Byong Guk's simple code, his brash optimism, his faith in the power of a few students to change their world. He left his friend at the library and spent the rest of the day deep in thought, watching the gathering rainclouds.

# CHAPTER NINE

Joel went up to Seoul on Thursday, the fifteenth of May, to catch a train to Kwangju, there to be reunited with Paul. In his backpack he carried his portable shortwave radio, which had lately become his constant companion. His bus from Anyang traced a circuitous course through Seoul's southern suburbs and finally joined the mass of traffic on Taepyong Street, the eight-lane boulevard which, a mile south of the capitol building, passed directly in front of Seoul Station.

Traffic slowed to a crawl a half-mile short of the station, which was un-usual for mid-afternoon. Joel roused himself from his book and listened to the chatter of his fellow passengers. They spoke excitedly, in low tones, as schoolchildren do when they talk about misbehaving classmates who are sure to catch punishment. "Look at those guys" — "Where are they going?" — "He's got a stick, see?" — "What's he gonna to do with a big stick like that?" — "Look, they all have 'em!"

Joel looked out. Clusters of young men strode along the street confi-dently like frisky stallions, calmly accepting the awed glances of passers-by.

"What's going on?" he whispered.

The answer came when Seoul Station and its broad plaza came into view. The plaza, which Joel estimated to be the size of several football fields, was packed with a roiling sea of people. The crowd overflowed the plaza and spilled out onto the streets. He opened a window to listen: the cacophony of a multitude of slogans, all shouted at once, filled the bus. "Burn General Chon!" — "Trash the Yushin Constitution!" — "Democracy and Justice!" Large signs and banners echoed these slogans.

Traffic ground to a halt. "I won't get my train today," Joel muttered, and he set out to walk the remaining mile to the Peace Corps office. He man-aged to reach the first intersection north of the train station, where traffic blockades had been set up on Taepyong Street.

249

The unmistakable rumble of diesel engines came from around a corner and grew louder as armored personnel carriers and buses sped in close formation to cleared areas of the street. Riot police filed out. They wore the familiar gray-green body armor, wide-flanged helmets, and heavy boots. They also had gas masks clamped over their faces and carried large metal shields. Shiny black jeeps pulled up behind them, their roll bars mounted with tear gas launchers.

The appearance of the police caused a stir among the students. The chanting stopped abruptly, then just as quickly began again with renewed intensity.

The riot police hung back, waiting for reinforcements. Clusters of students began to march brazenly up toward City Hall and beyond, on the same street, toward the Capitol. More joined in from a side street. A column of women, carrying signs identifying themselves as students from Ehwa Women's University, flooded the triangular intersection bounded by the Seoul Plaza Hotel, City Hall, and the old Doksu Palace. Their appearance created a sensation.

"*Yoja do! Yoja do!*" they shouted. Women, too!

Joel followed along with the students only because he could not break away from them: the press of people around him was so great that he could hardly move. The best he could do was keep pushing slowly toward the edge of the crowd, hoping to escape down a side street and take refuge in the British embassy compound nearby.

A woman at his side screamed through cupped hands: "Kill General Chon! Kill him! Rip his guts out!" Others around her took up the chant and marched forward, jostling Joel along with them.

The police had sealed off one end of Taepyong Street. It was now completely cleared of civilian traffic. A double line of riot police, backed by tear gas launchers, stood along the east side of the street. The students lined the west side in disordered masses. They made brief forays into the middle of the street to hurl stones and Molotov cocktails. The police stood their ground, waiting for the order to move.

That order came when a pack of two dozen students broke away from the crowd. They pranced into the street, whooping it up, emboldened by the police's stillness. Hardly had they reached the middle, however, when a squad sprinted toward them and, easily surrounding them, fell upon them with heavy batons. They rained blows upon the students and then rejoined their unit. Three students were left lying on the pavement, barely moving. Four were captured and hustled roughly behind the lines of the police. The rest retreated, yelping with pain and fright, clutching broken arms and bleeding heads.

The incident spurred the students to attack again at several spots along their front line. Shouting angrily, they moved in large formations into the street. The police retaliated with greater force and brought more students into custody.

Joel watched the spectacle with numb fascination. The students had chaos on their side; the police had order on theirs. Each was probing the other.

A voice, distorted loudly through a bullhorn, shouted an order, and those police who had not yet put their gas masks on quickly did so; another order, and the tear gas generators on the black jeeps were turned on. The jeeps started running along the street's center lanes, leaving billows of white gas trailing behind them.

A tickling sensation in Joel's throat suddenly erupted into searing pain. His eyes flooded with tears and mucus flowed from his nose. He stumbled blindly to the side of a nearby building. Some students were prepared for this; they had tied wet handkerchiefs around their faces. Only slightly disabled, they carried their rocks to within throwing distance of the police, let them loose, and scurried back to their own lines. Those who came unprepared for the gas hacked and sputtered, and cried out in pain; most of them had experienced tear gas before, as Joel had during his years in college, but this gas was different. It burned their lungs so much that they nearly lost their ability to run. Joel caught the eye of one sufferer. Her look told of shock and fear. "What is this?" she managed to utter through a fit of coughing.

The gas worked well for a while: the students retreated to the side streets and forced the stranded civilians to run even faster to get away from them. The police did not pursue them far. They quickly returned to their own lines to await further orders.

Joel ran to an alleyway just off the main street. There he found a cluster of students, about fifty in number, standing quietly, watching. Most had found something to cover their faces with. They seemed to be resting. He stood with them, relieved to be in a relatively quiet spot. He used the moment to take his handkerchief from his pocket, wet it from a helpful student's canteen, and press it against his face.

"*Kaja!*" Let's go! One of the students near the curb raised his fist and, with a loud war whoop, led the entire lot out onto the street. They carried Joel along like a cork on a wave. He had gone several yards out onto the street before he knew what was happening; he desperately fought his way to the rear of the ambush and ran back to the alley, more out of breath than before.

Time moved ever more slowly as the fighting grew in intensity. The two sides lost themselves in war lust. More and more students, their reactions slowed by exertion and the effects of the gas, got caught by the riot police. They were beaten mercilessly in the street, in full view of their comrades at the curb, then hustled into buses to bleed and moan while the police went back for more. The police flaunted their brutality. One very tall member of the squad captured a dazed student and, while staving off a shower of rocks with his shield, kicked the young man in the groin and the head until his heavy boots sent him in a motionless lump to the pavement. He and the policemen around him pantomimed laughter and dragged the student back behind their lines, leaving a swath of blood behind them. Other policemen along the line watched the spectacle and repeated it.

A line of abandoned buses was parked in the street not far from where Joel stood. A band of students looked inside one of them. "The keys! The keys are still in this one!" They pried open the door and scrambled in. With a sputter and a belch of smoke out the tailpipe, the blue-and-white bus came to life. Cheers and chanting followed it as the student in the driver's seat ground through the gears and sent it careening nearly out of control across the street. Joel watched in horror. Whether intentionally or not — he could not tell which — the bus blindsided a squad of police. The thud-thud of contact with the first pair of policemen and the flopping of a body beneath the wheels carried sickeningly to Joel's side of the street. Some of the students around him gasped in horror, but most went into a paroxysm of cheering that turned to rage when the bus finally ground to a halt and came under attack. The hapless driver and his passengers were thrown out of the bus. Their heads crashed against the pavement. The policemen surrounded them and rained kicks and punches on them. All this was done in full view of the students. When the police left, all that remained of the deed was a few of the many splotches of blood that covered Taepyong Street that day.

Joel had seen enough — more than enough.

He rushed away along with a cluster of middle-aged men to the subway station near the Seoul Plaza Hotel. He tried to descend with them into the station, but his way was blocked by hundreds of people who, like him, were trying to catch a train to escape the riot. He fought his way down into the packed ticket area. Some people shoved change into the ticket booths and ran to the turnstiles without waiting for their tickets; others vaulted over them without paying.

A fresh wave of gas tainted the air and drifted down upon them. Joel cursed himself: he had forgotten that tear gas is heavier than air and will build to high concentrations in low areas. Soon the crush of people reversed and became a stampede trying to get out. Once again he was carried along until he emerged into bright sunshine.

He now found himself, however, on the same side of the street as the police and well behind their positions: he had been turned around underground and had crossed the street down there. Being upwind of the action, the air was not so bad. Curious onlookers milled about.

Mark Follett was there, pacing briskly back and forth, straining to see.

"Joel! Hey, Joel! Over here. Can you believe it? Can you believe it? This is big, man. It's big."

"Were you over there?" Joel asked. "Did you see the fighting?"

"Well, no ... but you did? Holy shit, tell me about it. What did you see?"

Joel knew that Mark wanted only to be appalled, to be entertained by the mayhem and whatever atrocities Joel would speak of. He shook his head. "I want a drink." They ran a few blocks further east to the vast underground shopping complex beneath the Choson Hotel.

"What is this place?" Joel wondered as he and Mark descended into a darkened cocktail lounge. Clusters of well-dressed businessmen, many of them Westerners, huddled in conversations over drinks, talking calmly about matters that did not seem to excite them. A pianist in the corner tinkled out a popular Barry Manilow tune. Joel and Mark quieted down somewhat in the somnolent, smug atmosphere.

"I wish that guy on the piano would find something else to play," Mark whispered. "So what did you see out there? Molotov cocktails? The thing with the bus?"

"You don't want to know," Joel replied, "and I really don't want to talk about it."

"Come on. Can't you see how amazing all this is? It's incredible!"

Just then a commotion began outside the smoked glass wall that separated the lounge from the arcade's walkway. A student, his eyes red and swollen from gas and his head streaked with blood, fell against the glass and slumped to the floor leaving a long red smear behind. The customers gasped but did nothing to help; a couple of them laughed nervously. Joel shook his head in disbelief.

"They have no idea what's going on out there," he muttered to Mark. "The sons of bitches sit in here making their deals, drinking together, having fun, and just down the street the riot police are killing and maiming people. I don't believe this. I don't believe it."

More students, all battle-weary and carrying rocks or sticks, and helping each other along, started pouring into the underground arcade. The pianist stopped playing. Several of the businessmen gingerly side-stepped the students and went away. The bartender, a normally relaxed man whom everyone called "Johnny," muttered bleakly that the democracy movement was about to drive him out of business.

"They're gonna send us home," Mark stated flatly. He could not take his eyes off the flow of injured students. "With all this going on, Peace Corps has got to send us home."

## *Two*

Seoul was quiet the next day. According to the international news that Joel monitored on his shortwave radio, the Korean government had publicly renewed its promise to reform the Yushin Constitution and allow free elections. In response, the students called off further demonstrations for the time being, believing that they had made their point. They were also recovering their strength: according to the BBC, about two hundred students had been seriously injured the day before. And that was only in Seoul — riots had also broken out in Taegu, Kwangju, Chonju, and several other cities, each with its own multitude of casualties.

Joel took the first available expressway bus to Kwangju. Paul and Mi Jin were waiting for him on the front portico of the Catholic Center downtown, taking refuge from a warm spring shower. He saw them first from a distance. Unaware of his presence, they looked to all the world like newlyweds. He ran up and embraced them warmly.

Paul looked tired. He sported a short red beard and had developed crow's feet at the corners of his eyes. Joel could not say that he looked unhealthy; on the contrary, he had never seen him so fit. Paul had a new look in his eyes, an appearance of amused world-weariness that made him look several years older.

It suddenly struck Joel that Paul, who had always looked up to him as a man of experience, had now turned the tables on him. Paul was a fugitive; he loved a woman with whom he had no possible future; of all the places he could have chosen to enjoy a few weeks of happiness with her, he had chosen the most volatile of the cities in Korea. Joel hardly knew whether to congratulate him on how well he was holding up or slap him on the back of his head for his stupidity.

"Leslie's coming, too," Joel said. "She should be here any minute. You heard about the riot in Seoul?" The happy mood of their reunion dissipated like mist under the sun. "I was there. It was like nothing I've ever seen before."

"We had a big *demo* here, too," Paul said. "Somebody estimated twenty thousand students. We didn't take part."

Leslie arrived just then. She caught sight of Paul from the bottom of the steps and turned pale, as if she had seen a ghost. Paul ran to her and gave her a hug that was as much to comfort as to welcome.

"Yes, it really is me," he said as he led her to the portico. "You remember Mi Jin, don't you?"

"Of course."

The four left the Catholic Center and walked up Kumnam Street toward the Provincial Office, or Capitol, which looked like a haphazard stack of white boxes at the terminus of the boulevard. Army tanks stood at the street corners. Riot police idled beside their buses in the nearby alleyways.

"Don't go looking for an inn," Paul said. "We've got you a room at ours."

They turned into one of the smaller streets off Kumnam Street and walked slowly through a vast open-air city market. It was larger than its counterparts in most cities, stretching many blocks parallel to the main street. "You haven't seen Korea until you've browsed the Kwangju Market," Paul smiled. He led them past stalls of every imaginable thing for sale: grains, ordinary and exotic seafood, cloth, pottery, roasted pig heads, and raw sea slugs ready to be eaten on the spot. The smell of cooking hung heavily on the air. The crowds moving through the narrow street on the busy Friday afternoon were enormous, but Paul strolled among the people with a confidence and easy grace that Joel had never before seen in him; he stopped here for some cheerful *repartee* with a woman selling sprouted mung beans, there to sample a piece of blood sausage offered by a smiling old man who all the while watched the antics of two toddlers, his grand-children. Paul and Mi Jin were known and liked among the shopkeepers.

Paul stopped at a streetside tent that served fried *mandu* dumplings and motioned to the others. "Let's have lunch. I'm starving.

"We were expecting you yesterday," he went on. "You couldn't get out of Seoul because of the riot?"

Joel described it to him, from the stopping of his bus to the scene in the underground shopping arcade. "I tried to stay out of the action, but I have to tell you, there were times I wanted to jump in with the students and fight with them. The police were brutal. They had no reason to do the things they did."

"I felt that way, too, at first," Paul said. "A lot of the fighting here in Kwangju went on just down the street from us. But I can't get involved, obviously. If I get caught, it's bad for me. And as for Mi Jin — well, she's just not as involved as she used to be."

Mi Jin, who had been talking with Leslie about news from Chindo, looked up at the mention of her name.

"I am interested, but not active. The help I give to the students is moral support and prayer. Besides," she said, playfully ruffling Paul's hair, "this friend of yours needs constant looking after."

Joel shook his head in disbelief. These two people had lost their jobs because of "political" activity — having acted with or on behalf of the very people who were emerging from the riots bruised and bleeding — yet they behaved like young lovers who cared nothing about the world beyond themselves. He was disappointed.

"I know what you are thinking," Mi Jin cut in. "You are thinking, 'She has turned away from the democracy movement.' That is not true. I care deeply about it. I have worked very hard for the movement all through college and beyond — for over five years now. Now I just want to take a rest. I want to lead a normal life for a little while. There is nothing wrong with that, and I will return to the movement when I'm needed. Until then, I still have many friends among the students and organizers. They know I support them. And besides," she added, "Paul is here. We live day by day."

She spoke without heat, but Joel felt chastised for not seeing the subtleties of their situation.

"What's going on now?" Leslie asked. "It looks like the government is being more moderate. What are your friends telling you?"

"No one believes the government. They are being moderate today — but who knows about tomorrow? We have been promised quicker reforms of the Yushin Constitution. In a gesture of good faith, the leaders of the movement canceled today's *demo*s. They are waiting to see what happens next.

"But I know what will happen; and it is too late to leave Kwangju."

## Three

The Tongbu Express Bus Terminal in Taegu was unusually quiet, even for a Sunday morning. Martin Budzinski noticed it the moment he stepped through the door and strode, unimpeded by any crowds of passengers, to the ticket window. The snack kiosks were closed. He racked his memory for some holiday he had forgotten about, but could think of nothing.

"A ticket for Kwangju, please?" he asked. The young woman behind the glass ignored him. She sat well away from the window, filing her nails and chatting with a friend.

"*Shilehamnida*." Excuse me. He rapped lightly on the window.

The girl looked up, annoyed, and pointed with her nail file at a sheet of paper taped to the window beside him. He could understand only a few words of it. A man in a gray suit sidled up to him and translated it into broken English:

"'Informations. By the order of Martial Law Command, bus service is quitted ... ?'"

"Suspended?"

"Ah, yes. Thank you ... suspend for Sunday, May eighteen, nineteen hundred eighty. Maybe they want everybody to go church!" The man laughed, and the lights of the terminal glinted dully on his dental work.

"I wonder what's going on." Martin muttered.

"Soldiers." The man stopped laughing and chuckled the way Koreans often do when they are nervous. "Soldiers taking all the buses somewheres."

## Four

Chong Il Man, Lee Byong Guk, and others on the Kwangju Students' Council fidgeted in a faculty lounge at Chonnam University on the same Sunday morning. Another student, still out of breath from a wild ride through the city on his motor-scooter, stood before them, telling them what he had seen.

"The convoy split up about a mile from the expressway coming into the city, close to where my parents live. I don't know where the smaller part went, but I followed the larger part downtown. They stopped at the end of Kumnam Street, on the far end from the Provincial Office. I didn't see anyone get out. They just sat there, hundreds of soldiers, waiting for something. Then I came here."

Il Man did not wait for him to finish; by the time he was halfway through the story he was already on the telephone to a friend in Seoul. Time slowed and then seemed to stop while they waited for an answer.

"Hello? Yes, hello?" Il Man listened for a moment, then slammed the receiver down.

"Shit! It wasn't him. And the voice sounded much older, someone I've never heard before. The bastards caught him. Shit!"

At almost the same moment a student at the far end of the room, who had been listening to a transistor radio, broke in. "Listen to this!"

The news from one of the local stations was being read by an unfamiliar voice who practically barked it out, as if commanding its audience to listen. It said that martial law had been broadened to cover the entire country, including the island of Cheju. The colleges and universities were to be closed indefinitely, effective immediately. Political gatherings of every kind and labor strikes were prohibited. The nation's newspapers and broadcast stations were to be watched for "false reporting" of the news. The decree, read in a husky, imperious tone by the Information Minister, ended with a warning: "Anyone who violates these rules, promulgated hereby as Martial Law Decree 10, shall be severely dealt with."

"You damned fools!" Lee Byong Guk screamed. "You fucking morons! Didn't I tell you this would happen? Didn't I tell you that General Chon is a damned snake? He dished out some sweet talk about reforms and elections and all that shit just to keep us quiet while he moved his troops into position. How could you trust that son of a bitch? *Eh?* How could you?"

Il Man ignored Byong Guk and turned to the rider of the scooter. "Where did you say the troops were?"

"Last I saw them, they were downtown."

"No doubt a portion of them have broken off to handle 'hot spots.' So it's only a matter of time before they make it here to the edge of the city," Il

Man said. He peered out the window toward the university's main gate. "If they aren't here already."

Another student, his face red with exertion, bolted into the room. "I just got off the telephone with a friend in Seoul. He's hiding out near Korea University. There was a strategy meeting at Ehwa University last night — a big one, over a hundred people. The police raided it with tear gas and batons, smashing everyone in sight. My friend had to break a window and jump out the back to escape."

This new revelation raised the tension in the room still higher.

"How many did they get?" Il Man asked.

"Twenty or thirty. He didn't know for sure. They put the students on a bus and drove them away. Some of them were unconscious. That's what my friend heard. He was running for his life with the others."

"We've heard enough," Byong Guk broke in. "We've got to do something now! General Chon's been asking for it — now it's time to give it to him. No more appeasement or compromise. It's time to struggle!"

Il Man controlled his sense of shame as best he could, for Byong Guk reminded him of how badly he misjudged the government. "I hope it's not too late. Let's all get on the phones. We have to gather as many friends as we can as quickly as possible. If they want a fight, we'll give them a big one. They're not going to shut down this university, and they're not going to enforce that evil decree without a fight. Martial law ends with us!"

## Five

Joel looked shaken when he and Leslie showed up for Sunday breakfast.

"I've been listening to the news on the shortwave, guys. There's trouble. Big trouble. Maybe we should think about moving to the countryside for a while." He told Paul and Mi Jin about the events of the previous night:

"There've been a lot of arrests. Kim Dae Jung. His grown son. Kim Jong Pil, the former Prime Minister — he's the head of the ruling party, for God's sake. Several members of Kim Yong Sam's party. A Reverend Mun, who's a popular religious leader. A former Army Chief of Staff under President Pak. Businessmen, politicians, former ambassadors, the list goes on. Big, important names."

"What about the students? The student leaders?" Mi Jin gasped.

"The police raided some meeting late last night in Seoul." Joel told what he knew, including the escape of most of them. "We've got to be careful. Martial law has been extended. It covers the whole country, top to bottom, including Cheju Island, and there's a whole raft of new restrictions. You can bet the students will be out in force to protest this."

The four of them rushed outside to have a look around.

Kumnam Street was quiet in the late morning sun. A few bands of students milled about on the street corners listening to radios and arguing among themselves. Most of the people walking about that morning had just got out of church and were roaming through the market in their Sunday clothes with their children, buying food for their dinners, oblivious to the events of the night before. Mi Jin smiled at a little girl in a yellow dress who was playfully hiding from her grandmother among large bins of grain and beans.

"It all looks pretty normal to me," Leslie said hopefully.

Angry shouts suddenly erupted from the middle of Kumnam Street. About thirty students marched together toward the Provincial Office shouting slogans, tentatively at first, but gaining strength as their numbers slowly grew.

"Release Kim Dae Jung! Release the student leaders!" they chanted. "Down with martial law!"

They had marched only one block when an armored personnel carrier rolled around the corner from the Sangmukwan, the Army Reserve office, and came to a halt before them like a heavy, squat insect. A tear gas cannon was mounted on its roof. A squad of riot police in gas masks, helmets, and shields followed it at a quick trot. Tear gas exploded from the cannon in a flurry of sparks. Several of the police carried tear gas launchers. They fired off rounds of canisters that traced purposeful arcs over the street and landed among the people watching from the curb. The onlookers scattered and ran into the market. The students broke up, then regrouped. Several of them ran to a construction site nearby to pick up rocks and bits of cement. They dashed through the clouds of gas, hurled their weapons at the police, then beat a hasty retreat to the curb.

Mi Jin and the Americans ran away, gasping for breath. Billowing clouds of tear gas, wafted far afield by a strong spring breeze, fell like a white blanket over the entire length of the market.

"Hey!" "What's going on?" Coughing and shouts of dismay rose from the narrow street. Men in pressed suits, women in satin *hanbok*s, and children roiled about among the stalls like ants in a mound that had suddenly been sprayed with smoke. They poured through the side streets and emerged along the length of Kumnam Street, coughing and spitting, angry as hornets, growing angrier with each new canister of gas that landed in their midst.

The police responded to the growing crowd with astounding nonchalance. One policeman, a lean, jumpy man who swung his armor about with abandon, broke ranks and ran to the crowd along one curb, shaking his fist, taunting the people, practically asking to be pelted with rocks. They obliged. His fellow policemen responded with more tear gas, and this further enraged them. Within minutes, this game brought traffic to a complete halt.

Kumnam Street swelled with an infuriated throng trapped among buses and cars that could not move.

Mi Jin and her friends stood in front of the Catholic Center; Kumnam Street, alive with over a thousand scrambling people of all ages, stretched out in the distance before them. She blinked away tears, then uttered a cry. A green line of men had formed at the large intersection about a half-mile away. They advanced, and as they got closer it became apparent that they were not riot police, but soldiers in combat gear. White bands were tied around their helmets; they wielded heavy black batons.

"Paratroopers!" Mi Jin cried. "See? Special Forces!"

"Jesus. This is too much. Let's get out of here," Joel said.

The crowd around them grew bigger by the moment. Most were ordinary people driven out of the market by tear gas, but students comprised a growing portion. They carried banners and chanted slogans as they pushed themselves to the front of the pack. A cluster of students soon took up positions opposite the straight green line.

Paul heard a distant command: "Get them!" and the soldiers began running toward the crowd. The students at the edge scrambled to retreat, but they ran up against the inner crowd that had not yet seen the charge. The soldiers waded into them, savagely waving their batons. The people in their path scratched ever more desperately to get away, but the press of abandoned cars hemmed them in. Some still managed to break out. The soldiers broke ranks and pursued them in pairs up the street and into the alleyways. They rained heavy blows with their batons on the people they caught; then they moved on in pursuit of others. The older people, and those whose movements were restricted by their traditional clothes, were the first to fall, bleeding and clutching their heads. A few lay motionless. Ones who were hit but could get back on their feet ran into the alleys. Blood coursed down their heads and soaked their clothes.

Joel grabbed Leslie's arm and ran up an alley. Paul and Mi Jin followed close behind. A dozen students followed them and quickly dispersed among the side streets. Behind them they heard the sharp *clop clop clop clop* of heavy boots upon the concrete pavement. A moment later a scream told them that one of the students had got caught and been mowed down; they dared not pause to turn and see.

The heavy footsteps recovered their rhythm and continued to gain on them.

They turned a corner and approached a small supermarket. Joel pushed the others through the door. Running past the surprised shopkeeper, they found the back of the store and stopped, desperately gasping for breath, inside the dark stock room. The pair of footsteps slowed down and entered the store. Harsh questions were asked of the shopkeeper, who tried to gather the words to answer, but at that moment a fresh scurrying of runners flew past the door. The soldiers quit the store and were gone.

"You in the back! Get out of my store!" the shopkeeper yelled. "Those soldiers almost beat the shit out of me because of you!"

Paul poked his head out of the stock room. "We'll leave, sir, but only if your back door is open."

The shopkeeper grumbled but acceded to the polite request. "Go! I'm closing up."

They worked their way slowly up the winding alley to their own neighborhood, where they hoped to find safety in their inn. At every sound of quickened footsteps, even imagined ones, they tensed and made ready to run. Now and then they heard groans and saw splashes of blood, but they never stopped for long until they came upon an old woman sitting on the ground, moaning piteously. Her hair was matted with blood. The gray satin of her *hanbok* was torn and dirtied.

"Grandmother," Mi Jin said. She knelt down and pried the woman's hand from her head while Joel examined her. "Please don't cry. We will help you."

"Those sons of bitches! Those jackbooted bastards, look what they've done to me. *Owwww, owww* ... my head hurts."

"She's got a nasty bump," Joel said, "and some cuts. But she'll be okay."

The woman looked up at the sound of his voice. "*Miguk salam?* Americans? What are you doing here? You shouldn't be seeing this. *Owwwww.* I was just going home from church, damn it. First they gas us, then they come beat us up. What did we do to them? They're devils, I tell you. The dirty bastards are sons of the devil ..." Paul knelt down and Joel lifted her onto his friend's back, piggy-back style.

"Come with us, Grandmother," Paul said. "We'll find you a doctor."

The nearest clinic was a three-story building whose sign advertised the services of a team of general practitioners. A mob of twenty or thirty wounded people and bystanders had gathered on the street outside. Several were beating on the locked door.

Joel saw some movement behind a window on the second floor. He threw a stone at the window and broke it. A head appeared, shouting angrily.

"Let us in!" Paul cried. "There are injured people out here!"

"Are you crazy?" the man in the window screamed back. "What if the bastards find out that I opened my doors to rebels? Eh? They'll put me out of my practice and arrest me!"

It took time and a number of vicious threats to get the doctor to open his doors; after the people came in, he locked the door behind them. "This is all we're taking," the doctor said as he took stock of the range of injuries before him. "And whatever you do, don't tell anyone where you got treated."

Horror followed horror as afternoon gave way to evening. Brutality fed upon itself: it hung over the city and seeped into every corner like an immense cloud of tear gas, burning up the senses and scrambling rational thought. The paratroopers never let up. Pairs of them made sudden, lightning-quick forays into groups of onlookers, swinging their batons. They never came back empty-handed: a student or some other young person was always dragged away, bleeding and limping, driven by blows. Once in custody, the men were made to strip down to their underwear and lie face down on the street until a transport truck arrived. These attacks were made not in the dark privacy of some back alley but on bright street corners along Kumnam Street in full view of onlookers. The paratroopers took pains to put on a show of bravado. They ignored the deep rumbling and occasional catcalls from the people around them. When each batch of prisoners was safely in custody they made more forays into the street, and so followed this procedure time after time until dark.

Paul, Mi Jin, Joel, and Leslie got home just before the nine o'clock curfew. By nine-thirty the streets were as quiet as a tomb, deserted by all but soldiers and riot police. The four sat together in the small room that Paul and Mi Jin shared. No one spoke; they ate a dinner that the landlady had made for them hours before but had since grown cold. Mi Jin fought back tears. Leslie comforted her as best she could while she herself trembled uncontrollably. Even Joel had lost the ability to be cynical, much less try to make an affectation of it: he could not believe all the things he had seen that day, nor could he yet grasp that those sights had shaken him to the core.

Only Paul seemed calm. He stood by the room's only window, sometimes looking up at the moon, sometimes watching the narrow street below. He touched his fingertips to his thumb, as if making calculations. Joel got up and joined him.

"What are you thinking?" Joel whispered. "A way to get out?"

Paul looked at his friend as if he had said something in Swahili.

"Out of where? Not Kwangju. You're kidding, right?"

" ... No."

"I can't leave Kwangju. If I leave I'd leave Mi Jin, too, and I'm not going to do that."

"But you're in danger here," Joel persisted. "We all are."

"I'm in danger wherever I go. No place is really safe except this room, with her. I'm staying for as long as I can."

## Six

Paul and Mi Jin left their room early the next morning and went straight to the Chonnam University campus. They saw clouds of tear gas billowing up over the main gate long before the gate itself came into view. The taxi-cab driver, who had taken back roads the entire distance from downtown, stopped a mile from their destination and refused to go nearer. "They've been stopping taxis and beating drivers," he said, "because they think we've been carrying students around."

"Then why are you giving us a ride?" Mi Jin asked.

"Because I hate those sons of bitches as much as you do." He grinned a gap-toothed smile. "Besides, at the first sign of trouble, I would've dumped you and lit out of here as fast as I could. No offense."

The pair worked their way around the edge of the conflict that was brewing outside the wall that surrounded the university. The students were trying to get in and the soldiers were blocking their way. Once Paul and Mi Jin worked their way well into the crowd of students — Paul estimated several tens of thousands along this road alone — they joined in the surprisingly well organized give and take of street fighting. The front lines of students charged the standing line of paratroopers, throwing rocks, bottles, and Molotov cocktails in small sections jabbing out into the street, like bee stings. The paratroopers responded with a charge toward the crowd; their tactic was to surround small cells of demonstrators, isolate them by chasing them down alleyways, and then drag as many as they could back behind their lines. The students tried to dilute the soldiers' force by attacking them on several fronts at once. This went on for hours in the morning sunlight.

Paul never lost sight of Mi Jin. He watched her constantly. Both had covered their faces with wet bandannas, like bandits, to help them bear the tear gas that swirled in the air like a heavy fog. Mi Jin's eyes, red-rimmed and weeping from the gas, were on fire. At times Paul stopped and marveled at this side of her that she had never shown him before. Mi Jin ran like an athlete; her small body tensed into a tough, mobile rock-launcher that nearly always hit its mark. Her language slipped into the profane, earthy *patois* of a coastal fisherwoman, full of ripe obscenities, which she bellowed at the top of her lungs. "This is her mother's voice," he thought to himself.

Suddenly the crowds around them became a screaming maelstrom of people running as fast as they could from the line of soldiers down the street.

"What's happening?" Mi Jin shouted.

"Run! Just run!" came the answer from a woman who did not break her stride. A moment later the white-banded helmet of a paratrooper appeared in an opening in the throng, not more than twenty yards away, approaching fast. Paul caught just a glimpse of the outline of an M16 rifle and a sharply pointed object jutting out beyond its muzzle. Mi Jin grabbed his hand and dived into the crowd. As he snapped his body around to follow, his hand whipped out and brushed against something sharp. Splashes of blood on the pavement followed them as they ran with the crowd, here and there jumping over huddled bodies in their path. The paratrooper pursued them for a few steps, then went after a slower student, a short-legged woman wearing a pink sweater and blue jeans. He lunged at her with his bayonet and she crumpled to the ground like a marionette whose strings had been cut. He paused to pull out his weapon, got his footing back, and ran after another.

Paul and Mi Jin scrambled into the first alleyway they could find and followed its winding course deep into a run-down neighborhood. The area was deserted. The clomping of pursuing footsteps never left them; they could not be sure whether they belonged to paratroopers or to others like themselves. The concrete walls played tricks on their hearing, amplifying and distorting the sounds in a mad echo chamber: corners that seemed to conceal running feet revealed an empty alley when they turned to look, while others that had sounded quiet were suddenly rounded by terrified students.

They paused for a moment, listened, then looked at each other. Paul had panic in his eyes and his face was pale and sweaty. His hand began to throb with pain.

"You've been hurt!" Fear quickly left Mi Jin. She cradled his hand. A three-inch gash splayed across his knuckles; the outer skin separated as a red trough that still bled. She searched her pockets and came up with a handkerchief, which she tied tightly over the wound. "We've got to get you to a doctor for stitches."

They joined hands and went back into the maze of alleys. The sound of footsteps sent them running again this way and that, first up one alley, then down another until they were completely lost. They ran until Paul tripped over a soft obstacle and went flying.

"*Oof!*" He regained his senses when Mi Jin screamed. He raised his eyes to stare into the face of a prone figure, its face covered with blood, on which he had fallen. It did not move. He jumped up quickly.

The body was next to a pile of twelve others, all motionless, blood flowing in a stream into a drainage ditch beside them. They were stacked like firewood, heads all at one end, some on their backs, some on their stomachs.

The sound of pursuit filtered up the ally.

"Hey ... one of them's moving!" Paul cried. A young man with rough, stubby features, wearing a high school uniform, stirred. Another body of a much larger man lay on top of him, and he tried unconsciously to push it away as a sleeping child would move a heavy blanket. He groaned softly.

They moved to the mound of bodies and grasped the one on top. It was heavy. They struggled with it for several minutes before they could roll it to one side.

"*Yah!*" A harsh voice shot out from the street.

"Christ!" Paul's eyes followed the sound of footsteps. A paratrooper brandished a baton and bore down on them with long strides.

"Jong Shik, we have to go. Come on!" Mi Jin grabbed his arm and pulled with unnatural strength. They ran for hours and finally, late in the afternoon, found their way home.

## *Seven*

"See this, Leslie? You have to push the skin together and pass the needle through..."

Joel was tending to the gash across Paul's hand in their rooms under the yellow light of a desk lamp. Paul had returned in a daze, discouraged from getting help at the hospital by the chaos he found there. Joel drew on his experience as a paramedic, boiling a sewing needle with a length of thread. He also made a mild saline solution with kitchen salt and boiled it, then used it to irrigate the wound. It was the best he could do. He worked without a local anesthetic; Paul came to himself under the pain of the needle. Mi Jin held him tightly.

"Will he be all right?"

"He'll be fine. It looks worse than it is. We need more antiseptic and dressings and antibiotics, though. And he should go to the hospital as soon as he can get in."

"There's a drugstore around the corner," Mi Jin said. "We can get those things there."

The drugstore lit the gray street with an abundance of fluorescent light gleaming off its white counters. Huge roll-up doors hung over the front like a garage. The street was relatively quiet.

"Leslie, get some bandages and creosol and first aid stuff — whatever you can find," Joel said. "I'll get some antibiotics. Hell, I can't believe it: I'm actually glad they're selling them over the counter. Paul, I could use your help.

"I was listening to the shortwave radio this morning," he whispered as they walked up an aisle. "It's getting worse by the minute. Fifty thousand people in the riots this morning. Five hundred people arrested, five dead bodies, even a dead child. You and I know it's far worse than that. Those bodies you saw won't ever be brought to light."

Paul said nothing; his mind was on the bodies and the live one he could not save. Joel understood and let him alone.

Leslie and Mi Jin met them at the front counter with their arms loaded, but only with odds and ends, items that others had judged not worth buying. "This is the last of it," Leslie said. "No surprise: there's been a run on supplies."

They were near the front of the store, at the cashier's station, when the sound of screams and rapid footsteps approached from the street. Paul became agitated and let out a deep groan of pain.

"No! No, not again!"

A young boy, not yet out of middle school, and bleeding from an ugly gash across his face, ran crying into the store. A lone paratrooper followed him with his baton raised for another blow. The druggist started to lower the metal door. The soldier had to duck to get in.

Paul sprang upon the paratrooper with a brutish yell. He grappled with him and tried to wrest the baton from his hand. Joel stood transfixed for a moment at his friend's impulsive act, but quickly joined him. Together they managed to hold the soldier away from the boy and push him toward the door. The soldier's eyes widened at the sight of the foreigners; this seemed to blunt the force of his attack. With one last shove, Paul and Joel pushed him out the door and watched him fall. The druggist, with help from Mi Jin and Leslie, slammed the door shut.

Joel saw an immediate change in Paul. Before the attack, he had been brooding over his first exposure to ugly, violent death and the faceless soldiers who brought it. Paul had got close enough to glimpse the eyes of this one, to see his young pockmarked face and to understand that even a paratrooper could lose a fight.

"We got him," Paul exulted. He beat his fists on the metal door and let out a whoop. "We knocked him on his ass!"

"Did you smell his breath?" Joel asked.

"I did. He's been drinking. How else can a human being do the things he's been doing?"

In days to come, as the crisis wore on, others who had been caught in close quarters with those men would make the same observation.

They left the drug store by the back entrance as soon as the coast seemed clear and made their way to the US Cultural Center, five blocks away. Its high brick wall loomed over the wrought iron main gate, which was closed fast. A Korean employee stood just outside, looking at the credentials of people who tried to get in. Paul recognized a few American missionaries and aid workers on the other side. Joel, Leslie, and Paul showed their Peace Corps identification cards and were admitted. Mi Jin was stopped.

"Are you a United States citizen?" the man asked, in English.

Mi Jin shook her head. Paul offered his passport. "She's with me, sir," he said. "I'm a citizen."

The man did not look at Paul's credentials. "No Koreans are allowed today. Only United States citizens."

"But I told you she's with me. She's ... my wife."

The man looked at him, then at her. "No exceptions."

"Joel, Leslie, you stay here. I'm leaving," Paul said. He walked out and rejoined Mi Jin.

Joel followed him out. "What?"

"I can't leave her."

Joel considered, then turned to Leslie. "I'm going with them."

"Come on, guys. Don't do this to me," she pleaded.

"You'll be safe here," Paul said. "You'll probably get a military escort back to Seoul. It'll be okay."

Leslie hesitated, crestfallen, and Joel ran back through the door. He put his arm around her and spoke gently: "Look, I know how hard it's been on you these past few days. Nobody will think less of you for getting out of here. Taking refuge here is the only sane thing to do."

"But I'm going to worry about you."

"We'll be all right. I want you safe." He kissed her forehead and went out again.

The man closed the gate.

## Eight

The back streets of Kwangju became increasingly clogged with people. Surprisingly few were of college age. They were parents, siblings, and relatives of the students who had been demonstrating on the big boulevards. Mi Jin, Paul, and Joel came upon a grandmother who, confident of her invincibility as an elder, harangued a gathering of other seniors on a street corner:

"Those sons of bitches are murderers! I don't know about you, but I remember the Japs all those many years ago when they ground us all into the dirt. The Japs never treated us this bad. They were devils, but this is ten times worse!"

Her audience murmured agreement.

"What makes it worse is that these bastards are our own people. Fellow Koreans, anyway — I hear they're really all Kyongsangdo lepers. What business does a Korean have killing another Korean? Eh?"

The three moved quickly along. Paul led them at a brisk walk, almost a trot.

"Where are you going?" Joel asked.

Paul said nothing, but pressed on as if looking for something.

"No, Paul. Not that pile of bodies! It's being guarded for sure. Even if you could get to it, the guy's probably dead now. Listen to me. Let's go home." He caught his arm and tried to pull him around.

Just then they heard the light scurrying of feet from around the corner. They hung back in a recessed doorway while a small band of students ran by, followed in a moment by a pair of paratroopers. A minute later, the *whack! whack!* and moans of a beating echoed back to them. The incident was short but violent. The students who got caught were ordered to remove their clothes and then herded away. When Joel, Paul, and Mi Jin rounded the corner they found bloodstained clothing and some fresh pools of blood on the ground.

"Hold on," Joel whispered. "Do you hear that?"

In a small chink in the wall, deep in shadow, lay a short man who wore the white headband of a prominent student association. A large wooden cross hung from a leather cord around his neck. He gripped his head and moaned. A dark mass of blood seeped down his back.

"He's from the theological seminary," Mi Jin said, reading the slogan on his headband. "*Yah!* Can you stand? Let us help you."

The man did not respond; he only let go of his head and tossed it spasmodically from side to side.

Joel ran his fingers gently along the back of his head and paused near the space where the skull meets the neck. "This is bad — very bad. He needs to get to a hospital right away. It's dangerous to move him, but we've got no choice."

"The University Hospital is close by," Mi Jin said.

With Paul and Mi Jin's help, Joel heaved the man gently onto his back. He carried him like a Korean mother carries her sleeping infant against her back, her hands clasped under its bottom.

They did not have to ask directions to the hospital: traffic told them where it was. A fast-moving stream of bleeding humanity flowed into the hospital grounds and strove to get the most seriously injured through the front doors. The gatekeeper had long since quit his post; he had been drafted into service inside as an orderly while the regular orderlies, those familiar with the phenomena of trauma, became nurses. Thus under the unrelenting influx of injuries, which strained the hospital to its limit, nearly everyone who worked there was promoted: orderlies became nurses, nurses worked as doctors, and all doctors became surgeons.

"Don't bring him in here!" a tiny nurse barked at Joel. "Triage is over there!" She pointed an imperious finger at the lobby next to the emergency room, which had been cleared of chairs. Joel set his load on the floor upon a blood-soaked pallet beside a rack of Hello Kitty children's books.

"My God," Paul whispered. "Look at this place!"

His senses reeled at the chaos around him. Everyone — medical staff, the injured, family members — moved in such a jumble that his eyes could not focus on any single object. The screams of pain and grief were hellish. Even the smell of the place held him transfixed, for it was an odd, unreproducible combination of antiseptic, urine and excrement from the dying, and the faintly metallic odor of blood.

Joel meanwhile was stumbling through an explanation to a nurse that he, as a paramedic, could be of great help. The nurse, who had been caught in mid-flight to an operating room, listened politely for a moment and then curtly told him to see an orderly if he had an injury. He had better luck with a doctor who hurried through next; the latter put him to work in an area which he called, with grim humor, "The Tailor Shop." It was a corner where patients had their lacerations cleaned and stitched up.

"I've got to go. I can't stay here," Mi Jin said. Paul first thought she meant she could not stand the sight of the blood and chaos. It later occurred to him that she was more angry than frightened, and that the best channel for her anger was the street, fighting as before. He left with her.

## Nine

The street fighting had escalated while Mi Jin and the others were at the hospital. When they emerged they saw columns of black smoke rising into the sky from diverse areas of the city.

A familiar voice rang out from a street corner while they pressed through a noisy crowd on Kumnam Street.

"Mi Jin! *Yah,* over here!" Chong Il Man glanced about furtively, then bounded out to meet them. His shirt had been ripped on one sleeve, and his shoulder was caked with dried blood. "Elder Sister, I heard you were dead. Thank God you're alive."

"What ... who told you I was dead?"

"No one in particular. It was a rumor. The rumors are flying these days, wild ones, and everyone believes them. I've heard that the soldiers are drunk, or on drugs."

"That one's true," Paul said. "I know."

Il Man gave him a respectful nod. "So you've gotten close enough to see for yourself. But that's only one rumor that's been proved true, and in just one case. How can we believe anything else of what we hear? The government tells lies about us. They lie to us. Our own people innocently spread half-truths that grow into the equivalent of lies. We have nothing to believe in."

"Take a look around you," Mi Jin said bitterly. She pointed at another assault by a phalanx of paratroopers just visible in the distance. "Isn't that enough?"

"Elder Sister, there's a meeting of what's left of the student associations. I'm on my way there now. You'll come, won't you? And the American can come, too. It'll be good to have some outside corroboration of the 'condition' of the soldiers. I warn you, though, Pak Jong Shik. Americans are not popular right now. I'll vouch for you, but you have to be prepared. Most of the people at this meeting will hate you because you are an American and because Jimmy Carter is backing General Chon."

A half hour later they entered Trouble House which, being deep within a poor neighborhood, was far from the fighting. Strongly-built students, armed with heavy truncheons, stood in pairs at the front and back entrances. The room, boisterous with argumentation, went quiet when Paul walked in.

"This is my friend Han Mi Jin, whom most of you know," Il Man said. "And this is Mister Pak Jong Shik, a friend of mine."

Some in the room, at a separate table near an open window, sneered. "How did he get a Korean name?" one of them said. "Give me a break."

Il Man patted Paul on the shoulder and continued. "The American, as I said, is a friend. He's on our side. I trust him."

"Ask him if his fucking government is doing anything to stop this atrocity upon the people of Kwangju," Lee Byong Guk said.

"I don't know," Paul replied, in Korean. "I haven't been keeping up on my government's actions."

"That was a rhetorical question, American. The fact is, your government is helping Chon Du Hwan and his clique by guarding the Demilitarized Zone while Chon moves his troops around. The Americans are making this crisis possible."

"No. You can't be right."

"I am right. The United States pulls the regime's strings in all other things. If the Americans really wanted the atrocity to end, they could end it today. All they'd have to do is give the word. They haven't. Would you like to see what your government is responsible for?" He picked up a sheaf of large photographs and threw them down on the table in front of Paul. "Feast your eyes."

The pictures were in black and white, and still damp from the developing bath. The detail in them was devastatingly clear. They depicted piles of bodies stacked grotesquely like firewood. One pile resembled the one he fell onto earlier. Other photographs showed stray victims splayed about on the streets like the aftermath of a tornado, their bodies left as they fell. One body was that of a boy dressed in a high school student's uniform. He looked very young, even for a student.

Paul glanced at the picture, looked again, and turned white.

"Jong Shik, what's wrong?" Mi Jin asked.

"I know this boy. Oh, God." He let out a long shuddering breath and closed his eyes. "His name is Pak Song Min. He's the son of my boarding house *ajumoni* in Mokpo. He was a great kid, like a little brother to me." He sat down hard and blinked away tears.

One of the students, a hard-bitten engineering student from Choson University, cleared his throat.

"Welcome to our land of misery."

After a pause, someone mercifully spoke up. "So where do we stand now? Shouldn't we be checking how many of our people are arrested, how many are killed and wounded, how many damned troops are out there? I feel lost without information."

They consulted among themselves, tallying the names of the leaders now arrested — those from whom they had not heard — and added to that number an estimate of the multitude of unnamed ones who had been seen in the hospitals.

"Well, we have a number," Il Man said finally. "But it's surely so inaccurate that it's almost useless. It looks like we've lost between fifty and sixty leaders so far, including a half-dozen from our group here and the rest from other student organizations. Arrested students in general — add another five to six hundred. That's a conservative guess. Wounded — add another thousand."

"I know where they're taking the ones they arrest," said one in the group. "Not to jail; there's not enough room there. They're holding them on the grounds of Choson and Chonnam Universities. I saw some being driven there in trucks. My aunt works at Chonnam. She says they've got them packed into classrooms without beds and with no food. She told me that none of them has eaten since yesterday morning. And most of them are wounded, kicked or beaten with sticks."

"We have to struggle at those spots," Byong Guk said, jumping up. "Set up more *demo*s. Let everyone know about it. Concentrate our numbers there and tell them we will not stand for it."

All present nodded in agreement, though no one believed for a moment that their demonstration would free the captives or ease their suffering in the slightest. Mi Jin prayed for a miracle.

"I need to find my friend's body," Paul said. "Can anyone help me?"

## Ten

The United States Cultural Center offered Leslie a level of physical comfort that she had not known in months. The library, an unadorned room with blue institutional carpeting, sturdy oak furniture, and the smell of book glue, could have been found at any small college in the United States. She shared it with two dozen other Americans, all chattering about the violence with which the students were defying the government. None of them seemed to know what they were talking about. Leslie wanted to shout at them, "No, no! You've got it all backwards. The soldiers are attacking ordinary people with clubs and bayonets! I saw them!"

After a while the Western sterility of the room became too much for her to stand: she craved some of the chaos to which she had lately grown accustomed. She left the building. A planter in the courtyard provided a place to sit amid the disorder of interrupted gardening. This calmed her slightly.

The odor of a distant tear gas assault wafted over the wall and stung her nose. Shouts of "Death to the American collaborators!" and worse came from students as small bands of them marched past. She started to cry, due in equal measure to the remnants of tear gas and to the tension that was just now finding release.

A movement nearby attracted her attention. Against the outer wall of the courtyard, perched on a large rock like an overweight sprite, sat a middle-aged American man. He wore a white short-sleeved shirt, tight around the middle, and dark trousers. He smoked an unfiltered cigarette down to its end until it threatened to singe his fingers.

"You don't want to sit there," he said.

"Excuse me?"

"You don't want to sit there," he repeated. Just then a rock about the size of a softball arced over the wall and landed less than a yard from Leslie's feet. A lone voice outside shouted an obscenity against the United States.

"That's why. The fuckers have been doing it off and on all day." He shifted his weight on the rock and adjusted his trousers around his seat, but did not invite her to sit down. "Name's Bob. I'm with AID. That's the Agency for International Development."

"I know. I'm Leslie. Peace Corps."

"A social worker," Bob snorted. "How come you're not out there being a do-gooder?"

"What?"

"Well, that's what you people do, isn't it? Me, I don't really give a shit about all the mess going on out there. I just want outta here. Got a wife and kid up in Seoul. They're Americans, not Koreans. We're gonna ship out pretty soon. I got a transfer. Not a moment too soon, if you ask me. Korea's the pits. It's a helluva place to live, isn't it?"

"Well, it's got its good points and bad points, just like everywhere else."

"Good points? Hah!" Bob spat. "Name one. You can't eat the food. The Koreans I work with are assholes, corrupt like you wouldn't believe. The place stinks. Hell, the whole country smells like *kimchi!* The Koreans, they eat that shit all the time, and then something in it comes out of their pores, like sweat. My poor wife, she almost fainted when she stepped off the plane."

"Believe me, it's not as bad as all that." This man provoked an instant dislike in her. She had her own criticisms of the country — though milder and more delicately expressed — but she took umbrage when someone else voiced theirs, someone less entitled than she to harbor criticisms. God above, do I sound like that? she wondered. She quickly changed the subject.

"I'm surprised there aren't many people here yet."

Bob shrugged. "They're all at work, I guess. Most of 'em work in hospitals, you know. Kwangju is big on Catholic and Presbyterian hospitals. Me, I don't give a shit about this place. I'm tellin' you the truth, now. All the people gettin' beat up here got it coming. The government wouldn't be steppin' in if there wasn't serious trouble goin' on. Like the North Koreans. They're behind all this. I say to hell with 'em. I got nothing keeping me here. As soon as that evacuation bus pulls up, I'll be the first one on it."

The strange little man's mention of the hospitals, and of the other Americans' duty to work in them during the crisis, called to mind Joel stitching up the wounded. She suffered a sudden pang of remorse. One of her life's few clear choices suddenly rose before her. It frightened her, because she knew that the right decision would put her back in danger. She thought of Joel, then gazed at Bob, who had paused to light his third cigarette off the stub of the second. She took a deep breath, wished him luck, and left the compound through a side door.

## Eleven

Paul and Mi Jin found Song Min's body in a makeshift morgue in the gymnasium of a nearby high school. It lay covered with plastic in a wooden coffin. In traditional fashion, a ball of cloth had been stuffed in its mouth to prevent his soul from re-entering and animating his body. But this preparation, along with the appearance of the eyes — left open, looking surprised — was too gruesome for Paul to bear. He hurriedly pulled the lid of the coffin up and closed it. Only then, looking up, did he notice the rest of the room. Droves of weeping, shouting relatives filled it to overflowing. Seven other coffins lay in two neat rows. Most were covered with Korean flags. A few relatives had placed photographs of the dead — school pictures or snapshots — on top of them.

Mi Jin went away for a few minutes while Paul sat by Song Min's coffin and prayed. She came back with a votive candle and a large flag. He spread the flag over the coffin and lit the candle on top.

"It's too bad we don't have a picture of him," Mi Jin said.

"Oh. I almost forgot." He searched through his wallet and finally produced the school picture Song Min had given him months ago in Mokpo, the one that came with the written admonition on its back never to forget him. He propped the portrait against the candle and prayed again. Mi Jin put her arm around his shoulder and, when he finished, they talked about the boy's life. They left an hour later. The sun was just going down.

## Twelve

When Joel returned to the inn from the hospital later that evening, he found Leslie sitting in the gloom upon a cushion on the floor, her knees pulled up under her chin, listening. At the sound of the his steps, she bounded up and fell into his arms. He stroked her hair for a long time until Paul and Mi Jin came home.

The four spoke little, out of exhaustion and a reluctance to evoke the horrors they had seen that day. Eventually they fell asleep, all in the same room and fully clothed. They spent the night waking up at every sound, as animals do who fear predators.

A strained quiet ruled the night outside their rooms. The strictly enforced curfew had sent most people home or into hiding. But in the distance, to the north, where the universities were, the breeze occasionally brought whiffs of conflict, the whispers of chanting that faded in and out as the wind changed direction. Everyone's dreams reflected that sound, and also the sounds burned into memory during the day: the tear gas cannon, the angry buzzing of the crowd, the clatter of heavy boots on pavement, the cacophony of unrestrained grief.

Joel could sleep least of all. Sleep had come hard for him since childhood, when somehow he had gotten into his head the notion that sleep was a nightly rehearsal of death. He went to the window, lit a cigarette, and strained to hear the fighting that still went on.

## Thirteen

Paul, Mi Jin, and Leslie awoke the next morning to the hollow sound of a voice on Joel's shortwave radio.

"The BBC says about forty people have been killed, and a hundred injured," Joel said. "We all know that's short of the mark." He left it on that station until the announcer moved on to another story.

"I was listening to the local news a while ago. You might find this interesting." He switched to the AM band and tuned in one of the local stations.

"The city of Kwangju is quiet this morning after unprecedented attacks by hooligans against police over the past two days. Injuries from hurled rocks and bottles have caused dozens of injuries among riot control personnel. Thanks to their restraint in dealing with the demonstrations, police have reported no deaths on either side of the conflict and few injuries among the renegade students."

The announcer's voice droned in the background while Mi Jin's face went red with fury. "How can they say such a thing?" she sputtered. "How can they lie like that?"

They left immediately to go to the nearest radio station.

The maze of streets around their building was choked with thick black smoke. Paul counted a half-dozen overturned and burning cars on Kumnam Street. People milled about watching the fires. Paul and Mi Jin ran the next few blocks.

The crowds grew thicker as they went. Mi Jin heard snatches of angry talk as they moved along:

"They've taken my daughter away, and I don't know where she is."

"My next door neighbor got bashed in the head by one of those goons. Now he's in a coma."

"Last night I saw a body being dragged behind a troop carrier, stripped naked and bleeding."

Every word drew the people closer together in fleeting camaraderie as they cursed the paratroopers and the government that had unleashed them upon its own people.

Paul stopped when the mob became too tightly packed for them to go farther. A column of black smoke rose from the windows and roof of the broadcasting station. The students near the edge of the fire danced for joy; they had apparently started it. "No more lies! No more lies!" they chanted.

"What happened to the people inside?" Mi Jin asked of no one in particular. In seeming answer to her question, a dark figure appeared in the building, silhouetted against the flames. It looked like a portly man in smoldering rags that were once a business suit. The figure staggered among the blackened furniture and then threw its head back in a howl of pain. It dropped to the floor and was lost.

"Hurrah!" the crowd shouted. "Hurrah! No more lies! No more lies!"

Mi Jin buried her face in her hands and fought to get away from the building. "My God, my God!" she screamed when Paul caught up with her. "What are we doing? Oh God, what are we doing?"

Paul hurried her away from the mob and headed up toward Kumnam Street; from there he meant to take her home. She held her hands over her mouth and choked as if ready to vomit. They turned the corner near the Provincial Office and looked up the street.

Kumnam Street stretched out before them in a roiling sea of people as far as the eye could see, even past the distant spot where the paratroopers had launched their first attack. Paul heard later that two hundred thousand people, a quarter of Kwangju's population, including businessmen, house-wives, workers, and the elderly, had gone out to demonstrate against the government. The roar of the protests was deafening. Others just entering the street stopped and stared, too, astonished at their numbers.

## Fourteen

Mrs. So, the *ajumoni* of the inn at which so many Peace Corps Volunteers had stayed over the years, wiped drops of splattered paint off her arm and stepped back to admire her handiwork. On a large white western-style pillowcase — a gift from a volunteer long ago for which she had no further use — she had daubed in crude red letters:

"Don't waste any time! Give blood right now!"

She knew the wording left much to be desired, but she wrote the way she spoke, and for a woman who had not read a complete page of anything since middle school, she did not consider it half bad.

"What are you doing, Omma?"

Mrs. So jumped. Her daughter came in. The young girl's eyes widened at the sight of her mother's project.

"You messed up one of the fancy pillowcases!"

"*Yah!* Never mind. It's for a good cause. We never used it, anyway. Many, many people need blood today. The hospitals are running out."

"Are you going out to march, Omma?" The girl's eyes gleamed with amusement and eagerness. The amusement came from knowing that her mother had never before cared about anything beside gossip and the price of food at the local market, and yet now she was turning into a positive rebel. The eagerness came from an ache to go out herself, for a number of her friends had already slipped away from home to march in the huge rallies that even now could be heard faintly, far off in the distance.

"*Aigo,* what do you take me for, you little pup? I wouldn't be caught dead following that rabble around. No —" She motioned toward the open front door. In the courtyard stood a circle of middle-aged women like herself, dowdy in their respectable clothes, all carrying home-made banners. "We're going to walk through the neighborhood with our signs. Where's my stick to hang it from? Ah, there it is. We're not marching, we're going shopping. The signs will just be there to remind people to do the right thing."

The daughter clapped her hands and pranced gaily out of the room, overjoyed at the change in her mother.

## Fifteen

As the character of the demonstrations changed, from students to ordinary citizens, so did the character of the leadership.

Almost every organization in the city — civic, professional, and religious — appointed a committee to deal with the crisis. Clerics met and for once did not dwell on the theological points that separated them: they knew that just as many Baptists were fighting and dying as were Roman Catholics and Buddhists. Trade unions, merchants' associations, and even ladies' flower arranging clubs resolved either to support the demonstrators or to take direct action against the government troops. Even the local chapters of the pro-government Saemaul Movement that dotted both the city neighborhoods and the countryside participated by turning a blind eye to its members' activities and suspending meetings until further notice.

Representatives of the most active committees met in a spacious church auditorium on the outskirts of the city at noon on Tuesday, two days after the beginning of the crisis. Under a haze of cigarette smoke the room quickly became a madhouse of shouts and boisterous debate that the church's Baptist pastor tried in vain to control.

"Look at these old farts," Lee Byong Guk remarked angrily to Mi Jin and Paul when they arrived. "What right have they got to be calling the shots now? That's what they intend to do, you know, but they've got no right to. They weren't getting themselves killed out there from the beginning, like we students were."

The public address system went on, and the "One, two, three, *yaaah* ..." of the technician brought a little order to the room. When no one stepped up to the microphone for several minutes, the noise and arguing began again, this time over choosing a leader. The arguments went on for nearly half an hour, after which time it was finally decided that all they needed was someone to stand up there and manage questions from the floor. The church's pastor reluctantly took the job. The loudest speakers got recognized first.

"I got something to say about how the taxi drivers were treated last night!" shouted a small man who was wound as tight as a knot, his neck muscles bulging underneath his driver's uniform. A number of men surrounding him, all in similar uniforms, urged him on. "Let him speak! Go on, get up there!"

"I am Kim — well, you don't need to know my name," he said, not in the least intimidated by the crowd. "I'm a taxi driver. Those damned soldiers have been rougher than hell on us drivers. Those sons of bitches started coming after us because they thought we were carrying students to the *demo*s. I don't give a shit whether that's true or not — I didn't carry any — but they got me anyway. A whole squad of 'em charged my cab while I was taking some older people to Buk District. They smashed my windshield. I don't know what happened to my passengers after they dragged them out, but I can tell you they beat the shit out of me." He lifted his shirt and displayed several red marks and an elastic bandage wrapped around his ribs. "The same thing happened to a lot of drivers — more than I can count. You should hear the stories going around among the drivers."

"So what are you gonna do about it?" yelled someone in the audience.

"I'll tell you what we should do. We should get our asses out on the street and join the protest. Did you see the crowd a little while ago on Kumnam Street? We should be out there with them!"

The audience was disposed to adopt any plan that involved action, no matter how ineffective or dangerous. After some discussion, they decided that a protest convoy of taxicabs and buses should wend its way through the streets from Mudung Stadium, on the west side of the city, to Kumnam Street downtown. Volunteers were asked for. Paul and Mi Jin eagerly raised their hands.

After that, a seemingly endless stream of comments and exhortations came up, most of them of little importance. Some speakers whipped the crowd into a frenzy, acting like angry cheerleaders. Others spoke in varying degrees of eloquence about some fallen comrade. One major piece of business was Byong Guk's reminder that nearly eight hundred student demonstrators were still being held at the Choson- and Chonnam University campuses and had to be freed. A massive demonstration was organized for later that night at those spots.

Almost as an afterthought, and quietly, a group of men was put together to try and negotiate with the martial law authorities for an end to the violence. They called themselves the Citizens' Committee and hardly anyone noticed their presence.

## Sixteen

The convoy of taxicabs and buses got underway early the next morning. A blue and white city bus was already rumbling with life when Paul and Mi Jin got on board, accompanied by its driver, a Mr. Choi. He was a cheery, open-faced fellow whose only nod to the unusual circumstances of the day was to remove his white gloves. In all other respects, from his neat blue uniform to his green Saemaul cap, he was a model of neatness that put his fellow drivers to shame.

"Let me drive," Paul urged, and Mr. Choi good-naturedly agreed.

"Remember the order of gear shift positions, young sir," he instructed. "First is up, second is down, third is over and up. Shift as fast as you like. This bus can take it."

"Are we ready?" Paul called out. He climbed into the well-worn driver's seat and let out a gleeful cowboy whoop. "Passengers will please remain seated while the bus is in motion. C'mon, you guys out there! Get a move on!"

The convoy lurched to a slow start and took a few turns around Mudung Stadium to pick up some late joiners. Paul used the time to get accustomed to the feel of the bus. When the line of taxis and buses emerged in a straight line going straight downtown, the crowd of several hundred people watching from the sidewalk burst into wild cheers.

The trip went smoothly for the first mile. Excited throngs of people lined the streets and cheered them on. Soon after that, however, the troops discerned the purpose behind the convoy and moved in toward the vehicles.

"Keep your speed up, sir," Mr. Choi warned. "If you don't, we'll be stopped." Paul knew what he meant, and his enthusiasm quickly evaporated. Mi Jin, sitting behind him, put her hand on his shoulder.

What if the bus is surrounded? Paul worried. What if a soldier steps out in front of me and I have to stop or run him over?

"Don't stop for any reason," Mr. Choi said, as if reading his thoughts. "Run the bastards down if you have to. That's the whole point of this drive!"

"No it isn't," Paul said.

"Follow the bus ahead closer, Jong Shik," Mi Jin urged.

As they approached the center of the city the convoy moved slower and slower, partly because their way was blocked by overturned cars from previous riots, partly because the troops had started to take concerted action against them. Tear gas wafted through the open windows of the bus. Paul, Mi Jin, and Mr. Choi tied wet handkerchiefs around their faces. As their speed declined still more, the troops banged against the sides of the bus with their batons.

Finally the convoy ground to a halt. Soldiers broke the windshield of the bus ahead of them. They tore open the doors and dragged the occupants out. The crowd of demonstrators that had lined the streets began to react. Like an ocean wave, it began to surge beyond the curb. The more able-bodied students in front raised their long sticks and rocks and charged.

A soldier ran up to Mr. Choi's bus and slipped his fingers into the door. Two more came to help him and they managed to pry it part-way open. Mi Jin screamed.

"Get up! Get up, Jong Shik!"

Mr. Choi had prepared himself for this. From behind the driver's seat he withdrew a baseball bat and bounded for the door. When the first trooper stuck his head through, Mr. Choi clubbed him in the face, sending him reeling back into his comrades' arms. Just then, a band of students rushed the soldiers and cleared a small path outside the door.

"Now! Get out now!" Mr. Choi yelled.

Paul grabbed Mi Jin by the arm and dived out the door. He collided with a student, and felt the student's elbow smash painfully into his jaw. Mi Jin stumbled against a soldier, but because he was distracted by a student preparing to throw a large rock, she pushed against him and jumped away. Paul and Mi Jin fought their way through the crowd. When they reached the curb they looked back. The student with the rock had smashed open the soldier's face; Mr. Choi, bloodied from the side of his face to his belly, reeled into a band of soldiers and was swallowed up by them. As far as they could tell later, after repeated inquiries, no one ever saw him again.

## Seventeen

"Hell, look at how they've got this place locked up!"

Chong Il Man made the remark to no one in particular, and did not expect a response as he stood across the street from Chonnam University' main gate. Two lines of soldiers and a pair of tanks stood guard on either side of the gate. Armored personnel carriers, trucks, jeeps, and buses were parked at intervals along the high wall that encircled the campus. Between the soldiers and the wall a long helix of barbed wire glinted orange and red in the light of the setting sun. The guard detail seemed content to stay on its side of the street. A small but angry crowd of demonstrators milled about opposite them.

"That's the biggest prize they've won in this whole sick business of theirs," a woman in the darkness said. "That and the students they're holding in there."

A breeze blew in from the east, fragrant with the aromas of the moist earth and new flowers on Mount Mudang. For a moment it overpowered the fumes from the diesel engines downwind of him. Il Man breathed it in deeply, eager to take pleasure in something, anything at all.

The sound of cymbals and drums and chanting came out of the distance, softly at first, but with rising urgency as it moved through the streets toward the university. Il Man could hear the newly arriving demonstrators before he could see them.

"Death to Chon Du Hwan! Free the students! Free Kim Jae Kyu!"

They repeated it over and over until they turned a corner and marched down the street toward the main gate. There were about two thousand of them, by Il Man's estimate. They did not slow down as they reached the gate.

"Free the students! Free the students!"

The soldiers began to take notice. Some scurried away to consult senior officers in the rear. The front line put their riot batons in their belts and unslung the rifles from their shoulders.

"Free the students! Free the students!"

The protesters did not slow down. By the time they came within a block from the gate, five troop carriers swung into view. Paratroops jumped out and hustled to form a new line. They all carried M16s at the ready.

"Wait for my command!" Il Man thought he heard the commander shout. The troops knelt silently on the sidewalk. The column of marchers proceeded relentlessly. Their shouting almost drowned out the cymbals and gongs they carried. "Free the students!"

"Ready ... Fire!"

Il Man was not sure what happened next. A volley of loud pops and bursts of smoke erupted from the soldiers' line. Screaming broke out all around him. He fell to the ground while the marchers scattered like minnows fleeing from a stone flung into the water. Another volley of gunfire went off, then another. He got up unhurt and raced with a group of marchers into an alleyway nearby. He did not look back to see how many people had fallen. To his shame in later years, he ran like everyone else, trying to put others between him and the shooting, praying that someone else would catch the bullet that was meant for him.

## Eighteen

The first of the wounded reached Chonnam University Hospital a few minutes after the firing started. Joel and Leslie were exhausted after a long shift. They started to put their suture needles and instruments away or into the autoclave. Joel remarked that the triage crew seemed to have got better at their jobs, for the work load seemed to have leveled off or even diminished.

The first gurney clattered through the swinging doors and stopped in the hallway. A nurse looked, gasped, and barked at an orderly to bring a doctor and prepare an operating room. Doctor Ko, a dapper man even in a soiled lab coat, asked what the problem was, and then snapped into action.

"Mr. Joel," he said, without looking up. His face had turned pale. "Come here. This is a gunshot wound."

No sooner had he spoken than another gurney came in, then another. The first patient, a young woman with a gaping chest wound, gasped for breath. Joel rushed to the newcomers and found another chest wound, three hits in the arms and legs, and one in the head. The last one looked dead already.

"Mr. Joel, I think there will be many, many more wounded tonight," the doctor said while trying to stanch the flow of blood from the first woman. "Tell me, did your paramedic training include surgery?"

Joel grabbed an IV bottle from an orderly and inserted the needle into her arm. He shook his head. "Nothing like this. But I can assist if you need me."

Dr. Ko nodded. "Please get scrubbed, and hurry. This is going to be a long night."

## *Nineteen*

The events of the next several hours were lost in a city-wide fog of mounting panic. The panic expressed itself in desperate actions that at any other time would have been unthinkable. The shootings at the university, which were repeated elsewhere through the night, led increasing numbers of citizens to think that more than mere protest was called for. "Think of an intruder in your house," ran the argument. "If he started killing your children and your wife, wouldn't you have the right — no, the obligation — to stop him any way you could? And if your bare hands weren't enough, wouldn't you use whatever weapon you could find?"

Hardly any private citizens owned firearms. The only exceptions were the occasional hunting rifle or target gun that could be obtained only after getting permits from local authorities, often through fantastically large bribes. Most citizens never missed what they never had. So when the need for deadly weapons arose in the early hours of May 21st, 1980 — ironically, Buddha's birthday — students gathered in numbers and swarmed upon the numerous police- and military armories throughout the city. The first armory to fall belonged to the local police force in an isolated ward of Kwangju. When a band of students, led by a close friend of Lee Byong Guk, surrounded the building's front gate, the guards beat a hasty retreat indoors. They emerged a few minutes later out a back door, dressed in civilian clothes. Somebody stopped one of them a block away.

"*Yah!* Aren't you a policeman?"

"Hell, no. Are you crazy?"

The students rushed in and quickly cleared the building of the M1 rifles, body armor, and tear gas canisters that were stored there in abundance. They also got a truck and two jeeps.

This marked the beginning of the insurrection, three days after the troops had first entered the city.

# CHAPTER TEN

Only a pair of armored personnel carriers were parked at the street corner across from Kwangju City Hall, about a quarter-mile down the boulevard from the train station and quite distant from Kumnam Street and the universities. The orange light of dawn on Wednesday, May 21st, brushed the top floor of the gray structure. Seven soldiers kept an eye on the early traffic and lolled about, smoking. A wet spot on a wall nearby showed where they had relieved themselves during the night. They were armed, but in the quiet of the morning they had slung their weapons well out of the way across their backs. After all, their comrades had beaten the student protesters to a bloody pulp over the past few days; a couple days more of mopping up and they would be going home.

Lee Byong Guk led a tight knot of students, all males, around the corner shouting the usual slogans: "Death to General Chon! Death to martial law!" They chanted in an easy, rather jaunty rhythm, by all appearances enjoying themselves. The students at the periphery of the group pumped their fists in the air in time to the chant; those inside kept oddly still.

One of the soldiers, a frog-eyed youngster from Chollado, noticed the marchers and motioned to his fellows to come round. The squad leader was at the wall finishing his business; he hurried back with his pants open.

"Halt!"

"Sure, we'll halt!" Byong Guk cried. "Now!"

At the signal, the students in front fell to their knees. Those behind immediately raised rifles to their shoulders and took aim. The fusillade lasted only a few seconds. The students were poor shots. Most bullets went far off the mark; yet enough found their targets to mow down most of the soldiers before the latter had time to lay a finger on their triggers.

Byong Guk led the students to the bodies and stripped them of their helmets and weapons. He scampered to the top of a personnel carrier.

"Hey, does anybody know how to drive this thing?"

## Two

Paul and Mi Jin had breakfast that morning at a noodle stand near their inn, in the marketplace that had done only sporadic business since the assault the previous Sunday. The owner, a sprightly grandmother who was hard of hearing, let them eat for free in exchange for a promise to spread the word that her place was open for business.

No sooner had they sat down than a couple of young men ran by. They stopped when one of them recognized Mi Jin.

"Elder Sister, something wonderful has happened. We're armed. We've got weapons!"

"What! Where did you get weapons? What kind have you got?"

"Not us, Elder Sister. Some other guys broke into an armory and stole guns. They even have vehicles."

"Have you seen this?" Mi Jin asked.

The two glanced at each other. "Well, no. We heard it — on very good authority."

"A rumor," Paul muttered. "Every rumor is 'on very good authority' because it's what they want to believe."

An hour later, however, another acquaintance found them and motioned them to follow him to a darkened storefront deep in the alleys of a neighborhood near the train station. The area reeked of engine oil and old timber; inside, the room smelled of metal and gunpowder. A student from Ehwa Women's University, hardly more than a girl, sat at a desk and scribbled names in a ledger. Chong Il Man came out from a back room, a riot policeman's helmet perched on his head at a rakish angle.

"So it's true," Mi Jin gasped.

"Elder Sister, and Jong Shik! You found us. What do you think about this, eh? We've got guns in the back. Wait here."

He bounded into the back room and emerged with an M16 in the crook of his arm and several ammunition clips. He handed them to Paul.

"You can sign this out."

Paul considered for a long moment, thinking of the bodies he had seen, of the beatings and senseless pursuits, and of Song Min's body in a coffin, and struggled with the temptation to take it.

"No," he said at last. "I can't do that." He handed it back.

"You don't know how to shoot?" Il Man asked, bewildered. "I thought all Americans love guns."

"Of course I know how to shoot. I used to go hunting with my father every year. But I won't shoot at people. I'm sorry."

Il Man nodded and went back to his duties. Students lined up at the door and spoke to the girl at the desk. Every weapon was signed out with a stern warning from one of Il Man's lieutenants that it must be fired only as a last resort, and only at soldiers; it was to be returned as soon as the crisis was over.

"These are the rules," he said. "They're the same everywhere. Follow them."

## Three

Within hours, gun battles started breaking out all over Kwangju.

Joel and Leslie blinked in the sunlight when they emerged from the hospital. Joel had spent all night and most of the morning in surgery; Leslie, still wearing her bloodstained white lab coat, had filled in for a nurse who had been put on triage duty. She was numb from the sight of endless mangled bodies, many of which were women and children.

The street outside the back door was reasonably quiet, as most of the emergency cases went to the front. To get back home, they had to walk a few blocks to the Provincial Office and cross Kumnam Street. The nearly constant *pop-pop-pop-pop* of gunfire made them edgy.

The street was strewn with wrecked cars. Banners littered the ground, as did scattered bits of bloody clothing. Markedly fewer people went about on the streets, in contrast to the multitudes that had come out the day before. Still, Joel and Leslie kept a keen eye out for soldiers and for masses of students who might draw their fire.

"You'd better take that lab coat off," Joel said, and helped her. "Let's not make ourselves a target." He took her hand and they walked close to the walls, ducking into doorways as they went.

They were several blocks away from the Provincial Office when they saw smoke rising from some buildings a couple blocks away and heard gunfire nearby.

Leslie clutched Joel's arm in fright. He squeezed her hand.

"There's an armory down there," he said. "Why would there be fighting in front of an armory ... ? Hold on, I've got to see this."

"Are you crazy?" Leslie gasped. "You'll get us killed!"

They stopped within a block of the fighting and hid themselves well in a space between two buildings. From this spot they had an unobstructed view of the action but were somewhat protected from stray gunfire. The sun, shining down in distinct rays through breaks in the clouds, illuminated the protagonists as if on a theater stage.

A group of a dozen or so students hid behind cars across the street from the featureless building that housed the armory. They emerged at intervals to throw Molotov cocktails and rocks over the wall. Others hid in the doorways of an office buildings next door. A tight knot of soldiers and policemen hid behind the armory's cement wall and its metal gate, which remained resolutely closed. An occasional arc of smoke followed a tear gas canister lobbed out onto the street.

Soon an armored personnel carrier barreled around the corner at breakneck speed. Joel caught sight of it out of the corner of his eye as it passed by. It seemed ragged somehow, and roughly driven. A second later, a loud cheer sprang up from the students. Joel stepped out onto the street, against Leslie's protests, to look again. The personnel carrier was festooned with banners; this accounted for its frayed appearance. "Death to General Chon!" the banners read. "Troops Out of Kwangju!"

"My God. Those are students driving that thing!"

The personnel carrier stopped in the middle of the street in front of the armory. Its brakes failed to set, and it rolled a few feet before they were applied properly. The rear door opened. A student, looking faintly ridiculous in an ill- fitting riot control helmet and a sweatshirt, poked his head out and led a half-dozen others out. They clumsily carried M16s. Without taking aim, they fired at random into the gate until return fire stopped. Joel saw men running away down the alley behind the armory as fast as they could go. They wore civilian clothes, but their boots were government issue.

Several students tried to open the gate, but it was locked and bolted. They called out insultingly to those still inside to give themselves up. If they didn't, they yelled, they would be ripped to shreds the moment they got in. No reply came back. The students beat on the metal gate in frustration. The personnel carrier started up again, belching smoke from its tailpipe. With its rear ramp still down and flinging sparks up from the pavement, it backed up, lined itself up with the iron bars, and lurched forward. The gate buckled and a large gap opened up, but in hitting the wall obliquely, the vehicle had wedged itself into the opening and could not pull out.

"*Sheesh!*" Joel said. "What a bunch of idiots."

The students scampered over the hood of the vehicle into the armory compound. Joel and Leslie heard several shots fired. A few seconds later a student emerged carrying aloft a bloodied jacket. The others cheered; Leslie buried her face in Joel's arm.

After much grinding through gears and scraping against the wall, the personnel carrier finally came free and moved away. A few minutes later an army truck and another personnel carrier rumbled out onto the street. In the rear of the truck Joel saw rifles stacked in disorderly piles. The students climbed onto the trucks and banged their loaded rifles against the sides. With a bloodthirsty yell they careened down the street and out of sight.

## Four

Word soon spread through the awakening city on Thursday morning that the students were armed.

The armories in Kwangju became targets for rebels who now rode fearlessly up and down the streets in military vehicles covered with revolutionary banners. The paratroopers and the regular riot police could not defend them all; those officials who took the larger view admitted privately that in arming itself so thoroughly against the threat of invasion by North Koreans, the nation had inadvertently supplied armaments to domestic rebels. One by one the armories fell, until a mass of organized students became an unskilled but formidable enemy. The paratroopers, who numbered about ten thousand at the time, began to fear themselves out-gunned.

Army helicopters hovered over the students and the raucous crowds whose demonstrations grew bolder by the hour. Soldiers dropped leaflets over them. "Don't be swayed by the actions of the small number of criminals and hooligans who are leading your beautiful city down a dangerous path," the leaflets said. "We know that the great people of Kwangju have nothing but contempt for their treason." The message ended with an order to go home and stay there. Far from blunting the demonstrations, the leaflets inflamed the crowds to greater fury. "If being against criminals and hooligans means killing innocent women and children, they can go fuck themselves!" shouted one man, a taxi driver who had driven in the convoy the day before. Several students who had rifles fired them into the air. The helicopters backed off.

A major gun battle erupted on Kumnam Street, centered near the Provincial Office, in the early afternoon. At the sound of the first shots the wide boulevard quickly emptied of people. Paratroops and students took cover behind overturned cars and in doorways and alleys. Several groups of students commandeered rooms in the upper stories of the buildings along the street. One group, led by Lee Byong Guk, knocked the windows out of the Delicious Tabang, the place where until recently Mi Jin had worked. Two young men, both barely out of their teens, whose combat training extended little beyond childhood games, died shortly thereafter next to the shattered rose-colored windows.

Paul, Mi Jin, Leslie, and Joel had no choice but to stay indoors. Even though their rooms were two blocks away from Kumnam Street, they were still terrified of being hit by stray bullets. Twice during the day they heard a distant report that was echoed by the sound of concrete chips flying from the wall outside. The *ajumoni* offered a little comfort when she appeared at the door with a hammer and a handful of nails.

"Drive these into the window frame," she said reluctantly. "I heard that people are hanging mattress pads over their windows to keep the bullets from coming in. Just be careful not to harm the wall!"

They did as she instructed, and the room was suddenly plunged into darkness. They turned on a desk lamp and sat on the floor. The sound of Joel's shortwave radio did little to encourage them: the local news was warped, and the more accurate news from overseas was depressing, or outdated, or both. No one felt like talking. This tiresome situation lasted for hours.

Occasionally a commotion in a nearby building broke through the quiet. The thin walls carried the sounds of breaking doors and screams of pain as if they were just down the corridor. At such times, when it sounded as if soldiers were going door to door in the neighborhood in a mad effort to round up every possible enemy, Paul, Joel, and Leslie shoved Mi Jin into the cramped bathroom and held their blue-and-gold American passports aloft, prepared to wave them at an intruder and shout *"Miguk salam! Miguk salam!"* American! American! at the top of their lungs. They never had to put their plan into action.

The shooting stopped later that afternoon.

## Five

They emerged onto a street that bustled with people. For the first time since the beginning of the crisis, the mood was upbeat, even cheerful. Mi Jin sensed it immediately.

"What has happened?" she asked of a woman who wore an armband of Honam College. "What's going on?"

The woman smiled. It was the first smile Mi Jin had seen in more than three days. "You haven't heard? The paratroopers are leaving. They're giving up and running away with their tails between their legs!" Those nearby who heard her let up a loud cheer.

Joel grabbed Leslie's hand and walked quickly up the block to Kumnam Street. Paul and Mi Jin followed close behind. A faint sound of tanks, personnel carriers, and trucks behind the cheers of multitudes drifted through the side street.

The slanting rays of the setting sun illuminated the vehicles as they moved in procession toward the far end of Kumnam Street. The heat of their exhaust warped the sunlight above them.

"They're leaving!" said a middle-aged *ajumoni*. "I can't believe it, but the sons of bitches are leaving. Good riddance!"

"But where are they going?" Joel asked. "And when will they come back?"

"Who cares?" the lady replied, but her face clouded over as she thought about it. "Who cares?"

## Six

"Oh, my God. My God."

Joel and Leslie gasped together at the scene before them as they approached the hospital. Streams of screaming, bleeding people descended upon the emergency room, brought there by any means available: on flatbed pushcarts, in the arms of friends or relatives, even hobbling in under their own power. Once inside, they cried out with cursing and pain for immediate attention; the ever-present feisty little nurse herded them all into the triage area.

The wounded occupied every inch of floor space. Streams of blood flowed freely over the floor faster than the few remaining janitors could mop it up. The cries and screams were hellish, but Joel thought he heard an odd undercurrent of moaning that vibrated with hopelessness. He later discovered that many of the wounded had lain where they were for over twelve hours and received only rudimentary care. Their wounds had anesthetized them into a long, low stupor.

"Mr. Joel! Miss Black! You've come again!"

Dr. Ko greeted them eagerly, his face sagging with exhaustion. He spoke slowly in a raspy voice. "There is so much to do. Thank you for coming. We need all the help we can get."

"Doctor, I'm so sorry," Joel said. "I should have come sooner ..."

The doctor brushed off the apology. "It was too dangerous to go out. I completely understand."

Joel grabbed a lab coat and started looking at patients in the triage area. Many of them had been hastily bandaged and left there the night before; an oppressive odor of leaking body fluids hung in the air. It was only through the work of family members and good Samaritans that a massive outbreak of infection had been averted in the hospital, for they had kept all the patients reasonably clean of urine and feces. Even so, by now the floor had turned completely red with blood. He had to walk carefully lest he slip in it.

Leslie immediately set to work, too. She had much less training than Joel, but she proved herself a good nurse. When changing dressings and stitching cuts, she lost the fearful, furtive look that Joel had once found so unappealing in her. She attended so strictly to her duties that she looked almost calm in the face of the horrors around her. He caught her eye once and gave her a nod; she allowed herself a sigh in return and then went back to her work.

An hour into his shift, an orderly tapped Joel on the shoulder. "Please, American sir, would you help me carry something?" It was the corpse of an overweight student. Even Joel's height gave him barely enough leverage to heave it from an examination table onto a gurney. They covered it with a sheet and wheeled it down the corridor to a freight elevator. Joel turned to leave. "Excuse me, but I'll need help when we get there," the orderly said.

The morgue was not unlike any of the other hospital morgues Joel had seen: a chilled room with a few steel examination tables; refrigerated drawers for bodies; a cabinet for instruments, tools, and reference books. What struck him immediately when he walked in, though, was the pervasive smell of death. The magnitude of the stench did not surprise him: bodies were everywhere. They lay cold and white, paired up on the examination tables, wrapped neatly in sheets on the floor — even in the drawers, which the orderly had opened hoping to find more space, they lay squashed together like lovers, two to a drawer.

"We try to keep their modesty by putting only males together and females together," the orderly explained with a sigh. "Not that it really matters to them now."

Joel and the orderly heaved the new body onto the lone unoccupied examination table, where a worker quickly came, gloved and gowned, to wash it with antiseptic. Joel knew that the washing away of dried body fluids — mostly caked blood and exudate from a gunshot wound to the gut — was at best a temporary measure against the spread of infection from the remains. The man washing the body seemed to read his mind:

"We've got to get rid of some of these. Burned or buried: I say burn them. By the time a proper funeral can be arranged and we get some graves dug, most of these will be rotting." He pointed out a drawer marked with red tape. "That one died of gangrene from a wound. He stinks to high heaven. The refrigeration on that drawer happens to work the best. When we open it, it'll be to take the body away to cremation. It's the only way."

Just then a flash of blue-white light lit the room for an instant, then another. Joel crouched and reflexively covered his head, but the source of the flash quickly came forward. In the corner, near a pair of heavily laden tables, a fair-haired man was taking pictures.

"Hey! Hallo!" the man spoke in a heavy accent. "Are you German? No? English? American?"

"American."

"Ah. My name is Gunther Loeb, *Der Spiegel*. Do you speak Korean?"

"A little."

"Great! Then maybe you can translate for me."

"Well —"

"How do you do, sir?" he reached out to shake the orderly's hand but quickly thought better of it. "I am a journalist from Germany. Can you tell me how many bodies you have in this room? And may I take a picture of what's in those drawers over there?"

Joel translated, but then began to guide Loeb out. "Look, this really isn't the time or place for taking pictures. Let's have a little respect for the dead —"

"Let him take pictures," the orderly said.

"What?"

"Let him. How else will everyone out there know what's going on here?" He beckoned to Loeb and led him to the stacks of drawers, opened one, and invited him to take a picture of its contents, two young men whose once well-muscled bodies were beginning to bloat. Joel turned aside while Loeb shot three photographs; he agreed with the orderly's reasoning, but still could not bear to watch the intrusion.

"These two died the day before yesterday, when the first shots were fired at the university. Now that it's safe to reopen the temporary public morgues, where people can claims the bodies of their relatives, we'll be putting many of them out in coffins. They'll have to be disposed of within another day or two. The warm weather we're having is making the decay go faster."

Loeb scribbled notes hurriedly. "Where are these public morgues located?"

"School gymnasiums so far. I fear we might have to move them outdoors before long. There are so many bodies."

Joel, who had become possessive of the crisis, and reluctant to share it with others who had no history of involvement, said to the orderly, in Korean, so Loeb would not understand, "Why are you talking with this foreigner?"

"Because he's the only journalist who's bothered to ask questions and write down the answers. Maybe you haven't noticed it, sir, but there are many American and Japanese reporters roaming the city, asking questions. Nobody from any Korean newspaper has even shown up. The Korean press is being forced to tell lies. Only the foreigners are telling the truth about Kwangju."

## Seven

The old Citizens' Committee, which had been practically disbanded while the students were engaging in gun battles with the paratroops, came together again in an auditorium on the second floor of the Provincial Office building. A number of the members were surprised and even a little disappointed that the interior of the large white building was not opulent, as they had imagined, but was actually quite ordinary, not unlike the well-worn ward offices and health centers which they had all seen before.

The sound of a noisy celebration reverberated through the empty halls. Papers from vandalized offices littered the floors. When Paul and Mi Jin climbed the broad staircase to the auditorium the noise grew louder until, at the door, it burst out like a blast of wind. Revelers threw official papers in the air like confetti. Someone had brought cases of *soju* and of *makkoli*, and many were beginning to get drunk. The public address system had been turned on; between chants and revolutionary songs, a string of slurring speakers vilified the martial law authorities and General Chon and praised the courage of the citizens who had taken up arms and killed the enemy. After half an hour of this, Chong Il Man went to the microphone and tried to speak.

"Listen, everyone, we must start organizing. Can you hear me? Now that the soldiers are gone ..."

The hall erupted into hysterical cheering. Il Man had to wait several minutes before he could continue.

"We must start organizing ..." The excited chattering of the crowd drowned him out again. No one paid attention.

"Listen! It's time to stop this self-congratulatory bullshit and start talking about important matters!"

The hall suddenly quieted to a low, faintly resentful buzz.

"Sorry to spoil the celebration," Il Man said, "but we have to face a new reality. We have won a battle. We have not won the war. What we do next will determine whether we live or die. Now is not the time to become a mob. We cannot turn our city into an insane asylum. We cannot let chaos rule."

"Why not?" laughed a shaky voice from the floor. "Look what law has done to us already!" Others laughed and nodded in agreement.

"Because if we show any sign of lawlessness, if we give in to chaos, the bastards who did this to us in the first place will have an excuse to come back in and exterminate us."

The hall turned silent at that statement.

"Put yourselves in the position of the martial law bastards," Il Man continued. "They swoop in last Sunday after killing all hopes for democratic reform. They turn Kwangju into a slaughterhouse. The people rise up together and fight back, even killing many of their best soldiers, and they have to retreat. That can't sit well with them. They are looking for an excuse to come back and kill us all. The only thing that stands between us and them is the attention of the outside world.

"There are dozens of foreign journalists now in our city who can spread the word about what's really happening here. Believe me, they are this very minute preparing reports that they will transmit back to their TV networks and newspapers at home. They influence people in powerful countries. Our best hope lies in them. It's a slender thread, to be sure, but it's all we've got. And what will happen if they show pictures of rioters, of lawless rebels shooting guns into the air, riding around in army trucks and jeeps, destroying the city in which we gained victory? The world will think we are nothing but rabble, unable to take care of ourselves, completely divorced from any noble ideals. They'll turn their backs on us. The next slaughter will be done in broad daylight, and no one will care. The world will think we had it coming."

After an interval of silence, someone asked, "What should we do?"

Il Man had their approval, and he knew it. His spirit leapt. "First of all," he laughed, "let's clean this place up!" He picked up a handful of papers from the floor and stuffed them into a trash bin. "Clean up the building. Clean up the streets, the city. We need to reinstate the Citizen's Committee and come up with some acceptable form of self-government. We're not a lawless mob; we'll have laws all right, but ones that make sense, like laws against vandalism and public drunkenness. All the weapons that were taken in the last couple days must be returned and issued only to those people who will be organized to defend our city.

"I don't know how much time we've got to show the world what we're made of. All we can do is start now."

## Eight

The meeting ended just before midnight. The Committee drafted a dozen resolutions, only a few of which had any importance to the survival of the city. These measures set up rules for managing weapons and created committees for organizing clean-up crews and blood banks. The rest of them condemned various government figures by name and denounced the actions of the martial law authorities.

Paul and Mi Jin walked home through remarkably quiet streets. The celebrations had gone on through the evening hours, and by rights should have continued late into the night; however, a universal exhaustion took over shortly after dark and people retired to their homes to catch their first full night's sleep in days. The tiredness even overcame the anxiety that would not leave them, the knowledge that a growing deployment of troops still stood at the city limits. The only revelers still out when the pair walked up to their room were the die-hard fanatics whose adrenaline had not yet been used up.

Paul watched Mi Jin while she drifted off to sleep. The light of a waxing half-moon streamed in through the window and dusted her face in a cold, clear nimbus. He had never seen a sight so beautiful. Her skin was as pale and delicate as blue celadon, utterly priceless. He let out a long sigh of contentment, the first he could remember in a very long time. It woke her up.

"*An cha?*" she asked. You're not asleep?

"I was thinking, that's all."

293

She brushed his face with her hand. He did not know that his eyes betrayed worry. "Do not worry, dear. We will survive this."

"No. That's not what I was thinking about. I was seeing how lovely you are, how dear you are to me. We have to stay together, no matter what happens. We belong together."

"Yes," Mi Jin smiled.

"'Trouble is the seed of joy,' right? Well, when this trouble is over, we'll have joy to spare. No more running, no more fighting. Our life will be normal. Normal. Can you picture that?"

She rolled into his arms and held him tightly. "And what will we do?"

"We'll go to Chindo, where I'll finally meet your parents."

Mi Jin shook her head.

"No? Then I'll take you home to Indiana. We'll go to the places I loved when I grew up: that wonderful old Columbian Park, where there's a round swimming pool the size of a city block; the old-fashioned candy store downtown, across the street from the courthouse which, by the way, is the ugliest building in the world, all frilly and busy with a gold-colored dome, like somebody from the candy store got drunk and concocted it from caramel and gray icing and mustard. We'll go to my old church, where you can see for yourself what an ass the minister is. And to Purdue — I'll show you the fountain in the plaza that sprays water according to how hard the wind is blowing, and the old brick buildings with red tile roofs. We'll visit my aunts and uncles and cousins — there must be hundreds of them — spread out all over the countryside from Delphi to Attica to Crawfordsville, and they'll love you, too." He sighed. "Would you like that? ... Mi Jin?"

She had slipped off him and regained her former place, resting quietly on her pillow, fast asleep, still with that beatific smile.

A distant chugging of an army truck broke the stillness of Paul's thoughts. His heart leapt in momentary terror that the paratroops had returned. A moment later, when the tranquility of the night returned, he lay motionless, his face clouded with worry. An old nagging thought came back to him, one that first came to him during the worst days of fighting, when he feared most for Mi Jin's and his own safety: that life is delicate and transitory, and that trying to confine it to a plan is as impossible as tying up a river in a package. He covered Mi Jin and himself with the thick blanket and fell into a light, disturbed sleep.

## Nine

In Seoul, at the Peace Corps office, John Atwood sat in his overstuffed leather chair and gazed straight ahead. Mrs. Kang fumed and fidgeted in her seat at the opposite end of the coffee table.

"How many volunteers got out of the area yesterday?" he asked.

"Four. One from Wando, one from Naju, and two from Changsong. Leslie Black and Joel Reynoso were not with them. They are still in Kwangju."

"Well, have you tried to find them?"

"I've done everything I can, John," she said, trying to sound pleasant and confident, and failing at both. "I called the US Cultural Center. They were invited to leave the city, but they refused."

Atwood hammered the arm of his chair with his fist. "Why? What are they up to? What are they involved in? Are they safe?"

Mrs. Kang chuckled nervously. "John, from the way you are looking at me, it seems that you are holding me responsible for their safety."

"Maybe I am. You're in charge of their program. You were supposed to keep an eye on the mess down there, and order the volunteers out at the first sign of trouble. There's been plenty of trouble, hasn't there? So where are my volunteers?"

"John, I assure you they're safe," she said. She struggled to control the panic and rage that shook her voice. Imagine this American accusing me of lack of diligence, she thought. Out loud she began: "My husband —"

"Who is a highly-placed official in the government, I know." Atwood interjected.

"My husband knows what is going on there. Casualties have been extremely light. Less than fifty people have been killed, most of them policemen and soldiers murdered by the rabble and the North Korean agents. The numbers of wounded are not that great. Hardly worth speaking about."

Later that afternoon, after calming Atwood with assurances she knew were empty, Mrs. Kang found out from a hasty telephone call from the Ministry that her husband had lost his position. Everyone in Prime Minister Shim Hyon Hwak's cabinet had resigned, in the words of the official announcement, "to take responsibility for failure to maintain domestic calm." Mrs. Kang's husband was caught in the penumbra of that mass resignation. Within an hour of that event he had been called into the office of his benefactor, the outgoing Minister of Health, and told the news. He had expected it; and since he had powerful friends and a good reputation, he greeted the news with equanimity. His wife, however, fell apart. When he called her, she screamed at him, begging him to fight the resignation. In the end, worn down under the strain of finding the Kwangju volunteers and the sudden diminishing of her own position through her husband's bad luck, she closed the door to her office and collapsed. Atwood found her there a while later insensible, staring blankly at the wall and whispering to herself. He ordered the driver to take her home. He felt sorry for her, and as pity can drive away fear, she never dominated him again.

## Ten

A coalition of leaders, split between older moderates and younger militants, formed from among the large crowd that had celebrated the retreat of the army the night before. They called themselves the 5.18 Citizens' Committee of Fifteen. 5.18 referred to May 18th, the date on which the crisis had begun. It had a strongly Christian bias, for two of its moderate members were clergymen and most of the rest were practicing Christians. Still, a wide gulf divided them.

"I hear you students tortured a wounded paratrooper in the hospital yesterday," said Reverend Kim Nam Ho, a prominent minister at Kwangju's largest Presbyterian church. "I object to this atrocity. If we treat people like that, we are no better than they are."

"Let me tell you something, Reverend," said one of the militant members of the Committee. He had been in the room during the interrogation and had even delivered some of the blows. "If Lee Byong Guk were here — and I can't imagine why he's not, considering he's got more leadership in his little finger than all the rest of you combined — he would tell you that he was expressing the justifiable fury of the people of Kwangju. He also needed to get to the truth —"

"Yes, but truth at what cost? And to respond to your veiled criticism of the Committee's decision not to invite him to serve, let me say this: we can't let our anger rule our actions. Lee Byong Guk doesn't seem to understand this. The only way to survive this crisis is to be more clear-headed, more reasonable than the forces that want to kill us."

Byong Guk's man muttered that that view was nonsense, but he made no effort to disrupt the proceedings. In the end, the Committee made a list of seven demands which they intended to take personally to the martial law commander in the region, a certain General Nam:

One: No more deployment of combat forces.

Two: An acknowledgment by the military that they used excessive force in the suppression of demonstrations.

Three: The release of all students currently held in detention.

Four: Compensation for all the deceased and wounded.

Five: No blame placed on the citizens of Kwangju.

Six: No reprisals against the people after the crisis is ended.

Seven: All these demands broadcast unedited by radio to the entire nation.

They arranged to meet with General Nam later that evening at the edge of the city.

## Eleven

"What's that? You said somebody called?"

Lee Byong Guk was distracted by the paper he was reading, the list of demands by the 5.18 Citizens' Committee of Fifteen. He did not like it. It had obviously been drawn up by a moderate, and while no one could argue with most of the points, it was overall too weak. It exemplified all that he thought was wrong with moderation: too soft, too local, too open to interpretation. Moderates tended to compromise too easily — why bother with negotiation, he thought, if you give half your position away by the time you're done? Better to take a stand and refuse to budge: argue on principle, not on fleeting practicalities. In the present age, compromise with evil was simply unthinkable. Even so, neither he nor his fellows suggested any alternate demands.

"A bunch of students from Seoul National University called," the young student said. "About thirty of them. They started out on a trek to Kwangju to show support for us."

"Oh? Where are they now?" Byong Guk asked.

"In Sogu District, quite a way from here. They're close to soldiers out there. They want an escort downtown."

"Where's the line?"

"As far as we know, the soldiers are stopped at the edge of Sogu, a few blocks from the school where the students are holed up. These guys — little pussies from rich families, I'll bet — are scared shitless. They heard we have guns, and they asked for protection."

Byong Guk thought for a moment, then nodded. "A few blocks, you say? It's close, but we'll pick them up."

Seven young men, the best Byong Guk had, all fully armed and ready to fight, piled into the first of a pair of army trucks. The canvas cover over the back flapped a noisy goodbye to onlookers as they sped away.

The line between the mass of soldiers and the people of Sogu, the western district of Kwangju, was a silvery coil of barbed wire that Byong Guk could just make out as the trucks got closer to their destination. Soldiers, looking like green specks on a gray backdrop, milled about on the other side. The space between him and the barbed wire was completely empty of people. Nothing but a few breeze-driven scraps of litter moved there. The line drew a sinuous boundary that followed straight boulevards in some places but nearly surrounded pockets of neighborhoods in others. In one such pocket, at an elementary school, the group of students from Seoul National University waited anxiously for rescue.

"Take it slow," Byong Guk commanded the driver. They crept through the eerily silent streets. In the distance, some of the soldiers noticed them.

One of them reached for a field telephone. Seeing this, Byong Guk had a change of heart. "No — move it! Let's go!"

The driver gunned the engine. The truck skidded into the dusty schoolyard. A knot of students stood inside the front door and sprinted outside before the dust settled.

"We're glad you're here," their leader said. He jumped into the cab with Byong Guk while the others squeezed into the back of the trucks. There were more of them than Byong Guk had expected. They packed themselves tightly, too tightly. Neither the students nor Byong Guk's men could move. The trucks spun around to head back out the gate. "We've been here since yesterday, during the worst of the fighting."

"Why didn't you move out after they passed by?"

"There was too much danger. Who knows where they've got soldiers hiding? We couldn't take a chance going it alone. When we heard you were armed, we knew you could get us out of here."

Byong Guk curled his lip. "So you share your danger with ..." He stopped in mid-sentence. Out of the corner of his eye he saw a spot of green moving along a rooftop across the street. He turned to look. Suddenly several more came up. Rifle muzzles popped up into view a split second before the firing began.

"Go! Move it!" Byong Guk screamed, but the trucks sped forward only a few feet before bullets started ripping through the canvas roof behind them. Screams broke the silence of the neighborhood while sunlight streamed through the tattered remnants of the covering. A few of Byong Guk's men managed to pull themselves from the tangle of wounded. They leaped out and, taking refuge behind tires and the truck's chassis, fired blindly back at the soldiers above. The bullets rained down from both sides, however, and within a minute everyone who had been in the back of the trucks lay dead or mortally wounded. Byong Guk's driver, bleeding from a wound in the leg, struggled to maintain consciousness and get the vehicle moving again. The leader of the Seoul students had died at the first shot; Byong Guk pushed his body out the door and set up to return fire. He did not last long, either. By the time the truck had lurched slowly to relative safety, Byong Guk had died.

## Twelve

At about the same time that Lee Byong Guk and his men were meeting the stranded students in Sogu District, a small convoy of cars moved slowly to the eastern edge of the city. Festooned with white flags of truce, they stopped at the barbed wire that stretched across an intersection. A paratrooper sauntered up to the lead car. "What do you want?" he demanded in low Korean.

"I am with the 5.18 Citizens' Committee of Fifteen," Reverend Kim Nam Ho replied. "General Nam is expecting us."

"Wait here."

Mi Jin and Paul watched anxiously from a car further back. A reporter with *The Los Angeles Times* rode with them. They saw the general come to the checkpoint and motion the car through a makeshift gate.

"We will not go over there," Reverend Kim called out. "We must meet with the general on this side of the barbed wire."

General Nam stood impassively, rigid as stone. His aides chattered angrily among themselves.

"That's it," Paul thought. "We're dead." He closed his eyes and prayed.

The argument between Reverend Kim and the soldiers went back and forth for nearly half an hour. The general and his staff were loathe to meet the rebels halfway; the convoy, on the other hand, feared that once they crossed the line they would not be allowed out again. They finally agreed to meet in the middle of the road, in the midst of an area described by the large coil of barbed wire. Everyone, including Paul, Mi Jin, and the reporter, got out of the cars. Twenty people crowded cheek-to-jowl in a tiny section of the roadway.

"General Nam, we represent the people of Kwangju," Reverend Kim said. "We have come to present a list of demands for the safety of our citizens and the restoration of the Republic." He brandished the sheet of paper and read them off one by one in a loud voice. In the surrounding silence Paul heard the *click-whirrrr* of cameras: several soldiers on the other side were taking photographs of the delegation. He wished he had not allowed Mi Jin to talk him into coming.

General Nam's reaction to each of the demands could be gauged by the degree of curl in his lip. When the Reverend finished reading, the general reluctantly accepted the paper from him and handed it back to one of his men. A group of officers glanced over it and broke into laughter.

"Reverend." the general said, "the government of the Republic of Korea has no quarrel with the good citizens of Kwangju. The problem is with the impure elements who clearly have the solid backing of communists. So you see, one of your demands, 'No blame on the people of Kwangju', has already been met.

"However, your other points are irrelevant to the crisis. You have no standing to dictate how the martial law authorities deal with criminals or how the government compensates the few people who have been accidentally injured in the fighting. We have nothing to talk about …"

Paul's nervousness subsided somewhat as the meeting wore on. He listened closely to the speeches of both sides, all of which were prefabricated and meaningless. Reverend Kim spoke of democracy, of freedom, of brotherhood, and sounded faintly ridiculous in the presence of soldiers and

tanks; General Nam spoke of North Korean agents and communist sympathizers to people who were clearly neither. The absurdity thickened as
speech piled upon speech. Paul soon realized that the two men were not
there to negotiate but to state positions, to draw their own boundaries. After the meeting ended they would return to their fellows and claim that they
did their best to bring an end to the crisis, but that the other side would not
listen. In the end, nothing would change. He made this observation to Mi
Jin.

"I know," she sighed. "I should have expected no more."

During a lull in the meeting, General Nam noticed Paul and the reporter, the only Western faces in the crowd. The tone of his voice, oily and malevolent, sent a chill of fear up Paul's spine and then made him blush. "I
wonder why Americans are getting involved in these talks," he said. The
*click-whirrrr* of cameras started again, this time pointed at him.

## *Thirteen*

The 5.18 Citizens' Committee of Fifteen called for a rally to be held that
evening at sundown in the open plaza near the Provincial Office. They
planned to summarize the events of the past days and show the people the
list of demands they presented to General Nam. Mi Jin went alone; Paul
had gone to the university hospital with Joel and Leslie. "To make myself
useful," he said.

The rally started peacefully enough under a darkening slate-gray sky. The
air had a cool, sticky feel and was completely still. The older members of
the committee mounted a makeshift rostrum wearing white sashes with the
words "5.18 Citizens' Committee" written across them in blue. They wore
Sunday suits with white gloves and looked like rather stodgy dignitaries at
an awards luncheon. The younger, more militant members of the Committee eschewed the suit, sash, and gloves, opting instead for the casual attire
of the classroom. One student, a member of Lee Byong Guk's faction, had
not wanted to join the others on the dais to begin with; when pressed to go
up, he wore a captured riot policeman's helmet. When he made his appearance a swell of approval went up, and it took many minutes for the crowd
to settle down.

Reverend Kim eventually got up to talk.

"God has delivered His judgment on the men who sought to kill our
spirits and kill our bodies! He heard the cries of His servants, saw our blood
running in the streets, and He could bear it no longer. He lifted up His
servants — the young men and the young women, the workers and the
housewives, the elderly — and with His mighty hand he smote the evil-
doers. To Him belongs everlasting praise!"

The crowd roared its agreement. Mi Jin, mesmerized and swept up in the moment, joined the other Christians in the park in cries of "Hosanna!" and "Praise be to God!" Those who were not Christians momentarily forgot that they were not, and allowed themselves to be carried along as well.

"Many of you are wondering what happened at my meeting with General Nam this afternoon. Well, let me tell you this: He got an earful from this humble old preacher!"

He waited for the cheering to subside, and continued.

"I want to confess something to you. Until our little gathering of cars and taxicabs drove down those deserted streets to the stout ramparts of the soldiers, I never truly understood how Daniel felt when he entered, naked, the den of hungry lions. Now I do. I sing praise to God for keeping us safe in that time of danger. For while we were there we were sure that we would be arrested at any moment.

"We met with General Nam under the open eye of heaven. He is a man of hard heart. He looks upon us as impure elements, as hooligans, as communists and communist sympathizers!"

The crowd shouted and booed. Gunther Loeb, the reporter from *Der Spiegel*, watched from the edge of the plaza. He understood nothing of what the Reverend was saying, but he marveled at the way he used his oratory to hold the crowd like a wild animal on a leash, sometimes letting it out and sometimes reeling it in.

"What does he know of us?" Reverend Kim demanded. "What does he know of Kwangju? What does he know of ordinary people? Here is a man of privileged background. He attended the Military Academy with his cronies, among whom we find the soldiers now running our country. He was hardened in wars in foreign countries. Now he is ordered to sweep into our city, kick us, beat us, and kill our people. We fight back — we fight for survival. That's not a criminal reaction, not a communist reaction. It's a human reaction! What is so hard to understand?"

Just then a fight broke out on the dais. One of the older members of the committee had looked askance at the lack of tact displayed by the student who wore the riot policeman's helmet. The youngster had bragged loudly that he had taken it off a dead body. This amused many of his cohorts nearby, but left the older man in a bad state. He asked the student three times to remove it. The student refused. He told him once more to take it off. The student again refused, using an obscenity. The older man grabbed at the helmet, and succeeded in getting it off, but the student responded by throwing a wild punch. After a struggle, the old man lay on the floor of the dais and nearly fell off before others of both factions intervened. The tussle was over in a few minutes, but it left the crowd angry and out of sorts. Arguments broke out along the fringes, and only with strenuous talking and cajoling did Reverend Kim bring the proceedings back to order.

"We must control ourselves," he pleaded. "Are we not better than the soldiers whose only language is violence?"

This was not the only disruption during the Reverend's speech. A few minutes later a group of students dragged a man screaming up to the rostrum and threw him on the ground before it. The militant members of the committee watched impassively, and it was the opinion of many afterwards that they had planned what came next.

"This bastard is a spy!" yelled one of the students. Someone reached up and switched off the power to the public address system on the rostrum so that Reverend Kim's pleas for quiet would go unheard. The man on the ground was youngish, long-haired, dressed in what once was a natty sweater and jeans. His face was now bloodied, his clothing stained and rumpled.

"Let me go! I'm not a spy — I'm not a spy!"

The student who had brought him forward grabbed a megaphone and shouted into it; the feedback from the device so garbled his words that no one past the first few rows of people understood him at all. The rest could hear only scattered words like "spy," "Special Forces," and "sold out."

"Don't listen to him!" the man screamed, weeping, but no one heard him. "I'm not a spy!"

The crowd vibrated with excitement. Their interest in the drama grew and with it grew the desire for revenge for the atrocities of the last several days. A number of students pressed forward and tried to reach him; others spat at him and showered him with obscenities. "You fucking killer!" someone screamed. "We'll send your body back to Chon Du Hwan with your heart ripped out!"

Reverend Kim pleaded for order through the dead microphone, forgetting that he could not be heard. Someone finally found the controls and turned it on.

" — have no killing here! We'll have no killing here! Somebody help that man!"

A dozen large, solidly-built students, members of a moderate faction from the theological seminary, moved in and shoved their way to the man. He had got up and been pushed down several times, and was bleeding from fresh injuries. The bodyguards surrounded him and fought off attacks from smaller students. The rally ended in this way, with confusion and discord.

Mi Jin watched all this and wept. She returned home, unutterably saddened that her beloved movement was dissolving before her eyes.

Later that night, the 5.18 Citizens' Committee of Fifteen disbanded. The older men and moderate students were sent home without a word of thanks from the militant students, who quickly set up a "5.18 Struggle Committee."

## Fourteen

Paul remained Mi Jin's source of hope and solace.

"How was the rally?" he asked. Mi Jin did not answer for a long time. When she did, there was unutterable weariness in her voice.

"Not what I expected. People are going mad. It's almost as though it's not our fight anymore."

"What do you mean?"

"There's so much confusion out there. Nobody's in charge."

"Reverend Kim?" Paul prompted.

"He tried, but the students just aren't following the Citizens' Committee. Maybe it was a mistake for them to form their committee in the first place. They're too moderate."

"The students were the ones who armed themselves and fought," Paul said. "I can see how they'd feel entitled to run it their own way."

"Whatever."

"I've got some news for you," he stammered. "I was passing through the emergency room on my way to the lab. We got a transfer patient, a student who'd been shot up badly. He said he was in a truck picking up other students stranded near the edge of the city. He was the only survivor of a group of thirty-eight or so. Among the ones who died was — Lee Byong Guk."

Mi Jin took in a sharp breath and spun around. "No!"

"I saw his body later in the morgue. There were at least twenty gunshot wounds in him."

Mi Jin fell into Paul's arms. He stroked her hair.

"Byong Guk had a following," Paul said. "His death caused a huge stir in the hospital."

Mi Jin sighed. "That's what he wanted. He's a hero."

"Not a hero," Paul whispered. "A weapon. Nothing more."

She squeezed Paul so tightly that he gasped for breath.

Joel and Leslie came in a little later, hot and tired from working at the hospital. The uneasy peace that had come to Kwangju did not bring an end to casualties: patients who had come in over the past few days needed continuing care, and there were still scattered firefights and ambushes. Byong Guk's party was a conspicuous example.

"Well, here's the Lab Man," Joel greeted him cheerfully. "You should know, Mi Jin, that your boyfriend is a top-notch laboratory technician."

"Top-notch ... ?"

"The best. The diagnostics and blood typing came back quick and accurate. We got blood transfusions going in half the time. Paul saved some lives today."

Paul brushed off the praise. "The regular lab techs were off doing other things; I just took up the slack. What I really wanted to do today was to get out and treat patients, like you guys did."

Later that night, in bed, he thought again about his work in the hospital. Was I too hard on Dad when I refused to go to medical school? he wondered. Images of the suffering he had seen came to mind, and of the care Joel and the doctors had given to relieve it. He had heard more than enough political speeches recently, and seen too much politically motivated bloodshed. In the hospital he saw the people who helped, the ones who fought to restore health.

"Maybe Dad was right," he sighed, "in ways he can't imagine."

## Fifteen

"So you see, we're doing a pretty good job of running this city."

Chong Il Man was leading Paul, Mi Jin, Joel, and Leslie up Kumnam Street past rows of battered buildings. The windows had been blown out of most of them; some were streaked with black soot from the fires that had ignited when gunfire knocked over propane and kerosene heaters indoors. On the sidewalks the sunlight refracted through mounds of glass shards. Students, children, and elderly people were sweeping them up. On the street, a few burned-out skeletons of cars still rested lopsided by the curb. These, too, were being removed: mechanics from a local trucking company attached cables to them and pulled them onto flatbed trucks. Still elsewhere, middle-aged women — Mrs. So, the inn *ajumoni*, among them — planted new flowers in the faux wood planters that lined the street. Planters that had been destroyed were replaced with simple flowerpots. The entire stretch of the street looked almost cheery.

"You're certainly doing a good job of making it look pretty," Joel said, impressed.

Il Man laughed lightly. "Your remark barely covers a more serious comment. You're wondering if substance is keeping up with appearance. Come with me."

They walked into the small plaza that fronted the Provincial Office. A pair of armed students watched them closely but stood at ease when they recognized Il Man. The group went indoors. Just off the lobby, in a vast room that had formerly been filled with counters and desks for filing all manner of papers with the government, two rows of gurneys had been set up, each one occupied by a volunteer blood donor. A line of people waited their turns while nurses flew from station to station.

"Are you ready to give blood today?" Il Man asked.

"You bet," said Paul.

Later on, Gunther Loeb caught up with them as they were leaving the building. He was breathing heavily from exertion. "I have been walking around all day," he said. "I just came from the edge of the city. Did you know there is a body in the No Man's Land?"

Il Man paused while Paul translated. "Yes," he sighed. "There is nothing we can do while the troops stay within firing distance."

"'No Man's Land'?" Mi Jin asked.

"The space out there between the citizens' line and the troops," Joel said. "I know the place you're talking about, Gunther. It's about five hundred yards wide at that point. Nobody goes in there for fear of being fired at by the other side. Sort of like the Demilitarized Zone."

"And I'm sure the troops think we are the North Koreans in that scenario," Mi Jin said ruefully.

They continued their walk, accompanied by Gunther, who took photographs constantly. In choosing subject matter, however, he favored the ruined, burnt-out shells of cars and buildings.

"No, no," Il Man protested. "Look at this over here. We have citizens guarding important buildings like the Provincial Office and the banks. They're armed, but they pose no threat to the people."

Indeed, they saw old women and housewives carrying bundles of food to the students who manned their makeshift guardposts. The boys set aside their weapons and smiled wanly as they accepted the provisions. They looked weak and exhausted from days of constant guard duty.

"When do you think the troops are going to come back?" Gunther asked bluntly.

"We don't know," Il Man said. But we are determined that when they do come, peacefully or not, they will find the city better than the way they left it."

# CHAPTER ELEVEN

The uprising began to unravel shortly after that, not because the government's resolve had grown stronger, but because outside forces had finally come together to put an end to it.

Chief among these forces was the United States. On the surface, relations between the governments of Korea and of the United States had always been more than cordial; however, it became increasingly clear to the international community that a rift had recently opened between the Korean government and the established, comfortable democracy abroad. Jimmy Carter had repeatedly said that he would consider human rights abuses when formulating American foreign policy. This gave the student movement in Korea a measure of hope that their struggle would bear fruit. But the Cold War made the Carter Administration's best intentions untenable: a weakened South Korea, the reasoning went, would be an inviting target for a North Korean attack. It had a policy of promoting human rights and an obligation to support the current government of Korea. It could not do both.

The students' hopes died with the news, announced over radio and television with much fanfare by the Korean Ministry of Information, that the United States had released four battalions of Korean troops from the Joint Forces Command on the Demilitarized Zone and allowed them to travel south to Kwangju, there to join the mass of fresh troops preparing to save Kwangju from the "thugs" who, according to the Korean press, were running amok in the city like little warlords. A less incendiary, probably more truthful report came from the BBC over Joel's shortwave radio: the United States had reluctantly acquiesced to something that General Chon would have done anyway — as he had done during his *coup d'etat* last December. In return, Ambassador Glysteen and General Wickham had demanded that "maximum restraint" be employed when the retaking of Kwangju eventually occurred.

An angry crowd confronted Paul when he was walking near the Provincial Office with Joel.

"Why are you Americans getting involved in this?" one student demanded. His left arm was wrapped in bandages that had turned grimy from going too long unchanged. "What the hell is your government trying to do, kill us?" He spoke in English. The people around him muttered darkly in agreement, waiting for him to translate Paul's response.

Paul had just heard the news himself. "I really don't know what's going on! Trust me," he protested, in Korean. The fluency of his speech surprised and mollified them a little. "If what the radio says is true, I think my country is wrong. Terribly wrong. We should be cracking down on the martial law assholes who started this whole fight!" The crowd liked his remarks, and after scattered apologies, they let him and Joel continue on their way.

When he and Joel returned to their rooms, Mi Jin was there listening to the shortwave radio. Her lips pursed and turned white when they entered the room.

"You heard the news about the United States?" she asked.

"I heard the something had happened, but I didn't know what it was. I gather General Wickham did something the people around here didn't like. Something about sending troops?"

Mi Jin explained in clipped, sharp sentences.

"What a bunch of fools." Paul closed his eyes and rubbed them hard. "They don't know what they're doing."

"It's politics, pure and simple," Joel said bitterly. "The fate of one city in Korea doesn't count for much when you're trying to keep an ally fat and happy."

An urgent rapping at the door interrupted them. They froze until they heard a familiar voice.

"Mr. Pak, Elder Sister," a young student, one of Chong Il Man's couriers, opened the door a crack and spoke through the opening. "Something terrible has happened. Elder Brother Il Man is in the hospital. He's been attacked!"

"It's really nothing," Il Man said. He lay fully clothed atop the blankets on a bed at Chonnam University Hospital. His left thigh was wound up in bandages. The dark rings under his eyes betrayed exhaustion more than pain. His room, which he shared with six other wounded, was on the top floor of the building, directly under the .50 caliber machine gun the students had mounted on the roof. When it was quiet, he could hear the youngsters up there clanking the bolt in play and talking about what they would do if they saw soldiers coming.

"What happened?" Joel asked.

"It's crazy. I was walking in a corridor of the Provincial Office when someone came up behind me and stabbed me in the leg with a ball-point pen. That's what it turned out to be; we didn't know what it was at the time. You should have seen Jong Nam here — the fellow who brought you — trying to suck poison out of my leg! Looking back, it was pretty comical. But we didn't know. The doctors looked at it. All that got in was a little ink from a pen. They told me that the only poisoning I had in my body was 'toxins from lack of sleep,' as one of them put it. So here I am, in the company of heroes, trying to rest. My friend Jong Nam over-reacted, I'm afraid."

"Who would do such a thing?" Mi Jin wondered.

Il Man shrugged. "Not everyone is behind the movement, or behind me or my faction. It's inevitable. Every revolution winds down, devolves, as people lose sight of their ideals and give in to their fears. It hardly seems possible that our big rally of two hundred thousand people was only a few days ago. That was a great thing, a great feeling, wasn't it? Everyone together, everyone demonstrating against one enemy. It didn't last long. It never does."

"No," Mi Jin agreed, her voice mournful.

"Some people say that the government is embarrassed that Kwangju is better run now than it was before the uprising," Il Man said. "They're trying to cause a little chaos around the edges, just to keep us humble. I don't really agree. It's just winding down ... It's winding down."

Il Man's voice had softened into a raspy mumble. Paul gathered that the doctor had given him a sedative, and that it was now taking effect. "General Chon is going to get bolder now that the Americans are behind him. Sorry, you guys, but I think your president is an asshole ..."

He drifted off to sleep.

## Two

Signs of a quickening continued through Sunday, exactly one week after the troops' first assault on Kwangju. The weather had turned foul, which was typical for May: a casket lid of heavy clouds clamped down on the city and a steady drizzle made walking outdoors difficult, for the moisture fell and swirled about from below so that even those carrying umbrellas soon got drenched. The miasma muffled every sound, even the occasional *pop-pop-pop* of far-off gunfights that broke out and quickly ended. The various rallies planned for the day were canceled or sparsely attended. Almost everyone who did not have guard duty stayed indoors, at home or at a *tabang* or a bar. This was how an unexpectedly large portion of the population saw President Choi Kyu Ha's address to the nation.

Paul, Mi Jin, Joel, and Leslie spent the day at Trouble House, packed in with a multitude of students who, if not for the weather, would have been out demonstrating. The day's gray light made Venus' breasts on the *bas relief* by the door seem too small to notice, and that put many of the boys into a deeper gloom. The television in the corner was on, tuned as always to whatever channel had news, its volume turned all the way up. One of the few pleasures left to the besieged was the cleansing outrage that exploded whenever a reporter or government official talked nonsense about Kwangju.

Suddenly the room went quiet. Even those who had been deep in conversation turned to the television set. Mi Jin broke off in mid-sentence and held her finger to her lips.

"What's happening?" Leslie asked.

"A speech by President Choi," Paul said. "Coming up in a minute."

The screen went black for a moment, then came back, filled with a black and white still photograph of the president. Choi Kyu Ha's tired, raspy voice, being cut off from any image of a moving, living person, sent a chill down Mi Jin's back. The voice merely repeated what the martial law commander had been saying all along: that the majority of Kwangju's citizens were blameless pawns in a bid by communist-inspired malcontents to disrupt the nation and put all the people in danger of attack; that the issues causing unbearable heartache in the beautiful city should be resolved through negotiations; that "maximum leniency" would be shown to all who laid down their weapons and surrendered peacefully. In almost any other circumstances, the students at Trouble House would have greeted the speech with hoots and jeers; the weather outside and a profound weariness on the students' part, however, quelled such displays.

"Why is his photo giving the speech?" called out one student with half-hearted wit. "Where the hell is he?"

The fact that the address was obviously pre-recorded and delivered over a static picture of the man completely distracted everyone from its contents and fueled a rash of speculation.

"He's in jail," said one student. "General Chon couldn't trust him because, you know, he did try to start some reforms."

"I'll bet he delivered the speech with a gun to his head," agreed another.

The speculation went back and forth well into the night. Weary students who had been guarding the Provincial Office came in, were briefed on the situation, and then joined in with new arguments of old positions. As the night wore on, the queerness of the episode grew in their minds like a tumor.

"Something's going to happen," Mi Jin said gloomily. "I'm afraid the end is coming."

## Three

That night Mi Jin and the Americans sat in Joel's room and listened to one shortwave broadcast after another. Night seemed to come early under the thick shroud of clouds; by six o'clock it was almost too dark to see across the street. The news about Kwangju, when it came, was bad. The Korean government had made it clear to whoever would listen that their patience was coming to an end.

"Paul, let's go for a walk," Joel said.

They strolled along the broad expanse of Kumnam Street, which was lit murkily by weak bonfires and the few street lamps that had not been shot out. The cold droplets continued to swirl, to permeate the air in a coagulation of mist. When Joel spoke, his voice was heavy with the same murkiness, the same coldness.

"This can't end well, you know."

Paul said nothing.

"Once the troops come back — and they will, you can be sure of that — everyone will be in trouble. Everyone who helped the uprising."

"Like Mi Jin."

"Yes, like Mi Jin."

"Why are you telling me this?" Paul demanded in a low voice. "Don't you think I know it?"

"Do you? It's getting worse by the hour. This new Kwangju — this hodgepodge that the students are convinced is some paradise of communal spirit — is dissolving. We all knew it couldn't last forever. Yet here you are, getting closer to Mi Jin hour by hour. Like you're married, for God's sake. Have you given any thought to the future?"

"Jesus Christ, you're the cruelest son of a bitch I've ever met," Paul said, his voice rising. "I love her, right to the end, whether that end is tomorrow or the day we die. Why can't you understand something as simple as that? What would you have me do, pick up and leave? Abandon her? I don't know what your definition of love is, but it sure isn't the same as mine."

"I'm sorry."

"So am I. Let's just forget it, okay?"

They walked a few blocks in silence until, quite unexpectedly, Paul heaved a loud sigh and cleared his throat.

"No, let's look at this. Let me ask you something, Joel. What the hell do you think love is?"

Joel had never been asked the question so directly. He had trouble finding an answer. "A relationship that grows over time, I guess. Some warmth and a physical relationship, maybe ..." He shrugged.

"No wonder you think I'm crazy. It's more than that — more than sex, or friendship, or even a future together. No. It's a motivation, a striving, an act of creation. It moves and shakes and burns things up and then it creates them all over again. If it lasts for a lifetime, or a year or a day, so what? Is a child less human if it dies in infancy?"

Joel could not find his voice to make an answer. His own definition was tired and static, one that he had accepted without question. Paul's love was as much an act of defiance as of creation, a living thing of muscle and sinew that challenged more than gave comfort. Joel faltered in the presence of such a force.

## Four

Worrisome glimpses of new developments came in the person of a courier from the United States Cultural Center. The courier, a middle-aged Korean man who wore his trousers well up on his stomach, in the young men's fashion of the day, and drove an impressive Ford Bronco, came to Joel's rooms with a look of annoyance clearly written on his face.

"It took a long time to find you guys," he said in perfect English. He addressed Joel and Leslie and nodded toward Paul. "Who's he? I was told to look for two Peace Corps Volunteers."

"I'm a friend, just passing through," Paul said.

"American?"

"Yes."

"Well, this is it. All Americans are being evacuated from the city. This is your last chance to get out."

Mi Jin gasped. "Does this mean the government is going to retake the city soon?"

The man ignored her.

"Are the troops coming back?" Joel repeated.

"I can't say," he shrugged. "I was just told to come here to pick you up. A bus will be ready to go in a few hours. You can read whatever you want into that."

Paul moved closer to Mi Jin and looked at Joel. "Do we have to come with you right now?" Joel asked.

"You don't have to come at all, if you don't want to. It doesn't matter to me."

"We're not going," Leslie piped up. The sound of her voice, silent so far, startled them. "Joel and I have patients at the hospital. We can't leave them."

Joel smiled and drew her to his side. "That's right," he said. "If we get to the Center before you leave, we'll go with you. If not, so be it. Thanks for coming."

"Whatever." The man, irritated at making the trip for nothing, left. All eyes fixed questioningly on Leslie.

"I knew Paul wouldn't leave without Mi Jin," she said. "And Joel wouldn't leave without Paul. And I won't leave without any of you."

## Five

Many memorial services were held the next day for those who had died since the beginning of the massacre. Mi Jin and Paul attended the one held at the Sangmukwan, the National Guard armory that had supplied many weapons to the uprising. Someone had cleared its large auditorium of pro-government posters and set up a small altar on the stage. White flowers mounted on dozens of wreaths filled up the rest of the stage, their aroma overpowering the old stink of metal and grease. Several strong men had crated in a good-sized organ from a nearby church. People came in their Sunday best and by the time the couple got there the room was full of the quiet rustling of gauzy women's *hanboks*.

Reverend Kim Nam Ho, the man who had led the unsuccessful negotiations with the martial law authorities, announced the first hymn. The organ boomed out the first bars of a familiar, majestic melody, and the crowd joined in a swelling of voices:

*A mighty fortress is our God,*
*A bulwark never failing;*
*Our helper He, amid the flood*
*Of mortal ills prevailing;*
*For still our ancient foe*
*Doth seek to work us woe;*
*His craft and power are great,*
*And, armed with cruel hate,*
*On Earth is not his equal.*

A noticeable change came over the congregation, and most notably in Paul, as the hymn went on. The naked defiance in Martin Luther's words seemed to clear the air of doubt. People who had come to the memorial service under a cloud of despair, fearing that the next service would be for them, stood straighter and seemed to regain hope, however fleeting. Paul remembered the words from his Sundays in church back home. He sang them in English, at the top of his lungs, louder with every verse:

*And though this world, with devils filled,*
*Should threaten to undo us,*
*We will not fear, for God hath willed*
*His truth to triumph through us;*
*The Prince of Darkness grim —*

*We tremble not for him;*
*His rage we can endure,*
*For lo, his doom is sure,*
*One little word shall fell him.*

*That word above all earthly powers,*
*No thanks to them, abideth.*
*The Spirit and the gifts are ours*
*Through Him who with us sideth;*
*Let goods and kindred go,*
*This mortal life also;*
*The body they may kill;*
*God's truth abideth still,*
*His kingdom ours forever!*

"Brothers and sisters in Christ!" Reverend Kim cried out from the podium, shunning the use of the microphone. "'Greater love has no man than this, that he lay down his life for his friends.'" He knew the cleansing power of emotion: with alternating modulations of sentimentality, outrage, and adoration, his long sermon drew tears from most of his listeners in a long, loud misery of weeping and beating of chests. Mi Jin clutched Paul's arm and wept, too.

Paul watched the faces around him. Some wept anew louder than before; some shouted with grief and rage. Onlookers yet untouched by tragedy in their own families found themselves moved as much as those who had lost all. Paul tried to stay outside the emotions of the place, to stay strong for Mi Jin, but soon he, too, succumbed to the moment and to something that Reverend Kim said, almost in passing:

"To hope and to act — that is our duty in times of trouble. To give in to despair is a crime, an affront to those who lost their lives here."

## Six

Paul proposed to Mi Jin when they got home.

He took a small felt-covered box from a corner of his backpack and rubbed it nervously while he spoke in faltering words about his love and his wish to spend the rest of his life with her. He blushed at the triteness of his words, appalled that such an important declaration should be couched in such inanities; Mi Jin, not knowing anything about tired expressions in English, warmed with joy at the sentiment behind them. He showed her the ring, a cheap pastiche of silver and onyx with something that looked like a diamond chip in its center.

"It is beautiful," she whispered. "When did you buy it?"

"The night before I escaped from the airport and started on my way here. I couldn't afford ..."

Mi Jin interrupted him with a long kiss.

"I want to us to be together forever," she said. She slipped the ring on her finger and admired it at arm's length.

"As I was about to say, I'll get you a nicer one as soon as ... our situation improves."

Mi Jin smiled, then started to giggle like a schoolgirl. "We've got to tell somebody! Let's tell Joel and Leslie."

"I'll go get them ..."

"No! We must do this right." She trundled him out to the supermarket down the street and filled his arms with steamed red bean buns, pound cakes, and other confections from the store's nearly depleted shelves. Then she asked the shop-owner if he had any champagne. "No," he replied, "only *soju*, and not much left of that." They bought four bottles and rushed back home.

Joel and Leslie paused at the spectacle spread before them. On a low table, Mi Jin had torn small slips of paper into rough approximations of hearts and pasted them in a ragged frieze around its edge. She had piled two dishes high with every available candy and snack cake, all arranged in orderly piles that reminded Joel of traditional Korean burial mounds. Paul invited them to come in and sit down.

"We have news for you," Paul said shyly. Joel and Leslie glanced at each other in morbid silence. "We're going to be married. This is our engagement party."

"We're happy for you," Leslie said. She went to Mi Jin and hugged her. "We wish you the best." She ran back to her room to get her camera.

Joel's congratulatory handshake carried an unspoken message: "Didn't you understand what I said to you?" Paul's reply came in a low whisper: "You just don't get it, do you?"

"Now sit together, you two. Joel, get out of the picture. Heads together. That's right. Smile!"

Mi Jin, allowing one of her rare smiles, was radiant. Paul, equally happy, gave a defiant smile. This was the photograph that Joel and Leslie kept for many years after.

## Seven

An urgent knock on their door brought an end to the celebration.

"What a relief! You're still here." Chong Il Man wiped large drops of perspiration from his forehead, the result of a dash from the Provincial Office.

"Why shouldn't we be here?" Paul asked.

"It's the rumors," Il Man said. "The latest is that the last of the Americans were evacuated from the city a short time ago. People take that as a sign that the government is about to attack."

Paul and Joel glanced at each other. Joel spoke up:

"Actually, Il Man, it's not a rumor. We chose not to go."

Il Man's face fell, then hardened in that mask.

"What is it?" Mi Jin asked. "What else have you heard?"

"Nothing; it's just that more and more rumors are starting to prove true. Remember even a few days ago, when they spread like wildfire among the people and always turned out to be false? Time after time, we got word that the troops were on the move, sometimes in the middle of our rallies, and the crowds panicked. We always felt tense and maybe a little silly afterwards. Now it's different." He went to the window and pointed toward the hills to the west of the city. "We got word a few hours ago that paratroopers were being dropped into the fields outside the city. We checked it out, and it was true. Others near the siege border reported that they've seen more helicopters flying around; they saw stretchers being loaded on them – apparently the government is evacuating its wounded from their field hospitals. That's another bad sign. Now we've got the last Americans being evacuated. Well, almost the last. The troops are on the move. We had all better get ready."

When they went to dinner shortly afterward, Mi Jin and the Americans did not go far from their inn. The mood of the people they met on the street had indeed changed. The optimism that had swept everyone up after the expulsion of the paratroopers last week and buoyed them briefly during the memorial service had dissipated: now they were glum and tense. A few students on the street corner talked big about their battles against the soldiers and bragged half-heartedly about what they would do to them in "Round Two." A pair of older men, neither of whom had supported the students during the uprising, laid bets with each other on the day and hour that the city would be retaken. Other men, drunk from the bar next door, came over and joined them. The bets ranged from that evening to three days hence. No one wagered that the troops would stay away.

## Eight

"They're insane, you know." Joel stubbed out one cigarette and lit another one with a shaky hand. The radio in his room blared out an abomination of a song called "Funkytown" from AFKN, the American armed forces station; Joel felt ready to kick it across the room.

"How so? They're happy, and that's what matters," Leslie said. "I admit I was as shocked as you when they said they're getting married, but what can we do? I just pray that it turns out well for them."

"It won't."

Leslie took another look at Joel. The face that had grown dear to her had become lined with worry. In his worry he scowled, and his scowl made him look angry. She put her hand on his cheek and drew him toward her. They rested there until he calmed down.

The music was suddenly broken by a pair of distinct chimes followed by a moment of dead silence. Joel had heard it many times before: AFKN used those tones to introduce bulletins and requests from the Red Cross to find lost servicemen; they invariably sent a chill down his back.

"This is a special bulletin to all United States citizens residing in the Republic of Korea. The United States Embassy is directing all military and non-military personnel to refrain from traveling to Kwangju, South Cholla Province and its surrounding communities until further notice. American citizens currently in Kwangju should remain indoors and not venture outside. The United States Embassy through the Armed Forces Korea Network will keep you informed of all further developments."

Joel's body tensed. Leslie let out a gasp and started shaking.

"They're coming," she said.

## Nine

Joel did not tell Paul and Mi Jin what he knew. He did not want to spoil their celebration.

Mi Jin was a member of a group of students who gave themselves the unwieldy and somewhat pompous name of "The 5.18 Provincial Office Defense Committee." They guarded the building in shifts, standing at the broken-out windows dressed in captured body armor and helmets, rifles ready, scanning the distance for signs of attack. Mi Jin did not know how to hold a gun, much less fire one, and her petite frame could not support the helmet and padding; she played a supporting role, fixing coffee and snacks for those who were forbidden to leave their posts.

"Don't go to the Office tonight," Paul pleaded. He pulled her to him and kissed her. "They'll find somebody else to work your shift. Stay with me."

They undressed and soon fell into a sound sleep.

Mi Jin awoke near midnight. She was sweating, and at first wondered if she were ill. Only after sitting quietly for several minutes, listening to Paul's rhythmic breathing, did she remember a fragment of the dream that had awakened her.

Her grandmother had come. She and Mi Jin held hands and walked together in a field of azaleas and forsythia. The mist toward which they walked seemed pleasant enough at a distance, like an early morning fog in summertime, but behind it a thick breeze wafted up vague noises of distress and the odor of smoke and blood. At the moment the gray mist engulfed them, Mi Jin's eyes had flown open.

She shakily poured a cup of cold barley tea from a brass kettle and sipped it. The air in the room was unbearably close. She put on jeans and a sweater, kissed Paul, and went outside.

The cool night air cleared her head. She soon forgot about her dream. Thoughts of Paul and their future as a couple, a married couple, pushed the dream from her mind. In her new mood of optimism she had a sense that everything would work out well for them. She turned to walk toward the Provincial Office.

"I might as well take my turn on duty after all," she said.

The students were glad to see her. She went from window to window, chatting with each young guard, asking if they needed anything.

"So you've come after all," a fellow named Lee said. He was one of the small circle that was close to Chong Il Man. His natural diplomacy had helped smooth relations with the leaders of other factions among the students. "Il Man went home already. He was tired, very tired, and he wasn't looking forward to the long trip to his house. You look good, Elder Sister, like you're happy about something."

"I am," she smiled.

## Ten

Paul awoke with an odd buzzing sound in his ears, and in his state between sleep and wakefulness he wondered who had turned on a fan and why it seemed broken. Only after he sat up did he realize that the sound he heard was of helicopters flying in formation along the length of Kumnam Street toward the Provincial Office; their *flap-flap-flap-flap* shook the window as they flew overhead. He looked toward Mi Jin's spot on the bed, now empty.

"Mi Jin?"

He wondered if she had merely got up to use the bathroom, and rapped on the door.

"Mi Jin?"

The room was empty. With a rising sense of panic he ran to the hallway and called her name. The commotion brought Joel and Leslie running.

"What is it?" Joel asked.

"Mi Jin. She's not here!"

Just then Joel heard another wave of helicopters flying overhead. In the background, in a rising crescendo of vibration, the deep-throated rumbling of a column of tanks began to shake the building. He and Paul had heard the same sound and felt the same vibrations on the night President Pak was assassinated, when martial law was first declared.

"They're coming back."

"Where's Mi Jin?" Leslie cried.

The answer came over the public address system mounted on the high walls of the Provincial Office. Mi Jin's voice rang out, a human solo over the cacophony of machinery:

"Get up! Get up!" Her voice quavered with fear. "Brothers and sisters of Kwangju! Arm yourselves! They're coming!"

"Mi Jin!" Paul made a dash for the door, but Joel caught him and held him tightly. "Let me go! Let me go, damn you!"

"No!" Joel shouted. A series of deep reports, *thud ... thud ... thud* rattled the windowpanes. The tanks were bombarding the Provincial Office.

"Get up!" Mi Jin continued. "Come to the defense of your city! Come —" Her voice stopped.

"Mi Jin!" Paul ran to the window and flung it open. "Mi Jin!"

A squad of paratroopers was trotting along the street below, their rifles held before them at the ready. At the sound of Paul's shouting, one soldier took aim and fired. The bullet, purposely mis-aimed, *ping*ed against the brick wall above the window and showered Paul with dust. Joel pulled him inside and wrestled him to the ground. It took all of Joel's strength to keep his friend from getting back up.

The bombardment of the Provincial Office and the firefights in the streets lasted a couple hours, until dawn started to light the horizon. Pockets of resistance formed and then dissipated, popping up and then retreating and resurfacing elsewhere. The government, armed with an almost ridiculous number of tanks and men, made quick work of the retaking of Kwangju. Within a few hours after Mi Jin's voice last rang out over the city, the fighting ended and Joel and Paul were able to go out. They headed straight for the Provincial Office.

The streets swarmed with soldiers and with watchful citizens who, emboldened by an hour without the sound of gunfire, allowed their curiosity to get the better of them. Aside from soldiers, there was no one on the streets between the ages of fifteen and twenty-five. Everyone in that age group seemed to have disappeared.

Joel gaped at the Provincial Office as they approached. The number of bullet holes that pocked the walls had doubled since he last saw them; in addition, black streaks above some windows testified to fires that had gutted the interior. They ran first to the front door, but the steps were packed with soldiers who allowed no one to pass inside. They turned and ran down a side alley, hoping to find one of the service entrances in the back.

"Where do we go once we get inside?" Joel asked. Paul shook his head and pressed on.

The pair did not have to enter the building. In a corner of the alley, under guard by a single reservist, lay a pile of bodies. Joel and Paul stopped.

Several of the people there were known to them, including the eager young man who only a couple days before had rushed to Paul's rooms to tell him of the attack on Chong Il Man; he lay near the bottom of the heap, his face and chest covered with blood. Paul searched the mass breathlessly, nearly ready to faint. Joel held him and suddenly felt him slump in his arms.

Mi Jin lay motionless on top, on the far side, her body splayed like a rag doll across three others. Her eyes were closed and her face was pale with the pall of death. Save for a badly mangled left leg, she seemed relatively unharmed, and this gave the impression that she was not dead, but asleep. Paul uttered a cry and tried to go to her, but Joel held him back. Joel managed with great difficulty to move him over to a shadowed doorway where they could stand and watch unobserved. The guard, whose back was turned to them, stood in a slouch, his head down. Joel turned his gaze back to Mi Jin and watched her intently, unblinkingly, burning her image into his memory. When she moved, he thought it was an optical illusion. Her head moved again and he roused Paul.

"Did you see that?"

Paul looked up and held still, watching. She moved again, tilting her head and opening her mouth in a moan they could not hear.

"Come on!"

Paul sprang to her side. He cradled her and held her face close to his, eager to find confirmation that she was alive. She let out another moan, a weak one. Joel felt for a pulse and raised an eyelid to peer in.

"She's in shock. She's lost a lot of blood, but not enough to kill her. She needs to get to a hospital, quick!"

Without another thought, Paul picked her up like a baby and started to run into the alley. A harsh cry stopped him.

"*Yah!* What are you doing? Put it down!"

Paul turned and stared at the guard.

"Paul! Put her down for a moment," Joel said. "Maybe I can talk with him ..."

"Mr. Kim?" Paul said. "Laboratory Mr. Kim?"

The guard stared at Paul. A flash of recognition lit his eyes.

"Do you remember me, Mr. Kim?" Paul continued. He walked toward him, still holding Mi Jin. "I worked with you at the Mokpo Health Center. We did lab work together."

Mr. Kim nodded and looked around, hoping no others soldiers were watching them. He did not lower his weapon.

"This woman is still alive. She's my *yak hon ja*, my fiancée. We we're going to get married. Please let me take her to a hospital. She'll die if she doesn't get care. Please, Mr. Kim!"

A dozen considerations wrestled in Mr. Kim' mind in the next moment. His training had taught him to obey orders without question, and he had been ordered to secure this damning human debris of the paratroopers' work. On the other hand, Paul was a friend and the woman still lived. Above all — and this eventually swayed him — he himself was a Chollado man, no friend of the Kyongsang bastards who killed these people here. He nodded quickly and turned his back. The last Paul and Joel heard of him, as they ran up the alley, he was telling a squad of paratroopers around the corner that everything was quiet.

## Eleven

"This looks bad. Very bad," Dr. Ko muttered as he examined Mi Jin's leg. Joel worked near the head of the gurney in the emergency room, looking after her vital signs. He had found her blood pressure to be dangerously low, and was now setting up a transfusion. "Not good at all."

A foul odor filled the examination room when the doctor cut open her pants leg and peeled it back. Paul recognized it immediately. "Gangrene, isn't it?"

Dr, Ko nodded. "Already. This infection has grown remarkably fast, as gangrene sometimes will. We don't have the equipment to save the leg."

"What do you recommend?" Paul asked.

"Amputation. I can have a surgeon do it right away."

A nurse rushed in and whispered something in the doctor's ear. He swore softly and gave her some hurried instructions.

"The government is sending troops into the hospital," he explained. "They are arresting as many as they can, even ones who are seriously injured."

"Can we hide her?" Joel asked.

"Let me think, let me think ... I know. Take her to the Infectious Diseases ward. They won't go into that area if we tell them we've got a case of typhus or leprosy or something in there. Go ahead."

With the help of a nurse, Paul and Joel wheeled Mi Jin into a small private room. Its walls were bare and white. White daylight flooded in through a frosted window. The room's brightness hurt Paul's eyes when he first came in, and caused Mi Jin to cry out until Joel ran to the window and drew the shades.

"It's all right," Paul whispered. "Can you hear me? Can you hear me?" She moaned again, more softly. "We're going to take good care of you, honey. You're safe. You're safe."

Mi Jin settled into a deep sleep.

The operation started within minutes. Paul waited in her room, pacing its narrow width, as if caged. An hour later, Leslie came to the door and threw her arms around him.

"Thank God she's alive! How is she?"

Paul told her. She cleared her throat and proceeded uncertainly:

"I've got bad news, Paul. I just got a call from Mr. Atwood. Peace Corps found out about us three, how we stayed here after being told to evacuate. They know about you. Needless to say, they want us to come to Seoul right away. Especially you."

"I can't."

"I know."

"Listen," Paul said, "you guys should go back. The game's up. There's no reason for you to stay. I don't want to drag you deeper into trouble than you already are."

Just then an orderly and a nurse wheeled Mi Jin back into the room. They lifted her onto the bed. The bedsheet covered her body closely in a contour map of creases and wrinkles; it fell off precipitously above her left knee.

"Oh, God," Leslie gasped.

"Go on, you two. I mean it." Paul pushed them toward the door. "I'll see you someday soon, I hope. Until then, thank you for all your help. Now go."

"I'll talk to Mr. Atwood," Joel called from the doorway. "He'll get your side of the story. That's a promise."

## Twelve

Mi Jin had been delirious all day, thrashing in her bed and calling out meaningless names. The amputation wound on her leg had broken open, but because of the shortage of nurses and the uproar in the hospital it had gone unnoticed. It soon began to suppurate. Paul could do nothing but try to keep the wound clean. He dreaded the leg becoming gangrenous again. There was little he could do but worry, hold her hand, put cool rags on her forehead, and take her temperature from time to time. She was burning up with fever.

Mi Jin finally grew quiet. In the warm light of late afternoon Paul lay in exhausted slumber. Sitting in an armchair beside Mi Jin's bed with his head slung back at an angle, he let out short bursts of snoring that made Mi Jin jerk with discomfort: in her delirium she imagined the rasping to be the sound of the doctor's saw once again cutting through her bone.

Mi Jin's eyes opened and she thought she heard the sun speaking from past the horizon: "Come away with me to the west. Sleep forever."

She closed her eyes again and tried to will the doctor to stop sawing on her. Violent spasms rocked the feeling part of her while her body remained immobile. She felt herself straining to break out of a straitjacket.

"Let me out!" she cried, but no sound came from her lips. "Let me out of here!"

The slow step-step-step of a Kyongsang paratrooper on the street below quieted her. The light from the window became gray-blue as the hospital fell into gloom. When nearly all light had left the room, the beloved voice came:

"Jin-a. It's time to go."

"Grandmama!"

Mi Jin opened her eyes and sat up. The room was bright. She saw more clearly than she had ever done before, as if the air around her had been cleansed and polished. She understood every feature of her surroundings with extraordinary clarity: a smudge on the wall that had once been made by an errant wheelchair attracted her attention. "Of course," she whispered. "It has a history. It belongs there!"

"Come with me, Jin-a."

Grandmother, clothed in the white linen country *hanbok* in which Mi Jin best remembered her, stood at the foot of the bed and held out her arms.

Mi Jin smiled and stood up. She was wearing a *hanbok* like her grandmother's. Her leg was whole again. Her discarded body, as still as stone, lay on the bed.

She moved effortlessly and faced Paul, who was asleep in the chair. She paused before him.

"You must come." Her grandmother's gentle voice was firm.

"Paul," Mi Jin said. A flicker of uncertainty passed over her face. The name had become unfamiliar to her. "Jong Shik?"

A moment later she moved on. She no longer knew him, nor the body on the bed, nor anything anymore.

## *Thirteen*

"I can't believe you left Paul alone like that," Leslie snarled when they stepped outside the hospital and started walking toward the train station. The words came out hard as flint. "Some friend you turned out to be. The moment he needs you most, you up and leave him with a dying fiancée, soon to be arrested ... do you always leave people like that — worse off than you found them?"

"Let's keep my personal history out of this," Joel said. "I'm not going."

" ... What?"

"What do you take me for? You're right: a friend wouldn't think of leaving at a time like this. That's why I'm going back to the hospital as soon as I put you on the train."

"Then I'm staying, too," Leslie said.

"No. You're going to Seoul and heading straight for Atwood's office. You have to tell him what happened here. Everything. Don't let Mrs. Kang stop you — this is for Atwood alone. I'll come up with Paul when — well, when it's time to come up. It probably won't be long."

They walked along Kumnam Street with their arms linked.

"I don't want to leave you," Leslie whispered.

"I don't want you to leave, either," said Joel with surprising tenderness. She had managed a feat that he thought could never be done: she had become dear to him. He had often belittled this frightened, troubled woman in the months before the Uprising. It was only during recent weeks that her courage had emerged: it shone in her steadiness at the hospital and in her refusal to leave the city during the worst of the fighting. Admiration was for Joel only a step away from love, and just as rare. He put his arm around her as they walked.

A commotion was forming ahead along Kumnam Street. Crowds of spectators lined the curb. In all the jostling, though, there was little sound of talking. No one had anything to say. Most of the noise was the familiar rumble of tanks.

"What's going on?" Leslie asked. Joel craned his neck to look up the street. A neat line of tanks, banners flying from their turrets, processed in single file toward the Provincial Office. The sight took his breath away: the line stretched the entire length of the street, half a dozen long city blocks, and still the tanks turned one by one onto the street in the distance. "No wonder the bastards won," Joel thought, and he realized that this was exactly what the government wanted the residents of Kwangju to think.

Army trucks filled with soldiers joined the procession along with armored personnel carriers and jeeps carrying military officials. One jeep stood out from the rest, both by its running flag and by the mass of soldiery surrounding it. The sight of the stiff figure of a man riding in the back caused the quiet crowd to grow quieter still, and sullen.

"General Chon!" people whispered among themselves.

Joel looked closely at the man. The general took no notice of the stares and whispers of the spectators. He sat ramrod straight, motionless, looking neither left nor right. Joel thought he looked smaller in real life and thinner, and rather commonplace in his features; he was vaguely surprised that Chon was a human being at all, composed of color and substance.

The train station, too, was quieter than usual. A squad of well-armed paratroopers guarded the front door. A far greater number of national guardsmen patrolled inside. Few people traveled; those who did were held under close scrutiny. An orderly squad of young women, obviously brought in from outside Kwangju and dressed in crisp attendants' uniforms, swept up broken glass under a bank of bright floodlights and the watchful eye of a movie camera.

"I'd better get back to Paul," Joel said when they stepped outside to the platform. "Mi Jin's probably waking up by now." He gathered Leslie into his arms, kissed her, and held her. He let her go only after a nearby group of soldiers whistled disrespectfully. He dived back into the crowded station and disappeared.

Joel returned to the hospital after dark to find Paul gone. Mi Jin's room was empty.

"Where are they?" he demanded of a nurse.

"*Cho yojanun tola kassoyo*," she said. The lady passed away. "The American man left after we took her body away. I don't know where he went. I'm sorry."

Joel slumped heavily onto a bench in the hallway. He lowered his head and, after many attempts to control himself, wept as a child does, without restraint.

## *Fourteen*

Joel had to return to his room at sunset, when curfew came. He hoped Paul too would come in for the night, but was not surprised when he did not. He set out at first light of the following morning to look for him.

Paratroopers were everywhere. They now seemed to outnumber the ordinary citizens of the city, most of whom were hiding in their homes.

An unnatural silence gripped the streets, broken only by the rumble of military vehicles. But running beneath it all, just above the level of hearing, was the droning of vast, unquenchable grief. It found voice at first in the old people and the children, for it was they who ventured out to the public morgues looking for sons, daughters, grandchildren, and parents. The soldiers, for the most part, either ignored the keening or could not hear it. Joel heard it; and as he walked the alleyways and streets in his search for Paul, he fought with all his might the urge to succumb to it.

The largest makeshift morgue, one of many throughout the city, occupied an alleyway between two burned-out buildings not far from the hospital. About thirty coffins were lined up in three rows. Most were closed, bound in cloth, and tied with white ribbons. Relatives shrouded some of them with Korean flags and set framed photographs of the dead upon them.

The cries of mourners created a hellish din in the echoing concrete of the alleyway. In the event of a normal death, grief would play itself out at home, under a roof, within a circle of friends and kin. Kwangju's grief, in contrast, spilled outdoors under the open sky. Nor would the burials be private: the dead were to be interred together in a public graveyard the next day. Local reservists stood guard and saw to it that no one disobeyed that directive.

The reservists were almost to be pitied. They had no respite from the entreaties of people to look the other way so that sons' and daughters' bodies might be taken away and laid to rest decently beside their ancestors. When the men had first come on duty they had refused the requests firmly but politely, hardly able themselves to understand the scene before them. Later, as the long day passed and some of the bodies began to stink, the calluses that had been building up over their emotions all day led them to refuse sharply and with threats.

Many of the plain wooden coffins still lay open, *mi hwak in*, "identification unconfirmed" daubed on them with crude letters. The interior plastic shrouds pushed down far enough to display the white faces inside. Several of the bodies that had become badly decomposed were completely wrapped; they would have to be taken away soon, identified or not.

At intervals, a family that had been making the rounds of the city's morgues would stop beside an unidentified body, peer in, and recognize one of their own. At first they could utter only a muffled "*Ommo!*" of shock and disbelief. Then a piercing shriek would rend the air for a moment, subside, and finally mingle with the sound of bitter sobbing that had filled the morgue since dawn.

The stench of death penetrated everywhere. The soldiers smoked cigarettes constantly to mask it.

A little boy, lured away from his grandmother's side at his father's coffin by the bewildering smell and confusion around him, shuffled aimlessly among the coffins, a bottle of Coke in his hand. He noticed two coffins set off by themselves, and went to them to investigate. He lifted the plastic wrapping that hung out of the closest one and peeked inside. A young man lay there, his face blackened and caved in on one side. The child screamed in terror and ran back to his grandmother. She struck him savagely for having wandered away. The boy spent the rest of the day at her side, whimpering.

Paul stood unnoticed in a doorway across the street from the morgue at dawn when the orderlies brought Mi Jin's body from the hospital. He had stood, hidden in the shadows, beside her body since then. Her body had been placed in a plastic bag and put in a coffin cruelly marked *mi hwak in*. The morgue attendants had set it on the ground a little apart from the other dead. It was clean, and had been shrouded with care, but they knew that the microbes that had killed Mi Jin were still consuming the body long after her death. The smell by the end of the day would be intolerable.

Hours passed. Paul did not move.

No one came to claim Mi Jin's body. The coffin still lay open and ignored by all but those who, looking for their own kin, peered into her coffin; they glanced down, handkerchiefs over their faces, and trudged away. Somehow the rag that had been stuffed in her mouth — under an old superstition, to keep evil spirits from entering the body and animating it —

had gotten loose and fallen out. Her mouth lay partly open, as if she were about to say something.

The Kyongsang paratroopers who kept an eye on the reservist guards were burdened neither with grief nor with respect for the dead. When not talking among themselves, they stared and grinned blankly, still showing the effects of courage-giving drugs and alcohol. Walking past the coffins on their way to other duties, they exclaimed "*Waugh!*" and clowned expressions of disgust. They made loud jokes about dog feces.

Paul saw it all and remained impassive. Under normal circumstances, he would have been consumed with anger over such a display, whether the body were of a loved one or not. But these were not normal circumstances. An observer might have seen his outward calm as shock, pure and simple, but it went beyond shock to an unquestioning acquiescence to the turning of events. It had begun yesterday when Paul first noticed the swelling beneath the bandages on Mi Jin's leg. Hours later, when the smelly, bubbling exudate started to appear, he realized that her fate was beyond human control. He saw how horribly she suffered in her inhospitable body, and he at last felt relief when she left it. He could not, however, shake the feeling that some part of her essence remained with the body. That is why he took such pains to follow it as far as he could to its place in the morgue.

Joel finally found him at mid-morning after checking all the other morgues in the area. Without greeting or preamble, Paul talked in a soft monotone about the arrangements he had made: for the inclusion of her name in a Requiem Mass to be said the next morning; for cremation as soon as possible; for the arrangements he could not make, among which were notifying her family of her death. Through it all he maintained the somber, sedate manner of one whose elderly wife has died after a long illness, calmly doing what needed to be done because he was the only one left to do it. Joel stayed with him until late afternoon, when a woman from the hospital came to remove the body for cremation.

## *Fifteen*

"Paul, I have this for you."

Dr. Ko called Paul and Joel into his office the next day. Paul was still unnaturally quiet and his eyes were red with sleeplessness. The doctor took a wooden box from a cabinet and placed it on his desk.

"The nurse who admitted Miss Han to the hospital, Mrs. Yun, did as you requested," Dr. Ko explained. "She went to the authorities and claimed Miss Han as a relative. We had her cremated and brought her ashes back here." He motioned to Paul to take the box. "She ... the ashes ... are yours."

"Thank you Doctor," Paul said, "and please thank Mrs. Yun for her kindness. It must have been difficult for her." He reached for the box and was surprised at how light it was — almost weightless. He placed it gingerly in his backpack.

"We have to go back to Seoul, you know," Joel told Paul when they left the hospital.

"Not yet."

"You want to stay in Kwangju? Why?"

"No," Paul replied. He thought for a moment and said, "I want to go back to Mokpo. But first ... come this way."

Paul took Joel's arm and led him away from Kumnam Street, which was still crowded with soldiers, and deep into the alleys not far from Chonnam University.

"I know where you're going," Joel said, "and I don't think it's a good idea."

Paul did not hear, or was not listening. He pressed on until he turned the corner of a quiet side street and gazed upon a burned-out building whose sign swung from its fixture like the sword of Damocles. The plaster *bas relief* of Botticelli's *Venus* lay on the ground, dirtied and broken like the bodies they had seen throughout the city. Trouble House lay in ruins.

"Let's go," Paul murmured.

Joel trudged after him toward the bus station. Why is he doing this? he wondered. Reliving Trouble House, and next Mokpo — like he's willing his life with Mi Jin to flash before his eyes, as if he were drowning.

They had walked several blocks when suddenly a hissing, scraping noise shot out from the dark corner of a deserted food market.

"*Hsst! Hsst!* Come this way!" whispered a familiar voice.

Chong Il Man emerged briefly from the shadows, just long enough to be seen and recognized by the Americans and no one else, then jumped out of sight. He leaned unsteadily against a wall. The flash of sunlight across his body revealed a contusion on his chin and a large gash whose swelling deformed one side of his face into a hideous mask.

"Il Man!" Paul cried. "Are you all right? Let us help you."

"No. I'm wanted." His voice was husky, his speech slurred with pain. "If they find me, they'll probably kill me. Eventually."

"What are you going to do?"

"I wasn't at the Provincial Office that night, but I heard Mi Jin's voice, as if in a dream," Il Man said, oblivious to the question. "Where is she?"

"She died."

Il Man slumped even farther than before, to the point where Joel stepped in to hold him up. "My God ... my God," he groaned. "I don't know what to say. I can't ..."

"What will you do now?" Joel asked. "Where will you go?"

Il Man motioned to the low mountains on the horizon, just visible through the chinks in the alleyway, in a wide gesture that nearly knocked him over. "To the hills. Those of us who survived — there are damned few of us — are going to the hills, to fight again someday. And we will fight. Kwangju will not be forgotten. We Koreans take everything to heart. We hold grudges, long ones, grudges that nurse our pain through years and generations. Kwangju is not dead." With that, he squeezed Paul's shoulder and turned to rejoin the shadows of the street.

## Sixteen

A brisk spring wind blew up behind Mount Yudal in the first minutes after dawn. It followed the main spur of the mountain southward, sweeping down onto Mokpo Harbor below. It nearly straightened the trees that were accustomed to bending over in deference to the prevailing winds; now they stood at semi-attention, like a line of aged soldiers, the spirits of the peasant-warriors of Chollado's past.

Paul and Joel climbed the stairways of the mountain cautiously in the shadows. Paul walked especially slowly, for every step, every landing provoked a thrill of recognition: here he fell in the darkness one night long ago; here Mi Jin caressed his bleeding hand; there she put his arm around her shoulders and used her strength to take the weight off his injured foot. He gazed long and hard at those landmarks.

"How about this place?" Joel asked when they reached a pavilion halfway up the mountain.

Paul shook his head. In this pavilion he and Mi Jin had stopped and talked, where Mi Jin had sung; it was where he first knew he loved her. Many times later she had told him how she treasured this spot. He strained to see in the semi-darkness. A young couple had come and were leaning on the railing, looking out over Mokpo's harbor and the sea. Were they people or were they ghosts from Paul's memory? He could not tell. He thought he heard a small voice on the wind singing slowly, tenderly, like a lullaby:

Seh no yah — seh no yah
*We live in the mountains and the sea;*
*To the mountains and the sea we go.*
*If it is happiness, give it to the mountain;*
*If sadness, to your love.*
*If it is happiness, give it to the sea;*
*If sadness, to me.*

"Not here. Let's go up a little farther." He shifted the wooden box under his arm and turned to look again at the pavilion. It was empty.

They reached a rocky ledge fifty feet above the pavilion. Mokpo, the city that he and Mi Jin had loved, stretched out below, a distant and indistinct jumble of streets and houses. Paul told Joel to stop. Pink light was beginning to color the clouds overhead.

Paul walked out on the ledge and opened the box containing Mi Jin's ashes.

"Do you want to say a few words?" Joel prompted.

"I've already said them." Paul took a deep breath and plunged his hand slowly into the gray powder. His fingers stirred the ashes. He closed his hand around some, held it out at arm's length, and let it go.

The wind swirled Mi Jin's remains into a vortex around Paul's hand, nearly doubling back on it as if to make a last goodbye. Then it flew out in a white cloud over the mountain and the sea, and over Mokpo. After a few handfuls, Mi Jin was gone.

# EPILOGUE

Eighteen years passed.

Night had long since fallen on the aging ex-volunteers gathered on Joel and Leslie Reynoso's backyard patio. Evan Barker, the volunteer whom Mrs. Kang had thrown out of Peace Corps, was there. Mark Follett, now a high school principal, was on his summer break. Sarah Conlon had arrived late and planned to stay through the weekend. She was no longer a Conlon, though, having left Theodore years before. That surprised no one.

Martin Budzinski, now paunchy and blind in one eye, brought a bottle of *soju* he had found at an Asian food market. Almost everyone took a sip of it for old times' sake, but nobody finished it off. It sat in the middle of the table, a spot of green among the brown beer bottles, until Jenny — Joel and Leslie's teen-aged daughter — dared to take a swallow of it. She sputtered and coughed and without thinking poured the rest of it into a flower-bed.

Several other ex-volunteers came to the reunion, all showing signs of age. Their graying hair at first lent a curious sense of agitation to the affair, shocking everyone that the passage of time had done its damage while they weren't looking. They hurriedly filled each other in on all that had happened since they last met, and by the time the conversation had become free-wheeling and spontaneous, as in the old times, they ceased to see the years' toll on each other. Only Jenny, watching the party from the kitchen window, wondered how such a collection of senior citizens could have done something so daring as to join the Peace Corps.

By and by the party began to wind down. Clusters of ex-volunteers slowly took their leave to local motels, to meet again in the morning. Midnight passed. It was in this darkest hour of the night, when the breeze guttered the candles out, that the name of Paul Harkin came up.

"I wonder what became of him," Sarah said dreamily from the shadows. "We wrote for a while when he was still in Korea, but his letters stopped suddenly a few weeks before the Kwangju affair started."

"Then you never heard what happened?" Leslie asked. She quickly sketched out the events of the Uprising — the blood-soaked hospital wards, the temporary victory of the citizens, and Mi Jin's sad end.

"Every now and then we get a letter from him," Joel said. "After Peace Corps he went home. God knows what agony he went through in his parents' house, alone with his memories. But then he did something that surprised me — at the time. Now I can't think of anything else he could have done. He went to medical school. He did residencies in pediatrics and public health. Then he joined a French relief organization called *Medicins sans Frontiers*, Doctors Without Borders. He spent his first few years in the Sudan, then in Eritrea and Guatemala. I'm not sure where he is now. Who knows? Maybe he's in North Korea, treating victims of the famine. Wouldn't that be something?"

Eventually even Leslie and Sarah, who was staying with them, went into the house to go to bed. Joel sat out alone, looking up into the clear sky, watching the stars so fixedly that he could almost see their slow wheeling across the heavens. The talk of Paul and Mi Jin had revived a pang of bitter regret in the center of his stomach, a feeling that the Koreans would call *han*. He missed Paul, and he missed Mi Jin, and the ache he had carried with him all these years came from knowing that he would never get them back. A brief, startling glint of a shooting star solidified his musings into a question.

Had Mi Jin died in vain?

"Trouble is the seed of joy," Paul used to say. On the face of it, the old adage was coming true: Korea had had free elections since 1986, though for a while it had elected leaders little better than old Pak Chong Hui. Most recently, in the elections of 1998, the people had elected Kim Dae Jung, that formerly condemned hero of Mokpo, as their president. Joel had drunk a toast when that news came; Mi Jin would have done the same, for she had played no small part in his eventual victory.

He still was not satisfied. If, as he believed, the present moment is the unchanging goal of history, Mi Jin's sacrifice would have to be for something more than a single election, or for an improved government, or even for democracy itself. Fleeting changes in a nation's institutions were not good enough. He could not bear the thought of Mi Jin dying for anything less than some eternal benefit.

The question brought Paul to mind. "Why are you doing this?" Joel had once written in a letter he later wished he could take back. "Instead of running around the world homeless, a charity doctor, living just above the poverty line, you could be making a good living in the States."

"You just don't get it," Paul had replied. "You're a paramedic. Why should I have to explain it to you, of all people? The child you save today may be a scientist or leader or who knows what else someday — and, just as importantly, he's the vessel of his ancestors' genes. It's the same here, only the conditions are far worse. A little help goes a long way — maybe for generations to come. What's so hard to understand?" Reading those words, he remembered Paul on a dank night in Kwangju during desperate times, explaining love with a reproach, trying to put words to a force he knew so naturally.

Perhaps Mi Jin had not died after all.

The stars continued their course through the sky. Joel watched the Milky Way and replayed scenes of Paul and Mi Jin's life in his mind. They came one by one, each more searingly dear than the last. And in the end, under the infinite eye of heaven, the world seemed to him bound up tightly in slender filaments of joy.

# GLOSSARY

The Korean language is rich in words that cannot be adequately translated into English. I have tried to use English equivalents wherever possible, but to use them in every case would rob the story of much of its Korean flavor. Here is a quick reference of Korean words used commonly in this book.

*A note on the Romanization of Korean words:*

I have made no attempt to follow any of the schemes now in use for converting Korean script into English spellings: they are either unwieldy or distracting, and I doubt whether the typical reader really cares whether Mokp'o, Mogpo, or Mokpo is the better match to the Korean original. My goal is merely to guide the reader to a fair approximation of standard Korean pronunciation using the simplest English sounds. The only added guidance I would give is that 'u' is pronounced as 'oo' in m*oo*n and 'a' is always pronounced as in f*a*ther.

| | |
|---|---|
| *Agashi* | A young, unmarried woman. Used both as a description and as a term of address. A *tabang agashi* is a waitress in a *tabang*. |
| *Aigo!* | An expression of surprise, pain, or frustration. English equivalents range from 'Oh, dear!' to 'Damn!' |
| *Ajumoni* | Any married or middle-aged woman. Used both as a description and as a term of address. Also, the proprietress of a small business. A shorter, more familiar term of address is *Ajumah*. |
| *Appa* | "Daddy." |
| *Bangchop ham* | A counter-intelligence box by which citizens may anonymously drop a note to tell officials about the suspicious activity of others. |

| | |
|---|---|
| *Chollado* | Either of the Cholla Provinces of Korea — North Cholla and South Cholla. Kwangju is the capital of South Cholla Province. |
| *Demo* | Short for demonstration. |
| *Gochu* | The spicy red pepper, which is dried and ground into powder or made into a paste called *gochujang*. |
| *Han* | A feeling of bitter regret or overpowering emotion. |
| *Hangul* | The Korean alphabet. |
| *Kae sekki* | A son of a bitch. |
| *Kibun* | A person's mood, psyche, or mental state. |
| *Kimchi* | Cabbage or vegetables combined with spicy red pepper, garlic, onion, and other ingredients and allowed to sour over time. Similar in some ways to sauerkraut. |
| *Kwajang* | A section chief in an office or organization. |
| *Soju* | A clear, potent alcoholic beverage akin to American "white lightning." |
| *Makkoli* | A traditional milky-white alcoholic beverage brewed from rice. |
| *-nim* | An honorific appended to a person's title. |
| *Nunchi* | The state of the soul as read in one's eyes. |
| *Omma* | "Momma." |
| *Ommo!* | An expression of shock or surprise. |
| *Putak* | A favor. |
| *-shi* | An honorific appended to a person's name. |
| *Shi pal* | An obscenity equivalent to the English "Shit!." |
| *Sojang* | The chief of an office or organization. |
| *Tabang* | Literally, a tea-room, but most of them also serve coffee and other drinks. As Koreans typically do not entertain any but their closest friends in their homes, the multitude of *tabang*s serve as meeting places for conversation or business. |
| *Yangban* | A person of noble blood, or one who behaves as one. A gentleman or gentlewoman. |

# ABOUT THE AUTHOR

William Amos was born and raised in Madison, Wisconsin, where he graduated from the University of Wisconsin. After college, he joined the US Peace Corps and served in South Korea from 1979 to 1980. Upon his return, he earned a law degree from Loyola University of Chicago. He currently lives and writes in Boise, Idaho.

Made in the USA
San Bernardino, CA
24 November 2017